Contorted Nightmare

Alexandria Bugaj

Edited by: Sean Leonard (Reedsy)

Trigger Warnings and Thank You Message

Caution, Readers: This story contains mentions of blood, gore, drowning, possession, parental death, torture (kind of), some adult language, sexually explicit content, and mentions of death in general. If you or the person you're gifting this book to is sensitive to this type of material, this may not be the book for you. To everyone else, enjoy **Contorted Nightmare**!

Thank you to everyone who supported me, I finally did it!

Chapter One: Contorted Nightmare

"Sometimes human places create inhuman monsters."
—Stephen King

My oar fought for control of the kayak after the current became too fast for me to handle.

"Stay calm, Mia!" my father shouted. "We're almost out of it."

I was terrified, trying desperately to slow down. It was my first time out in the river, despite my mother's warnings of a flood about a week back. I felt like a fish trying to swim up a waterfall, utterly hopeless to my situation. Finally, just like he told me, we came to a patch in the water that was calm, and an instant wave of relief washed over me. As we sat there, he eyed me over to make sure I was alright. I think I almost had a panic attack. The only problem, I realized then: I wasn't anywhere near the dock to get back out.

"Can we just rest here for a bit?" I asked him as I used my oars to keep me in place.

"If we rest here, then we won't get to the best part before sundown," he responded. "Remember, there's a lot you wanted to explore."

I groaned, but I knew he was right. Up the river, about twenty miles from where we started, there was a deserted warehouse, some old apartment buildings, and one of the most infamous hospitals in history, Beacon Medical Center. After a bridge collapsed in town, the only way to get there was by boat. Despite the remote location, it was on the paranormal channel at least ten times a month because people were so fascinated with the energy of the building. They talked about demons, and how people left there with scratches on their backs. There were even YouTubers who went there illegally just to experience the haunted nature of it. I wanted to be among them.

I remember watching a live video of someone exploring the hospital when I was six. I stumbled across it by accident, after I tried to hit a fly off my dad's touch-screen computer. It started with this man in his mid-twenties who had a GoPro strapped to his head as he walked through the eerily creepy floors. He spoke softly, but fear was evident in the tone of his voice. Surprisingly, he went in alone; I couldn't imagine being in that horrible place by myself. I stared, transfixed by what was happening, and held my favorite teddy bear in my arms. Besides the dim light he had illuminating his way, it was pitch black. The only sound echoing through the decrepit place was his footsteps. He walked slowly at first, shining his flashlight all around himself, but then he heard what I assumed to be a low growl and took off running. I covered my eyes, and my whole body began to shake.

"Oh no," I said to myself. A few seconds later, I heard a loud crash, and saw that the floor had caved in beneath him. He barely held onto the beams of the upper floor, and his struggling only seemed to make it worse as more and more rubble fell down around him. I squeezed my eyes shut in fear, and when I opened them again, bright red eyes were peering back at me. Then the screen went dark, with the sound of a blood-curdling scream in the background. Quickly, I got up and hid behind my chair as if that thing would hop out of the screen. When my dad came back in from doing a mechanic job, he found me gripping the back of the chair in tears. He got me some butterscotch ice cream to calm me down, and it helped somewhat, but it was in my nightmares later that night.

At first, I didn't believe the video was real, but when I saw his face on a missing poster about two weeks later, my curiosity and fear of the place only seemed to grow. As I got older, my dad realized my fascination and helped me by buying every book, magazine, and pamphlet he could find describing the history of the gruesome building. Eventually, through my research, I found out that the video I saw became part of a police investigation for murder. I couldn't believe it when I heard the police chief come forward showcasing the video and saw that someone edited the eyes and the growling out. Somehow, I was one of the rare few to see the truth. What was going on with that place, and why was someone hiding what happened that day?

I had about a million questions, and I knew the only way to find out was to go there myself. After some convincing, my dad finally agreed to take me as long as I promised we'd leave if anything bad happened. We packed face masks, flashlights, bug spray, some water, a few towels just in case, a first-aid kit, and an old video camera my mom lent to me.

All I wanted was the truth. Looking back on it now, I wish I would have let that go.

"What do you want to do, kid?" Dad asked me as he spun around my kayak and did laps around me. *How does he have so much energy?* I thought as I looked at my own reflection in the water, then pushed forward to let him know I was ready. "Good choice."

It took us about an hour to get there through the rushing river. I was still nervous, but I felt safe with my dad. The light shined through the trees, illuminating the blue-green water below us. I could hear birds chirping, and the sound of toads on the shoreline.

"This is beautiful," I told him as the water began to slow down again. He just smiled with this proud look, then stopped dead-still in the water behind me. It took me a moment to notice, but when I did, I turned around. "Everything okay?"

He nodded and pointed in awe above us.

"I see the hospital, straight ahead!" he yelled. I looked up, and there I saw the intimidating building that haunts my dreams to this day. The hospital poked out from the trees, revealing just how dilapidated and nature-exposed it was. Moss, vines, and water damage showed the building in a different light than what I saw in my research.

Beacon Medical Center, a building with a history a hundred times worse than it looked. Besides the missing YouTuber found mangled and covered in blood, when it was still open, many people died there. There were diseases, a plague, and extremely inexperienced doctors. The patients were basically human lab rats. Reading that during my research sent chills down my spine.

Ahead of us, I could see a guard tower where a security team set up camp, and right at the base of the docks was a sign that read: *No trespassing! All violators will be—* The rest of the sign was covered in black spray paint. In big, bold letters, the sentence was finished with the word ***KILLED.*** For a moment, my blood ran cold, but when my dad used his oar to drag my kayak toward him, I snapped out of it.

"Here, let me help you out," he said, extending his hand to pull me onto an old wooden dock. It was worn out, revealing the water beneath in some spots. *In most scary movies,* I thought, *a hand would appear from the water and try to pull me in,* so I was pretty shaky when I peered into the cracks. Before we left the docks, I grabbed my backpack from beneath the straps on the kayak and sprayed the two of us down with bug spray.

"Let's take our time," Dad said, as we contemplated where to go. "I don't feel like getting arrested today." I nodded and began walking toward one of the apartment buildings. It felt like it was frozen in time. There was a street sign, and some old lampposts lining what would have been the road through the little town. It was called Vista Street, and the sign was bent in half like someone had tried to tear it off. The first apartment we came across, ironically, had the number 666 as the address. There was more graffiti on the outside walls, and strangely enough some paint cans were left sitting in a pile by what I assumed to be the garage. To my shock, they were all still full.

"Why did they leave their cans here?" I asked, playing with my hair nervously.

"Maybe they got caught?" Dad replied with a shrug as he pulled on the front door. Of course, it was locked, no surprise there unfortunately. We walked around until we found an open window on the second floor. "Want me to boost you up?" he asked, pointing with his thumb. I looked up at the balcony beneath the window, and it made me nervous. It looked decayed, and the metal beams were rusted; it probably wasn't going to be very stable.

"We should probably find another way inside." I said, feeling anxious. I began searching around until I came to a door falling off its hinges. The wind slammed the door against the brick wall outside repeatedly as it hung there. A few feet from it, the security team had placed another sign in front of the door, this time with no paint splattered across it. "Let's go in here!"

"Alright, but be careful, kid. For all we know, the guards could be inside." Slowly I pulled the door open just enough to squeeze inside, and I jumped when it fell and crashed to the ground.

"Oops," I said with a grimace. Dad didn't seem to share my worry, instead he just chuckled and made his way past me.

"Nice going, now they definitely won't know we're here."

I laughed along with him and followed him into the complex. Inside, there was a single light on the bottom floor that was dangling by a frayed wire. It was blinking rapidly, which didn't bode well for vision's sake. I decided to pull out the flashlight I had stowed away in my bag, and it definitely helped. The hallway consisted of fifteen doors. Most of them still looked decent. They were yellowish, brown-colored doors with a small peep hole near the top of each one. For some reason, they were kind of creepy looking.

"Pick a door, and meet me down the hall," Dad said, aiming his flashlight down the corridor. I nodded, and slowly made my way toward room 108 (the second closest to me). For some reason, that door called to me. I didn't know why, but it felt different than the rest. The floor beneath creaked with each step and I couldn't help but think back to the live video when the floor gave way. *Is there a basement to this building?* I wondered, feeling a little worried. I shook the thought off and started to turn the knob when I heard Dad call my name.

"Mia!" he called quietly.

"Yeah, Dad?" I answered with the door cracked open.

"Be careful, okay, kiddo?"

I nodded and walked inside. At first, the room seemed to be pretty boring. The sheets on the large queen bed inside were stained with what I hoped to be water damage. (Looking back, it wasn't.) Beige wallpaper lined the walls besides a small space where the previous owners decided to be spontaneous. They painted a mural of a young girl reaching toward the sky where a monarch butterfly was stretching its wings. I stood there for a moment to admire it, then decided to rummage through the drawers. I opened the first couple drawers to see small kids' clothing, and again my mind went to all the worst scenarios. *What if the demons took them? Clearly something must have happened to make them leave all their belongings,* I thought as I saw more and more leftover stuff. There didn't seem to be much else besides an old teddy bear with one of its button-eyes missing. I picked it up and twirled it in my hands. It felt nostalgic as I held it. It looked just like mine. A small brown bear with a red bow around its neck. Stuffing poked out between my fingers where a small piece of thread was dangling. I thought about taking it with me to fix it up, but I ended up putting it back.

Before I left the room, I checked the nightstand by the bed and found a pamphlet I'd never seen before. It was for Beacon. I started reading about an accident in the west wing when a loud knock at the door made me jump.

"Find anything good?"

"Geez, you scared me!" I exclaimed, feeling like my soul left my body. "I found a pamphlet from Beacon. It says something about an accident in the west wing, but it's torn."

Dad walked over and examined it as if holding it up to the light would reveal a new section.

"Maybe the other half is around here somewhere. Keep looking. I'm going to take a look upstairs," he told me, and his voice began to drift off as he walked away.

"Wait! What if something's here?" I asked, still reeling in fear from the jump scare from earlier.

"Don't worry," he said calmly. "I'm sure—" He stopped mid-sentence, as a loud bang came from behind us inside room 113. He put his hand to his lips and motioned in that direction. Instinctually, he stepped in front of me and began walking toward the door. I saw the shine of his pocketknife, and immediately my mind went on a tangent again.

What if we open the door and the room is empty? That would mean ghosts are real, right? No, it could just be the building settling. Or we open the door, and there's some kind of ax-wielding maniac in there. Or...

"Mia!" Dad whispered loudly, breaking me out of my trance once more. "The door's open." Cautiously, I peeked inside, and it looked like we had just walked into a crime scene. *I guess I can cross ax-wielding maniac off my list.* I made a mental note as I walked farther inside. The mattress from the queen bed was torn to shreds, leaving only streaks of cotton in its wake. Next to it, a glass nightstand was completely shattered. Along the floor, I saw muddy footprints spread far apart, like whoever made them was in a hurry. They led straight for the closet, and they were still wet, meaning this had just happened. My curiosity got the better of me, and I slowly tiptoed toward the closet.

Once Dad saw the scene laid out before us, he gestured toward the hall. "Maybe this isn't such a good idea," he whispered before noticing I wasn't stopping. I had to know. The creaking of my shoes filled my ears and made me shiver with each passing moment. I heard Dad's footsteps approaching, but before he could do anything, I was shoved to the ground with such force that it took my breath away. A moment later I gasped as a very beat-up guy came tumbling out right on top of me, looking as if he had just escaped a war zone.

"Why won't you die?!" he screamed as he shoved what looked like a broken chair leg toward my chest. In a blind panic, Dad pushed him into the wall and quickly helped me to my feet. The boy blinked rapidly and groaned in pain, seemingly trying to reassess what just happened. "Please, no." He slowly raised his head until our eyes met. His ragged breathing turned slightly calmer, and I watched as he leaned back against the wall. "Oh, I thought you were *something* else."

His voice became quieter as he spoke, and his body slipped down the wall. I caught him before his head hit the floor, but when I looked at him, I realized it wouldn't have mattered anyway; he was out cold. His dark brown hair fell over his face like curtains, covering both eyes. Mainly his wounds seemed to be scrapes and bruises, but one very large one across his chest caught my eye. I knelt down and saw what I assumed to be a giant claw mark. The wound was pretty deep, and it genuinely scared me that he might die. I turned around and absentmindedly watched as Dad looked through his backpack, thinking about what could have done this to him that got him so scared. *Maybe the stories about the demons are true?* I thought, swallowing down a lump that formed in my throat. Finally, Dad tossed his backpack down and groaned with a frustrated look on his face.

"What's wrong?" I asked him a moment later.

"I thought we packed a first-aid kit," he responded. "Where is it?"

"I haven't seen it since we left the car." I remembered grabbing it, but as I dug through my bag, I didn't see it anywhere either. "What do we do? He looks like he could die!" My hands began to shake again as I reached to the boy's neck to check his pulse. It was slow, but it was still there. I breathed a sigh of relief and sat down hesitantly next to him.

"We'll have to look around for supplies," Dad said, lifting the boy up in his arms. Ironically, I saw the hospital in the distance, and wondered if we should take him there. I knew it was abandoned, but maybe there was something we could use. "Let's get going, we don't know who or *what* did this." I nodded and grabbed our backpacks before following him into the hall. As we came back out, I noticed the blinking light went out. Considering most of the windows were covered with paper or boarded up, it was pitch black. So I used the light from the backdoor to find our flashlights. When I did, I gasped at what I was seeing. The walls looked as if they melted in the summer heat. There were bricks falling out in certain places, and there was some kind of black ooze dripping from the ceiling.

"What is this stuff?" I asked Dad, who was a short distance away. I didn't want to touch it, but my shoe got stuck in a large goopy puddle. I pulled until it came loose, and then stumbled against the barely stable wall for support. He didn't respond to my question; I turned around to see his flashlight aimed above me.

"Mia, don't move," he whispered, almost quietly enough to make no sound at all. My heart raced in my chest as I took in the creature that was now right above me. It looked human, but its limbs were contorted and bent in weird directions as it dragged itself across the ceiling. There was some sort of huge bloody growth on its back, making it look insanely big. Its mouth had at least two rows of teeth, and a large slimy tongue poking out. The part that made me shudder was that it didn't have eyes. I realized just then, the boy must have been talking about this creature when he attacked me, because I could see a gaping hole in its chest where it had been stabbed. Meaning I had stepped in its blood. In my head, I was screaming; a scream so loud I was sure it would shatter any glass around me. Out loud though, I was holding my breath, hoping the thing would leave. With each step it took, it made a squelching sound. Horror filled every fiber of my being as another brick came crashing down right beside me.

It growled, and this dreadful-smelling liquid fell out of its mouth and dropped directly on my shoulder. The moment it hit me, it took everything in me not to scream as it burned my skin off. The smell of my burning flesh filled my nose and my eyes started to water as I struggled to stay silent. I turned my head toward Dad and saw him toss a brick down the hall. I don't know if it was pure luck, but the creature fell for it and slowly crawled away, leaving a trail of blood behind it. Once it was out of sight, I stopped holding my breath and let out a sob as I checked my shoulder. My face felt warm and I knew then if I had waited any longer, it could have been much worse.

"Are you alright?" Dad asked as I bent over with ragged breaths. I just shook my head and felt my skin with the tips of my fingers; it felt charred.

"It hurts," I cried, as I tried to catch my breath. "What was that thing?" He shrugged and set the boy down to tie a piece of cloth he tore off his shirt over the wound. I grimaced, and he closed his eyes sympathetically.

"Sorry, kid. Let's get out of here before that thing comes back." He picked up the boy slowly, trying not to make any noise, and we walked in the opposite direction of the monster. We unlocked the front door and stepped out into what looked like the beginning of a storm. I could see the trees in the distance swaying in the wind, and a light rain was picking up. I looked around, trying to decide where to go, when I saw a lightning strike come down close by. The rain started coming down harder as we debated, and soon it was pouring.

"Come on, we have to get out of the rain." Dad pointed toward one of the other apartment buildings, number 648, with his free hand, the other still supporting the boy on his shoulder. As we ran toward it, my socks became drenched in water. I sloshed through the puddles until we made it to the awning of the next complex. Once I was out of the rain, I scrunched my shirt up and got as much water out as I could. I could see more lightning in the distance, with the occasional loud boom overhead. It wouldn't have been so bad—I loved storms—but with the rain and thunder came this high-pitch screeching from every direction including right above us. Those things were everywhere, and we were left with only one choice. Run like hell.

Chapter Two: Beacon Family Secret

The two of us ran as fast as we could back to the dock. I tried to see the bright side of how cool a story this would be, but we were left distraught when we saw the scene laid out before us. Our kayaks were smashed to bits, leaving a mess of splintered wood. The oars were slowly floating downstream, and my phone was submerged beneath the water. I groaned as I bent over to try and salvage it, but when I pressed the button, it didn't even flash. All my pictures, research of Beacon, phone numbers, everything: gone.

"No," Dad said, in shock as he came to stand beside me. The rain continued to pour down, pushing what was left of our kayaks even deeper into the water.

"W-what should we do now?" I looked at him as I crossed my arms across my chest for warmth. He sighed, and after a moment of looking around, he pointed right back to where we came.

"We have no choice but to wait out the storm, and hopefully when the guards come, we can get some help. Once we're inside, I'll see if I can find us some dry clothes. If we're lucky, they'll be here in the morning." I nodded, and we made it about halfway back when I remembered the signs and shook his arm.

"Maybe he has a boat we could use," I shouted over the rain, gesturing to the boy in his arms. "I don't want us to get arrested." Again, we came to stand under the awning and he looked at me sadly.

"I don't either, kid. But if he doesn't have anything, we won't have a choice. As far as I could see, our kayaks were the only ones out here. The current is too fast to swim across, and we need to get your arm checked out." I nodded once more, and very slowly pushed the door open. This time it looked much more pleasant. The ceiling light was still intact, showing a brightly lit hallway of doors.

"At least we don't have to worry about them hiding in the darkness this time," Dad said reassuringly. I wasn't totally convinced we were alone, so I tiptoed around. Down the hall, I could see a rusted sign that read, *laundry chute*, and felt a glimmer of hope.

"There might be some dry clothes down there," I said, pointing with my good arm.

"Help me find a place to put him down first, my arms are getting tired," he responded, gently tossing him up to get a better grip. I ran, almost forgetting those things were there with us, and went to open an apartment door. Before I even opened it, a rotten smell hit my nose, and I found out something was blocking the door. *I hope that's not a body,* I thought, gagging as I pulled it shut again.

"Not that one. Do NOT go in there," I said, feeling queasy. Dad chuckled and walked past me to try another door. It felt good to hear him laugh, it almost made me feel better. Slowly he pushed open the next door, and I was pleasantly surprised. "It actually looks...nice?" I said. There was a small leather couch in the living room and an old box TV that looked presentable, despite being caked in dust. The kitchen was connected to the room, and the only two rooms inside were the bedroom and the bathroom. I prepared myself to see another stained bed, but my mouth almost fell open when I saw a clean twin bed. The blankets were understandably old and wrinkled, but otherwise it was clean. *They must have lived alone,* I thought as I gently sat down.

"I think this'll work," I told him, and moved so he could set him down.

Once he did, he stretched his arms out wide, and said," Ahhhh. Much better." I managed to laugh a little and walked toward the door.

"Will he be okay by himself?" I asked, looking back at the boy. His chest slowly rose and fell as he slept. He looked so peaceful, I almost wished I could join him. Dad looked back at him, unsure, so I sat back down on an old computer chair near the bed and waved him on. "I'll stay. If anything happens, yell for me. Okay?" I told him, and he nodded as he flipped his pocketknife open and shut again anxiously.

"Same goes to you, kid," he responded as he left, leaving me alone with my thoughts. While he was away, I walked around the apartment, looking through the drawers. Most were filled with utensils or school/office supplies. Then I found a sliding metal drawer filled to the brim with old letters dating as far back as 1953.

I dug through it and found an acceptance letter to Beacon Hospital Staff. It read:

Dear Martha Evans,

Congratulations, you've been accepted to a very competitive position as a surgical resident here at Beacon. This privilege is not given to just anyone; only the best of the best make it into our program. You should feel proud of your accomplishments, as you will help shape the—

I stopped reading as a drop of water hit the top of the page. I looked up and saw a huge water mark on the ceiling. Relief washed over me as I realized it was only rainwater, but as I began to read again, I heard growling and scraping sounds upstairs. I knew it must have been one of those things, and I swallowed hard as I imagined it falling through the ceiling. Shaking myself out of it, I continued reading:

...you will help shape the future of medicine and you will hopefully become a part of history in the making. Unfortunately, we are in the middle of a pandemic right now, so we ask that all new employees and applicants wait until next year to begin their journey with us. This is a very unfortunate setback, but we will contact you upon being cleared by the board. We hope you understand, as the safety of our staff and patients is our number one priority. It is my goal to see you here as soon as the spring of 1989, and have you integrated as soon as possible. Again, thank you for your interest in being a member of the Beacon staff, and we wish you a safe, healthy year in the meantime.

Signed,

James Beacon.

I couldn't help but gasp when I realized the Beacon family had written this. It was pretty well known that they died in the 1990s from a fire, so I felt like I was holding history. I flipped it over and saw a scribbled message in red ink. ***"The Beacons are evil."*** My breath caught, and I continued digging. I was so invested, I needed to know more. Beneath the pile of letters was a torn newspaper clipping; just like I thought, it was about the fire. "Beacon Family Killed in

Tragic Fire at Family Estate." Something didn't feel right, so I stowed the letter and newspaper clipping in my backpack. It was still wet, but I found a dry pocket and folded them up to fit.

I searched around a little more, but soon I gave up and plopped down on the chair again. Dad came back about twenty minutes later dressed in some old jeans and a purple retro-looking bowling shirt.

"You look nice," I mocked, and he rolled his eyes playfully.

"Oh, you love it." He tossed me an outfit and put down another dry set for the boy. "Go ahead and get changed, I'll see if I can wake him." I nodded and dragged my wet-pant legs to the bathroom. The outfit he gave me was a pair of blue jean capris and a daisy-covered tank top. He even managed to find a jean jacket, and somehow it fit just right. They all smelled really nice too, as if he used fresh dryer sheets. It must have been sitting in the dryer for a while though, because they had a slightly filmy feel to them.

When I finished changing, I came out and saw the boy was awake. He wiped his eyes and strained himself trying to sit up. With a groan, he clutched his chest, and I saw that Dad had wrapped strips of a ripped towel around him.

"W-where am I?" he asked, forcing his body into a sitting position. He must have realized we carried him somewhere because he seemed calm. "Are we safe?"

"Yeah, we're safe, kid. I'm Tim, and this is my daughter, Mia," Dad told him, gesturing to me as I emerged from the bathroom.

"Mia," he repeated, looking me up and down. "You're beautiful." I couldn't help but blush. Dad, on the other hand, wasn't so amused.

"Here's some dry clothes," he said, tossing them coldly into the boy's arms. "The bathroom is next door, go get changed. If you can stand up." He nodded and craned his feet over the side of the bed with a yawn.

"My name's Oliver. Sorry that I attacked you both earlier, I was scared." Slowly he peeled himself off the bed, and Dad's expression seemed to soften as he realized just how bad off, he was.

"It's alright, you couldn't have known it was us," Dad responded, giving him a sympathetic look.

Once Oliver was up, he stretched with a grimace. "Do you have a bandage?" he asked, as he looped his fingers around the towel scraps. They came back with blood on them, making me shudder.

"No, we tried looking for one in our bags, but we must have forgotten our first-aid kit in the car." I told him and saw Dad tearing more towel strips for him to switch out with.

"These will have to do for now," he told him, and Oliver smiled gratefully before shutting the bathroom door. "Once he's done, we'll ask him about a boat to get out of here, but let's try not to get our hopes up." I nodded, feeling tired, and sat back down on the computer chair. I couldn't help but yawn as we waited. It was getting late, and although I didn't want to stay in that dreadful place overnight, it became more and more likely that we wouldn't have a choice. About ten minutes later, Oliver came back and leaned against the bedroom door frame. He was wearing a gray pair of jean shorts, and a navy-blue T-shirt with some rock band I didn't recognize.

"What now?" he asked, rubbing his eyes again.

"First things first, do you have a boat we could use? Our kayaks were smashed to bits," Dad asked, hopeful of returning home soon.

"I was hoping you did. I've been stuck here for a while now." He came and sat down on the floor with his back against the wall opposite of me.

"How long?" I asked as worry seized my heart. He seemed nervous that I asked, and let out a deep, pained breath.

"About a month." Something about the way he looked told me he was lying, but before I could ask, Dad chimed in.

"There's no way. The guards haven't come to check the place at all?" Again, Oliver looked nervous, and pulled his knees into his chest.

"I don't want them to," he muttered under his breath, making me wonder what was going on.

"My ears aren't the best, kid. Can you speak up a bit?" Dad seemed completely oblivious to his sudden change, but I wasn't so quick to dismiss it.

"I just said I haven't seen anyone. We should probably find a place to—" Before he could finish, he was cut off by the sound of cars outside. I looked out as my heart leapt into my throat and saw army trucks coming over a metal bridge they had craned over the water. I felt an instant wave of relief wash over me when I saw them.

"Yes, we're safe!" I exclaimed happily. It felt like the nightmare was finally over, but as soon as I got to the door, Oliver grabbed my arm and gave me this unsettling, terrified look that sent goosebumps up my arms.

"Don't, they'll shoot you," he said a moment later.

"What? Why?" I asked him as he ran over to the front door of the apartment and peeked out.

"I can't explain it, but if you and your dad want to make it out of here alive, we should hide."

"I don't understand, kid, what's going on?" Dad came and joined him by the door. Finally, he seemed to catch on as he placed his hand on his shoulder. "Whatever it is, you can tell us. It's okay." He didn't answer; instead, he shook his head and showed me his hands, which were covered in black paint. *How did I not notice that before?* I felt dumb as I realized the warnings were from him.

"That was you?" I said, feeling shocked, as more and more fear built in my chest.

"Yes, please believe me. They. Will. Kill. Us!" I nodded, and grabbed Oliver's hand as Dad led us down to the laundry room. At first, I felt anxious when I got to the bottom of the steps. There didn't seem to be too many places to hide, but then I saw all the laundry hampers and dumped them all out, creating a giant mound of clothes on the floor.

"Will this do?" I asked, as Dad came to realize my plan. Oliver nodded, and we buried ourselves in clothes. And not a moment too soon; a few seconds later, I heard footsteps descending the stairs. I was so scared, I held my breath and imagined myself back at home with Mom, safe and sound. No matter how hard I fought it though, bile began to rise in my throat, as this horrible smell hit my nose. Some of the clothes weren't washed, and I felt sick as I laid down beneath them. I couldn't tell what was happening, but I could hear the sound of clothes hitting the ground and knew they must have been looking through them. *No, go away,* I pleaded in my head, swallowing a lump in my throat. I felt my whole body go numb when they tossed the only shirt covering my face, revealing two men in camo with big guns.

"Where did that little brat go?" one said, eying our pile of clothes.

"I don't know," another responded. "We'll get him back in containment soon." He groaned and reloaded the shotgun in his hands, dropping bullet casings on the ground.

"Soon is not soon enough," the first snapped back, and I watched as they jogged up the steps again. I waited until I heard the sound of the laundry room door shutting before I pushed the clothes off me and saw my dad and Oliver come out panting.

"What was that about?" I whispered, turning a shotgun shell over in my hand.

"Me," Oliver said plainly, and turned his back to us. "My name is...Oliver Beacon." My whole body shook when I registered what he said.

"That's not possible. The Beacons are dead!" I looked to see Oliver shake his head and turn back toward me.

"They're using our blood to make those...things. That's why they want me. My family has a genetic mutation that they're implanting in people." He turned his arms around, and clear as day, I could see scars and bruises where they drew his blood from. "I just want to be free."

Chapter Three: Toxic Blood

"Mysterious fire took the lives of the Beacon family." I remember the day I saw it on the news. I was six at the time. It was a pretty normal day, at least in the beginning. Mom and Dad were inside making dinner while I played in the yard. I had just gotten out of school, and I knew exactly what I wanted to do. There was this beach set I begged my parents for, and after saving enough, I was able to buy it with my allowance. It had everything. A little red shovel, a purple castle mold, a starfish mold, a sand sifter, a mini rake, a seahorse mold, and a crab mold. I was so excited, the moment I got home, I ran to the garage to finally open it. The garage was filled with my parents' stuff. Packing boxes stuffed with tools, collectibles, letters, and some of my drawings I gave them. It was where pretty much everything was stored. I stepped inside and was disappointed when I realized I would have to go searching. It was nowhere to be found.

I started by opening a box labeled *summer*. It was so dusty that even touching it left a print where my hands were. Slowly I pulled open the lid, and...nothing. It was filled to the brim with old pictures, my favorite being my parents' wedding photo. I sighed and replaced the lid. From there, I had to step over Dad's riding mowers to get to the other boxes. I saw it like a game of "floor is lava," and hopped up like I was climbing onto a giant rock. I jumped from the first one to another, and my heart leapt from my chest when one of them started up on their own.

"Ahhh!" I screamed, stumbling off the mower. When I landed, I stared at my hands as if I had done a magic trick. A few seconds later, Dad came running in.

"What's wrong? I heard you scream," Dad said, as he stepped over the mowers to pluck me up.

"The m-mower! It started by itself!" I told him, burying my head in his chest as my body started shaking. He just laughed and set me down outside the mess.

"Don't worry, kid. It's just automatic. It starts up when you sit on it, as long as the keys are there." I looked, and to my relief they were there.

"Oh," I said with a nervous smile. With another chuckle, Dad leaned down and planted a kiss on my forehead.

"What are you trying to get? I'll help you." I told him about the beach set, and without a moment's hesitation he found it sitting on a shelf by the back wall. "I figured you'd want it, so I put it up for you." With an excited look, I took it from his hands and ran to the back yard as fast as I could.

"Thanks, Dad!" I yelled, and waved as he went back inside.

"You're welcome. I'll call you when dinner's ready, okay?" I nodded, and practically jumped in the sand box. It took me a minute to get the set open—the netting was super strong—but when I did, a whole swarm of baby spiders crawled over my hand. I screamed and flailed my arms up and down as they swarmed up my body. Like the heroes I knew my parents were, Mom and Dad came running out and sprayed me down with a hose to get them off. That should have been the first red flag, but after Dad sprayed me and the set down, I went right back to the sand box as if it didn't faze me.

Slowly, I filled the castle mold scoop by scoop, determined to make a sandcastle. I even planned to build a moat around it using hose water, but something felt off. I dug as deep as I could go, and still didn't see the bottom. Usually, I would see a black tarp, but this time it just kept going. Eventually I gave up on the castle, and decided to see just how deep I could dig. I was maybe four feet down when my shovel became stuck in something goopy. I pulled on it with all my strength until I was able to get it loose, and saw it was caked in a thick black substance like the blood from those monsters. To my shock, it just kept pouring out, flooding the sandbox. I dropped my shovel and heard a sound almost like a pounding heart as I backed away. *Was that a body?* I thought, feeling like I had just stumbled into a real-life version of my parents' horror movies. I ran crying back to the house and went straight to Dad, holding onto his leg as if the world was ending.

"What happened?" Dad asked. I didn't really know what it was, so I shrugged and pointed at the sandbox through the kitchen window. I was almost certain I saw a shirt beneath all the goop, but I was too scared to know for sure.

"There's something d-down there!" Again, Dad picked me up, and Mom knelt to my eye level as we all peeked out the window.

"What was it, sweetie?" Mom asked as she mixed Ragu sauce into the meat she had browning on the stove.

"I don't know, but it was scary." They both seemed confused as we looked out and rain began to pour down.

"Hopefully, this rain will chase whatever it is out. If not, I'll check tomorrow. How about you and I play board games while Mom finishes making the spaghetti?" I couldn't help but perk up when I heard about dinner, so I nodded and followed him into the living room. We played Monopoly for about fifteen minutes, then we heard Mom scream. Both of us threw down the board pieces we were holding and ran. When we got to her, we saw the spaghetti sauce splattered on the floor like a fresh crime scene, and Mom standing over it with a horrified look on her face.

In front of her, the TV was on, and a young blonde lady holding a mic stood outside a house engulfed in flames. Firefighters were battling the heat with everything they had and about fifty police cars were surrounding the place.

"Mysterious fire took the lives of the Beacon family this evening. Police are unsure of what started the blaze, but as you can see," she said, gesturing to the house," our local firefighters are still doing all they can to stop the fire from spreading. Their family—" With a click, Dad turned the TV off and held Mom as she sobbed into his shoulders. She worked with the Beacons. She had every right to be devastated. Dad didn't yell at her, especially knowing her history with their family; instead, he helped her over to the kitchen table and I helped him clean up the mess. When we finished, he went back to her and just held her as she cried.

I don't know why, but something told me to look outside as they held each other, and I saw the sand from the sandbox being thrown into the air. I took deep breaths, looking between Mom and Dad, like, *are you seeing this?* Then I saw a bent and clearly broken leg come out. Then an arm, and another, until I saw a young boy, maybe eight or nine years old, in a navy-blue shirt and green khaki pants emerge from the hole. I was sure if I opened the door, I would have heard the sound of bones cracking as he turned to face my way. When he finally did, he stared at me with this blank expression as the rain poured down around him. It took me a second to notice a black stain along the front of his shirt, and I fell onto the floor with only a whimper. A moment later, he tilted his head at me and smiled, revealing razor-sharp teeth. Then he took off, crawling across the back yard like a dog until he scrambled over our fence, leaving a smear of black goop along the outer wall.

When I stared at Oliver right then, that was all I could think of.

"Mia, are you okay?" he asked me nervously, and I nodded as I slowly came out of it.

"I'm sorry I dumped this on you, but I didn't know what else to do," he told me as sweat formed on his forehead.

"Don't worry, kid. You're safe with us. Right, Mia?" Dad nudged me, and I nodded once more.

"Yeah, we'll protect you. Besides, I have about a million questions to ask you, and I can't do that if you're locked up." He chuckled softly, and a relieved look washed over his face.

"Thanks. As for your questions, let's get somewhere safe first. Then I'll happily answer them all, okay?"

"Sounds like a plan."

"Where is 'safe,' exactly?" Dad asked, standing on a couch to peek out the basement window. I don't think any of us really had a plan on where to go next. We just stood there in an awkward yet nervous silence until Dad spoke up again. "Our best option seems to be finding a way across that bridge, but those military creeps are everywhere. I'm not letting either of you get shot, so I'll distract them while the two of you run." My mouth fell open. I couldn't believe he was even insinuating we'd leave without him.

"No, we're not leaving you. We can go together. If we just sneak carefully—"

He cut me off with a wave of his hand and started walking toward the steps.

"I'm not risking that. I'm a strong man, I'll meet back up with you again." Tears fell down my cheeks and I ran to hug him.

"I swear, if you don't make it..." I stopped as he pulled me close and kissed my forehead. It scared me when I felt his lips were quivering.

"I'll make it, I promise. Oliver," he called, waving him over to join us. "Take care of my daughter. Get her out of here." He gave Oliver's shoulder a squeeze, then handed him his flashlight. I tried not to panic, but my mind was filled with dread and what ifs. "I'll run by the window. Once I do, don't stop until you make it across that bridge. Got it?" We both nodded, and he gave us one last smile before he left us there in the basement. I felt so scared, but I knew we had to be strong. Quietly, I pulled my backpack off and prepared myself to run by grabbing my flashlight. Oliver must have known I was worried, because as soon as I stood back up again, he nudged my arm.

"We're going to make it, we all are," he told me as we stared out the basement window. I nodded to him and took a deep breath. As we waited, I closed my eyes and listened to the sound of rain coming down. The gentle tap against the windowpane almost felt comforting. I remembered feeling his hand in mine as we stood there, and I silently thanked him. A few moments later, the gentle tapping turned to loud splashing, and we saw boots racing past our window.

"Run!" I told him and pulled his hand up the steps. We only got to the second landing when I heard a gunshot. My whole body froze, but Oliver didn't let me stop. We ran straight through the apartments and burst out the front. We stopped for a brief moment beneath the banister outside and saw Dad weaving through the cars as they took shots at him. I didn't want to leave him, but I knew right then we didn't have a choice. I felt grass hitting my ankles as we ran straight toward the bridge. We snuck past their cars, and through the overgrown apartment parking lot, until a bullet flew by my head. I screamed and turned around to see a woman in a white lab coat chasing us.

The sound of the rain was no longer enough to help me, and soon thunder rumbled across the sky as the storm became worse. In the distance, I could hear those things screeching as if the thunder was their battle cry.

"What do we do?" I asked, panting as we jumped through puddles. Oliver looked behind us and sucked in a panicked breath.

"Don't look back!" he shouted, pulling me along as he ran full sprint ahead. More gun shots, screeching, and a gross squelching sound came from almost directly behind us. We ran onto the bridge, and we must have gotten maybe ten feet in when it started to shake. "Oh crap," Oliver said, as we both seemed to realize the bridge was being lifted.

We hugged onto the sides, staring down at the racing water below us as it went higher and higher. I looked down as the bridge seemed to come to a stop about twenty feet in the air, and my mind started racing again. *What if we drown or they catch us? Or what if—* My thoughts were cut off when Oliver grabbed my hand and pulled me into the water with him. Before I hit the surface, I heard a scratching sound like nails on a chalkboard and realized there was one of those things on the bridge with us. The water was super cold, and it felt like ice traveled up my spine. Even worse, I couldn't keep my head above the surface. I gasped for air and thrashed my hands around in the water as I tried to get to safety. Just like Dad said, the current was way too fast to swim in. I was so busy trying to get to the surface that I didn't even notice the distant screams. To my relief, I felt a hand grab mine as the water tried to force me farther downstream. I was shocked to see Oliver digging his hands into the mud at the surface, and he groaned trying to pull me in. Finally, I managed to dig my hands in by his side, and we both crawled onto the surface panting and coughing up water.

"I-I heard a scream before we got up here. Was that you?" he asked once we managed to catch our breath. I shook my head and glanced around as we washed the mud off our hands. Only then did I remember Oliver's wound. I could see a red stain on the front of his shirt, and I got really scared as I came over to take a look. It seemed to hit me when I realized he was breathing super hard. He was in pain.

"Oliver, are you okay?" I asked as I came to stand in front of him. He just shook his head and groaned as the rain seeped into his wound. "Hang on, I'll rewrap it for you." Hastily, I pulled out my bag, which I was surprised to see even made it, and tore the last remaining towel into strips. It was soaked, but at least it was better than nothing. He didn't fight me as I lifted his shirt and untied the old bloody rags. I tossed each one to the ground as I worked, then slowly wrapped the new ones around his body. When I was doing one of them, my fingers grazed his skin, and he grimaced. "Sorry," I said apologetically, and continued, feeling my face heat up somehow. Once I finished, I pulled them all tight and pulled his shirt back down.

"Thanks," Oliver said, panting.

"You're welcome," I said, forcing a smile to make him feel better. Neither of us were sure where to go. There was nothing around us but trees, and I couldn't even see the hospital on the other side anymore through the rain.

"I'm so cold," I told Oliver as I began to shiver.

"I know, I am too." Our teeth chattered as we decided which direction to walk in, and we leaned against each other for warmth. We walked for maybe twenty minutes, sloshing around in the mud, before we managed to find the dirt road those military guys came in on. *Did the water really drag us that far downstream?* I thought as we stopped along the edge of it. About twenty feet away I could see people in army uniforms, soldiers or guards, huddled around the crane with umbrellas, and we ducked behind a tree as we heard them talk.

"You're an idiot, Thomas. Those brats could have drowned. Do you have any idea what they'll do to us if we don't bring that kid back?" a woman yelled, standing mere inches from the guy she was talking to. I could almost swear his glasses were touching her face.

"Look, I'm sorry. I didn't think they'd jump."

"You're sorry? Did you hear that, guys? He's sorry." I watched as she violently shoved the man to the ground and kicked him when he tried to get back up. “I hope they find him and make you choke on his blood! As for me,” she said, spitting on Thomas,” I’m going to go find Oliver and put him right back where he belongs.” Angrily they stormed off, leaving Thomas there sprawling in the mud.

When it was over, I saw Oliver was pacing back and forth. I heard him suck in a breath while they were talking, but I didn’t realize why until a couple seconds later. He pulled me to the side and weirdly started looking me up and down.

“What's the matter?” I asked, as he pulled my hands up to his eyes.

“Are they burning?” He stared at them quizzically, then grabbed my arms and began running his fingers along them.

“Is what burning?”

“Your hands! Are they burning?” Suddenly I remembered what he said back in that apartment, and my whole body went numb. *Am I going to turn?* I thought, as I remembered his blood running down my fingers. Each rag I pulled off echoed in the back of my mind; then I remembered Dad helped him too.

“No, not even a little bit,” I told him, honestly. Besides the shaking, I didn’t feel anything.

“You swear?” he asked, stopping to stare me in the eyes.

“I swear, Oliver. I don’t feel anything. I’m okay.” I tried to stay calm in order to not freak him out more than he already was, but he began to pace again anyway. Then I heard a voice behind us and turned around in a panic.

“You touched his blood, didn’t you?” It was Thomas. In the time we were talking, he stood up and managed to get a few feet from us without us noticing. I watched in horror as he aimed the flashlight on his gun directly at my chest and walked a little closer.

"Stay back," Oliver said, placing himself in front of me. "She's not one of them!" he screamed, but Thomas didn't believe him.

"If she touched your blood, she will be. Move!" he instructed angrily. Oliver didn't budge; instead, he backed up closer to me.

"I'd rather die!" he yelled. "She's fine! Her arms aren't even red."

"That's not possible. She must be feeling something." He lowered his gun slightly and looked between the two of us as Oliver guarded me. Once he was close enough, I saw one of the lenses on his glasses was broken, most likely from the shove. "Let me see," he said, waving his arm for me to come to him.

"Put the gun down first, and then I will," I told him as I stepped around Oliver. Slowly, he pulled the flashlight off the top of the gun, then dropped it. I was scared, but I came over to him anyway. Almost too aggressively, he grabbed my arm and shined the flashlight over it, revealing black veins along my arms. I sobbed when I saw it, and stumbled back, falling into Oliver.

"Look! She's done for. You should put her out of her misery." He kicked the gun to Oliver, and I saw him cry as he thought about what to do.

"Oliver, please. I feel fine," I told him, reaching out to grab his hand. He shook his head and grabbed the gun, putting distance between me and him. I watched as he pulled the gun up and aimed it between my eyes. "No, please," I whimpered, feeling faint as Thomas came and literally held me in place.

"Do it." I tried to struggle in his arms, but he was much stronger than I was. I kicked and thrashed, and even tried to bite his arm as he held me, but he wouldn't let go. Across from me, I could see Oliver was fighting his mind. He stared up at the sky, rain pouring onto his face, and sobbed. Then Thomas spoke up again. "Look, it's already spreading." I looked down as he held the flashlight to my right leg and showed the black veins to Oliver. "Do it!" His scream seemed to echo as the gun fired. The sound of the bullet leaving the chamber made my ears ring, and then my body hit the floor.

Chapter Four: Trapped in Beacon Hospital

When I woke up, I found myself in a small room about the size of a walk-in closet. Inside there was nothing but an old twin bed, a sink, and a toilet. The sound of the gunshot echoed in my mind as I woke up, and I almost instantly put my hand to my forehead. *Did he miss?* I thought as my fingers came back with nothing on them. Speaking of my fingers, my breath caught when I saw my whole body was covered in black veins. I put my hand to my chest, and still my heart was beating. Slowly, I got up, and saw a glass window hanging over the bed. I couldn't see anything but my reflection, so I knew it must have been a two-way mirror. Weirdly, my hair was pulled into a ponytail, and I was wearing a navy-blue jumpsuit. I was relieved to see that, besides my veins, I looked and felt pretty normal. *Why was I different?* I wondered as I pulled my cheeks open a little more to look at my teeth. Then I heard a voice and snapped my head up to see a speaker on the ceiling.

"Good morning, Subject 851," I heard a woman's voice say overhead. "My name is Polly, and I'm going to be taking care of you. You were infected about twelve hours ago, but lucky for both of us, the blood seemed to have very little effect.

For now, we must follow proper protocol procedures and keep you contained, but I assure you, you will be very well taken care of. I'm sure you heard that gunshot before you fainted and are filled with questions. Unfortunately, Officer Thomas Lewin, the man who was holding you, had to be taken out. He acted recklessly with you and Subject Zero and had to be relieved of his duties. The speaker above you works both ways, so if you have any questions, now's the time. You fall under my jurisdiction, so I'll be here."

I paced back and forth in my tiny cell as I took in everything she was saying. I knew Subject Zero meant Oliver, and I was both shocked and relieved to learn the gunshot wasn't from him. After she finished talking, I played with my ponytail as I tried to process the fact that there were over eight hundred infected. *Are we dealing with an apocalypse scenario?*

"Okay, I have a lot of questions."

"Go for it, I'm all ears," I heard her say, and I sat down on the bed as I let everything come out.

"First, I need to know about my dad. Is he okay?" The last time I saw him, he was being chased by the army guys and some of the infected, so I swallowed hard as I prepared myself to hear her answer.

"I'm not sure. We did find a man on the island," she told me. "Scruffy guy, mustache, black-gray hair, and he was wearing a 1980s bowling shirt."

"Yes! That's him." I stood up and put my hand on the window. "Please tell me he's okay."

"Subject 850, your father, was shot by our commanding officers after he tore into a researcher's body." I shrieked and pressed myself against the wall in the room. I shook my head and started crying, when she continued, "He was presumed dead, but almost an hour ago, after they took his body down to the morgue, they found him going nuts down there, and there was no sign of a wound anywhere. He's down the hall locked up, but I don't think the man you knew is there anymore." I sobbed into my arms as she spoke and saw flashes of him going up the stairs again, smiling. *I love you, Dad,* I thought as I started to hyperventilate.

"I'm sorry, I know this must be hard. If you'd like, I can hold your hand if that would bring you some comfort." I saw a little box in the glass window open, and her hand came through in a plastic glove. It almost felt dehumanizing, but I took it anyway. Somehow, it helped.

"I have more questions," I managed to choke out after a couple minutes. "What about Oliver, or Subject Zero, Is he okay?" I heard her take a breath over the speaker before she spoke up again.

"I see you picked up on that," she said, as a loud clicking sound came over the speaker. "Unfortunately, I am not allowed to give you any updates on him, or I'd lose my job. The only thing I can tell you is that he is back in confinement with his family where he belongs." It made me feel sick. I remembered Oliver telling me he wanted to be free, and how he didn't want to be used. I really wished that I didn't take her hand.

"Why are you infecting people? I don't get it. Why are innocent people being turned into...monsters?" I heard the sound of footsteps around her and people whispering, then she came back. *Was I being watched?*

"I can't answer that either," she stated flatly. I sighed, feeling frustrated.

"What's going to happen to me? Can you tell me that?" I snapped, and again I heard whispering.

"You will be kept here in containment for another 30 days, and if you don't mutate any further in that time—"

"I'll be set free?" I asked, talking over her. All I wanted was to go home to Mom, but they had other plans for me.

"No, 851. I'm sorry, but you're never leaving here again. You're a special case. Most infected turn within an hour. In that time frame, their bodies start mutating and they grow a taste for flesh. But you... Well, it's been twelve hours, and while you have black veins, you are otherwise normal. You will be kept here for research, and that's final." I heard the speaker cut off, and I tried asking more, but no one answered. *Is this really the rest of my life?* I cupped my legs into my chest and sat there for hours with nothing but my thoughts.

I didn't know how much time passed, as I lay on my back staring at the popcorn ceiling above me before they came back. Of course, I tried the door once or twice, hoping to get a miracle and see I wasn't locked in, but I was. I was so bored, I almost wished to go back outside with those things again. They were the real victims of these people; being turned for research is absolutely horrible. Finally, I got up and glanced around, despite knowing I could only see myself. Out of pure boredom, I put my hand in the glove, and I felt like my soul left my body when the other side opened. The speaker started ringing, forcing me to plug my ears, before I heard the woman's voice from earlier come on.

"Here's your dinner," she said, putting what looked like a blue school lunch tray in the box and sliding it toward me. On it, there was turkey and gravy, mashed potatoes with little chive leaves spread into them, peas, and a small carton of OJ. The smell of everything made my mouth water, and I gladly dug in. I could hear the speaker making feedback sounds as I ate, but I ignored it and savored every bite.

"Are you done?" Polly asked, once I ate the last bit of gravy off my tray. I nodded, and she opened the box again. "Put it in." I did as I was told, and to my surprise the door opened. Without so much as a second thought, I rushed out and, almost instantly, I felt something stab into my back. They shocked me.

"You're gonna be a difficult one, aren't ya?" I lay there on the floor panting and glanced around the hallway as Polly lifted my arm and put a hospital armband on my wrist. She was wearing a white lab coat and scrubs. On her badge, I saw the name *Polly Swines,* with *Level Five Clearance* written below it. As my eyes focused, I saw a hallway full of rooms, each of them labeled with a number. Sure enough, a plaque was above my door with my assigned number. *Does that mean I'm eight floors away from Oliver?* I wondered, as drool fell out of my mouth uncontrollably. "Congratulations, your new name is officially 851." I looked down at my wrist band, and just like she said, it had the numbers in bold on the top with my home address being Beacon Hospital.

"No," I said panting, as they stood around me on the floor. "My name is Mia." Polly shook her head and knelt down until we were face to face.

"Mia doesn't exist anymore. Shock her again." I felt the prongs against my back, and somehow it was worse the second time than the first. I decided right then, as my body convulsed on the floor, that I hated that woman. Just like everyone else in this horrible place, she was evil. When it was over, she grabbed my chin in her hand and said, "Let's try this again. What's your name?" I was determined not to let them break me, but I knew if I told her what she wanted to hear she would leave me alone.

"851," I said finally, making her smile like she had won. One of the other doctors knelt down and wiped the drool away from my face as I recovered. It was a kind gesture, but I had already made up my mind about these people.

"Good. Lights go out in an hour. After that, I don't want to hear a peep out of you. Got it, 851?" In my mind, I punched her—her and the other doctors—but I couldn't even stand on my own right then. A punch would do nothing more than embarrass me. I nodded, bowing my head to the floor, and then I was lifted up and shoved back into my bed. I barely stopped myself from falling off with all the force they used and had to shield my head from hitting the wall. My body felt weak as I sank into the mattress. The one-hour warning didn't matter, because I fell asleep before the lights even went off.

I spent eight days in there, getting little to no outside contact. The only time I got to see someone was when I got breakfast, lunch, and dinner, or when I needed a shower. It felt gross having to use the bathroom when I knew someone outside could be watching me, but I had no choice but to live with it. I was beyond bored, so I kept myself busy with anything I could. I would swing my pillow around, jump from the bed to the floor, mess around using the mirror, and just try anything to stay stimulated.

On the eighth day, I woke up to a mic feedback sound again. I groaned and put a pillow over my head, but then the feedback turned to a ringing causing me to roll onto the floor.

"Ugh," I said with a groan as I peeled myself off the ground. When I looked up again, I saw my breakfast was placed in the box. It consisted of eggs, bacon, a container of mixed fruit, and some apple juice. I ate each bite of the meal and yawned as I stared at myself through the glass. *Yep, I definitely have bed head.* I laughed as I popped a grape in my mouth. Little did I know that was the last thing I'd eat for at least a few days, or else I would have eaten slower.

After I finished, I slid the tray into the box like normal, but this time the door opened. Instinctually, I pressed my body into the wall and waited until Polly came strutting inside with a coffee in her hand.

"Nice to see you learned your lesson from the first time. Come with me, it's time to hit the shower." I nodded, and Polly led me past the rows and rows of containment cells. Inside, I saw all kinds of different mutated creatures. Some big, some small. I had to hold my hand over my mouth when we passed by a cell with blood and guts on the window. To my relief, we came to a room right past number 830, and she handed me another jumpsuit and a towel. "You got ten minutes to wash up and get dressed. They have you scheduled for some kind of test around 7, so hurry up."

"What about soap?" I asked, and watched as she pointed her thumb toward the room.

"It's already there."

"Right," I responded, and pushed the door open. Usually, she would hand it to me, but I guess this time was different. There were about ten stalls, and one of them was already taken by what I assumed to be another doctor, since I saw her lab coat sitting on a bench in front. It was pretty nice there. The floor was covered in blue and white tiles, and the smell of lavender body wash filled the room as steam rose to the ceiling. With a sigh, I reached around the back and unzipped my jumpsuit, pulled the rubber band out of my hair, and left my dirty clothes on the side while I washed up. It felt relaxing as the warm water fell over my bare body like a waterfall. Every time I got in the shower, I felt human again, like I was back in reality. But then I started to wonder. *How is this happening? Wasn't Beacon Hospital in ruins?* My mind was racing again with curiosity, but I swallowed down the thought. Even if I was going to be there forever, I was determined to never talk to Polly again unless I had to. Finally, I finished and wrapped the shower curtain around myself as I grabbed my towel. To my relief, no one was there. Once I dried myself off and put my new jumpsuit on, I saw the other worker's badge flipped over on her uniform. At any moment, Polly could walk in, or she could come out, but I knew I had to try. I tiptoed over, flinching with each sound I heard her make, until I got to it and unclipped it from her lab coat.

The name on the badge was Emma Marie, and just like Polly, she had level five security clearance. I didn't have any pockets to hide it, so I clipped it onto one of the straps on the back of my jumpsuit and left.

"Took you long enough. I told you ten minutes," Polly snapped when I walked out. I saw her peeking at her watch and blushed when I saw at least twenty had gone by.

"Sorry," I said, feeling flustered. We started to walk back toward my room when I heard a door slam down the hall, and saw a couple men approaching us, some in camo and the rest in scrubs.

"You'll be going with them. But don't worry," Polly said, putting her hand on my shoulder as they reached us, "I'm sure you'll be fine, 851." She gave me a fake smile before she turned to them and handed me off. Part of me wished I could become a monster, just to get a chance at wiping that smile off her. *Is that evil?* I thought as they led me down the hall. I couldn't help but feel nervous as we all crowded into a sketchy-looking elevator. Weirdly enough, besides the monsters, this was the worst-looking part so far. All the button lights went out, and the mirrors inside were covered in handprints. Although I got weird looks from the officers, I stared intently at them until I saw a little one that was smeared almost all the way down. They looked pretty old, and I almost missed it. Then something hit me. *Are they infecting kids too?* I glared at them as the elevator took forever to go between floors, and luckily, they confirmed one of my suspicions: I was on the eighth floor.

I felt saddened for the victims, and even though they weren't there, I put my hand where the kid's hand was and said a silent prayer. Then I realized the men were gone. I gasped and stood up, coming face to face with a little girl in a pink dress.

"Hi," I said, not knowing what to do. "Are you lost?" She shook her head before she pointed at the mirror behind me, and I saw a different reflection there than what was really happening. It was her. She stood there leaning on her toes as she held a man's hand and tugged on his pant leg with the other.

"Daddy," the little girl's voice echoed, "will the surgery take long? I want ice cream." The man shook his head and knelt down to her.

"Not long at all, and when you come out, I'll get you the biggest waffle cone they have. How's that, Lilly?" he asked as he poked the little girl's nose, causing her to giggle.

"Deal," she said, pressing her hand against the mirror. "Race you to the waiting room." I saw her go running out of the elevator before it changed again, and we were in the O.R. I saw the little girl lying there with a gas mask on her face, staring up at glow-in-the-dark stars they glued to the ceiling. I couldn't hear what they were saying, but I watched as they turned the gas on, and her eyes slowly closed. A few moments later, one of the doctors stepped in with a syringe with some kind of red liquid inside, and I knew it was their blood. I watched in pure agony for the little girl, as the doctor grabbed her arm and injected it into her veins.

"Subject 385, starting now," he said, stepping back. Not even ten seconds later, her body started changing on the table. Her arms started growing what looked like huge blisters, until they spread to the rest of her body and took over. The creature tore itself off the table as if the gas wasn't enough, and in an instant the people jumped to get her contained. It didn't work. She tore through five doctors before a man in a military uniform came in, saw the carnage around him, and shot her clean in the chest. I couldn't even move. Just like that, the little girl excited for ice cream was dead over some dumb experiment. I turned around with a tear falling from my eye and saw a wound had formed on the girl's chest.

"Don't let them hurt you like they hurt me and Daddy," she said, taking my hand. With her other hand she gestured toward the elevator door, and I turned around to see the military men step out. I tried to join them, but for some reason I was stuck in the elevator. I watched as they walked into the hall, and then I saw the little girl's father run up to them.

"How'd it go? Is she okay?" the man asked, holding a slip of paper with his daughter's patient number on it. The doctor in the front shook his head and spat out the worst lie I've ever heard.

"We couldn't get her to wake up from the anesthesia. She's gone." The man stood there shocked, and put a hand over his mouth, rightfully horrified.

"She just came in for a broken wrist," he said, looking the doctors up and down. "What did you do?"

"Like I said, sir, we did everything we could. She just couldn't come out of it." The man began to sob into his hands and stared up at the ceiling before he pointed his finger in the doctor's face.

"You're monsters! You killed my daughter, and I'm going to make sure everyone knows it."

"Fine, you want to see a monster? I'll show you one," a woman's voice said, before I heard a gunshot and saw the man fall to the floor in a pool of blood. At first, I couldn't understand why I recognized her voice, until she turned around and I nearly threw up. It was my mom.

I screamed and stumbled back against the mirror, breaking it on impact. When I looked up again, I was back in the elevator with the men again, and they were all staring at me.

"What did you do that for?" The mirror had a large crack across it, starting at the bottom where the girl's hand was all the way up to the ceiling. I couldn't even answer. I just shrugged as I realized how horrible these people truly were and leaned my head against the glass. Before long, the elevator reached the first floor, and although I felt like I could barely stand, I had no choice but to walk with them as they ushered me out of the elevator. As we came out, I saw an old rusted E.R. sign pointing to the right and a sign for the O.R. to the left. Just like the little girl, we went left. Besides a pair of double doors they had to swipe their badges for, it was pretty much a straight shot there. I was led into a room with nothing but a small table and two metal chairs. One of the doctors pulled one out and gestured for me to sit. I didn't want to, but I felt like I had no choice. They were all armed.

Some time passed before the doors opened again and another doctor walked in with a familiar face.

"Oliver!" I gasped and tried to push my chair back to hug him, but one of the doctors held my shoulder down with one of his hands. *What's going to happen?* I thought as they shoved him into the chair across from me. All I wanted to do was talk to him, especially when I saw he was a lot paler since we last spoke, but they had other plans.

"Are we ready?" an older doctor asked, glancing around. My whole body began to shake as they all loaded their guns and nodded to give him their approval. Before I could prepare myself, the doctor grabbed my hand and sliced a long cut right beneath my middle finger down to the top of my wrist. I whimpered in pain as the blood began to spill, and I saw they did the same thing to Oliver. Then the doctor grabbed our hands and forced them together. We were both scared, but I felt my heart pound faster as Oliver intertwined his fingers with mine. His lips curved up as he saw it had no effect on me, and I felt him rub his thumb across the back of my hand. I realized right then that I would go right back to being locked up again. I would never see Oliver again, never get answers, and never see the light of day. So, I smiled sadly at him before I closed my eyes, fell out of the chair, and faked convulsing against the floor. When I was finished, I held my breath, and they all swarmed around me as I played dead.

"Mia!" Oliver yelled, and I heard a loud thud where he was. A moment later, I felt someone put their fingers on my neck and suck in a breath.

"There's no pulse. She's dead!"

Chapter Five: Escaping the Basement

At first, I questioned what happened as they lifted my limp body off the floor. Then I realized the little girl from the elevator was there, and she had put her hand over my neck. The feeling of her cold hand hovering over me sent shivers down my spine. I could hear Oliver sobbing, but they held him back, even going so far as slamming him against the table. I peeked my eyes open and saw him fighting them as tears fell down his eyes, dropping onto his shirt collar.

"She's not dead, she can't be!" he shouted, and all I heard before I was carried out of the room was, "Please, check again." If anything would have broken me, it would have been Oliver's voice turning to a whisper in the end. It took everything in me not to move as the doctor turned the corner with me. I wanted to take in a full breath, but I had no choice but to take small ones so he wouldn't see my stomach move. I felt like my heart was going to pound out of my chest as we turned down an unlit hallway. For the first time since I entered the building, I finally saw the darkness I feared so much as a kid.

"Don't be scared, you're going to make it," I heard the little girl's voice chime in from behind us, and I felt a small bit of comfort, even though it only got worse from there. The walls were peeling, it smelled like death, as if I was being walked into a giant unburied cemetery, and from the floor to the ceiling there was nothing but dirt and dust. I squeezed my eyes shut as soon as I saw fungus and mold growing, and they began to water as I fought back the urge to gag. All I could hope was that this wouldn't affect my lungs too much. Finally, the man stopped, and I heard him open a door before setting me down inside a small dumbwaiter. I had no idea where it was going to take me, but the rotting smell only grew stronger as it sent me down. I reached the bottom and my heart instantly dropped. I was in the morgue.

All around me I could see silver freezer doors, and some of them were open, revealing either empty pull-out drawers or a white drape over the metal tables inside. Slowly, I stepped out of the dumbwaiter, and peered around only to narrowly avoid slipping on a pool of blood beneath the opening. I sighed and took a deep breath before I began walking forward again. The floor had plain white and black tiles, and the ceiling was discolored to an off-yellow color. There were long fluorescent lights hanging by wires, and for the first time it hurt my eyes trying to adjust to them. Other than the freezers, I was surprised to find there was nothing else in the room besides two human-sized tables covered in peeling green paint and two bedside tables with equipment on them. There were some beakers with unknown liquid in them, a spray bottle, a scalpel, a power saw, needle and thread, and a rib spreader. *Ugh, gross,* I thought as my mind began to think up what they did here. *Definitely wouldn't want to be involved in that.*

The room was bright, but I was completely on edge. I crept forward, leaving bloodied footprints behind me, until I heard a clunk. In a panic I scanned the room, turning in every direction, but nothing moved. At least, nothing that I saw.

"It's okay, Mia," I told myself. "You got this." I swallowed hard and took maybe three more steps before I heard an alarm go off. I gasped and looked around. Before long, I realized there was a sensor in front of the dumbwaiter, and I had tripped it. "No, no, no," I muttered to myself. Then I began to hear footsteps, and a voice outside.

"Another body?" a man's voice asked.

"Yep, I'll get it," a woman replied. My hair stood up on end as I glanced around the room and realized I had nowhere to go. I knew I had to hide, so I did something I knew I might regret. I ran to the first open freezer door that I could reach, pulled the tray open, and after a lot of hyping myself up, I laid down on it and used my hands to close it just enough that no one could see me. A second later, I heard the doorknob jiggle and then footsteps as someone came inside. I watched out the crack in the drawer and saw a shadow pass by, then it was quiet. A moment later, I heard the woman's voice again.

"What did I tell those idiots about sending down an empty—" She stopped mid-sentence with a gasp, and I heard her take two steps before she spoke again. "What the hell?" At first, I thought she was leaving when I heard her footsteps recede, but I wasn't so lucky.

"Hey! The body's gone! Someone come help me find it." My breath caught in my throat as I remembered the footprints I made on the floor. I was terrified. Then it got so much worse. The footsteps grew louder and more frequent. I realized there was more than one person in the room, and I swallowed a hard lump down in my throat.

"The footprints are all around the freezers," the woman told them. I peered out and the light from the crack was covered, telling me someone was right in front of me.

"Easy solution, shut them all and turn the temperature down. If something's here, or...someone, we'll know pretty quickly."

"Got it," the woman responded, and before I could manage to climb out, my door slammed shut, sending the drawer all the way in. It felt like I was shoved inside a coffin, and as I turned in the metal box, my breathing picked up. I was in full panic mode, and I knew I had to get out fast. With my feet, I gently pressed on the door, but it didn't come open. It was locked. Then it began to get cold, very fast. I was so scared; I hugged my arms around myself and tried kicking harder until I got to a full shiver a couple minutes later. At first, I thought the cold was all I had to fear, until the walls around me began leaking black ooze into my drawer. It started as small droplets like rain, then it began to gush. I gasped and pressed my body as far from it as I could, but it didn't seem to do any good. It began to fall on my jumpsuit, and it felt like lying in an icy pool of Jell-o. I screeched and arched my back, trying to avoid getting submerged in it, but it was coming down so fast there was no way to avoid it anymore. Even worse, the liquid didn't fall like normal. It clung to my skin, like it was clinging to warmth. Once it covered my arms and I realized I couldn't move them anymore, I knew I had to call out.

"Help! Someone, p-p-please!" I shouted, kicking the door with all my might. My body began to shake violently beneath the sludge, so I gave it one last effort and screamed at the top of my lungs. "HELP!" This time they heard me, although I gargled some of the liquid when I called out the last time.

"There's someone in there," I heard a man's voice say, and a moment later, the drawer was pulled open. As warmth began to return, the liquid began to fall over the sides until most of it was gone. I was sure it was seconds away from covering my whole body.

"Holy hell, she almost drowned in there."

I coughed and tried to sit up, but I felt drained. "Please don't hurt me," I pleaded through gasps of air, but they didn't listen. They seized me by my arms and legs and dropped me onto a rusted green table. My body felt weak and cold, but when they started trying to strap me down, I knew I needed to fight again.

"N-no. Let go of me!" I demanded, kicking and punching in all directions as they tried to pin me down.

"Stop fighting, it's over!" a man's voice said. I couldn't see his face, but he sounded stern and angry. I shook my head, and although I was outnumbered, I fought with every ounce of strength I had in me.

"We need some help in here!" the woman screamed, slamming one of my arms down hard like she planned on breaking it. I whimpered and pulled it back, only to have it yanked out of its socket. *Am I going to die here? Will I end up with Dad? NO, keep fighting, Mia. Oliver needs you.* I screamed as loud as I possibly could, making them all cover their ears. It only gave me a small window, but once they were back up it somehow got worse. One of the other doctors sprayed me with a thick green liquid. It smelled and tasted vile, almost like a skunk spraying me. My lungs and eyes burned. Sucking in air only seemed to make it worse. I was so disoriented, they managed to get one of my legs strapped down before I started thrashing again.

I was about to give up after seven draining minutes of fighting for my life when I managed to kick one of the doctors into the table next to me. I turned my head, and through the haze and the tears I saw the spray bottle hit the floor and explode into a thick gas cloud. The doctors and I began coughing, and soon they ran out of the room, leaving me traumatized and extremely shaken up. I was sobbing as I pulled myself up and unstrapped my leg, but again, no matter how tired I was, I knew I had to escape. My body felt weak when I hit the floor, so I fell into a heap and laid there for a few seconds. Slowly, I dragged my limbs across the floor and waved my arms as much as I could around myself to try and dissipate the smoke. Once I reached the door leading out, my body began to shake again. I was feeling light-headed. I leaned my head against the door, sighed, and pushed it open.

I had no idea where I was, but I managed to drag myself down a long hallway full of locked rooms until I came to two identical-looking hospital wings. I peered down both sides, and eventually ended up going right. I'd made it maybe six feet past the hall opening when I heard someone yell, "Hey!" My heart leapt into my throat, and I used the door frames to catapult me forward, almost gaining enough speed to get to a full run. I felt as though I was in a wetsuit, and the skin on my legs burned from chafing. Blindly, I turned into the first open door I could find and collapsed on the other side.

Somehow, they didn't see me and went straight past. I sighed with relief and took a second to recover before I used a wooden beam embedded in the wall to pull myself up. I grimaced when I saw the stain my body left behind. Oh, the things I would have done for another shower right then. Slowly, I got up the courage to open the door, but something told me to turn around when I heard a clunking sound right over my shoulder. I was a bit shocked when I discovered a woman chained to a hospital bed.

She looked to be about forty years old, but she was stunning either way. I could tell just by looking at her that she looked just like Oliver, and my face fell. *How could they keep his family down by the morgue?* I looked over at her again and saw that she had wires and tubes connected to her arms.

"Who are you?" she said, shifting uncomfortably in her bed. At first, I didn't know what to say, but then I pulled the door closed again and stepped closer.

"Mia," I told her as I eyed the tubes on her arms that led to a blood bag. "Are you a Beacon?"

"Yes, my name is Lynn. I think Oliver told me about you. He said you protected him, that you saved him. Is that true?" I nodded and came to stand by her bedside.

"Are you his mom?" She chuckled lightly and pressed her head into the pillow.

"Is it that obvious?"

"You look just like him," I said with a smile, and I put my hand over one of the straps. "Is there anything I can do to help? I have a keycard," I said, showing her the one I stole. "I can unstrap you and help you escape."

"Not without the rest of my family." She swallowed, pulling on her arms a bit. "I'm sure you're in enough trouble as it is, baby. You're drenched and... Look at you, you're shivering. There's a set of blankets in the closet, why don't you wrap one around yourself?" I nodded and pulled out a thin blue blanket. Once it covered my exposed skin, I began to feel a bit better, although I felt bad about staining it.

When I came back to her bedside, she continued, "I don't know how you made it down here but helping us will only get you killed. Get Oliver out and leave this place. For good." I shook my head and started unstrapping her, but she stopped me by pointing at the monitor. "If I get unhooked for even a second, the alarms will go off. I'm sorry, there's no saving me." I felt sick again as I stepped away from her, but I swallowed it down and walked to the door.

"Where are they keeping him?" I asked. It felt like I'd cried too much these last few days, I just wanted one happy moment. I pressed my head against the door frame and took a breath before I turned back to her. "I had to fake my death to get down here, and he saw it happen," I had to tell her, and I saw her face instantly fall.

"He's probably so scared," she said painfully. "He's three doors down on your left side. They barely let me see him anyway. It's been years of in and out, and he's suffered so much. He deserves peace, promise me you'll give him that?" I couldn't hold it in anymore. She reminded me of Dad, and I had to hug her. I came back and wrapped my arms around her far-too-thin body before I spoke again.

"I promise," I whispered as we both cried together. To think that the first time I met Oliver's mom would probably be the last hurt even more. It took me a second to pull myself together before I finally asked, "Do you know the way out?" She nodded, and told me about an

elevator that only works by keycard. The only problem was the level of security clearance. She told me level five should be enough, but she wasn't sure. I took a deep breath and squeezed her hand before I turned to leave again.

"Tell him I love him for me, okay?" I nodded and mustered up one last smile before I swiped my card, peered down the hallway, and left. Slowly I made my way toward Oliver's door and stopped in front of it. I closed my eyes and thought up a speech. I knew he wouldn't understand, but I made a promise, and I intended on keeping it. After a moment, I swiped the card and pushed the door open. When I looked inside, I saw Oliver had himself pressed up against the wall in the room with his face buried in his knees. He looked up with tears flowing down his face, and I saw bandages over his cheek. One of his eyes was swollen and looked to be black and blue, making me instantly sad. *Is that from him fighting them?* I thought, as I pulled the door shut behind me.

"Stay back, you said you would let me grieve. Please go—" He stopped once he realized it was me, and a look of utter shock hit his face, like he was looking at a ghost. "Mia!" Before I could even prepare myself, he practically tackled me into a metal filing cabinet from excitement. I hugged him back and buried my head into his shoulder. I was so happy to be able to hold him that I nearly forgot the urgency of the situation. We weren't apart for that long, but as far as I was concerned, he was all I had left. My mom was involved in the evil of this place, and I wanted nothing to do with her. When we separated, he put his hand on my cheek and looked me up and down.

"How are you alive? I saw you die," he said, then saw my jumpsuit and got confused.

"I faked my death to escape," I told him, and just like his mom, I showed him the card.

"Where did you get this from?" he asked, his eyes widening as he took it from my hand.

"I stole it from a doctor in the showers." He sucked in a breath, then he gagged. I was confused at first, until he stumbled back and said, "Maybe you should go back to the showers, that smell is awful." He gagged again, and I erupted in giggles as he opened his little armoire closet and took in deep breaths. "What is that from? God, that's bad."

"First of all, rude," I said, pulling him out of the closet and gently shoving him into the bed. "Second of all, I paid the morgue a visit." I could see his eyes were watering, and I would have laughed again if I hadn't heard the sound of the door handle jiggling.

"We've got trouble," I told him.

He gestured to the closet and whispered, "Hide, quick." Without a moment's hesitation, I jumped inside and pulled the door shut. I sat there beneath a closet full of jumpsuits and empty hangers, and I heard footsteps right outside. All I could hope was that my footprints wouldn't give me away again.

"We've got a security leak," I heard a moment later. "If you've seen anyone come inside or run by you are advised to tell us now, because if we find out on our own, there will be severe repercussions."

"You told me you would leave me alone," I heard him respond, seemingly angry.

"And we will, but first I need you to confirm—"

"I haven't seen anyone," he snapped. "My head's been buried in my knees for the past hour."

"Got it, sorry for disturbing you." Before the man left the room, I heard him whisper, "Brat," under his breath, and I couldn't help but wonder if Oliver heard him too. Once I heard the footsteps recede and the sound of the door shutting, I slowly eased the closet door open until he told me the coast was clear. With a sigh, I stepped back out and stayed at a distance so Oliver didn't gag again.

"What's the plan?" he asked me as he showed me the ID badge again.

"We have to go at this alone," I told him as I pulled a swivel chair from their computer station and sat in front of him. "I met your mom, and I found out your family has an alarm set to their monitors." Oliver seemed to take this hard as he realized just what I was saying. "She told me to tell you she loves you," I said finally, and a look of pure defeat crossed his face.

"We're going to leave them for good, aren't we?" he said, meeting my eyes as he waited for my answer.

"She made me promise I'd take care of you." Quietly he sobbed and looked down at the floor. I didn't want to disturb him with the smell, but I needed to comfort him. So, I came and sat by his side. He leaned his head against me and sniffled as he tried to stop himself from crying.

"We'll have to take care of each other then," he said, finally taking his bandaged hand and wrapping it around mine. The smell didn't seem to matter then as we sat together. We were just two strangers bonded together by a nightmare world. I didn't know what the future held for us, especially since I couldn't go home, but I was determined to escape for good this time. Once we were both ready, I used the ID badge to open a color-coded filing cabinet full of medical supplies. I started by grabbing gauze, bandages, some alcohol wipes, and some safety pins. Since we didn't have pockets, we had no choice but to carry it all in our hands. It was a little hard to swipe the badge at the door, but I managed to hold everything up against my chest as I lifted my free hand.

Once the door was open, I peered around the doorframe, looking left and right until I saw far down the left hall there was a group of doctors talking to a man in a military uniform.

"Where's the elevator?" I whispered, looking back and forth to try and find it.

"It's right past them," he responded with a sigh as he peered over my shoulder. "We have to find a way to lure them away." I pressed my forehead against the doorframe as I let my mind wander. My first thought was to throw something near the morgue hallway and hide, but I was too scared that we would get caught. That's when I realized they were getting closer as they checked more and more doors. *They wouldn't come back down this way, would they?* I swallowed anxiously and began to pace back and forth as Oliver used his back to hold the door.

"You're not going to like this, but I have an idea," I said as I saw him lean into the hall.

"Let me hear it." He looked down at me as I stepped past him and pulled on his arm with my free hand.

"I think the best way to lure them down here is to set off an alarm," I told him gently, "but I want you to get a chance to say goodbye first. Knock on the door when you're ready, okay?"

I swiped the keycard for the last time on his mother's door, and I heard him whisper, "Hey, Mom," before I shut the door as quietly as I could. I lowered myself down to the floor and pulled my knees in to avoid being seen. Somehow, I completely forgot what the woman did to my arm, but as I sat there, I got a crude reminder when I felt a jolt of pain. I groaned, and with a grimace, I popped it back into place. It was painful, but again I had to ignore it. My eyes began to feel heavy as I waited for him. A few minutes went by before I heard the knock come, and I stood up to unlock the door with a yawn. When he emerged, he had two clear drawstring bags, one slung over his shoulder, and the other he held out for me.

"I unstrapped her," he said, helping me load the supplies into my bag. "She said she'll set off the alarm once we're ready to run." I nodded, and once I put the bag around my back and helped him load his bag, he knocked twice against the door to give her the signal. As fast as we could, we pressed ourselves against a door on the opposite side of the hall and heard the alarm echo over the loudspeakers secured to the walls. I could hear their shoes squeaking against the floor tiles as they bolted down the hall like they were on a basketball court, and we both sucked our stomachs in to stay hidden behind the door frame. My whole body tensed up when about ten military, two doctors, and three guys in hazmat suits ran directly in front of us, but Oliver squeezed my hand as my breathing deepened. We waited until they all packed themselves inside the door like sardines before we peeled ourselves away from the doorway and took off. Unfortunately for both of us, it wasn't long before they caught on, and I heard the screams of Oliver's mother as she fought them with everything she had.

"Don't touch my boy!" I heard her say, followed by the sound of glass breaking. I could feel the adrenaline pumping in my veins. This was our one chance, and failing wasn't an option if we wanted to see the light of day again, so I used my foot to kick a medical cart at them, causing a collision. I could hear the frustrated huffs and puffs behind me as I repeatedly pushed the button for the elevator.

"Come on, come on!" I said anxiously as I watched the numbers go down. The hallway was littered with syringes and tubes, causing them to slip over and over again. *Will this buy us enough time?*

"Uh...Mia?" Oliver said as I pushed the button in as far as it would go and heard a loud Pop behind me. I turned around to see what I could only describe as an abomination, peek its giant head around the corner and pop the lights above itself as it tilted its head at me. It had a large slender frame with broken ribs protruding from its body, and limbs longer than the hallway between us. Its eyes looked pale white and soulless, while the rest of its face below its nose looked rotten and decayed. We both stood there frozen as it gripped the wall with its oddly large hand and turned its head back and forth. A moment later, one of the army guys used the wall to pull himself up and pulled out his shotgun from his holster.

"Hey, ugly!" I almost felt relieved, until in one fell swoop it grabbed the man up by his ankles, struggling and screaming, and dropped him into its mouth. Before I could make a sound, Oliver pulled me into him and put his hand over my mouth as we both shook in fear. The sound of the thing gulping quickly overshadowed the screams. Then the elevator opened. To my horror, it stopped what it was doing and came barreling toward us. I wanted to pull away, but I felt Oliver shake his head against me as he physically held me in place. It stood directly above us and roared, making the hallway rumble with its loud voice. I peered up at it and felt like I was being pricked with pins and needles as goosebumps made their way up my arms. I thought we were in the clear, until it lowered its head down to where we were, staring me directly in the eye. My heart physically leapt to my throat as its claws dug into the brick wall on either side of us, like it was caging us in. All I could feel then was Oliver's shaking body against mine, his breath against my neck, and his hair brushing up against me as we cemented ourselves against the ground. Then, by pure luck, I heard another glass break behind us, and it turned around in a violent fury. We didn't waste a single second: I pulled him inside the elevator and hit the door close button. I heard another scream, but the door shut before I saw anything else happen.

Even after the doors were closed, I couldn't stop shaking. I knew then that if I would have moved, I would have turned out just like that military man inside its stomach.

"Oliver, you just saved my life," I mumbled, still reeling from shock.

"Don't mention it," he replied, panting as he wiped a bead of sweat off his forehead. Normally, I would have tried to muster a smile, but I couldn't. Instead, I used the elevator railing to prop myself up as my knees wobbled beneath me. I took a few deep breaths, and used all the strength I could gather in myself to get back up. All that adrenaline, and I finally crashed. It was hard, but I managed to come to a standing position and shakily grabbed the card off the elevator floor. I could only imagine what would have happened if I'd lost it, so I pressed it against my lips before I swiped it. I nearly collapsed again with pure joy when the light on the card reader turned green, and Oliver hit the button to go up. We only had one floor to go, which didn't leave us with a lot of time to prepare. I almost considered hitting the emergency stop button so we could sit there for a moment, but I was too scared they would come for us. It took a lot of courage for me to let go of the bar and pull myself away from the wall, but I managed to do it as I got in a running position.

"Get ready," I told him as he pulled himself off the floor behind me. Deep down, I knew escaping the island wasn't going to be an easy task, but I was prepared to fight for our freedom no matter what it took.

Chapter Six: Leaving Beacon Island

I heard the elevator make that familiar ding sound and began mentally mapping out the island as I waited for the doors to open. Once they did, we raced right past the reception desk and straight through the double doors at the front. The first thing I saw was a barbed-wire fence surrounding the building like a prison, and a chain around the front door with a heavy-duty lock hanging there. The parking lot right outside was filled with cars, although most of them were infantry carrier vehicles or trucks. In the distance, I could see a clearly sick little boy being ushered in by a doctor. I wanted to scream for him to run, but we had no choice but to slide under the first car we could see as we were followed out of the building.

"Security breach!" I heard a man yell and saw him frantically running across the parking lot. Within seconds, every available officer and security member was running around looking for us. Somehow, I felt safe, lying there on my stomach. I wasn't locked up and there were no monsters, it was just us watching boots run by us over and over again.

"Mia?" Oliver whispered as we sat there watching.

"Yeah?" I turned my body a little so we were both angled toward each other, and he chuckled as we came face to face.

The rocks beneath me slid as I moved, and I knew that later I was going to have indents in my skin.

"I have a feeling we're going to be here for a while," he said, solemnly, "so maybe we can get to know each other?"

"I'd love that," I responded, and we did just that. I told Oliver all about my home life, what it was like at school, my experiences, and fun things I liked to do. He listened to every word, although we both shifted around uncomfortably. Then I told him about my dad, and he smiled. In both our eyes, he was a hero. I wanted to make sure he didn't die for nothing, he deserved that much. Oliver was heartbroken when he found out that he was Subject 850 and that he turned. He told me that he felt like it was his fault, and I shook my head.

"You're not the monster here, they are. Including...my mother." His face changed to a genuine shock, and he implored me to say more. I told him what I saw with the little girl and her dad, and how I felt genuinely sick when she shot him. I was sure he would look at me like I was crazy, especially since I told him I was talking to a ghost, but he believed me. In a way, it was understandable, considering what we've seen, but if someone had told me this story, I would have thought they were out of their mind. I've always believed in ghosts, and maybe even demons, but this was way different.

"If we can make it to that gate, do you think we can find something to smash that lock?" I asked him as I shook pebbles off my arms.

"I think that's our only option. Smash the lock and pray for a miracle when we reach the shoreline." I nodded and sucked in a breath as I prepared myself to go back out again.

Slowly, we army-crawled our way out and ducked behind the truck bed for cover. I don't know how long we were beneath that truck, but I could see the sun was starting to go down. The sky was a beautiful pinkish-red color, and it reminded me of this old rhyme my dad used to tell me as a kid. "Red sky in morning, sailor take warning. Red sky at night, sailors delight." I wasn't sure if that meant the water would be calmer or not, but I took it as a good sign.

"Let's get going. I don't want to stick around to see Beacon Hospital at night," Oliver said, nudging my arm as I stared up at the sky. I nodded, and the two of us creeped along the side of the cars. It took us maybe ten minutes to reach the gate from where we were, but it was locked up tight. I could tell someone had come in recently because I saw muddy tracks out front, but whoever was let inside probably took the keys with them. More than likely it was that little boy's family. All I could hope was that once we escaped from here, we could tell someone and get their whole operation shut down. "Hang on, I'll look for a rock," he said. "Keep an eye out."

"Got it." As he walked away, I looked back and forth between each little opening to make sure no one was coming. I don't know what happened to those army guys, but the parking lot looked clear. *Maybe they gave up.* I wasn't sure, but I felt a little bit of hope rise in my chest as Oliver came back toward me with a giant rock.

"Hopefully no one hears this," I heard him mumble as he came back to the gate, lifted his arm, and smashed it against the lock as hard as he could. His face quickly turned from calm to frustrated when it didn't break. He swung once, picked it up again, and swung twice. Nothing. Finally,

I came up and held out my hand. I had so much pent-up anger from Polly, the little girl, my mom, all those innocent lives taken, all of it, that I pulled my arm back and crushed it like an empty pop can. The lock fell on the floor in a pile, and I heard Oliver huff behind me. "I think I broke it first," he said, crossing his arms. I just chuckled and shoved him playfully through the gate.

"Yeah, yeah," I teased, and I could hear him dragging his feet behind him as we walked away. From afar, the island always looked so tiny to me. Little did I know, we still had a couple miles between us and the shore. We walked on for a while, passing an old restaurant called "Denny's Dinner," a convenience store, and a giant warehouse. I could only guess what horrors were in store inside each of those places, especially the warehouse. For all I knew, it was filled with food or something good, but I swallowed those thoughts down and focused on the muddy path. That's when I started to hear rocks tumbling, and a gentle knock coming our way.

"Car! Take cover," I told Oliver, and followed him behind the trees. We stood there hugging this big pine tree as a small red SUV pulled down the road, and I sucked in a breath when I recognized the back license plate. It was my mom. Before she passed us, I saw an ID badge hanging from her rearview mirror and felt nauseous. There was still a small part of me that thought what I saw wasn't real, or that she was forced. What I saw then only cemented my fears. She really was evil. I think my heart shattered when I saw a sticker on the back windshield. It was me standing between Mom and Dad, holding their hands. Dad bought it the day I was born and put it on her car as a surprise. It hurt to know I would never get that back, so I pulled Oliver away as I fought tears and anger. Even then, Oliver knew me well enough to tell something wasn't right, so he stopped me.

"Do you want to talk about it?" he asked, using his finger to lift my chin up. I stared into his eyes and laced my fingers together nervously.

"That was her," I told him, digging my nails into my palms as I fought back my emotions. I didn't want to cry, or shake, or feel mad anymore, I just wanted to be at peace. The only problem was that peace was no longer an option.

"Don't," he said, cutting through my darkening thoughts. Confused, I looked up at him again and saw this deeply saddened look cross over his face. "You don't have to fight it in front of me. Cry it out, jump, throw something, scream... Well, maybe not that, but you get the point. You've been through hell, we both have. So right now, I want you to let it all out, because we..." he said, taking my hands in his, "are escaping tonight, no matter how scary it gets. And I hope your mom takes every bit of offense when I say you take after your dad." I chuckled and pulled him into me. It took me a minute to regain my composure as he held me and pressed his lips against the top of my head, but once I did, we set off again. I felt relieved when we finally made it back to the apartment buildings. We still had about a mile between us and the water, but it was close.

Once we passed complex 666, I could barely contain myself when I saw a boat at the edge of the dock. It was a small white motorboat, with the name *Jumpin Fishstix* on the side and a sticker of a swordfish dangling on a hook. We ran up to it and peeked inside, but no one was there. I could see it had a cooler full of different types of pop, beer bottles, and ice. It must have been here for a while because the ice water was starting to leak out of the bottom. The two of us climbed up and walked around as it bobbed in the water. Up front near the controls, there was a wooden crate filled with equipment. I saw an EMF reader, a polaroid camera, some motion detectors, and a lot of salt.

"What is all this stuff?" Oliver asked, as he pulled out a motion detector and jumped when it went off.

"Ghost hunting equipment, I think. Probably from another explorer coming to check out the island," I responded. I was shocked, though, when I saw the keys were still in the ignition. I wasn't expecting much, but I went over and sat down on what I liked to call the captain's chair and turned the key. The engine sputtered a few times, making a sound like a horse neighing, but somehow it actually turned over.

"Ha! It works!" I exclaimed, feeling excited. The boat didn't have that much gas in it, but I held out hope that it had enough to get to Dad's car. "What do you think? Go for it?" He came and sat down in the chair next to me and nodded as he handed me a cold cream soda in a glass bottle.

"Go for it." I smiled and broke the top of the bottle on the side of the boat. As it fizzed, I took a sip and smiled as the familiar taste hit my tongue.

"Mmm."

"Good?" Oliver said mockingly as I gulped it down.

"Even better than I remembered." He chuckled and took the bottle out of my hands. I gasped and went to grab it, but he held it out of my reach. "Hey!"

"It's against the law to drink and drive, you know."

"Ha, ha," I responded, before I pulled it back and floored the gas.

"Woah." I nearly broke out laughing when he grabbed the metal bar on the side of the boat and held on for dear life. "Have you ever driven a boat before?"

"Nope." His face turned bright red, and I had to admit it was pretty funny. It took me a minute to figure out the controls, especially considering there were so many switches, but I managed. Luckily for both of us, the water was much calmer than when I came in, and for the most part, it was a pretty smooth ride. Considering it was nighttime, though, it was a lot more eerie than before. I could hear the sound of owls hooting in the distance, and cicadas buzzing. The trees loomed over us like large claws, with their branches flowing in the wind. It was unsettling how quiet it was, so we decided to talk again.

"Wanna hear a joke?" Oliver said, turning around and around in a circle in his swivel chair as he stared up at the sky.

"Depends, is it good or bad?" I glanced over at him, and he shrugged.

"I think it's pretty good."

"Okay, shoot," I said, and started thinking of my own joke as he spoke.

"Why did the scarecrow win an award?" he asked, smiling from ear to ear. I shrugged and readied myself to hear a dumb answer. "Because he was outstanding in his field."

"That was so bad," I said, fighting back a giggle.

"Let's hear you tell one then," he scoffed, and crossed his arms over his chest playfully.

"Okay, um... What do dogs eat for breakfast?" I asked, thinking of a joke my dad told me years ago.

"I don't know," he said, leaning forward like I was telling a story.

"Woofles." He groaned, and I turned my chair back toward the water as I let out little laughs. Somehow, we made it to the docks at the park after about twenty minutes of goofing off. Slowly, I let off the gas until we drifted up to the dock and anchored us right by the ramp. Before we left the boat, we stocked up on drinks and grabbed some leftover ice to chew on as we walked away. I wasn't surprised when we got to the top of the hill and saw two wooden gate doors with red reflectors on them were closed and locked up. More than likely the park rangers just finished closing up the park before we got there. We glanced around as we climbed over the little doors, but there was no one around.

"This way, my dad's car should still be here," I told Oliver, and ran as fast as I could to the far end of the parking lot. Dad bought a permit for us to sit there overnight, since we were going to be exploring, but it was more than expired. I saw seven tickets beneath the windshield wipers, and a one-day warning to remove the car before they would tow it at our expense taped to the window. I could only imagine what Dad would have said if he saw these. More than likely he would have groaned and said something along the lines of, "Don't tell your mother." I chuckled just thinking about it and pulled the wipers forward to grab them.

"Ouch, fifty bucks each," Oliver said, standing over me to look.

"I don't think we have to worry about these anymore." Without so much as a second thought, I balled them up and threw them in the nearest trash can. Compared to everything that happened the last few days, a few tickets didn't really bother me.

"Mia, I don't mean to be the bearer of bad news," he told me, as he pressed himself against the glass and peeked inside, "but we don't have keys." Somehow, I completely forgot that part. I sighed, and he stepped aside while I yanked on the handle. My dad's car was pretty old, so the door was known to get stuck. I managed to get it open, but just like he said, no keys.

"Let's rest for a bit," I said, and reached across the dash to open the passenger side door for him from the inside. Once he was next to me, I leaned back in my seat and turned on my side toward him. "I'm tired." I yawned and wiped my eyes as they started to water.

"Me too," he responded, squeezing his eyes shut. "Maybe we can sleep here for the night, and get help from the rangers in the morning?"

"What do you think they'll say about this?" I held up my arms, and he exhaled deeply as he looked me over. My veins were black all over my body, and I knew it looked concerning.

"I'm sure we'll come up with something. We're so close, we can't fail now." I nodded, gave him one last smile, said goodnight, and drifted off. I don't know how much time passed as we slept, but we both jolted from our sleep when we heard a knock at the window. I squinted when I saw a flashlight shining into the car and stretched as I sat up.

"Hi," I mumbled as I pushed the door open.

"Hi, is this your vehicle, ma'am?" a ranger asked, looking back and forth between the two of us.

"It was my dad's, sir, but he passed away." I swallowed when I said the last part, and the man's whole demeanor changed from angry to embarrassed in a matter of seconds.

"Oh crap, I'm sorry. My rangers were freaking out thinking someone just left it here. Did it just happen?" I nodded and pulled the lever for the seat to go back up.

"Yeah, we went kayaking and had an accident. I l-lost both him and the kayaks." The man turned and said something to the other ranger, before he turned back to us scratching the back of his neck nervously.

"I know this isn't what you want to hear, but I'm gonna need your statement. I can only imagine what you're going through, you and your boyfriend? Brother?" the officer asked, gesturing to Oliver next to me.

"He's my...friend," I told him, as I peered over my shoulder to see Oliver's face had turned bright red.

"Right, let's get you to the ranger station and we'll wait there for the police to arrive. Are either of you injured?" he asked, pulling out a small notepad.

"She is, sir," Oliver said, gesturing to my shoulder that looked like a mess of burnt scar tissue.

"Ouch, what happened there?"

"A...fire," I mumbled uncomfortably. "I got too close to it and burnt myself pretty badly."

"Looks more like you fell in it," he said, scribbling frantically in his book. "Probably needs to get disinfected, it doesn't look too good." I heard him gasp, and squinted again as he accidentally shined the light in my eyes. "I don't mean to frighten you, but what's going on with your skin?" He aimed his flashlight at me, and his eyes widened. "Are you feeling sick at all?"

"I've got a medical condition." I lied, swallowing down a hard lump in my throat.

"Oh okay, you had me worried there for a moment. Come with me, I'll drive you two up there." We nodded, and he led us back to his car while he spoke to someone over his walkie about towing Dad's car for us. For the most part, the rangers didn't say much during the drive. The main ranger—or warden, as he told us—asked us why we reserved a spot, how we ended up there (since there were no other cars there), and if there was anyone he could call for us. We told so many lies just then, I couldn't help but feel guilty. I told him I didn't have any family, and Oliver was all I had left. In my eyes it was the truth, but I had a feeling Mom would somehow find out about this. Oliver told him he was an orphan and we met through mutual friends. As we spoke, the warden kept peering back at us through the rearview mirror, while the other scribbled in a notepad. After that we rode in silence, until we came to this little town called Hunter's Villa. The town that started it all, or in better terms, started the beginning of the outbreak.

Chapter Seven: Falling Into Hell

When we entered the town, there was a huge sign that said, *Population 87,* and showed a large ginger-haired man in a ripped flannel flexing his muscles. I chuckled as we rode by it, and Oliver gave me a playful look over his shoulder like he thought it was funny. The view was beautiful. Pink cherry blossom trees and weeping willows hung over the town entrance on either side of the street leading into the small bustling city. We rode past a Jerry's Toy Store where a little boy was showing his dad a Transformer in the window, a wedding boutique full of stunning dresses, and a food truck that made my mouth water as the smell filled the air around us. I pointed out the window as we drove on, and just by pure coincidence I saw the warden glare at me through his visor mirror. I started to feel very uneasy, and it was almost as if the town began to change with my feelings. I began to see barriers and police officers ushering people through the back alleyways. Something told me they didn't believe any of our story, so I gently nudged Oliver.

"Something's wrong," I whispered, glancing between him and the ranger ahead of us.

"What do you mean?" he asked, confused as he turned away from the window. I took a deep breath, and gestured back out the window where an officer was aiming a gun at a young girl. Slowly, he began to notice it too, and we both looked up to see the officer had turned around completely, taking his eyes off the road, and staring at us as he floored the gas.

"I never thought I'd see one of you infected in my car, but here we are," he said, ominously looking me up and down. I felt extremely unsafe and leaned against Oliver. Behind him, I saw the speed going as high as eighty-five, and my mouth fell open.

"I'm not infected. Please, watch the road!" We came up on a statue of a man with a bow and arrow aiming at the sky, and blasted right through it, shattering it on the ground.

"Ahhh!" Instinctually, I screamed, and the man covered his ears as if I let out a screech.

"You're not infecting me today, demon!" he yelled, turning back around, and swerving wildly through the street, narrowly avoiding some pedestrians as he drove over a traffic circle. I could hear the sound of the tires scorching the ground, and realized just how crazy this guy was as the speedometer rose to a hundred.

"Mia!" Oliver screamed, pointing in a panic straight ahead. I turned my head to see the man was driving us directly toward a *Bridge Out* sign, and my whole body went into shock. Our window of escape was dwindling by the second. There was a field right before the bridge, but I knew if we somehow missed, neither of us would make it. Either way, we didn't have a choice. Without so much as a second thought, I reached over Oliver, threw the door open, ripping it off its hinges in the wind, and shoved him out just as we came to the field. Before I hit the ground, I hugged my knees and rolled in a ball down the hill toward the water. I groaned as my body bounced over and over again, sending jolts of pain in every direction. I couldn't stop rolling. My eyes became blurry, and I tried to call out for Oliver, but no sound came out. Worst of all, I could taste blood in my mouth. No matter how much I tried to fight it, my eyes eventually closed, and it all went dark.

I woke up in my own house. I found myself on the floor with a newspaper beneath me covered in drool, and saw all the furniture was taken out, leaving stained spots in the wood. It felt disorienting as I sat up and tried to regain my strength, but once I did, I looked down at the paper to see the fire story. Confused, I tilted my head and peeled it off the floor. *How did I get here?* My body felt like Jell-o, so I had no choice but to use the wall to pull myself up. Outside I could hear thunder rumbling in the distance, and I limped my way to the glass sliding door that led to the back yard. *I could have sworn the rain had stopped before the crash... The crash!* I looked around in a panic until my eyes rested on a familiar little boy. It was the one we saw before we left Beacon, only his body was completely see-through.

"What happened to you?" I asked, taking a few shaky steps toward him. The boy just stared at me with a scared look and ran out the back door.

"Wait!" Somehow, I gained the strength to run after him, and raced outside in an attempt to catch him. I was even more confused when I saw the back yard was completely empty. *Where did he run off to?* I thought, cupping my hands around my mouth.

"Hello?" I called, looking around. No one answered. The first thing I laid my eyes on were some lanterns sitting on a rusty metal table underneath the house awning. Beside them, I could see a thick stack of papers, and before I could even go to investigate them, the wind picked up, sending them flying all over the yard. I gasped, and soon came to the realization that they were all missing posters. Women, children, men, all kinds of people. The stack was so big, I felt like they were coming out of nowhere. Each one had a tear near the top of them, like they had been nailed up but were torn back down. *Are these all the victims?* I thought, feeling sick as they flew over the fence into the night sky. My mouth fell open again, and through the paper screen, I could see the boy and the little girl from the hospital playing in the sandbox. Her giggles were loud and infectious as they threw sand at each other. Then they both stopped, and the girl screamed as her chest began to bleed again. My eyes widened, and I went to walk back there when she pointed toward the fence.

"He did this." I pushed through the papers blocking my view until I finally saw Oliver. I was in shock when I realized he was wearing the same clothes as the boy from my childhood. *Was that real?* I thought, remembering the horror of what I saw that day. He sat on one of the fence posts, swinging his legs. Even from across the yard, I could sense something wicked was emanating from him, a dark energy, and swallowed hard. I told myself he was my friend and shook the worries away as I walked toward him.

"O-Oliver?" I called, shivering from fear "Are you—" Before I could finish my sentence, my feet sunk into the ground. I heard what I could only describe as a swallowing sound when what I thought was water began to devour my lower body. It didn't take me long to realize it wasn't, as I tried to pull myself out and only managed to lodge myself in further.

Just like when we were in the river, I dug my hands into the dirt, and began screaming for help as the ground literally began to swallow me alive. I clawed and kicked and flailed wildly until Oliver came and stood over the hole, peering down at me from above. I began panting as I sunk deeper and deeper, and the goop around me became heavy on my body.

"Help," I pleaded, reaching my hand up to him as the goop rose to my neck.

"Sorry, Mia, but it's time to drown." His eyes turned pitch-black just then, and his voice distorted. I watched in horror as he put his foot on my head and forced me down. The goop filled my mouth and nose, and the only thing I could do was let out one final scream beneath the surface as my lungs gave out.

I thought I was dead, but somehow, I awoke again to Oliver giving me CPR. Instantly, I sat up and coughed up water.

"Thank God. You're alive!" I heard him exclaim as I tried to catch my breath. My eyes were blurry at first, and my lungs burned as I coughed up the last remnants of the murky water. Slowly I came out of it and found myself on the bank of the river. I glanced around me, and saw the ranger's car was almost fully submerged, leaving only the back end sticking out. I began to shiver and leaned my head against Oliver as I recovered from the shock of what had just happened. *Was it all a dream?* He held me and choked back his sobs. I looked up at him, and he gave me this heartbreaking smile that made my heart jump.

"Hey," he said, wiping the tears away from his eyes. "I was so scared I lost you." Like me, he was covered in scrapes and bruises, but somehow, I seemed to get the worst of it.

"O..." I spat out a bit of phlegm as I went to talk. Everything hurt, but I knew we weren't entirely out of the woods yet. I must have sat there for at least five minutes just breathing and wincing as my chest ached with each exhale I took. It didn't take me long to put the pieces together and realize I rolled into the water, but I was still confused. *What happened to the rangers? What about the police we saw? Are they going to come for us?*

"Oliver?" I finally managed to say.

"I'm here, Mia." he said reassuringly, and before I could even collect my thoughts, he picked me up and limped toward the roadway above us. For once since this whole adventure began, I felt speechless. Whether it was shock or exhaustion from tumbling out of a speeding car, I couldn't muster up the strength to say anything more. Instead, I tucked my head into Oliver's chest and just squeezed my eyes shut. I could only imagine what people would think if they saw us. Two college-aged adults wearing the same outfit, covered in scrapes and bruises, limping through a field. We looked like we came straight out of a scary movie, and if I was being honest, I felt like we were living in one too. The little bit of sleep from the car helped somewhat, but neither of us were in good condition. When we made it onto the street, Oliver stopped dead still. I looked up at him, and a look of pure terror crossed his face. Slowly, I turned my body around in his arms, and saw fire and smoke gathering in the sky, cars crashing into buildings, and people running frantically through the streets. It was a small town, but everyone was gathered in the middle of the city as pure chaos broke out. *Is this the start of the apocalypse?*

Chapter Eight: In the Dark

By some miracle, we managed to escape the city before things got any worse. After the mayhem and chaos ensued, he limped into town with me in his arms until he found a truck someone had left running. I felt unsettled when I saw a bullet hole in the passenger side window, but at that moment it seemed to be our only option. In the distance, I could hear gunshots, and Oliver jumped a few times while we tried to get settled. I was too scared to sit up front with him, considering I already got us in trouble once, so I used this fluffy winter jacket they had stowed under the back seat as a pillow and laid down in the truck bed. The two of us took an aspirin or two for the pain, and we had to share some water, considering most of our supplies got dumped. I thought we were ready, but I heard the sound of Oliver hitting the dash before he jumped back out again.

"I'll be right back," he told me at the last moment and ran off. I grew instantly scared, and watched as he ran into the mess. The once-beautiful town was now full of looters and police, and although I hadn't seen any yet, I was sure there were monsters too. My breath quickened as time dragged on. Twenty minutes went by, and still, I didn't see him. I almost got out to go after him until I saw him come running out of this little clothing store called Minair. I sighed and let my head fall into my arms. When he came back, he tossed a pile of women's clothes into the back and a hairbrush; some of the shirts had short sleeves, some had long. He told me he didn't know my size, so he just grabbed whatever he could find. I was grateful.

"Go ahead and get changed, I won't look," he said with a wink, making my face turn bright red. Smiling, I knelt down in the truck bed right beneath the back window, and unzipped the old, blood-covered jumpsuit. I broke out in giggles when I saw the bra selection he picked out. It was a cute attempt, but most were much bigger than I was. I managed to find three that fit snug against me. *Thanks, Oliver.* I let out one final laugh. It took me a second to figure out what to wear, but I ended up settling on a blue blouse with a marble-colored bar right below the neckline and a pair of gray cloth shorts. Then I brushed out a giant rat's nest in my hair. I wasn't even surprised when I pulled some cotton and seaweed out of my tangled mats. It took a few minutes, but I brushed it until I could run my fingers through it without getting stuck. Up front I could hear him moving around, so I sneakily peaked through the back window. I couldn't see much thanks to the seats, but I saw his bare upper body when he shuffled around. I gasped and ducked beneath the window. He was genuinely attractive, but he was thin thanks to the abuse he underwent at Beacon. I could tell he worked out by the way his stomach looked, and wondered, *do they have a gym at Beacon?* I felt embarrassed for what my mind was conjuring up. If I wasn't so scared of losing him, I might have hopped up there just then. Slowly I raised myself back up and saw him staring back at me through the rearview mirror. *Curse my loud movements,* I thought as the heat rose in my face.

"Sneaking a peak?" he asked, raising his eyebrows with a chuckle. I felt instantly flustered and sank back down into the truck bed.

"No," I said, and heard him laugh as he put the car in drive and set off down the road. As we left the town the way we came in, I saw a man in a dark-colored hoodie bust through the window of the toyshop and run off with the Transformer I saw that kid pointing at earlier. I felt sad at first, but right as we turned the corner where the trees were, I saw him hand it to the little boy and carry him off. I knew then it must have been his dad. *One small victory,* I thought as I put my hand on my heart and settled back down. I was scared that we would get blocked into the city by police, but we were lucky to find an opening in the barricades and escape.

I shivered as the wind blew over my body. I almost considered putting on a long sleeve shirt, but I knew once the sun came up, I would regret it. Ignoring the chill, I listened to the soft hum of the engine and the occasional thump as the car rolled over potholes. He checked on me a few times, but mostly we just had a quiet, peaceful drive. I stared up at the moon and the stars until eventually the sun started to come up. For the first time in days, I felt content. The pain was minimal, although I knew this euphoric feeling probably wouldn't last long.

We must have gotten at least a few hours outside the city before I started to hear the engine sputter.

"Are we out of gas?" I asked, peeling myself up with a yawn.

"Almost," he responded, "but don't worry, the store owner inside the clothing shop gave me some money. I told him we were in trouble, and after he saw the chaos outside, he gladly helped us out."

"How much?" I asked and saw him hold a thick stack of mixed bills including hundreds at the top. My eyes widened and I felt instantly relieved.

"Enough. He took the rest for himself, and I honestly can't blame him. I'll fill the tank up halfway, and we'll figure it out from there. It's probably a good idea we save the rest of the money for a hotel though, and...food. I'm starved."

"Me too," I told him, and my stomach growled as if on cue. "Can I come up there? Or do you think I should stay here?" I felt really self-conscious as I looked down at myself. The veins in my arms and legs looked strange. All I wanted was to be normal again. Even after we escaped the island, I still felt like a monster compared to him.

"Come on up," he said finally, pulling over to the side of the road.

"Are you sure?" I asked, gripping the back window tightly as I debated what to do.

"I'm sure, love. You look beautiful, even with dark veins. Remember that." I nodded, feeling giddy, and I felt my heart skip a beat as I slid down to the gate like I was on a playground. I wanted to be with him, and I knew the feeling was mutual when I stepped up on the passenger side and, before I could even sit down, he pulled me in toward him as I giggled again.

"You're trouble, you know that, right?" I faked a gasp, and looked up at him as he held me against himself.

"What did I do?" I asked, putting my hand against my chest.

"Everything," he whispered, kissing the side of my neck. He was teasing me, and I knew it. I began to shudder as his lips grazed my collarbone, and he stopped for only a moment, looking me up and down. To tease him back, I looked away toward the window, and saw we were in the middle of nowhere. There were no cars or street signs. The only sign of humanity around was rows and rows of corn. When I looked up at him again, he put his finger beneath my chin and held my eyes on him. His hunger was infectious, and I felt weak beneath his fiery gaze.

"You're mine," he declared finally, and my heart jumped over and over again as he climbed on top of me and began kissing my lips. His hands explored every inch of my body, and I watched as he traced the dark lines and scars across my skin. *Is this a dream? Am I dreaming?* I thought, as I felt him put his hand on my thigh and squeeze it gently. We didn't go much further than that, mostly because we were both so nervous, but he made me gasp a few times as his fingers danced along my skin.

"O-Oliver?" I said, feeling incredibly warm as he came back up to my face.

"Yeah, love?" He caressed my cheek with the back of his hand and gave gentle pecks against my lips as I tried to get the words out.

"What does this mean for us?" I asked him, as my breath caught in my throat.

"I want you, Mia. I want to be with you and fill your days with nothing but love and happiness. You deserve it, and I'll make sure it happens, no matter what. No matter how long

I have to wait. You're my Mia," he said, rubbing his thumb across my lips as I began to sob beneath him. "Are these happy tears?" he asked, wiping them away.

"Yes," I said, my body shuddering as I pulled him in tight. "Promise me you won't ever leave me." I started crying as I stared into his eyes. I realized then that I loved him, for real. In my mind I had thought I loved him because he was all I had. I thought I wanted to be with him because I was alone, but I was wrong. My heart yearned for him. I just didn't know how to put it into words. "You're my Oliver."

He smiled from ear to ear, and whispered, "I promise." A moment later, he grabbed my hand to put it against his heart. It was thumping wildly in his chest. I smiled and began running my fingers through his hair.

"Your hair is fluffy," I said, ruffling it up as I beamed up at him.

"You like it?" he asked, eyeing me again as his hands crossed beneath my body.

"Mhmm." He giggled as I played with a curl in his hair and grabbed me up.

"Come here, dork." He turned me so that I was on top, and kissed the top of my head as I buried it in his chest again. We must have laid there like that for an hour or more. I turned my body to the side, and he made a joke about how I was using him as a pillow.

"Yep," I joked back, and closed my eyes as he began to ruffle through my hair.

"As much as I want to lay here like this forever, it's probably not the best idea," he told me, kissing my forehead for the last time as he sat up.

"I know," I said sadly. "Want me to drive for a while?"

"I don't know, your driving scares me." Again, I faked a gasp and looked at him, offended.

"How dare you. I think I did pretty good for my first time driving a boat." He smiled and shook his head. Then he seemed to think for a moment, ruffling his hair nervously. I imagined the cogwheels turning in his brain, and laughed as he debated what to do. Then he sighed, slid toward me, and patted the driver's seat.

"Come on. I'll teach you." Silently I celebrated and climbed over him. A few years ago, Dad took me out driving, but he stopped when I almost crashed into a tree. Luckily, I wasn't driving that fast, but he still made fun of me for it.

"Seatbelt," Oliver told me, reaching over and pulling it toward my hand.

"Right." I clicked it in place and let out a breath as I readied myself to drive. I watched him turn the key until the engine sputtered. Then he gave me instructions.

"Press your foot on the brake and put the car in drive, but don't let go until you're ready." I nodded and did as he told me to. The car jolted a bit as I changed gears, but it didn't move.

"I'm ready," I said, and let go of the brake. It slowly crawled forward, and I felt a little scared as I heard rocks tumbling beneath it.

"Slowly push down on the gas, don't floor it." Again, I nodded, and felt a bit offended as he grabbed the handle on the roof. At first it was touch and go. Considering it'd been years since I last drove, I was pretty rusty. "Whoa," he said as I pressed down, and the car jumped forward.

"Sorry," I said with a grimace.

"It's okay, take it slow." Eventually, I got it, but he didn't let go of the handle until we made it to a gas station. When we got there, I felt this immense sense of guilt about the dream I had. I knew I had to tell him, so once I lined the truck up with a pump, I let it all out.

"I have something to tell you, and honestly, I don't know why it happened. It freaked me out, and I can't keep it to myself anymore." I felt my heart begin to hammer in my chest, and I fiddled with my hands as I struggled with the words.

"Is it bad?" he asked, looking at me concerned.

"Yeah, it's about a nightmare I had after the accident. It was about...you, but I swear I care about you, okay?" He nodded, and I let it flow out like a river. I explained it as detailed as I possibly could, even going so far as to tell him about the daydream or nightmare I had as a kid. It felt more like I was venting, and I watched his expression change from shocked to scared to confused. When I finished, he slumped down in his seat with a deeply hurt look. I thought I messed up and felt my heart shatter in two as I waited for a response.

"I would never hurt you," he said, putting his free hand on mine. "You're safe with me, I promise." I sucked in a breath and nodded. He pressed his lips against my forehead, and hugged me tight, washing the anxiety and fear away in a matter of seconds. I believed him, and wondered why I dreamt up something so unsettling.

"Thank you, love," I said, kissing him on the cheek gently.

"You're welcome," he whispered. "Want to come inside with me?" I looked and there was barely anyone around, but I still felt uncomfortable. *How would I explain this to anyone?* Oliver was super sweet, and I trusted him when he called me beautiful but going out like this felt wrong. "You don't have to," he said finally, "but I'll defend you no matter what, if you want to try. Eventually, you'll have to try anyway, right?" I nodded, and hopped out the driver's side door, ready to face anything that came my way. As I walked, I just kept telling myself I survived Beacon, I survived a giant monster in the basement, I survived the monstrosities on the island, hell, I survived a hundred mile an hour car crash. This was a cake walk.

The door made the familiar *ding* when we opened it, and although I felt worried, the cashiers weren't even looking. Together we went through the aisles and picked out snacks. Oliver grabbed some deli meat sandwiches, some water, and a few pops including more cream sodas, while I grabbed chips and candy. I pulled a bag of Reese's Pieces forward, but the plastic tab on the top got stuck on the edge of the bar. Annoyed, I pulled it as hard as I could until it went *pop* and the bag broke open all over the floor. I groaned and knelt down, dropping each one into the torn bag. I never realized how dirty a gas station floor was until I started taking them in and picked up more dust bunnies than candies.

After I stood up again, I saw Oliver shaking his head at me, and I giggled as we walked up to the register. We gave the cashier all our stuff, checked out, and walked to the door. Before we stepped out, I looked outside and saw this large diesel truck parked right by the doors. It had a metal bull-dog screwed onto the front and a sticker on the windshield that said, *Smooth Sailing*. At first it seemed normal, until this woman in a trench coat and combat boots stepped out, reached into the back of her truck, and pulled out a shotgun, completely unbothered by the crowd of drivers around her. That's when my smile faded.

"Oliver?" I swallowed and looked around the store for another exit. It didn't take me long to realize it was Polly. She had blood smeared on her cheeks, and dirt caked above her brows. I watched her through the cameras above the cashier as she cocked the gun back, loaded five shells into it, and tossed the strap over her shoulder like she was ready to go to war. I was scared. I knew no matter where we went, we couldn't escape danger. It felt like we were constantly in trouble, despite putting a whole city between us and Beacon. Luckily the cashier just finished, and we managed to get our bag and run out the back door before she came inside. I could hear the cashier yelling behind us about it being an "employee-only door" as Oliver slammed it open, grabbed my hand, and ran outside. We managed to make it back to the truck, but I couldn't get the key to turn over.

"We never pumped the gas," Oliver said as he smacked his forehead. "Run! Quick." He kicked the passenger side door open and came around to my side to get me. My body tensed up as we ran within a few inches of her.

"Get back here, you brats." I could hear the wind whoosh almost directly behind as she tried to swipe the backs of our shirts and missed. We ended up running behind the gas station again, down this thin, rocky path leading to the woods. I knew once we made it behind the veil of the trees we could use them as cover, but there was at least a few hundred feet between us and safety. We had no choice but to run off the path as she tried to take shots at us. Somehow, she kept missing, and I covered my ears as they began to ring from the gunshots.

"Keep pushing, we're almost there," Oliver assured me as he practically pulled me along. When we finally reached it, we snaked around the trees and jumped over fallen logs and tree stumps as we avoided her. She was wicked fast, and it scared me when I heard a twig snap within a few feet behind us. It didn't make any sense to me: *Why would she want to kill us if we were both important to Beacon?* I peeked over my shoulder and jumped as powder went right beside my head.

"Stop running, now!" I heard her shout. We must have kept running for another ten minutes or more. We just couldn't shake her. I started to feel aches and pain again and swallowed as I remembered the medicine was in the truck. Again, I heard another gunshot, and somehow managed to pull Oliver around a tree and into a ditch just out of her line of sight while she reloaded. Above us there was this small ledge with roots and dirt where she came and stood. I leaned against it, hoping and praying we would stay hidden. Oliver put both his hands over his mouth and pointed up with one finger. I nodded and held my breath as dirt came tumbling down the cliff. At first, I thought it worked just like the other times as I heard her footsteps recede. Then I found out just how wrong I was.

"You think I'm stupid?" Before we could react, she jumped down right in front of us, and we both screamed when she aimed the barrel straight at our faces and pulled the trigger.

Chapter Nine: Becoming Subject Zero

I waited for death to claim me. My eyes closed and I squeezed Oliver's hand in what I assumed to be the final moments of my life. Instead, I opened my eyes to see a thick puke green–colored smoke surrounding us. I tried to hold my breath, but I couldn't get out of it fast enough to save myself. It tasted foul, like a rotten tomato left out in the sun. It was almost exactly like the liquid back at the morgue, but a lot more potent. It left a raunchy and sour aftertaste in the back of my throat. We both coughed as the vapor seeped into our lungs. *What is this stuff?* I dropped to my knees and tried to crawl out of there. Just outside the cloud of smoke, I saw Polly squat down to look at us while we tried to get a breath of fresh air. A few minutes later, the cloud of smoke seemed to dissipate, but Oliver and I were still sprawled out on the ground. I tried to cough it out, but it wouldn't leave. That's when I looked over at Oliver, and saw his veins were just as dark as mine.

"W-what..." I choked, spitting more phlegm and a dark liquid out of my throat. "What did you do?" I could hear Polly laugh. It was a loud irritating sound, as if all my senses were heightened.

"I'm testing something," she told me as she came over, pulled out a finger stick, and poked my index finger. I grimaced and tried to turn my body, but I couldn't. I just laid there, reeling from fear, shock, disgust, pretty much everything all at once. Then she laughed again. "Ha ha, it worked! You're just like this idiot," she said, kicking Oliver on the side of his ribs.

"Ugh," he cried, cradling his side.

"Leave him alone." I tried to sound intimidating, but with her towering over us, I couldn't do anything to stop her.

"Oh right, he's your boy. Silly me, I'll do you instead." I whimpered as she kicked me over with the front of her boot so that I was lying on my back. Then she grabbed me by my hair and held my face so that it was level with hers. "I never told Oliver this, but I guess it's time you two knew. His blood is only toxic because they made it that way." I gasped as she took my head and turned it toward him and then back at her. "Just like you, he was immune. They developed this disease almost a century ago, but they couldn't find the right body—or bodies—to house it. That is, until the Beacon family came along. Without blood, the toxin doesn't work. It tastes funky but it has no effect. Once it mixes, it's a whole new ballgame, and now you're just like him. Another subject zero to exploit." I looked over at Oliver as we both took all this in. For almost his whole life he was in captivity, and he wasn't even born with it.

"Why?" I heard him ask, pounding the dirt beside him before he groaned and cradled his arm too.

"Luckily for you, my security clearance was upgraded," she said, holding up a level ten clearance badge. I gasped and tried to reach out for it, but she shoved my hand away.

“Nice try. I got this thanks to your little mess down in the basement, so I can actually say it now without my job being threatened. But not here. Who knows who's listening,” she said, acting nervous as she glanced around. “Besides, I got to get you two patched up and back in the gurneys where you belong.” I tried to think of ways to escape, but my hopes were short-lived when I saw the men from the elevator come and stand over us. Two of the army men approached us, and we both got defensive. I tried to kick one away, but he grabbed my leg and pressed a needle into my calf. Almost instantly I went numb, and he scooped me up, letting my limbs fall over his arms.

“No, Mia! Let her go!” I heard Oliver shout. I heard a loud thump behind us, but even that didn’t last long. Before I knew it, Oliver and I were carried through the woods straight along the path and shoved into a black van waiting behind the gas station. I wasn’t surprised when Polly took a bundle of ropes and tape and tied us up back there. The tape caught the hairs on my arms and legs, but she didn’t show even an ounce of sympathy. I tried to speak, scream, even make a little noise so that maybe we could get rescued, but nothing came out of my mouth besides spit. I knew we lost, but somehow it got even worse when I heard my mom’s voice just outside the van.

“You got 'em?” I heard her ask as she came around and peeked at us. Her eyes locked on mine for a moment, but I turned away spitefully, hoping she would get the message.

“Yeah, boss. Tied and ready.” *Boss.* My mind raced faster than a race car driver, and suddenly I started to wonder just how long she knew. *Was this all some kind of sick plan of hers?* I closed my eyes and allowed the cold metal of the van floor to hit my neck. *Did Mom plan for Dad to die like this? Did she think I was going to die too? Why is she allowing this? Why did she shoot that poor man?* There were so many things I needed answers to, but I wouldn't get the clarity I wanted until much much later.

"Good, don't hurt her. She's still my daughter, so if I see any of you raise a single hand to her, I'll kill you myself." I watched as she slammed the van door shut, and through the darkness I saw Oliver turn his head toward me and slowly blink his eyes as tears began to well up. Neither of us could speak or move much, but I knew he was trying to comfort me. I sobbed quietly and blinked back, before I let the darkness consume me.

We must have slept for a few hours or more. When I finally woke up, we were still on the road. I could hear rocks rumbling and tumbling beneath us again and felt butterflies as we went over bumps a few times. I laid my head against the floor and listened for a few minutes. *We must be on the highway,* I thought, sensing how fast we were going. I sighed and turned my head toward Oliver again, who was sleeping soundly. I found out that night he snored. I envied that. I was so tired, yet I couldn't manage to go back under again. Instead, I pushed my tied feet against the floor until I managed to gently lay my head against his chest. I listened to him breathe and noticed how labored his breathing was.

"I'm sorry," I whispered to him, feeling guilty that he got hurt to begin with.

"It's okay, love," I heard him whisper back, and whipped my head just in time to see him yawn.

"Did I wake you?" I looked up and saw his lips curve up.

"Yeah, but it's okay. I'm happy to be with you," he told me, snaking his tied hands behind my head. "I'm scared I'm going to lose you once we get back, Mia. I can't deal with that again."

"I know. Maybe I can reason with...Mom. I can try to appeal to her to keep us together. I know Polly won't, but she might." He nodded and gently pressed his lips against my forehead.

"I know you're angry with her. Are you sure you'll be okay?" My lips quivered as I thought about everything that had happened so far. *Could I really hate my mom?* As a kid she and Dad were my heroes, but now... I hated her with almost the same amount of passion as Polly.

"I'll try my best," I told him, burying my head into his chest. "I need answers anyway. But I won't let my heart get involved with her again. I can't."

"No matter how this goes, just know you will always have me, Mia. Even if they split us up again," he said, pressing his lips against my head. I could feel them quivering, so I tilted my head back up and kissed him gently.

"I know," I whispered, and we laid there with my forehead against his until the van came to a stop about five minutes later. I was so scared; I pushed my back up against the metal wall behind the seats as far away from the door as I could. I tried to look out the back windows, but they were tinted an insanely illegal amount. The only sounds I could hear were their muffled voices up front. "Oliver, I'm scared."

"I know. Just breathe, love. Let's not panic yet," he said, staring at the van doors intently. We both waited for movement, and somehow even when they finally did open, we still weren't ready. I gasped and pushed my body back against the metal, hoping and praying it would bend and give us more space. Deep down, I knew there was no escaping this, but I stayed pressed against the back until I heard a loud *zap!*

"Out, now!" Polly ordered, showing the familiar taser from up in the hallway. I whimpered and slowly slid down until she grabbed me by my legs and pulled me to the door. Oliver came next, and soon we were both sitting there staring at a modified version of Beacon.

"What happened?" I asked, taking a look around. It had bars over all the windows, barbed wire over the fences, and armed guards at the front door this time.

"We modified it," she said, tossing her shotgun over her shoulder. "Welcome home." She looked me up and down as she cut our legs free and had us follow her inside. She tied our hands together so that she pulled us along like sheep. It made me uncomfortable, because Oliver walked much faster than I did so I had no choice but to jog-walk all the way there. The building looked incredibly intimidating, like they turned it into a prison in our absence. I felt sick as I walked up to the doors, but I had no choice but to swallow it back down again.

"P-polly, may I talk to my... I mean, your boss please?" I asked her as we walked across the parking lot toward the door.

"No," she said, coldly. I recoiled, slightly taken aback by her rudeness, and opened and shut my mouth as I tried to find the courage to talk up again. I thought I could find Mom behind all the guards, military, and doctors, but she was nowhere to be found.

"Please, show me some sympathy. I lost everything. Let me talk to her!" I pleaded, pulling back on the rope around my hands so she'd stop.

"Don't forget where you stand with me," she snapped as she turned around and got almost directly in my face. Oliver tried to intervene, but Polly sneered at him before she turned back toward me again. "You are under my jurisdiction, so what I say goes. I told you no, and that's final."

"Why are you so cruel?" I asked, as a tear fell down my cheek.

"Because that woman pays my checks, and I'm not going to let you open your big mouth and tell her what I've done to you." She took my rope and wrapped it around her wrist like a dog leash and gave it a tug, pulling me ever so slightly closer to her. "You won't ever make a fool out of me again like you did a month ago when you left." *That was a month ago?* I gasped, utterly shocked.

"I won't, I just want to talk to her. Please, I—"

"NO! I said no!" I fell back against the dirt and began to sob as she raised her voice at me. She got so close in the end; she gave me a shower with her spit.

"Please be nice to her, Polly. She's scared," Oliver told her as he knelt down next to me.

"I don't care," she said finally, and pulled us as hard as she could so we had no choice but to stand back up and walk with her again. I knew then talking to Mom was out of the question, so I built up all the courage I had and stopped her one last time.

"Okay, I won't ask about Mom again, but can I please stay with Oliver? In the same room, I mean. I know he's probably under someone else, but I need him." My body began to shake as Polly turned back around again and luckily, I saw her face had softened some. She gave a pensive look before she pressed her forehead into her palm. Then she looked back up.

"I'll ask, but if your mother comes to you, you won't so much as utter my name to her. Is that understood?" I nodded, feeling a pang of excitement rise in my chest, and turned toward Oliver with a nervous smile. "Good." Finally, we made it to the doors, and we were greeted by two army personnel standing at alert with rifles.

"At ease, soldiers," Polly told them, and I swear one sighed with relief.

"I'll take the boy," the one soldier said, but when he went to reach out, she stopped him.

"They requested to be together, so I'll have to have a word with the boss."

"Oh, alright, keep him on a short leash. He's a pain in the ass," he said as I turned toward Oliver and saw his face turn bright red.

"Yeah, yeah. I can handle him," Polly said, dismissing them with a wave of her hand. For once, I liked her. She was still my enemy, but she didn't break her promise. It was sweet.

"So..." I said, nudging Oliver with my shoulder while Polly walked us around the first floor. "Mind explaining what he meant?"

"Hmm?" he asked, giving me an oblivious look.

"What did you do?" I joked, causing him to chuckle nervously.

"I may or may not have snuck out and stole a bottle of his expensive wine he had hidden in a mini fridge in the break room," he whispered in my ear. I covered my mouth as I giggled and eyed Polly to make sure she didn't hear.

"Was it good?" I asked him, with a mischievous smile.

"Mhmm. It was kinda fruity too. I ended up sharing it with my dad, and we laughed about it for hours...until the man came in and saw the empty bottle on the floor. Then I had to make a run for it. Trust me, they reprimanded me pretty badly for that one, but it was worth it."

"Ouch," I said, shaking my head. Before I knew it, we stopped in front of a meeting room and stood there while my mom spoke to one of the doctors. Polly glanced back at us while we stood there and silenced us with a wave of her hand even though we weren't speaking. I never thought I would have to treat my own mom like royalty, but right then it felt like it. About twenty minutes went by while we waited, and eventually we got impatient and sat down. After a few minutes of leaning our heads against the wall in silence, the doctor came running out, slammed the door behind him, and stormed off.

"What do you think happened there?" Oliver asked, as we all stood up again.

"No clue, but you are NOT going to go in there and annoy her any further. Behave yourselves," Polly told us, waving her pointer finger in our faces before she gently knocked on the door and pushed it open.

"Your daughter wishes to speak with you, miss." I saw Mom nod as she typed on her computer, and then she looked up and I felt my stomach fill with butterflies. *Why am I so scared? She's my mom, shouldn't I feel safe?* I took a deep breath and stepped forward.

"Cut them free," she told Polly, sliding a knife across the table. I don't know why, but my heart jumped when Polly cut our ropes in one swipe. *She's not going to hurt you,* I told myself, *not in front of Mom.* When I sat down, I felt the fear rise like acid in my stomach.

"Hi, Mom," I mumbled, tapping the table nervously with my fingertips.

"Hey, baby," she said, a little louder than I did. "I know how you must feel about all this, and I can't expect you to come and hug me, but I would like to talk with you. If you'll let me, of course?" Somehow, hearing her call me *baby* felt worse than hearing her get called boss. I began to chew on my nails, and Oliver quickly noticed and gently grabbed my hands in his, ignoring the looks Mom gave him.

"I have questions," I said, looking between him and Mom, "but I'd like to make a request first."

"Go ahead," she said, finally closing the screen on her laptop.

"I'd like to stay with Oliver. Not 'Subject Zero,' Oliver. Please. I've grown attached to him, and I don't want to be away from him."

"I can do that," she said with a nod. "I'll have Polly take care of you both."

"Thank you." I linked my hands together beneath the emerald-green glass table, and prepared each question like they were on flashcards in my head. "I need to know why you would support this. They're hurting innocent people. I don't get it."

"There's a lot at stake here, Mia. It's a huge operation. That's why I support it." She said it so matter of factly that

I almost lost my train of thought. *Did she not hear what I said about the innocent people?*

"Okay, what is *THIS* exactly? Oliver and his family have suffered for a long time, the least you can do is tell me why, right?"

"I suppose we owe you both that much," she said, glancing between me and Oliver. "Do you remember when you were little, and you screamed that something was inside the sandbox?"

"Y-yeah," I responded, feeling unsettled.

"Well, the day after that, your father and I went back out there to check, and it was covered in this thick gooey substance. We immediately called the police, thinking something bad happened, until it escalated and men in hazmat suits came out to investigate it while you were at school one day. They said it was some sort of toxin, and the officers who arrived on scene first all became VERY sick. For the whole day, they were out there collecting it for evidence, and eventually I found out that our house was built over an old lab. The government seized the toxin, and that day we found out that...Oliver and Oliver's family were buried beneath that box."

"WHAT?!" I said, jumping up from my seat.

"What do you mean I was buried?" Oliver muttered as he stared down at the table.

"Your family was involved in an experiment. Unfortunately, you passed over fifty years ago, on July 7th, 1971, and shockingly enough they buried you in secret without anyone knowing. We found the paperwork to prove it," she said, sliding a file folder containing his birth certificate and old lab documents across the table toward us. We stared in shock and my hands began to shake as I saw Oliver's birth date was in 1963. "The only thing that doesn't add up is what happened when Mia dug in the sandbox. She brought you back somehow. I think it has something to do with her being exposed to the toxin, but there's no way to be sure." I looked over at Oliver to see a shocked expression seize his face. He was terrified, and I couldn't blame him.

"So...how did we end up back here again?" he asked, visibly shaking in fear.

"Well, a member of the Beacon staff found your family wandering a few miles away from my family's home. Instantly, they seized you, and found you were a bit different than everyone else. You were turned. They kept you in confinement until they found out that by injecting you with the toxin again, you were able to go back to being the Oliver that people knew and loved. Without it, you and your family would turn in a month or less, depending on the circumstances. That's why we were very lucky to find you when we did. After that discovery was made, they made this whole persona for your family. Modified your birth dates so no one would freak out, and your family, Oliver, resumed working again as if nothing happened. Much much later, a few years after your family came back again, the government came to us and demanded that we use the toxin for population control. At first our staff was sickened that they would even mention that as an option, considering what the toxin does to people, but eventually military personnel began flooding in to force us. So, we had no choice but to fill in the blanks ourselves and 'kill' your family in a fire so no one would notice your scars. It's unfortunate, but without your blood, the toxin isn't fully viable. It only makes people sick. Your family essentially became Subject Zero, and it kept spreading until now. We have over 900 infected under our roof, and eventually we're going to run out of room here. If they give the word, we release them into a city and pick up the pieces after. That's what our job is. You and your father weren't supposed to get involved, Mia, but these things never go to plan, do they?"

I couldn't speak. I was in complete shock. Not only was she aware that Dad died, but she glossed over it like he meant nothing. She was involved with killing innocents, and she acted like it was a breakthrough. I felt revolted.

"I need some air; can I go outside?" I began to gag as I sat there and saw her wave her hand away without a care in the world. Oliver tried to follow, but Polly held his shoulder down. I glared at her, but I knew it would do no good. I ran, and the moment I reached the front doors, I threw up all the contents in my stomach. Afterward, I began to cry as I dry-heaved. I tried to stop myself, but I felt disgusted. *If Mom knew this whole time, why didn't she stop us from going to Beacon? Did she ever love us?* I spit in the grass to try and get the rotten taste out of my mouth. The officers watched me like a hawk as I knelt down in the bushes, clutching my stomach. All I could do was glare at them, and I saw one grab his taser before I turned my head back to the green leaves ahead of me. I hated them, I hated Polly, I hated the government, but most of all, I began to hate Mom too. I didn't care what they thought, I sprawled out in the grass on my back and stared up at the clouds. *Will this be the rest of my life? A vessel for their sick "population control" virus? No, I'm going to fight back.*

Chapter Ten: Finding a Cure

I stood up using the bush to support my weight, and started mapping out what I would do next. My stomach was still in knots as I came to my feet, but I ignored it and forced myself to stand. The guards seemed less on edge than before, and I even saw one laugh as they stood there talking to each other. I needed their attention, so I faked a groan and let myself fall to my knees so that I could scoop up dirt to throw at them. I had a plan.

"Help," I choked out, as I dug my nails into the grass.

"What's wrong, are you okay?" a guard asked, leaving his post to come over to me. The other guard followed, but he looked much more cautious than the first. When the first guard reached me, I didn't waste a single second. I threw it right at his face, disorienting him, and then jumped on the other's back. I wrestled the second guy for a moment before I ended up grabbing his taser and using it on them.

"UGH," they yelled before they dropped down and rolled in the grass, clutching their sides where the prongs had gone. I grabbed their gear and weapons before I ran back inside and slammed the door closed behind me. I knew they wouldn't stay down long, so I had to act fast. If I could find a cure for Oliver and me, we could be free for real. I didn't even know if there was one, but I had to try. The hallways seemed to blur together as I ran through them again, and I stopped in front of the meeting room once more. I had a small handgun on me, so I quickly turned the safety off, checked that it was loaded, then threw the door open.

"Put your hands where I can see them!" I demanded, and saw Polly and Mom give me a shocked look as they realized I was fully dressed in weapons and had vile running down my shirt.

"Where did you get that?" Mom asked as she stood up angrily.

"Doesn't matter, do it!" I yelled, stepping in front of Oliver. I watched them raise their hands and looked between them both nervously.

"Are we escaping again?" Oliver asked, taking pepper spray out of my belt.

"Not yet," I told him as we slowly backed up toward the door. "Where is the lab?" I yelled, aiming the gun between the two of them.

"Just down the hall to your left, but you'll need a security badge."

"Then give me yours!" I snapped at Polly. I wanted to laugh as Polly came to realize she was losing the same badge she had boasted to me about earlier. She groaned and tossed it at me, landing directly in my open palm. *Ha, I caught it.* I smirked before I left them there and raced with Oliver down the hall like she told me. We came to a set of double doors with a keycard reader outside and saw a sign that said *Beacon Laboratories*. It almost felt satisfying hearing the familiar *ding* again as I slid Polly's card and walked through, until Oliver stopped me on the other side.

"Wait, what's the plan here, Mia? They know we're here now, we should just escape again, like last time."

"We can't," I told him, and took in a deep broken breath. "We could have gotten into so much trouble if they hadn't found us when they did. You could have turned. I could have lost you!" I sighed, feeling defeated before I finally spoke again. "We have to find a cure. There has to be something in this lab we can use to fix this, and once we do, then we can run away again. For good this time." I squeezed his arm gently. He looked down at my hand and I wondered what was going through his mind.

"Are you sure you want this?" he said, giving me a genuinely broken look. His mouth was turned down and his eyes looked to be moments away from tears. "I was born way before you. I may not look like it, but I'm technically sixty years old. Do you really want this?"

"Of course I do. Oliver, I don't care about that. I like you, and you deserve a second chance at life, away from Beacon and the monsters. I want to give you that."

"Y-you really mean that?" he asked, and his lips began to quiver.

"Yes, I swear." I smiled, taking in a deep breath as we both cried together again. "Let's see what we can find before they come for us again. Okay?"

"Okay," he whispered.

The next few hours were hectic. After we rounded the corner, we saw rows and rows of glass windows like the upstairs areas. The first window had an old man in a white lab coat sitting at a desk dropping a blue liquid into a green beaker. At first it didn't seem to do anything until I saw the man scoot his chair back. After a few seconds, it began to fizz, and then it exploded, sending glass flying across the room. Somehow the man was lucky enough to avoid all of it, but the desk it was sitting on wasn't so lucky. It was destroyed. Many of the rooms were just like that. Men and women in lab coats dropping tiny, minuscule drops into another beaker and seeing it either explode, fizz, melt the beaker, or create bubbles. It seemed underwhelming at first, until we came to another meeting room just like Mom's and saw a group of five guys in lab coats arguing back and forth as a woman pointed at a slideshow with one single thing written in bold. *Top Secret: Reversing the Sickness.*

When I saw that, I didn't hesitate for a second. I busted through the door and all six of them turned their heads toward me.

At first, I was nervous. It was a bit intimidating how quiet the room became, then I took a deep breath, pulled Oliver inside, and gestured at him. "How do I cure him?" All of them gasped at once and began murmuring to themselves before I pulled the gun out and aimed it around the room. "HOW DO I CURE HIM?" I repeated, much more sternly than the first time.

"That's what we're trying to figure out," the woman at the front told me nervously, gesturing to a pile of papers in front of her. "We had the cure, then the government stole it from us when they started infecting people. We're trying to figure it out all over again." I sighed and sat down in one of the chairs at the end of the table.

"What are the chances we can get this cure now, or find the one they stole?" I asked, staring at her intently.

"Slim to none. They have the cure locked away somewhere private, and our people aren't even close to figuring it out yet."

"You mean, that's what they're doing out there?" Oliver asked, pointing toward the hall.

"Yes. As you can see, it's not going so well." I watched as she tilted her glasses up just enough so she could wipe her eyes.

"Who would know where it's at then?" I asked her finally, as I flipped the safety switch back on the gun.

"Probably those military *bozos* out there. Those idiots bust in here every day, just to make sure we're not doing anything we shouldn't. They scream at us to make sure that we blindly follow their orders, and I'm tired of it. It's either the soldiers or their commander, Simon Drear," the woman told me, folding her arms together angrily. "But be careful, we've tried talking to them, and so far, we've gotten less than nothing."

"Thanks, and I'm...sorry for...this," I told her, causing her to smile.

"Don't be. If one of us can find it, that's enough for me. Just make sure you tell us once you do, deal?"

"Deal," I said, before we went back out and heard them resume talking again. I knew there was plenty of military around; the only question was, which one? We left the lab again, and I kept the gun aimed ahead of me as we inched around the corners back out. I knew it was only a matter of time before the guards or someone came to catch us, so we stayed prepared. Oliver ended up taking the rifle off my shoulder as we cautiously treaded the nightmare halls. I don't think either of us intended on using our guns, but at least we were ready for anything they threw our way. I could hear him reloading behind me as we came into the main lobby area again and saw that no one was there.

"What now?" Oliver asked, glancing back and forth. Cautiously, I pushed on the front door, and heard a chain rattle outside. They locked us in. I groaned and leaned against the wall as I let my mind unravel.

"I guess we'll have to go explore," I told him after a few moments of silence. The hospital was an unnerving dead silence. There was no one around, and I couldn't help but feel unsettled as we creeped down the halls. There was no one in their rooms either, so instinctively we made our way back toward Mom's meeting room. When we got close, we saw the hallway was blocked by hospital beds standing up on end. Even worse, they were soaked in a familiar black goop. I thought they were hiding from us at first but seeing *that* told me otherwise. *What did they see when we left?* I thought as I came close to the beds and saw a large bloody print that definitely wasn't human.

I opened the door across the hall from the meeting room, hoping I could get in from the other side, but when I went through the other hall it was blocked off too. This time with desk chairs and tables. The barricade on this side was barely stable, and there was a monster's body flung over the top with its tongue out. It was still dripping, burning the carpet beneath. *NOT GOOD.* I swallowed hard and gestured for Oliver to take a look.

"D-do you think they're still alive in there?" I asked as I debated in my head if I should start taking the chairs down.

"I don't mean to sound like a downer, but I don't hear anything, Mia," he said, staring up at the body. Momentarily he gagged and covered his mouth with his hand.

"You okay?" I asked him, patting him on the back gently.

"Yeah, I'm good. Let's tear it down and see what we can find." I nodded, and one by one we pulled the desks and chairs down until they were low enough to get through. The door to the meeting room was wide open on the left side. I tried to peek in through the windows, but in our absence, someone had taken spray paint to them. We had no choice but to tiptoe toward the door. My heart was pounding in my ears like a drum. By now, I had been through so much I thought I would become numb to the feeling, but I was terrified. I peered around the closed right side door, and...nothing. The room was empty. I breathed a sigh of relief and stepped inside with Oliver.

"Let's check around," I told him. "I doubt they'd block off this room for no reason." He nodded, and we pulled open the heavy metal filing cabinets, looking for anything we could use. One was labeled *Green Room* and was filled with green file folders in alphabetical order. I pulled them out one by one and was shocked when I saw they were filled with the missing person flyers. Each one had patient records, and either were stamped in bright red stamp with, *deceased,* or in black with, *turned.* It felt sickening to flip through them, and I felt completely shattered when I saw Dad's file. I ran my thumb sadly across the page. It was a picture of Dad on a camping trip we went on, holding a huge walleye up in the air. He was never really interested in taking photos, just taking mine and Mom's. So, it was about the only one we had of him, besides one of him holding me as a baby.

The black stamp felt like another stab in the back on Mom's part; Dad didn't deserve this.

I sighed and folded it up neatly to fit in my back pocket. Curious, before I closed the drawer back up, I flipped through the files until I saw mine and Oliver's. I put them on the table and opened them at the same time. We both had the same stamp. It was blue, unlike all the others in the drawer. *Immune*, it said, in sapphire-blue ink.

"Whatcha looking at?" Oliver asked, peering over my shoulder as he came and looked at the files. "Oh, it's our files. I've seen those before." Under his watchful eye, I flipped a page until I came to his medical record. I watched him through the corner of my eye as I ran my finger down his chart and saw him chuckle nervously. For the most part it was full of toxin dosages, but there were a few notes detailing the abuse he felt here.

"I'm sorry," I whispered to him when I saw he was literally beaten by Beacon staff.

"It's okay," he told me, grabbing my hand. "They won't break me. They'll have to kill me first." I nodded, frowning sadly at him, before I closed the folders and left them there on the table. We went though the other drawers, but there wasn't anything else that seemed to catch our eye. I went around the room, looking up at the ceiling. I pulled up the carpet, moved the table with Oliver's help, but the room seemed untouched besides the lack of dust on the table. I was about to give up and suggest to Oliver that we look somewhere else when he called me over. It was subtle, but there was a very small scuff mark across the floor behind one of the file cabinets.

"Oliver, you're a genius!" I exclaimed happily and helped him push it out of the way. To both our dismay and surprise, there was a small square hole in the wall about the size of an average desktop computer that revealed a set of stairs leading down.

"You think that leads to the morgue?" I asked, scratching the back of my neck. *We barely made it out the first time, could we really survive a second?* I wondered as I peered down the ominously dark staircase.

"Only one way to find out," he replied as he squeezed his body inside. I didn't want to, but when Oliver jumped down and started to descend the steps, I knew I had no choice but to follow. Neither of us had lights. I was hoping the men had one on their belt, but we weren't that lucky. Somehow it was darker with my eyes open than shut. *Why? Just why?* I thought, staring upward. The only comforting thing was Oliver's slow foot falls ahead of me. I wanted to talk to him, but I was so scared I just listened instead. It took a good couple minutes as the stairs spiraled farther and farther down until we reached the bottom. "Yeah... We definitely aren't in the basement," Oliver whispered over his shoulder. I didn't know whether that was comforting or upsetting as we began to walk down a hallway shrouded in darkness. There were no doors, just a long empty hallway. Our footsteps bounced off the walls like a ball, and I began to feel paranoid as we walked on. I couldn't tell whether I was hearing Oliver's slow footfalls or someone else's.

"Oliver?" I called out after at least ten minutes of walking, before instant regret seized me. I covered my mouth as it echoed down the hall. It seemed to go on forever, the sound echoing farther down the hall than we had explored yet. He didn't respond, and my body went numb as I came to a stop to check if I still heard his footsteps and didn't hear a sound besides my own shaky breath.

"O-Oliver?" I whispered this time, glancing back and forth in the darkness. My whole body shook violently, but I very slowly started walking again as I called his name. I began to cry until I felt someone seize me and put their sweaty hand over my mouth. In a panic, I thrashed to try and get away until the figure pressed their lips against my ear.

"Shhh, it's okay. It's me." I stopped and leaned my body against him as I breathed out against his palm. "There's someone right ahead of us. I saw them go in the door up there," he whispered directly in my ear. I nodded, feeling relieved, and pulled his hand off my lips. Maybe ten feet away, I could see a tiny sliver of light I could only assume to be the underside of a door.

"What do we do?" I whispered, meeting his eyes.

"Keep your gun at the ready," he told me as he pulled the rifle off his shoulder again. We reached the door much quicker than I had anticipated. I felt like I had little time to prepare myself, but finally, Oliver turned the knob and threw the door open like we knew exactly what was beyond it.

"Hands in the air!" he shouted as we came into a very large room with a glass dome over top. It honestly looked like a college lecture room. *What is this?* I thought, as we came in guns blazing. Rows and rows of desks, lined up in a triangular fashion pointing at the front where an older dark-skinned man in an army uniform stood just like that woman, gesturing to a slide show. He had a thick gray-black beard on his face, and his hair was shaved short, revealing only the tips of curly ends on top. He had a sharp jawline, and despite his age, he looked good. The man had his right pant leg torn off where he did a sloppy patch up job, evident by the blood seeping through, but honestly, he was intimidating.

"Whoa, who the hell are you?" the man said, as the entire room glanced back at us. At the front, I saw Mom and Polly stand up. Mom had a large gash across her face, while Polly looked completely unscathed.

"I'm sorry, sir. That's my daughter," Mom said, pinching the bridge of her nose as she tried to hide her face away from him.

"Ahhh. Mia, is it?" he asked, taking a few cautious steps our way. I was apprehensive, but I nodded as I used my thumb to turn the safety off the pistol.

"And you are?" I asked, trying to sound intimidating.

"I'm Simon. Simon Drear," he said, bowing theatrically. "I'm pleased to meet you. I heard you two have been stirring up a load of deep shit."

"Yeah, we have. And we're not leaving here until YOU give us the cure. Where is it?" Oliver barked angrily, peering down at the man.

"Straight to the point," he said, waving his finger at Oliver. "I like you, kid."

"He asked you a question. Where's the cure?" I pointed the gun straight at him, causing him to chuckle.

"You weren't kidding, she is bold," he said, glancing back at Mom before he turned his attention back to us. "The cure...is locked up in an old mini fridge inside the storage building. But trust me, you don't want it. The horrors in there—"

"Don't care, how do we get to it?" Oliver said, narrowing his eyes at the man. If looks could kill, I was sure Simon would drop dead. "The front door's chained shut."

"Here, catch." The man tossed Oliver a small rusty key, and I stepped in front of him as he bent over to pick it up off the floor.

"There's a door right behind the white board. Take the stairs up and go out the red security door. That key opens the lock to the fridge. Good luck, you're gonna need it." We exchanged glances before we walked down the opposite row from where Simon was and ran straight toward the door before he could change his mind. Behind us, I heard someone whisper, "They're done for," and heard another laugh as I pushed the door open and ran up.

What horrors are there behind that door that are so scary, even the man who hid it tells us good luck? I knew what Oliver would say and, honestly, I wasn't ready to hear it.

"Only one way to find out."

Chapter Eleven: Warehouse of Horror

Somehow, getting to the warehouse was the easy part. We managed to get there about forty minutes after we left Beacon. It felt like we were walking to a battle. Both of us were dead silent, but every so often Oliver would glance over his shoulder at me as I stopped to look at things. For the most part, everything was the same, but I saw a poster hanging between two nondescript buildings. It was an advertisement for a new drug they were developing with a woman in a white lab coat giving a thumbs-up. Somehow, I knew exactly what they were referring to. The infection. It was a relatively new sign too, making me wonder just how many people they tricked into giving up their lives in recent months.

When we finally did get there, we stopped at the front door and, already I could hear noises inside. It was a two-story building, with at least forty windows on either side. It had to be at least a couple hundred thousand square feet, and from the window around the corner I could tell it was jam-packed with supplies.

"Where do we start?" I asked Oliver as we came back around the front.

"Not sure, but I have a feeling if we take the front door, it's going to draw a lot of attention our way." I watched as he went and peeked around the side and held up a finger for me to wait. "Be right back." I nodded, although he didn't see me, and glanced around as he did some digging. On the building across the street, Denny's Diner, I could see a flock of ravens gathering. Dad always used to tell me, when you see ravens fly in front of you, it's usually a bad sign. My family was always into ghost stuff and superstitions, so it made sense that I felt uneasy standing there. I watched impatiently as one of the ravens cleaned itself with its beak, before a loud bang came from behind me, causing them to get spooked and fly away. With a gasp, I turned around and glanced up at the door just in time to see it move with a loud *clunk*. I couldn't tell for sure whether it was the wind or something else, but I definitely didn't want to find out.

"Oliver, please hurry," I whispered to myself as I began to pace against the rocky ground beneath me. I knew he wouldn't leave me, but I was still worried. Impatiently I peeked around the corner and saw nothing. My feet dragged against the ground, and out of pure boredom I kicked up dirt and rocks, making a small dust cloud. A few minutes later, I peeked around the right corner again, when I felt a hand close around my shoulder.

"Ahhh!" I screamed, and tried to catch my balance, but ended up falling on my butt.

"Got ya." I looked up to see Oliver laughing as he held out his hand to help me up.

"I'll get up on my own. Thanks." I stood up and brushed myself off, feeling slightly annoyed that I let him get the jump on me.

"Sorry," he said with a nervous smile. "Just wanted to lighten the mood. I found a door on the left side. Luckily, it's unlocked." I nodded and brushed the dirt off my pants. When we rounded the left corner, Oliver led me through a tall overgrown patch of grass until we came to a small red door that had a faded *Emergency Exit* sign painted on it and a broken alarm overhead. Oliver held the door open for me as we stepped inside, and I felt an instant change in temperature. It was boiling.

"It's so hot," I whispered, fanning myself with my hands.

"Yeah, this is awful," he responded, wiping his shirt across his face.

"Let's try and—" My jaw fell open as we walked in just a bit farther and stopped when we saw the sheer amount of things in the warehouse. I realized right then that we were going to be here forever. "What do we do?" At first, he didn't respond as he walked a bit ahead of me and peered around. I came to join him and saw a giant tank in the center surrounded by tons of shelving units. There didn't seem to be any monsters...yet, but I was sure there were some there.

"I know you're going to hate me for this, but I think we should split up to try and cover more ground. This place is huge, we'll be here for hours if we don't at least try," Oliver said, scratching the back of his neck.

"I don't know..." I avoided his eyes. "I'm scared. He warned us for a reason, Oliver."

"I know," he said, peering around again. "How about we look around together for a flashlight, then we split. I'll stay close, I promise." I stared at him for a moment as I gathered up the courage, but reluctantly I ended up saying, "Okay."

The building wasn't completely pitch-black since there were holes in the ceiling, but it definitely wasn't pleasant walking around the shaded areas. We must have walked past three shelves, when all too quickly we found a brand-new package of camping flashlights with batteries wrapped in plastic.

"Oh no," I muttered to myself as he tore them open, put the batteries inside, and handed me one. I don't know if it was because of my body shaking or the frightened look on my face, but in that instant, he grabbed my chin in his hand.

"It'll be okay," he told me, gently kissing my lips. "Keep the gun close, and yell if you need me." I nodded, and although I felt weak in the knees, I turned around and started my search. The flashlights were really bright, so it brought me some comfort when I saw Oliver's beam through the gaps in the shelves. I aimed my flashlight up as I walked, scanning the upper levels, but there was no sign of the mini fridge. *What if Simon lied just to get us killed?* I wouldn't doubt this would be some sort of sick game to them, especially considering they still had Oliver's family in custody. I started to drag my feet again as a strong feeling of dread began to take hold of me. Then I heard a low growl. I glanced around in a panic, shining my flashlight in all directions, until heavy footfalls came from behind me. *That's NOT Oliver.* I knew the instant I turned around that I was going to see some sort of monstrosity, but what I saw left me slack jawed. Another giant monster. It had a face almost like a gargoyle, with oversized teeth sticking out of its mouth. It had four huge legs, and nails larger than both my arms combined. Somehow its eyes were the most normal part about it. They looked like a dog's eyes, with yellow-green irises and some black mixed in. It walked very slowly toward me and growled as it inched closer and closer. There was about a ten-foot gap between each shelf, and somehow this thing was big enough to dent the shelves on either side of it. As it walked completely unfazed by the damage it was doing, the metal made a loud creaking sound, as the shelves were literally being bent upward. *Was this thing EVER human?* I thought, as I shined my flashlight at it. That's when it seemed to hit me: *It's a giant infected dog.* The moment I turned around to run, the slow footfalls turned to quickened steps, and I soon realized it was charging at me. I got to the end of the shelf I was at and saw almost the same monster from the basement blocking my path. I was trapped.

"Oliver!" I screamed and turned back around. *If I have to face one of them,* I decided then, *I'd rather face the dog.* I looked up at it, just in time for the pooch to freeze directly over me. I could barely breathe. I slowly sucked in the thick dusty air, and frowned when it didn't move. It took me a second or two to realize it was asleep as it practically blew me over with its soft, yet gentle huffs. I let out a sigh, and with shaking hands I looked around with my flashlight until I saw Oliver laying on his stomach on a shelf right above it, a tranquilizer tube in his hand. I smiled and wiped a bead of sweat off my forehead.

"Thanks," I whispered, and came to stand on the bottom shelf below him to get a boost up.

"You're welcome," he said, dropping the empty tube by the sleeping beast. He pulled me up, and we sat there for a while peering around. Now that we were up a little higher, I could see all kinds of creatures jumping from shelf to shelf or walking along the floor beneath us.

“How are we ever going to find that mini fridge without getting ourselves killed?” I asked.

“I don’t know,” Oliver answered, sounding completely defeated. After a couple minutes aiming our flashlight around the nearby shelves and relaxing against the metal beams, he spoke up again. “Do you think the tank has keys in it?”

“Maybe, why?” I looked at him and saw a look of determination cross his face.

“If I can lure them outside, do you think you can find the mini fridge on your own? I’ll sneak by them and jump in the tank. Hopefully, we get lucky, and they were dumb enough to leave the keys in it, or else I’ll have to lock myself in.” I felt really uneasy about it, but I knew we had to try something.

“Do it,” I said, giving him an encouraging nod. “I’ll lure them away from the tank, but don’t be long, okay?”

“Got it,” he said with a smile before we hopped down together. Slowly, I crept toward the middle of the room and stopped dead when one of the big creatures dragged itself by me, leaving a slime trail in its wake. Once it was past, I took a deep breath and continued creeping forward, using the shelves as cover. I was about 20 feet from the center when I went through the shelves, finding a half-used foghorn canister and a roll of duct tape. It was risky, but I knew it would do the trick. Oliver was standing one shelf behind me, so I held them both up for him to see. He gave me a thumbs-up, then gestured to a small gap in the shelves behind me, just big enough for one of us to fit in. “Throw it and hide in there.” I nodded, and tore off a small strip of the tape, stuck it over the top, pulled it tight so it went off, and threw it straight over Oliver’s head.

"Run!" I told him, and watched in pure terror as every single monster in there came stampeding by me, single file, straight for the canister. Oliver ran down the opposite side, and I peered out just in time to watch him hop in the tank and pull the hatch shut. "Come on, come on," I whispered to myself as I peeked out of my little cubby hole. Finally, after a few minutes of plugging my ears, I heard the engine sputter and come to life. All the creatures went running toward it, ignoring the blaring foghorn, and a few began climbing on the top as Oliver drove it straight toward the front door. When he got close, the door came open automatically, and the creatures followed the tank outside. "Yes, go, Oliver!"

Cautiously, I climbed out of the cubby hole and began exploring the warehouse. I walked up and down the aisles, spooking a few birds that were huddled around, until finally I saw a whole row of mini fridges on the highest shelf, pretty deep into the warehouse. All of them were locked up with chains, leaving me no choice but to test them all. Each one came unlocked, but I started to get worried when I saw they were empty. One after another, I pried them open, and I began losing hope until I found a turquoise-colored one plugged in with an extension cord. *Right, the cure has to be cold!* Inside, I saw that some of the needles were used up, but most of them were still full, containing a blue-colored liquid. *Yes, now Oliver and I can be free.* I scooped up a whole handful and went to turn around, only to run directly into Simon.

"Bravo, you found it. Now, give them here," he demanded, putting his hand out. Three men came and stood behind him, each heavily armed to the teeth.

"No," I responded, slowly backing away from them. I attempted to get him away by kicking the mini fridge off the top shelf. It dropped for a solid second before I heard the glass break down below.

"That was dumb," he said, peering over the edge. "Mia, I'm not the one to mess with. Unlike Polly, I'll kill you." His words slid out of his mouth like ice. I felt an instant chill. This whole time I felt at least a little safe, knowing my mom was their leader, but right then, all my immunity slipped away. *Would he really kill me?*

"No, you won't." I swallowed, trying to call his bluff. Still, I continued backing up, but I knew the shelf was only so big. I didn't have much room left to slide back on.

"Really? Come on now, don't be like this, kid. You did good, now do as you're told." I looked around as they continued forcing me backward until I realized I had maybe four feet left. A whimper escaped my lips. This cure was our last hope, and I knew if I let them have it, I would lose Oliver for good. I heard one of them cock their gun and knew this was it. "Last chance, Give. It. Here," he said, coming to stand directly over me. My whole body was shaking, but I stayed brave and lay down over the ledge with my hand out.

"Drop the guns and walk away, or these go splat." The shelf was at least twenty feet in the air, and if I fell, I knew I would get injured or worse, considering there was nothing but concrete beneath me. A second later, I heard him, and his men erupt in laughter. Before I could even look up at them, I knew Simon was close. I managed to tilt my head just enough to see him knelt down by me. I instantly knew I made a mistake, and tried to get myself back up, but he grabbed me by my shoes and pushed me over the edge until the only thing keeping me from hitting the ground was him.

"Good, drop them. I wanted to destroy them anyway," he said, faking me out by making it look as if he was dropping me. "Ya know, kid, your mother and I are an item. The only reason you're still alive is her, but I can very easily change that." I was hanging upside down, staring at the ground. My body felt heavy, and I was scared at any moment he would let me go. Even worse, I watched as the handgun I had went crashing to the ground and broke into a million pieces. I tried grabbing onto the shelf, but he swung me away each time I got close.

"Please! Don't drop me," I begged.

"I won't, but I have conditions." He groaned as he heaved me up onto the shelf and threw me down almost effortlessly. All I could do at that moment was cry. I stared at his boots in front of me as I sobbed; he was definitely their leader. "Condition one, give me the vials." Again, I sobbed, but I obediently handed them to him with shaky hands. "Good job," he said, before ordering his men to lower their weapons. "Condition two, you're going to train with the other soldiers effective immediately, meaning, and this is going to sting... No more Oliver," he said in a sing-song tone as he turned away from me.

"What?" I managed to choke out and met his eyes, even though my entire body was shaking. "What are you going to do with him?"

"That boy is nothing but a nuisance. Even you can see that, I'm sure."

"No, he's—"

"I know, you love him," he said, cutting me off with a wave of his hand as he turned his back to me, "but work comes before love, Mia. You were never supposed to get infected, or even meet Oliver to begin with. Your mother wanted you here with all the other obedient soldiers."

"Mom...wanted this?" I managed to peel myself up and sat with my legs crossed as he spoke.

"Yes, you and your...father would have made excellent soldiers, but I'll settle for you." He seemed to stumble over the words as he spoke about Dad, and I couldn't help but wonder how long they'd been together. *Was Mom planning on divorcing Dad? Was she cheating?*

"H-how long have you and M-mom been together?" I asked, getting a little bit of courage.

"Not long, maybe about six months. I know it hurts to hear, especially because she didn't tell you yet, but they divorced over a year ago, Mia. They just didn't know how to break the news to you." I gasped as I came to take in his words. *Can I really trust what he is saying?* I hugged my knees into myself. "As much as I'd like to fill you in on what you rightfully deserve, training begins in an hour and I've got a brat to hunt down, so—"

"Wait! Can I make a compromise?" I stood as he sat down on the top ledge, ready to lower himself down.

"Depends on what it is," he said, turning back to me.

"Let Oliver be a soldier with me, please. Cure us, and we'll fight side by side." I heard him chuckle and got really nervous as I waited there.

"Speak of the devil," he said, and I gasped as I looked over and saw Oliver come running in, screaming my name.

"Please, give him a chance. I'll surrender to you, just don't kill him."

"Why not? But I'll need his word first, maybe then I'll say yes. Come on," he said, gesturing for me to follow him. I came to lower myself down by him when he stabbed me in the leg with one of the needles. I whimpered and clutched the spot, causing him to laugh. "Congrats, you've been cured." A moment later, he hopped down, jumping from shelf to shelf before he got to Oliver and grabbed him by the throat.

"No, stop, don't hurt him!" I pleaded as I followed his lead and jogged up to him.

"Stand down, soldier. NOW!" he ordered, turning his head ever so slightly until I froze behind him.

"Did you say 'soldier'? What did you—" I gasped as he squeezed a little harder, making Oliver choke. I took another step, and my mouth fell open when he effortlessly picked Oliver up at least a foot high and slammed him into a support beam.

"Move again and our deal's over," he snapped.

"W-what deal?" Oliver asked, glancing between him and me as he pounded his fist against Simon's arm.

"You and the girl are going to be soldiers, isn't that right, Mia?" I heard a whimper escape Oliver's mouth before I ducked my head in shame away from him.

"Yes," I said, finally.

"Mia, how could—" Again, Simon squeezed, cutting him off. He held out a vial and dropped it at Oliver's feet, making it break.

"No, you said you would save him!" I screamed.

"There's still one left, better hope the boy complies." I could see Oliver's face go bright red. I couldn't tell if it was from the lack of oxygen or from what Simon said. I didn't even remember stepping forward, but he yelled at me anyway. "Mia," he snapped, "step forward again and he dies."

I nodded, although his back was turned to me, and planted my feet firmly against the ground.

"Are you going to listen, or do I kill you right here?" I felt nervous as I saw Oliver's eyes lock on mine before he squeezed them shut and a single tear fell down his face.

"I'll listen," he choked out. To my relief, Simon dropped him and injected him with a needle. Just like me, he groaned and clutched the spot. Then he walked away from Oliver and pointed his finger directly in my face.

"You will learn. I'm your commander now, and if you or that boy EVER disobey me again, there will be hell to pay. Got it?"

"Yes, sir. C-can I go to him now?" I glanced between him and Oliver until he gave me the okay and then ran to him.

"I'll give you five minutes, after that I expect to see you both on your way to the training field."

"Yes, sir," we both repeated, although Oliver's came out as more of a broken whisper. I grabbed him up and held him against me as Simon walked away. I had no idea how to explain myself, so I buried my head into his shoulder and just repeated, "I'm sorry," over and over again.

"We're going to work for them?" Oliver whispered into me after a minute. It finally seemed to hit both of us as the words came out and I nodded reluctantly.

"Yes, but we're cured, Oliver."

"No, we're still monsters. You just made sure of it." He pointed out the door, and I felt an instant wave of nausea pass over me as Oliver yelled at me for the first time. "Get out!"

"But, Oliver, you don't understand—"

"I said get out!" Slowly I stood and gave him one last broken look before I ran away. I really was alone, and I didn't know if I could ever fix it. *Am I destined to be a monster?*

Chapter Twelve: Training with the Enemy

I'd never realized how scary it could be without Dad or Oliver with me. I heard so many noises on the way back that I was constantly jumping. The field was directly behind Beacon Hospital. I got to the front door after about thirty minutes of jog-walking, but Oliver was nowhere to be seen. Soon, I was greeted by the two army guys I knocked out before and felt instantly nervous.

"Hey," I said, coming to stand in front of them. "I'm sorry about what I did."

"Yeah, well, you're lucky the commander wants you alive." I nodded nervously and turned around, but still there was no sign of Oliver.

"Where'd the other brat go?"

"Um...we got into an argument," I told them before I went and peeked around the corner. A short distance away, I could see him marching toward me, so I turned back around. "He's coming now," I told them, avoiding their eyes as we all stood there and waited. Finally, Oliver came and stood next to me, but he looked as if he didn't want to be close to me.

"Finally, what took you so long?" one asked impatiently, peeling himself off the wall.

"Does it really matter? I'm here now, can we go?" I noticed he had his hands balled into fists, and I felt sad. I'd never seen this side of him before.

"Sounds good to us. Training starts in about ten minutes, so you're right on time. We just have to get to the back door." Again, we were led through Beacon, but this time neither of us spoke. I wanted to, but he seemed so angry I decided against it. All I wanted was to explain what happened. Instead, we walked through the familiar halls in silence until one of the soldiers pushed open the back door, revealing a huge field full of soldiers. There had to be at least a few hundred, maybe more, and most of them were our age. They all stood at attention, and I soon realized they were waiting for us.

"Soldiers!" I heard Simon yell the moment we came outside. "We've got some new recruits. We'll begin shortly, but first they have to get changed. Show your new comrades some support." The group cheered as Simon handed Oliver and I uniforms and gestured to a set of port-a-potties behind them. "Go get changed." We both nodded and jogged over to them. Once we broke away, I managed to pull him aside to talk, although he looked as though he wanted to chew my head off.

"What, Mia? What do you want?" he snapped, crossing his arms. I couldn't help but cower a bit, but I swallowed that down and kept my composure.

"How bad is it?" I could see his throat was red and swollen. I tried reaching my hand up, but he swatted it away. Somehow that hurt even worse than being yelled at.

"Why do you care? You seemed to have gotten exactly what you wanted."

"Please allow me to explain," I begged gently, holding his arm.

"What is there to explain? Do you not understand that we have to hurt innocent people now? It was one thing when it was my blood, because I had no control over that, but now we have to actually take part in this. I'm not okay with this, but you dragged me into it." He started to walk away, but again I grabbed his arm.

"Wait!"

"Mia, let me go." He looked me up and down, and in that moment I listened.

"He said he would kill you if I didn't agree," I spit out as he began to walk away. "I had to beg to get you here, doesn't that mean anything to you? I know this isn't what you want, and it's not what I want either, but if we have even the slightest chance of getting free, this is how we start. Please understand." I clasped my hands together and waited, but he didn't respond at first. Slowly, he turned his head back and gave a look with a mix between hurt and anger.

"What happened in there? This is your one and only chance to explain, so it better be good, because from where I'm standing, it sounds like you gave in because you were scared and you let him win. I don't see any new injuries on you, so tell me again how this wasn't your idea."

"You know what?" For the first time since I'd met Oliver, I was angry at him. I came and bunched up his shirt. I wanted to let out everything. How I was constantly saving him, how I nearly drowned, how I was attacked, but instead I told him the bare minimum. "When you left, he hung me by my ankles and swung me around as I cried until I gave in to his demands, because if I didn't, he would have dropped me headfirst twenty feet and I would have died." I heard him gasp, but I didn't stop there. "But then, even after I went through that, I managed to get the courage to beg him to keep you safe, to keep YOU alive," I said, poking my finger against his chest. "But forgive me, because I clearly wanted to become an evil killer soldier!" I stormed away just then, with him calling behind me, and slammed the port-a-potty door shut. No matter how hard I tried, I felt numb all over again, but this time it wasn't from fear.

Slowly I locked the door and began to undress. I was in complete shock when I saw myself in the mirror. I had so many marks and bruises. Both of us had endured so much, yet here we were at each other's throats. The calloused burn mark on my shoulder made me think of Dad all over again. I ran my fingers across it and thought back to the first monster we saw together.

"If only that one was our only issue," I said to myself before I snapped back to reality and noticed how sticky my skin felt. I used paper towels and hand soap to wash up a bit, then I pulled the new uniform over my bare body. My hair was a frizzy mess. It kept getting caught in my fingers as I tried to comb out the knots. Eventually, I realized it was no use. I would just have to deal with it. When I was done, I sat down for a moment and just breathed in and out. I didn't get too many of these moments the last few days, and I have to admit, it felt peaceful.

When I finally did come out, he was standing there, but instead of walking right back to him, I kept going. This time he didn't call my name, but I could hear him dragging his feet through the grassy field behind me. It was our first real fight. I knew it was bound to happen eventually, but somehow it hurt much more than I was willing to admit. Before we got back to the group, Oliver tried to stop me, but I shook his arm away just like he did me. *Does he deserve it?* I wasn't really sure, but my heart said yes.

"Mia?" I heard him whisper when I didn't stop for him. My chest ached when that happened, when his voice got shaky, but still I walked on until I got to the group. *Maybe a few days would do us some good.* I came and joined the formation, but Simon stopped Oliver when he tried to stand next to me.

"Why don't you go to the other side? Make some new friends, hm?" Simon asked him as if it was his first day of school.

"Mia's the only person I know here," he responded in a low voice. "Can't I just stay with her?"

"I think it'd be better if you split, at least for a few days. It won't hurt you, kid. Go on." He gestured for him to move along, but he stayed. He held his arms nervously around himself when everyone's eyes seemed to be on us right then.

"But, I'd really rather—"

"I said, go! That's an order." My breath caught in my throat as Oliver turned toward me for back-up. This would determine everything. Dad wanted Oliver to protect me, but I realized that it turned out the opposite. I loved him, but it felt like I was the one looking after him. The only thing I wasn't sure about, though, was whether that was a bad thing or not. *What if we only love each other because of the trauma we went through?* I knew what I had to do to know the truth, but I wasn't ready for the aftermath.

"Mia, I'm sure you've been with the boy enough. Why don't you go to the other side then?" Simon asked when he realized Oliver wasn't budging.

"Sure," I said with a forced chuckle. "A few days won't hurt." I didn't know whether I was saying that to me or Oliver, but either way, leaving hurt so much worse than I thought it would, and all I heard behind me as I walked away was a gasp.

Soon, I was surrounded by strangers. They were all huddled in circles. It felt like being back in high school again. Everyone had their own cliques, but I wasn't sure where I belonged. If I belonged anywhere at all. Nervously, I tried to integrate myself somewhere. I joined the first friendly-looking group I could find, but for the most part they ignored me. I was always an introvert. Even back in school, I didn't have many friends, so I knew this was going to be super hard. I kept going back and forth until Simon ordered us all to stand at attention. That wasn't so hard, but then he began yelling orders left and right. At first, I wasn't sure what to do, until someone grabbed my arm and gently pulled me backward.

A moment later, I was greeted by a soldier with bright red hair, and eyes so green they seemed to outshine the grass beneath us. Her eyebrows were dark and sharp, giving her an edgy look. She had a face full of freckles too, but she had smooth-looking skin, like she was drenched in moisturizer. Just like me, she had on a green and brown camo uniform and ankle-high combat boots with her pant legs tucked in. It really suited her, and I had to admit, I was jealous. She was really pretty.

"You're going to stand out like a sore thumb if you keep stumbling around like that, girl," she said, laughing a bit at my clumsiness. "My name's Gabby, and I'm assuming you're Mia?"

"Yeah, that's me," I said, worried about what she had heard. Although we were talking, we kept walking with the others until Simon said another instruction I didn't know how to follow.

"Hey. It's okay, follow my lead. I'm here for you." As Simon screamed things like, "About face," and other various orders, Gabby showed me each of the moves. It took a few tries as I tried to mimic her, but I eventually blended in with the crowd.

"Nice job, you're a natural." I smiled at her kindness, but I found myself distracted when, out of the corner of my eye, I saw Oliver fall over, stopping a few soldiers in their tracks behind him.

"Oh no," I said, under my breath.

"What's wrong?" she asked. I almost forgot I was with someone, and almost as if on cue, I said something that instantly struck a chord.

"I have to go help him."

"No, don't. You're just going to get yourself in trouble."

"But—"

"STOP!" I heard Simon yell, cutting me off. "ATTENTION."

"Sir, yes, sir!" Everyone yelled in unison, before we stood with our hands on our hips, waiting for his next move.

"Private Beacon," he yelled loud enough for everyone to hear, "do we have a problem, soldier?" He got almost directly in Oliver's face, and I swore I could see spit flying from where I was standing. I couldn't hear what Oliver said back to him, but I could see his lips move. "I can't hear you!"

"No, sir!" Oliver responded, this time the sound of his voice reached me.

"Then why are you AGAIN disrupting our training? Are you going to be trouble, private?"

"No, sir!" he yelled once more, but this time he didn't sound as confident.

"I didn't think so. Private Indi, come help him out." I watched as a very young-looking guy, who I assumed to be Indi, came and joined him. He didn't look any older than eighteen, like he was fresh out of high school. He was probably one of the youngest ones there, but there were definitely some older recruits too. I couldn't help but feel guilty for leaving Oliver on his own, but I knew we couldn't be together all the time. Even if I wanted to.

"Soldiers! At ease," Simon yelled before gesturing to some climbing equipment and an exercise course he set up. There were about ten sets of tires spread maybe two feet apart, some crawling sections with wires attached to little wooden pikes nailed into the dirt, a rope wall, and some climbing equipment to scale the side of Beacon Hospital. In all honesty, I hated the idea of being a soldier, but I was excited to show off my competitive side. Simon had us go one by one and told us that the person with the best time wins a prize. I wasn't sure what to expect, but everyone got really excited. While we were waiting for our turn, Gabby explained that the prizes were usually something worthwhile. I smiled and began to stretch as the line inched forward. We were maybe halfway between everyone, giving us ample time to prepare. I began to do jumping jacks when I felt a sharp pain in my head and colors blurred from my eyes.

"Whoa, Mia? Are you okay?" I tried to say something back, but with the hot sun beating down on my face, I felt overwhelmed. I cradled my head with my right arm, trying to fight it off. It was the worst headache I'd ever felt. "Mia?"

"Y-ea-h," I responded in my dazed state. A moment later, I hit the ground. My head was pounding, and it felt as if someone was using a jackhammer inside my skull. I heard voices, but I was so tired I ignored them and closed my eyes. Although I felt someone splash water in my face, the sleep finally took hold of me. I wasn't sure how much time passed, but I woke to someone screaming my name again.

"Mia!" It sounded echoey at first, as if I was dreaming, then it got louder. "Mia?!" I heard a man's voice yell and jolted awake. My eyes were crusted over when I woke back up again, but I definitely felt refreshed. "There you are. Why didn't you tell me you were tired, kid?" I yawned and slowly wiped my eyes until I saw Simon sitting on a chair next to my bed. The one person I was hoping to see wasn't there, and it almost broke me until Simon explained.

"I'm guessing you're looking for Oliver?" he asked, prompting me to nod as my vision returned. "He's asleep too," he told me, gesturing to another bed across from me. I sighed with relief and plopped back down again.

"How long have I been out?" I asked and felt pleasantly surprised when he poured me a glass of ice water. My throat felt so dry, it was as if he was reading my mind.

"A few days, unfortunately," Simon responded, shaking his head. "It seems like you and the boy really took a beating. He collapsed shortly after you. If you two had been under any longer, I would have had no choice but to have one of the nurses give you an IV."

"I–I didn't know you cared." I was genuinely confused. I pulled my knees into my chest and yawned again as I waited for his response. Surprisingly, he had a kind side, at least for a brief moment.

"Look, I may not be your father, kid, but I might become your stepfather one day. You and that boy caused me enough trouble to last me a lifetime, especially when you pushed that mini fridge off the shelf like that," he told me as he massaged a vein on his forehead. "But you can still be useful. You've seen a lot of those things firsthand, and as I've been told, they found you in the morgue covered in their blood. So, YOU know their weakness."

"Wait. Their weakness is the cold?"

"Bingo," he said, rocking back in the chair to kick up his feet.

"So, what do we do with that info? It's still summer."

"Maybe you could figure that out." He eyed me as if I would come up with an idea on the spot, but my brain was still foggy.

"I'm confused, I thought we, or...the soldiers were releasing these monsters into cities to hurt people."

"We are, Mia." The way he said it came out coldly. I couldn't manage to look him in the eye after that, but he continued anyway. "Our purpose is to turn as many people as possible. I'm just telling you how to protect yourself. This training isn't about protecting people. Once they're bit, it's game over. There's not enough of a cure to go around, and if you think those idiots in there are going to make more, you're sadly mistaken. What it's really about is—"

"Extracting the infected, once they complete the job," I said, staring down at the floor as it seemed to hit me. They really were evil. Standing by while hundreds of people were turned, only to clean up the aftermath. I knew that's what was happening, but to hear it being said felt so much worse. "I'm going to stop you." I said as I balled my hands into fists and shot him a glare.

He laughed for a good moment and tossed his head back like a TV movie villain. Then he spoke again, this time getting dangerously close to me. "And how do you intend on doing that? Don't forget, you and the boy may be cured, but it's really not that hard to infect you all over again, and this time, there's no cure to save your asses. You wouldn't want me to do that, would you?"

"No," I responded through gritted teeth. I knew there was nothing I could do to stop them, but it didn't make it any better that this was our future. Training was hard enough, but imagining myself standing by while other people suffered made me feel sick to my stomach.

"I didn't think so. Training will continue tomorrow morning. That should be enough time for you and zombie boy over there to recover. For now, go to the barracks. I'll let you know when he wakes."

"Can't I stay with him?" I looked up at him, and he crossed his arms angrily over his chest.

"What's it going to take for you to listen?" he yelled as he grabbed my arm and pulled me off the bed. "I am your general, I am your superior. When I give you an order, you follow it without question. Is that understood?"

"What would Mom think if she knew you were treating me this way?" I shot him an icy glare, hoping to intimidate him, but it didn't seem to work.

"I don't care. Drop and give me thirty. NOW!" A gasp escaped my lips as his thunderous voice echoed through the infirmary wing. I looked down at the floor, but I didn't move. That only seemed to make him angrier. A moment later, he grabbed my arm again and practically shoved me down onto the floor. I didn't want to comply, but then he put his foot on my back and pressed down.

"I'll give you until the count of three to start, or else." I closed my eyes as the first number came out. After two, I knew I had to try. Slowly, I pushed my arms up, and felt the pressure relieve a bit, but not all the way.

"One," he yelled. "Again." Slowly, I fell, and rose back up. My arms ached with each one I did, and after seven I whimpered.

"Can I please just do ten?" I cried, shaking beneath his boot.

"Keep going, you're not even there yet!" I nodded and felt a bead of sweat drip down my forehead to my nose. The last three were brutal. He seemed to press harder when he noticed I was struggling, but finally I got to ten and he stopped. Across from me I heard a creak as I laid there panting, and saw Oliver lower his feet over the edge of the bed.

"Leave her alone," I heard him say.

"Oh good, you're up," Simon said, and he turned and began walking toward him with a look of amusement. "Your turn, you wanna talk back to me too?" Slowly, I used the nightstand next to my bed to push myself up and saw Oliver peek over at me.

"No," he said, looking Simon up and down. He seemed to match his energy, and I couldn't help but crack a smile. "I believe I just said, 'leave her alone.'" He was speaking to Simon, but his eyes were on me.

"Oh, is that so, wise guy? Why don't you do me a favor then. Drop and give me twenty!" I watched Oliver's eyes dart to the floor, then to him.

"Okay," he said finally. I wasn't sure if he was trying to impress me, but he dropped down and quickly completed Simon's task. I couldn't help but watch him as Simon counted each one, then he got to twenty and stood back up as if it was nothing. "Your turn." The moment the words left his lips, I felt weak in the knees. I nearly burst out laughing when I saw a vein pop out of his forehead again. He probably hated us both, but to our surprise, he dropped down and outshined both of us.

"Wow," Oliver said, coming to stand by me as I counted his push-ups one by one. "He actually did it." I chuckled and finally, after completing fifty push-ups in under two minutes, Simon came to stand again.

"Don't challenge me unless you're willing to do double, private." Simon huffed in a hunched-over position before he took a deep breath, stood up, and eyed both of us. I didn't want to, but we had no choice but to shake our heads and back down. I wanted to step up to him, but I knew I couldn't do a hundred, especially not as fast as he did. "Go to the barracks, now!"

"Yes, sir." Walking back felt almost peaceful. The sun was just starting to go down, and the sky turned an almost orangish-red color. I stared up at the clouds as we passed through and watched them go by. As a kid I used to imagine shapes in them. My favorite one was a castle, although Dad said it looked like a blob in the sky. I missed those moments with him. Sitting in the grass in our back yard, just watching clouds roll by. I stood there and stared up; although I knew Simon probably wasn't too far behind, I wanted a moment to just be me again.

Oliver stopped about twenty feet in front of me and turned around when he saw I wasn't following. "Anything good?" he asked as he arched his head up.

"Just the clouds," I responded with a satisfied huff. "I like watching them, they're pretty."

"I do too, but I prefer the stars. They've always intrigued me."

"Maybe that's what I could get you," I told him, as I began to think of Christmas.

"What's that?" he asked, meeting my eyes again.

"A telescope. You can look at the stars, and I...can look at the clouds." I heard him chuckle and turned to see Simon coming up on us fast. "We should head back," I said, grabbing his arm. Luckily, when we took off again, Simon slowed down. I wasn't prepared for another fight. When we got there, I released his arm and was about to head inside when Oliver stopped me.

"Hey, wait up," he said, stopping me in the doorway of the barracks. In reality it was a giant storage building they converted into barracks, but it felt real enough to me. Simon walked past us, but he left us alone this time. I breathed a sigh of relief and returned my attention to Oliver. "I'm sorry," he told me finally, with a really sad look. "I didn't know what you went through. I thought you gave up. I should have known better. I deserved what I got, but I hope you know I was worried about you." He stopped and leaned his forehead against mine with a deep, painful sigh. "My whole life, I've always dealt with monsters," he said with a chuckle as he cupped my face in his hands. "I felt hopeless; honestly, I had no hope left. That is, until I met you. You and your dad showed me there is so much more out there, and I got greedy. I wanted to escape again. And I thought we had a chance, but I was wrong, and that's okay as long as I have you. I may not be free, but you are my escape. Please, forgive me." I felt my heart flutter as he finished his speech, and I nodded.

"I'm sorry too. I was cruel, and I shouldn't have acted that way toward you. You're all I have. I need you."

"Then you can have me," he whispered, kissing me as if we were apart for days. I completely forgot the door was open and jumped when I heard someone cheer.

"Yes! You two are so cute together." Gabby came to the door and looped her arm around mine when Oliver and I split a moment later.

"I'll be taking her," she told Oliver before dragging me away. I felt my cheeks flush, slightly out of embarrassment. Gabby was nice, but she was also a lot more extroverted than I was. Little did I know that besides Oliver, she would become my closest friend.

Chapter Thirteen: Infected City

About two and a half months went by in training, and despite my better judgment, it began to feel normal. Every day we would get up at five a.m. and run laps around Beacon, then we'd eat breakfast and do a training exercise using the equipment Simon's team built. After our morning exercises, we'd eat lunch, and we'd finish the day off by marching to Simon's chant. It was embedded in my brain, like a record on repeat.

During the chant we would march in a straight line, carrying rifles the army supplied for us. They felt heavy in my hands, and I couldn't help but wonder how old they were. I never bothered to ask, since Simon seemed almost unapproachable most days, but I knew based on the style they hadn't been made recently. They had knives attached to the ends of them, and around the edges of the barrel, at least on mine, I could see gunpowder. Around the trigger there were pretty engravings like swirls and vines that almost seemed buffed out, as if someone had tried to use a piece of sandpaper on them. Unfortunately, the number engraved into the side was destroyed, or else I might have tried to research it myself.

Oliver and I met up every day, but we also hung out with Indi and Gabby. It became our little tradition. All four of us would march together, and during our training exercises, we would time each other and gloat about who won. I began to love them, but when September rolled around that year, I found out just how ruthless they were. I never really questioned why they were recruited, but Simon made me question all of it.

"Alright, recruits! Attention!" It seemed like a normal day, but I noticed there were a lot more doctors and army sergeants around than normal.

"Hey, Oliver?" I asked. I knew I was risking another argument from Simon, but I was too curious.

"What's up?" he whispered, turning his eyes to the side.

"Any idea what's going on?"

"No," he whispered again, turning his head for a brief moment before he caught himself and straightened up again. "Stay on guard. Knowing Simon, it's not good." He was right. Simon liked to do these surprise training moments using real infected. All of us learned how sick he really was when he seemed to shrug off recruits dying. Since the start, we lost about fifty men and women. To me, it was heartbreaking, but Simon would just say, "They would have never survived out there," or, "It's all about survival of the fittest." Some began to notice his dark streak and tried to leave, but we learned pretty quickly that there is no leaving. About a month into our training, a soldier was killed by his hands when they attempted to walk off during training.

I never learned her name, but her death was still fresh on my mind as if it happened yesterday. She was maybe eighteen or nineteen, and when that day rolled around, she seemed restless. We had just finished a mission in one of the other abandoned apartment buildings, and when we got back, she couldn't stop pacing the floor.

"Hey, are you okay?" I asked, sitting up in my bed. Oliver and Gabby went for a run, so I was mostly left by myself. At first, she didn't say anything. Tears rolled down her cheeks, and she raked her hands through her hair like she was going to pull it out. "It's okay, you can talk to me." I stood up, and saw Indi shake his head as I came to stand in front of her. For the most part, Indi didn't talk much, but he was really sweet when he did. Part of me wanted to listen to him and sit back down, but I couldn't let her struggle on her own. "What happened?"

"My brother was one of the infected. I found the shirt patch I gave him for his birthday." She showed me a patch of a red guitar with his name attached to the bottom, and I winced when I saw there was blood splattered on it. "I had to shoot him," she managed to choke out. "I can't do this anymore."

She began to march away, and I knew I had to stop her. I ran up behind her, but she shoved my arm off and kept going.

"Wait, stop!" I yelled, trying to keep up with her. She went from marching to a full run, until eventually, when we got halfway down the side of Beacon, Simon stopped both of us in our tracks.

"Where are you going?" he said, narrowing his eyes and crossing his arms over his chest. "I believe I instructed all of you to either return to the barracks or the training yard."

"I'm going home," she said plainly, "and you won't stop me. I've had enough, this place is...evil."

"Really?" Simon asked, widening his eyes. Something told me this wasn't going to end well, so I gently squeezed the girl's arm.

"I don't think you should—" I tried warning her but was soon cut off by Simon's voice.

"Why don't we have a talk? Mia, would you mind informing the others to meet me at storage building 1105?"

"There's no need for that, we were just about to head—" Again I tried to protect her, but Simon shot me an ice-cold glare.

"Now," he seethed through gritted teeth. I was frightened as I ran back. I had no idea what was about to happen, but I quickly gathered everyone and led them along the gravel path to the first storage building, where we went looking for the cure. When we got there, the girl and Simon were talking out front, and I could see she was sobbing. He had a death grip around her upper arm, and I felt my heart instantly drop.

"Mia? What's going on?" Oliver asked, with an uncomfortable look.

"I don't know. Last thing she said was that she wanted to leave." Slowly, I pushed through the group, but I only managed to get a row behind the front when Simon called for attention again. Everyone but the girl listened, waiting for his next order.

"When you signed up for this position," he said, pacing back and forth in front of the doorway, "you knew the risks. Whether that be your own death, or the death of others. You were trained to take on the infected and either kill them or contain them. On day one, you took up an oath that you wouldn't leave until you were dismissed by me or another member of our staff, or you were killed in the line of duty. There are only two exceptions to that order, and those, as you all know, are Mia and Oliver. They didn't have that choice, but you all did. Today, one of you decided to break that oath. This young lady here is going to demonstrate what happens when you decide to...walk away from your duty. Like a coward." He seemed to say the last two words just to spite her, and we all watched as she fell to her knees and began begging Simon to stop, but he wouldn't. It was too late. I tilted my head down just enough to see the doors of the storage building open and managed to see one of the biggest infected mutants on the island. My jaw fell open as what looked like a giant pile of pinkish-red flesh convulsed on the floor. I wasn't sure what to think of it. It was ugly and slimy looking, but it didn't seem harmful. Then, Simon pulled the girl up from the floor, and pushed her inside.

"Goodbye, soldier," he muttered, saluting to the open door. At that moment, I didn't care about his order. I rushed forward, hoping to grab her arm and pull her away, but I was seconds too late. I heard a loud gushing sound as I pushed through the crowd and ground my shoes to a halt when I heard her scream. It was so loud; it made my eardrums vibrate. She was stabbed right through her stomach with a large stinger, almost like a scorpion. I saw her squirm, but before I could see the rest, Oliver grabbed me, turned me around, and pulled me into him, blocking my view. All I could hear behind me was a gross squelching sound and the other soldiers' cries. No one could believe that he would stoop so low, but I could. He was wicked.

I still remembered that day as we all stood there waiting for Simon to speak. My heart began to hammer in my chest, but soon he began.

"Hello, everyone," he said, seemingly preoccupied with a packet of papers in his hands. "As you all know, you were asked to be here for one specific job, and your time has come to begin. It's time that you all start the extraction process, so we can begin bringing in more infected than ever. In my hands, I hold your assignments. You will be given the name of a nearby city and will be transported with your fellow comrades by helios. Unless, of course, anyone would like to step down." I swallowed down a lump in my throat as a long moment of silence occurred. No one dared move, we all knew better, although Oliver and I squirmed a bit. "Good. Nice to see you're all ready to step up. The infected are being transported as we speak. When you get there, it should be over...for the most part. Stand by until you are given one of our direct orders," he said, gesturing to the team he had assembled up front. "Once we give you the all-clear signal, you will herd them into the designated transport vehicles using these." I turned my head to see him, and another woman hold up a crate of what looked like homemade bombs, a box full of pre-packaged gloves, and a crate full of assault rifles.

"These are dry ice bombs," he told us, using a pair of thick brown welder's gloves to carefully pull one out. They were made by using a plastic bottle filled with warm water, some dry ice that was loosely secured to the top, and a string to drop it in. "They will help redirect the infected and create a smoke screen for your team. They are very dangerous, so make sure you use them right. They can, and will, blow your arm off, got it?"

"Yes, sir," the group yelled back, saluting to him.

"Good. Now, I'm only going to say this once, do NOT kill the infected unless it is absolutely necessary. Have I made myself clear?"

"Yes, sir!" the soldiers yelled again, but Oliver and I stayed silent.

"Good, now line up!" Everyone here knew we were forced into doing this, forced into being the general's puppets, but it only seemed to hit us right then that we actually had to hurt people. My body froze up, but Oliver squeezed my hand and tilted my head toward him.

"Hey, it's okay, Mia. Look at me," he whispered as people pushed and shoved their way to the front. Most of the soldiers, sickeningly enough, seemed excited. It made my blood run cold, the thought of standing by while innocent people suffered, even after two months of training. I was scared. Slowly, Oliver guided me to the very back of the line and squeezed my hand hard any time he noticed I began to shake. "No matter what happens out there, we're not them. We're not the bad guys, they are." He pointed straight ahead through the crowd, and despite my growing fear, his words helped. I followed Oliver's arm with my eyes until they locked onto Simon and his associates. "Understand? You are good, Mia. Never forget that."

"We both are," I said, hoping to cement that in my mind before I finally allowed my body to turn toward the front. A moment later, Gabby latched onto my other arm and screeched excitedly.

"Don't worry, girl," she said, with the biggest smile plastered across her face, "I've got our assignments. No need to go up there. The four of us are together." She linked her other arm with Indi, but he seemed to shy away from it. *Is he nervous too?* I saw him scratch the back of his neck when he pulled away.

"I don't want to do this," I told them just then. There were ten helicopters waiting there to take us to our destinations, so it was really loud.

"What?" Gabby asked, cupping her hand over her ear. I didn't want to say it again, the look on her face was enough for me. She wanted to do this.

"Why don't you go ahead of us!" I yelled, as the different groups began filing inside. "I need to talk to Oliver."

"Got it, don't be too long. Simon might kill you." She was joking, but her words made my heart jump. *Would Oliver and I stand a chance of running?* I thought, as I began to chew on my fingernails. I was so nervous, I chewed too far in on my pinky nail and made it bleed. Unfortunately, they were doing multiple trips to pick up everyone since most helicopters can only fit four people comfortably plus luggage, but Gabby and Indi claimed one first. Meaning we had to follow.

"We have to go, Mia. Simon's doing a headcount," Oliver shouted when he noticed I didn't follow them. I turned my attention back up front and saw the leaders with clipboards.

"I can't," I said, as my breath caught in my throat. I started to hyperventilate, but a moment later, it got so much worse. My knees felt wobbly, so I used my hands to hold onto them, and took deep, slow breaths, though the wind from the helicopter blades was making it worse. Then I felt something cold against my forehead, and heard Oliver yell," No! Don't!"

I managed to muster up the courage to look up, just in time to meet the barrel of a pistol.

"Go! Now!" Simon ordered when I met his eyes. There was nothing there. The one shred of goodness I had seen in the infirmary was gone. I was sure, right then, that he was evil incarnate. My body gave one final attempt at giving up before Oliver grabbed me and helped me toward the last remaining helicopter on the ground. When I got in, the last two seats were in the back and it was a tight squeeze. The two crates were on the bottom, but the box had to sit next to us. Once I was in, I laid my head against the back of the headrest and closed my eyes. I had never been in a helicopter or airplane before, so that definitely heightened my fears. Gabby and Indi were up front, so it was just me and Oliver in the back. Once the pilot climbed in, he passed us all headsets, and after he did a few checks, the helicopter slowly began to rise. I listened to his every word over the mic, and used that to keep my heart from beating out of my chest.

"Hey, Mia? Are you ready for this?" I heard Indi's voice say. I almost didn't register it, since he was speaking so quietly, but when I did, I sat up.

"Uh..."

"Don't worry, this is going to be awesome," Gabby beamed, cutting me off. I could barely hold myself back this time as Gabby turned around in her seat. She had this sick sparkle in her eyes, and I couldn't take it anymore.

"No, it's not," I said, coldly shooting her a glare. She seemed to ignore my anger and continued on.

"What do you mean? We get to take part in herding zombies, what could be better than this?"

"Maybe not hurting innocent people? Maybe having a normal life? Or maybe...and hear me out on this one, not smiling while we fly to a city full of innocents who are going to die unknowingly when all we can do is stand there and watch as they get torn apart by the infected." The last line wiped the smile clean off her face. I was waiting for her to say something peppy again, but it became really tense instead.

"Simon's right, you two really are trouble. So here's what's going to happen..." Before I could react, she grabbed my shirt collar and dragged me toward the front seat, almost making me slide forward.

"Gabby, back off!" Oliver yelled, trying to separate her from me.

"Shut up, zombie boy. You two are going to grow up and do your damn job, because if you don't and you mess this up for OUR team, I might just let my gun slip and let another couple rounds fly that don't need to." The pilot turned his head in shock, but he didn't say anything. She took it too far, and even Indi began to fidget uncomfortably. I couldn't believe it myself. I stared forward in disbelief until eventually she turned herself back around with a loud huff. Oliver squeezed my hand again, and whispered for me to ignore her, but how could I? She was the first friend, besides Oliver, that I had made in this nightmare place. It felt wrong, and I almost apologized, although I felt in my head, I didn't truly do anything. When we reached the city, tensions were still pretty high, but it didn't even come close to what we were about to witness. We stepped out of the helicopter after some brief radio chatter and stood behind a yellow-taped barrier that said, *Police Line, Do Not Cross.*

"Stay here until you're given the order to cross. And...whatever you do, don't kill each other," the pilot told us before he unloaded the supplies, hopped back in, and left the four of us there alone. We all nodded and put on a pair of gloves preemptively. I was scared, mostly of what lay ahead for us, but something told me Gabby wasn't the most trustworthy with a gun either.

"So far, no noise," Indi said, cutting through my thoughts.

"Let's just hope it stays that way," Oliver said, gripping one of the wooden beams. When he finished, Gabby scoffed, and we all turned back toward her.

"You know it's not going to, so why even bother saying it? You just sound stupid," she told him, before she went up to the frontline and shoved him back.

"Hey!" Oliver stumbled back, and only barely managed to stay standing.

"Look, Gabby. You may be excited about this, but we have every right to feel differently from you. This isn't right and shoving us around or pulling on our shirts doesn't make it any better." She didn't respond that time, instead she shook her head and grabbed a gun out of the crate. Instantly the hair stood up on the back of my neck as she checked it for ammo. I didn't trust her, not anymore. She didn't do anything with it, but in my head, I was still screaming for her to put it away.

About ten minutes passed before we heard the first sounds of chaos. A scream, so loud it echoed through the town square. Quickly, without thinking, I ran to the gun box and pulled out my rifle. It was full to the brim with ammo, so I cocked it back, turned off the safety once I was past them, and aimed it out into the road.

"They said don't kill the zombies, Mia," Gabby chimed in immediately as I stood there on alert.

"I don't care," I responded, scanning the road ahead. No other sounds came at first, but then as I was about to step away and lower my gun, I heard a store alarm go off in the distance and saw a thick cloud of black smoke. I gasped and almost left the security line, but then the helicopter came back with four more soldiers. *Ugh*, I thought, as I began to pace back and forth. I knew I had to stop, but my heart was hammering in my chest. To distract myself, I ran back to the box and read about the city we were in. It was called Greenburrow, and it was a city with about fifteen hundred people in it. Fifteen hundred infected. That alone made me feel sick. They didn't deserve this, and I knew I had to do something to stop it. This time I charged forward and hopped right over the fence.

"Mia, stop!" I heard a few voices say, but I kept going until I made it about a block up the street and saw a woman get thrown face first through the window of a dress boutique called Daisy's. Her face was covered in blood and broken glass, and I wanted to help her, but before I could manage to get to her, one of the infected leaped out of the shop and slaughtered her right in front of me.

"Ahhh!" I screamed, and instantly let my gun fire. When it dropped dead, my mind jumped to Simon. I was going to suffer for this. All I wanted was to help people, but I couldn't help her. I turned around and began sulking my way back to the security line when I heard a distant voice. I looked up just in time to see Oliver hop over the fence and scream, but no sound came out. *Am I in shock?* Everything seemed to be in slow motion, then I was whipped back to reality in a flash when a bullet went flying by my left ear. I turned around with my heart in my throat and saw that the infected I thought I had killed was within a few inches of me. *Did I even shoot it? Did I miss it? I was about to die!*

"Mia, run!" I snapped my head up again to see a horde of infected was coming my way, and I knew I didn't have anywhere near enough bullets to cover all of them. There had to be at least a few hundred. Some were drenched in blood, probably from tearing into the townspeople, while others were missing limbs, hopefully from people taking them down. They heard my gunshot and were coming for me. In a panic, I bolted as fast as I could until Oliver grabbed my arm and used all his strength to drag me back to the line. The only problem: we weren't alone. They were still coming for us. I made it within ten feet of the line when suddenly I locked eyes with Simon. I didn't remember seeing another helicopter land, but he stood there, pistol in hand, shaking his head.

"How did I know it would be you that would mess it up?" he said with a disappointed tone before he aimed the gun right at us. Gabby followed suit, and to both our dismay, so did Indi. "You wanted to play the hero, now's your chance. Go on, go save them, but you're not coming back, either of you. You broke my rules one too many times. Now, you can either fight, or die trying."

Chapter Fourteen: Spreading the Word

"You can't do that!" Oliver yelled, making my heart rate spike. "They'll kill us!" I turned around and saw we had maybe sixty seconds to escape if we were lucky.

"How about this then, I'll give you another chance. But not Mia. You were trying to save one of my operatives; Mia, on the other hand, blatantly disregarded my rules and tried to save a civilian. You're out."

"No deal," Oliver responded without a moment's hesitation. "I won't abandon her, and I'd rather die than go back to working for you."

"Well then, be my guest. But let me make myself clear, if I hear so much as one gunshot, I'll order all the soldiers to find you and take you out. If you want to survive, then you're gonna have to run for it. Good luck, you're gonna need it."

"Remember what happened last time you told us that?" I responded with a devious grin before I ran off with Oliver. He looked back at me with a sly smile and raised eyebrows as we ran. He knew I was right. We were going to escape, I just had to figure out how. Our time was dwindling fast, but in the end, we ended up running through the last open alleyway between us and them. It was right behind a few restaurants, so the smell of fresh food was rising in the air, making my stomach growl. I thought that the soldiers behind the police line would give us enough time to make our escape, but Simon and the team tossed out a few dry ice bombs as we ran away, sending them straight after us. There wasn't much we could use to deter them, so we had no choice but to take every twist and turn we could. As we ran, we tried the doorways in the alley, but all of them were locked up tight. Luckily for us, the infected weren't that fast, but that didn't make them any less scary.

Then, right as we were about to escape, another group of infected came around to our front. I knew then that the sound of glass bottles breaking, and the other horde's constant groans and screeching attracted their attention. I looked back and forth between the two hordes before I realized there was only one remaining path.

"This way," I told Oliver. There were two abandoned buildings on either side of us, with brick walls covered in graffiti. The path ahead was blocked by a fence, so we had no choice but to veer right. When we turned, I hoped I would see another exit, but instead I ran straight into another fence.

"No!" I cried, turning to look behind me. "No, no, no."

"Mia, you know what we have to do," Oliver said, gesturing to the gun on my shoulder. I knew I had enough ammo to at least clear a path, but Simon was wicked and highly trained. *Can we take him?*

"We can't, Simon will kill us." I stepped back about five steps, and ran straight into the fence. No matter how hard I tried, the wood wasn't budging. Oliver joined me, but after five attempts, the first few infected came around the corner.

"Mia!" Oliver screamed, pressing his back against the wall as one got into position to lunge at us. They were the same infected from when we met. Some were climbing along the walls, while others were crawling or dragging themselves across the ground. The only difference was, unlike the one from the apartments, these had eyes. We had maybe ten feet between us and them, so I knew I didn't have much time to decide. Simon was an evil man, but I would rather take him on than a whole horde. As fast as I could, I began firing rounds in all directions. They began dropping like flies, and eventually I cleared enough room to burst through the wall. I used a whole clip of ammo trying to shoot through the wood. It was surprisingly sturdy, but when Oliver tapped my shoulder to tell me to stop, he kicked a hole through where the bullet holes were, and we managed to escape. We ran behind another line of buildings until, about five blocks up, we came out into the open street again. I could see the police line when we came out. It was empty.

"Where to now?" Oliver asked through deep breaths.

"We should find a way out of the city, fast, before Simon and the other soldiers find us."

"Got it," he responded, handing me a clip of ammo. "Grabbed it from the box before I left jumped over the line. Thought it might come in handy."

"You are amazing." I grabbed the clip and put it in my side pocket. I couldn't imagine myself killing a human, unlike Simon, but if it came down to our lives or theirs, I knew I would have to make a tough decision. We ended up losing what was left of the horde when we turned down another side street, and eventually wound up in the middle of a giant farmer's market. I felt an instant wave of relief wash over me when I saw a whole bunch of stalls full of fresh food. No one was around, so I grabbed an apple and instantly chomped down.

"Mmmm." I moaned, wiping a drop of saliva off my lower lip. We didn't have much fresh food on Beacon's little island. For the most part, we ate camping ration meals that a group of volunteers prepared for us, like freeze-dried chicken and rice or freeze-dried beef stew. Every day, they would pour two 24-serving buckets into a huge gumbo pot and throw in boiling water. For the most part they were pretty good, but it was nothing compared to fresh food.

"What's that like?" Oliver asked, raising his eyebrows.

"It's pretty good," I said with a satisfied nod. "Have you ever tried one before?"

"No, they don't have very many options in Beacon."

"Want to try it?" I held out the unbitten side of mine, and after taking a second to think it through, he took it from me and lifted it to his nose. It was a Red Delicious. My dad and I always liked Honey-crisp, but the box on the stall was empty. *Selfish monsters,* I thought to myself. *They couldn't have saved at least one?* With a headshake, I returned my focus back to Oliver again, just in time to see him take a huge bite, twice the size of mine, and moan.

"Wow," I said, with wide eyes.

"What?" he replied with a mouth full of apple. "There's still some left." With a chuckle, I shook my head and grabbed another one. I just barely got a few bites in when I heard the sound of someone's voice through what I assumed was either a megaphone or loudspeaker.

"Find them and kill them! Now!" I don't know what changed in me, but I wasn't scared anymore. I just groaned and threw down my half-eaten apple, slamming it into the pavement. I was tired of the infected and corrupt people ruining our moments of peace, so I grabbed a whole pile of apples up in my arms in protest.

"You know you can't take all those with you," Oliver told me with a chuckle.

"Yes, I can," I said, fully determined to find a way. I didn't have a bag or anything to carry them with, since the apple crates were nailed down to the stand they were on, but after a few moments of him watching me struggle, he came over and took half of them from me.

"Here, I'll help," he told me finally, shaking his head.

"Yes!" Admittedly we looked goofy walking down the road with huge piles of apples in our arms, but I was happy to have something go our way for once. We must have walked a few miles through the little town without incident before we came to the beginning of Greenburrow's evacuation efforts. As far as I could see, there were cars lined up, bumper to bumper, at a full standstill in the road. I could hear the sound of horns and people yelling obscenities at the people in front of them, although they couldn't move either. In the distance, I could see smoke, and as we got closer to the line of cars, the smell of burnt gasoline and diesel fuel hit me hard.

"Ugh," I groaned, and dropped my pile of apples in the grass just before the road.

"Yeah, it's pretty bad." I didn't mind it when he dropped his pile too. It smelled so strong; the fumes were making my head hurt.

"What do you think is blocking them?"

"I'm not sure," I responded at first, coming just behind the first car to stand on my tiptoes. I couldn't see much, but after taking a second to really think of his question, it seemed to hit me. "If Simon wanted to infect the entire city, he wouldn't just let them leave, would he?"

I heard Oliver suck in a breath behind me before he passed me and stood on his tiptoes in front of me. I knew he was a few inches taller, so I hoped he might be able to see something I couldn't. A second later, he surprised me when put his hands around my waist and said, "Here, tell me what you see." He lifted me up about four feet high, making me giggle. *Now's not the time, Mia,* I told myself in my head, swallowing down the tingles his fingers made me feel. I peered over the line of cars, and at first, I saw nothing for a long way out, but after I used my feet to pull myself up onto the first car that was luckily empty, I managed to see an overpass bridge covered in barbed wire from the top to the bottom.

"Bridge is out," I told Oliver. "They blocked it."

"The walls are blocking them in too, aren't they?" On either side of the street, they had these tall, tan-colored walls with vines engraved in them and the city's logo every few feet. I couldn't help but feel sick again. Simon knew what he was doing. He blocked the only way out of town by land, forcing them to either go back or get stuck in the massive line.

"Uhhh..." I stood up on my tiptoes again and tried using my hands as binoculars, but it was no use. I was just straining my eyes trying to look into the sun directly ahead of us. "I think so, I can't see too much farther," I responded, feeling a bit disappointed.

"It's okay, come on down." I nodded and slid down the back windshield. "I think we should follow the road. We have a gun, maybe we can help protect them."

"Yeah," I said, feeling guilt rising in my chest. "It just seems like anytime I try to help someone, it goes wrong. I watched that woman die, Oliver. I don't want that to happen again."

"The woman back in town, at that boutique?"

"Mhmm." I said, as my hands began to shake. I could feel tears welling up in my eyes, but before they were able to fall down my face, he grasped both my shoulders and held me out in front of him.

"Look at me," he said, staring into my eyes. "What happened to that woman is not your fault." I watched his eyes flick back and forth as he spoke and felt immense comfort when he let his hands go to run a finger down my cheek. "I knew the moment we landed, you would be the one to rush in to help people, and I was prepared to follow you into the crossfire, because YOU...yes, you, have saved me countless times. Do you understand that? Countless, Mia." I chuckled through a sob, and my bottom lip began to quiver before I managed to choke out a few words.

"I just don't want to be like them," I said, sucking in a breath.

"You aren't anything like them. I don't think you understand. You and your dad saved me from the infected back at the apartment, you helped bandage me up even though I had infected blood, you saved me from the ranger, hell, you faked your own death for me, not to mention you just saved me a few minutes ago in that alley," he said with a chuckle, gesturing that way. "Simon may have trained you to become a monster, but no matter what it cost you, you have always tried to be a hero. And you know what? You are to me. But if it's 'monsters' that Simon wants, why don't we give it to him?"

"What do you mean?" I said, wiping my eyes.

"We'll go car to car if we have to. Gather supplies and find a way to clear the bridge. Once we do, we'll tell everyone about their plan to infect people, and get them to spread the word. If people know about the infected before they strike, they can prepare. Get guns, barricades, or whatever else they need."

"We should tell them about the dry ice too, that'll be a huge help!"

"Nice thinking," he responded with a smile, holding out his fist. I bumped his fist with mine and stood tall again.

"For the record, you're my hero too," I said, as the confidence began to grow between us.

"Heh. Thanks, Mia." I nodded, and after taking a few deep breaths, we began knocking on the closest car windows with people in them. It didn't feel right opening the empty cars, so we just stuck to asking people. The first few cars didn't have anything in them. Most of the people we met in line were pretty kind when they heard we wanted to help, but a few yelled at us. I couldn't blame them; we probably looked like trouble dressed in army uniforms considering it was all we had. After checking about ten cars, we came to a red van with a family of five inside. The driver jumped and screamed when she saw my gun, so I had no choice but to lower it to the ground.

"It's okay," I told her, showing her my empty pockets. "We just need help."

"W-what kind of help?" the woman asked, glancing between the two of us.

"The bridge up ahead is blocked, they covered it in barbed wire. Do you have any supplies we can use to help clear it?"

"My husband's toolbox is in the back, but I'm not sure what all's in it. I wouldn't be surprised if he left his pliers at home. He's pretty forgetful." She chuckled and nudged her husband next to him, making him roll his eyes.

"Yeah, yeah. Say, are you two police or something, or are you from the army?"

"The army," we both said in unison, although it didn't feel real to either of us.

"But we're no longer a part of it," I chimed in when I saw him raise his eyebrows.

"Thank you for your service then, I'll go see what I can find." I nodded and followed him to the back. The trunk was filled with saltwater taffy wrappers, grocery bags, some suitcases, a couple open bags of chips, and his toolbox. "Hmmm, let's see." We both stood there as the man dug around, and eventually pulled out the pliers.

"Here you are. Hopefully these will help."

"Thanks, we'll bring them back to you," Oliver told the man before he tucked them in his pants pocket.

"You're welcome and take your time. Happy to have a few extra moments with the wife and kids every now and again anyway. Just be careful. If I were you, I'd try asking around for gloves, barbed wire is very sharp."

"Got it, thanks again, sir," I said before we walked on. For another mile at least, we tried talking with people, but most were beginning to grow irritable. It was a cool sixty-something-degree day, but after sitting in the sun for so long, it must have felt like an oven. I could see some people with their windows rolled up, while others turned their car off and were standing around fanning themselves with old mail or newspapers. Right about then, I really wished I grabbed a pair of gloves from the army supply box. It would have saved us both a whole lot of trouble.

We got about three miles in when we were met with a more violent group of civilians. Some of them were throwing glass and trying to push the cars ahead of them forward. I knew better than to ask any of them, so we moved on until we eventually came to an older man laying down in the grass playing blues songs on a guitar.

"Oh, thank God. Help has arrived. Please tell me you're going to clear this mess. It's been hours."

"Yes, sir," I told him. "We're here to help, but the bridge is blocked by barbed wire. Do you happen to have any gloves?"

"I'm guessing you mean work gloves?" he asked, raising his eyebrows.

"Exactly," Oliver said excitedly.

"Yep, I should have a collection of them in my truck bed, feel free. Most of them are used though, hope you don't mind."

"Not at all," I told him before I fished out two clean-looking pairs. They were huge on my hands, but as long as they protected us, I didn't mind. "Thank you so much, these are perfect."

"Good, I'm glad to hear it."

"Hey, sir, before we go, I have one more thing to ask of you," Oliver said, gesturing to my gun. "Have you seen...any of the infected?"

"You mean those nasty things? None around here, luckily, but the inner city was crawling with them. I was just visiting a relative before everything went to shit. I would give anything to have told them no, but I guess it's too late for that, huh?"

"Yeah," I said, sadly, "I'm sorry you had to go through this, but maybe there's a way you can help us while we clear the bridge."

"Oh really, how's that?" the man asked, setting his guitar down in the grass.

"Spread the word, tell everyone that the army is trying to infect people on purpose and that a man named Simon Drear is the one in charge," Oliver told him, gesturing ahead to the mess at the bridge. "He did this."

"Damn, alright." I wasn't sure how the man was taking this, but I knew we needed to spread the word somehow.

"And tell them dry ice or cold can kill the infected. It's your greatest weapon."

"Before I believe you, you two aren't in the army, are you? Cause you sure look like it."

"We were, but we managed to escape. They were keeping us as prisoners. I'd explain it all, but it's a long story." I nervously scratched my neck as the man stood up, but eventually he broke eye contact with a groan.

"Alright, I'll help you, but I want that," he said, pointing the base of his guitar toward my rifle. "If I'm risking my neck, I'm taking a weapon with me."

"Deal," I told him. Taking the weapon off my shoulder made me feel bare, but if it helped get the truth out, I was willing to try anything. I handed it to him and watched as he checked the ammo canister. Luckily, after a moment, he put the clip back in, bowed his head, and began to walk away.

"Go on, clear that bridge. But just to be sure, any other army members I see are clear to take down?" He turned his head back around and eyed us both. I wasn't sure how to respond. I wanted to tell him yes, but Indi was a good man. He didn't deserve to die, and I was almost certain he was forced to take aim at us. Oliver didn't say a word either, we both seemed at a loss. The man must have noticed our hesitation, because he coughed, making us look back at him.

"Well?"

"Uh, yes," Oliver finally muttered, prompting the man to nod.

"Anyone I should be aware of? That was a long pause." I looked over at Oliver nervously and saw him holding his arms over his chest with an unsure look.

"We had a friend there; his name was Private Indi. He's the only good one left." The man nodded, and after I went on to describe how Indi looked, he told us his name.

"Oh, the name's Rufus, by the way. Just in case we get separated." We both nodded, and after we introduced ourselves, he finally left and started making his way down the line.

"I'm glad you told him about Indi, because I wasn't sure if we should or not," Oliver said, taking in a deep breath.

"I know," I said before holding my hand out for him. He took it, and eventually we reached the bridge. It was surrounded by people. Some had cuts in their hands as they tried to pry their way through the barbed wire. It was a disaster.

"Stop! We've got pliers," Oliver told them as we picked up the pace to a jog. "Let us help so you don't hurt yourselves."

"Oh, thank goodness," a lady said. "I was worried they were going to lose a limb."

"No need to worry, we've got it covered," Oliver told them. "I'll cut through the first couple layers; you think you can get the rest?"

"Definitely." I felt antsy as I waited for him. We were finally able to help people and it felt good, but I knew it might come at a cost. If the government truly gave Simon and my mother their orders, there was a huge chance we would be playing with fire. I swallowed down those feelings as I waited for Oliver to cut the thick barbed wire apart layer by layer. After about forty-five minutes, we were about to switch since we were halfway through, but then a loud gunshot reached our ears.

"Cut faster!" I heard someone yell behind us. "Hurry!" I couldn't see who was speaking at first, but eventually the man came running back up to us. "The army sent the infected this way, people are running up here in droves," he told us as he caught his breath. When I heard that, I swiped the pliers out of Oliver's hand, and rushed back into the mess.

"You got this, Mia." I nodded, but I felt my heart begin to thump harder and harder with each snip. I pushed the layers away as fast as I could, but after a couple minutes of cutting, I began to hear screams behind us.

"Come on, kid," the man said anxiously as my hand began to cramp up. There were only a few more layers, but I began to feel nervous as the volume slowly increased behind me.

"They're coming!" A blood curdling scream cut through my thoughts, and I stopped momentarily to look back. When Oliver saw me, he knelt down and put his hand on my shoulder.

"Ignore them, be the hero I know you are. Come on." I nodded, although everything was building up in my body. Heart rate, sweat, shaky palms, time between breaths. It felt like someone was cranking up a dial, but finally, just as the large swarm of people reached us... I cut through the final layer.

"Go, go, go!"

Chapter Fifteen: Wanted Dead or Alive

When the crowd finally reached the bridge, Oliver and I had no choice but to blend in with them and run. Simon and his team came up on the top and began using the scopes on their rifles to search for us. He seemed so angry as everyone dispersed, especially since the bridge was the only way out of the city and we unblocked it. The man who took our rifle protected us with his body. He asked us briefly as we ran if we thought he should try to take aim at them, and although it seemed to cross both our minds, we turned him down. We didn't want to stoop to Simon's level.

"I'll find you brats. You won't escape my grasp!" Simon yelled through a megaphone. The sound of his voice was almost drowned out by the crowd, but I managed to decipher it. I looked back for a moment as we continued running away, but by the time I turned my head, he was already climbing down off the overpass. Shooting the infected was already bound to get us in trouble, but freeing the civilians felt like a nail in our coffins. We not only broke Simon's rule, but we saved an entire city from being turned into a sick science experiment. I could only imagine how many soldiers he would send to hunt us down. It made my skin crawl.

We ran for about ten minutes down the road, until the crowd started to disperse again. The road split off in two directions, and most of the crowd turned down the path with signs for a rest stop. I couldn't blame them, but me, Oliver, and a few others took the country roads leading out. Since we didn't have to worry about the infection anymore, we knew our best bet would be to go somewhere secluded. Part of me knew Simon would probably follow the biggest crowd. I just hoped it would buy us enough time to come up with a permanent solution. I was happy we were able to save the people of Greenburrow, but now our heads were on the chopping block in their place.

"So, where are you two headed off to?" I hadn't even realized Rufus came with us when we took the fork, but I was grateful that he did.

"We're not really sure," Oliver responded with a glance over at me.

"Simon's probably going to come hunting for us." I didn't want to face him again, but I knew it was an inevitable cost.

"Well, you're probably going to need this then." He pulled the rifle strap off his shoulder and passed it back to me. "I only saw that man for a second, but he's definitely not someone I'd want to cross paths with, and while I don't condone killing, I'd make an exception for that sick low life. Ya know, I...I watched my niece die," he said with a sniffle, as he put his hand over his mouth. "Do me a favor, and make sure that bastard gets what's coming to him. Can I trust you to do that for me?"

"Yes, sir," we both responded without so much as a second thought.

"I knew I could count on you. You seem like good kids. Keep a close eye on each other, okay? I gotta get home to my family, or else I'd come with ya."

"Thank you, sir. I don't mean to hold you up any longer, but were you able to tell anyone?" I asked him, as I swallowed down a hard lump again.

"You better believe it. I told a whole bunch of people. Simon Drear, right?"

"Yes, sir," I responded with a nod.

"That man's about to be on America's most wanted list. One of the people I told managed to snap a picture of one of those things and posted it for the world to see with his name plastered on the post. If you don't get him, someone else will."

"Thank gosh," Oliver said with a smile. It was actually a comforting thought, but would that really be enough to save us? For the moment, I took it as a win, but I knew it wouldn't stay that way forever.

"Be safe, you two." We nodded and waved as Rufus left us, and just like that, we were left on our own all over again. At first, we ended up walking for miles to try and find a place, but as we were walking a black Ford truck passed us with a boat in the back. We reached a stop light together, and although we knew it was risky, we hopped in and laid down on the floor inside. Eventually the truck moved again, and the cool autumn wind covered us like a weighted blanket. It felt nice, and I couldn't help but pump my fist up in the air with a quiet, "Woohoo!"

"Wooo!" Oliver screamed with me, before he pulled my body into his as we lay there and looked up at the sunset. It was a beautiful mix of blues and purples this time. I loved every minute of it. The only problem was that we were runaways all over again, but this time, there was nothing holding us back. There was so much on our minds, but at that moment the only thing we cared about was the present. The truck put a few hours between us and Greenburrow. We didn't talk much; instead, we just laid there with each other and looked up at the moon and the stars. After about hour four, though, we felt safe enough to hop out again. We sat up, and the moment we came to another red light, we hopped out and ran down the sidewalk. Luckily for both of us, it was pitch black by the time we climbed out. We had nothing but the moonlight and streetlights to light our path forward. Neither of us knew where we were, but that didn't seem like such a bad thing. I could tell we were in the middle of another city or town, but there weren't any signs around to tell us which one.

We followed the road through the little town and clung to each other like glue any time a car rolled by us too slow. We were definitely on edge, but it wasn't just because of Simon. If my mom sent people after us, I could only imagine what kind of trouble we would find ourselves in. Knowing my mom was involved with the infection and Simon was a huge step backward for me. For all I knew, she would be the one to send the army our way. *Would my own mother try to kill us?* I wondered, as I followed Oliver through the back alleyways in the city. I didn't tell Oliver my concerns, but I didn't think I needed to either. After what she did with Polly, her going a step further didn't seem like that much of a stretch. Eventually, it began to rain as we went farther in, so we knew we had no choice but to settle for a place. In the end, we found ourselves in a pillared alcove beneath a skyscraper. We didn't have much with us, so we ended up using cardboard to cover ourselves. The temperature that night dipped to the low fifties, making both of us feel freezing. I clung to Oliver as I slept; feeling his body heat against me gave me some comfort, but it was still mildly uncomfortable. I don't think either of us really slept well that night.

When morning finally came, I yawned and gently pried myself off the ground so I didn't wake him. I didn't want to leave his side, but I needed information. Before I walked away, I slid the gun beneath the box by his arm. Then I hit the streets. I wasn't sure what time it was, but I knew it was early because I could see people yawning and flooding into a small coffee shop called Paula Koala Caffeine. My stomach growled when I saw a lady emerge with an everything bagel. It looked so good, I almost wanted to ask her for it. Instead, I went up to her and mustered up a hopefully warm smile as I came to greet her.

"Hi, I know this is going to sound strange, but do you know what city we're in? Me and my boyfriend have been traveling for hours, and we're kinda...lost."

"Oh yeah, we're in Swinesdale."

"Swinesdale? Got it. Thanks," I told her. From there, I decided to try and find food for the two of us. The last thing I wanted to do was steal and create more trouble for us, especially in a bustling city, but the apples weren't enough. We needed to keep our strength up. I knew it hadn't been too long since we were at Beacon eating the freeze-dried food, but I had a feeling we were going to be there for a while. I started by eying the booths in the street. For the most part they were selling things like headscarves, hats, clothes, and other homemade items. As I walked, people shouted for me to look and browse their shop. I remember walking with my mom through a market like this, one time specifically, when I was five, being my favorite.

That day, she and I were looking for a Father's Day present for Dad. She held my hand as I looked out and glanced around all the shops excitedly. I always loved going shopping with her, because she would find every chance to make me laugh. As we walked down the causeway, she grabbed a teddy and held him just out of my reach.

"Mr. Teddy says, 'Hi, Mia,'" she said in an exaggerated man's voice. She liked to mock Dad like that too sometimes, and it always managed to bring a smile to my face.

"Hi, Mr. Teddy." I smiled wide and bounced on the tips of my toes as I tried to reach out for it.

"Here, he's all yours. Take good care of him now." She winked and handed me the teddy bear. Looking back on it now, I realized with a jolt of shock: that torn one I found at the apartment buildings was mine. *Did Mom plant that there for me to find? She said she didn't plan on us going to Beacon, but did she know we would explore the apartments?* I couldn't help but wonder as I perused the shops further. Finally, I came to a shop with tables and tables of backpacks under a large navy-blue tent. So far, we lost a few supply bags during our journey. This time, if I had to steal, I promised myself I would take care of it. The shop owner was following around a woman and her daughter. For a minute or two, I watched as she grabbed a few bags, looked at them, and put them back with a sigh.

"Not this one," she'd tell her mom, and the shop owner's face would fall a bit before she would repeat it all over again.

When I finally snapped out of it, I was holding a red bag. I hadn't even noticed I had picked one up. It was small, about the size of a kindergartner's bag, but after trying on the straps, I found that it fit. I was pretty sure it was one of those mini backpacks. That was all I needed. I looked over at the shop owner, who was so entranced by the two customers with a frown, she didn't even notice me there.

"I'll pay you back," I whispered, then I left. From there, I walked with a faster stride, but not a run, until I turned a corner and came to a clothing market. Somehow, I had completely forgotten that I was still in an army uniform. It felt sticky against my body. We'd run for so long, I could smell my body odor without even trying. It was gross. I decided to try and blend in with the crowd. I walked with a group of tourists, and when they stopped, I stopped. Luckily, it seemed to work. As they walked from stall to stall, I soon realized I couldn't take clothes from any of these. They were all facing each other, and they were set up where all the clothes were in baskets. It angered me. I wanted to blend in, and maybe even settle here. A home, a job, a fresh start, but instead I felt hopeless. Out of frustration, I kicked over this rusty metal bucket next to one of the stalls. It was filled with dirty brown water like it has been left there for a few months, and I absentmindedly watched as it trickled down and ran straight to a sewer drain. I shook my head with a sigh and started to walk away, when I felt a hand grab me from behind. I knew, just by feeling it, it wasn't Oliver, so I turned around with my mouth open ready to fight, until I saw an older lady standing there.

"Hello, sweetheart, you look lost. Is everything alright?" I looked down at the sweet old lady. She was hunched over, with a stained wooden cane in her hand that was beginning to wear away from too much use. She smiled up at me, and I found myself looking at her face as it twitched.

"Um... No. Not really," I told her, as my lips began to quiver.

"Oh, honey. What's the matter? You look too pretty to be so glum." She reached her hand up and slowly arched her head to look at my face. I knew just by looking at her that she must be around eighty, but I wasn't too sure. Normally, I would shy away if a stranger tried to reach their hand toward me, but she seemed trustworthy. After a moment, I knelt down, and she put her hand on my cheek. She had long burgundy-painted nails, and her hands were wrinkled. "What can I do to help?"

"Me and m-my boyfriend, we're homeless. We don't have anywhere to go, and we have no food or clothes."

"Oh goodness," she said, withdrawing her hand. "I can't allow that. Is the boy with you?" she asked, glancing around me.

"No, ma'am. He's still sleeping, we slept beneath that sky-scraper over there." I pointed my hand toward it and saw her follow my arm until her eyes connected with it.

"Wow, that's far," she said, squinting her eyes. "How about this, I'll get you some food and clothes, and you two can come work for me. I could use all the help I can get; my grand babies went off to college, and I can't do this on my own anymore. I'm getting too old. Say, what's your name, sweetheart?"

"It's Mia," I replied, shaking her hand firmly. Once we were done with introductions, she led me to her shop, and she had all kinds of hand-knitted clothes.

"For an old lady, I know what I'm doing, huh?" she asked with a laugh.

"Yes, ma'am," I replied with a smile.

"See, that's what I like to see. Your smile lights up your whole face."

"Thank you," I said, bowing my head.

"You're welcome. Now, let me just gather up some money for us, and we'll be on our way." I stood by and looked around at the nearby shops while she rummaged through her cash register. When I noticed, my mouth fell open.

"Oh no, I can't take money from your shop." I held my hands up until she turned around and held her cane up level with my face.

"Honey, I'm retired. This is all extra money I use to goof off sometimes. Besides, how are you going to pay for that bag?" I gasped, and my whole face turned red when she gestured to it on my back. When I looked, the tags were still hanging off the side, and I felt an instant wave of nausea and embarrassment wash over me. "Don't worry, honey. I'm more than happy to lend a hand. Now tell me, which shop did you find that at?"

"It's, um...down the way." I pointed and let my head fall. I knew she wasn't angry, but I still felt my heart hurt when she tore the price tag off and handed me a small wad of cash.

"Come along now, dear. We'll go together." I nodded and followed the woman like a scared puppy dog. I followed behind her as she led me back through. She didn't walk very fast, so I had to take half-steps to not pass her. When we rounded the corner, I pointed out the shop, and she instantly recognized it. "Oh, that's Dee. Don't worry, baby. She won't mind."

I felt a bit better when she told me that, but my heart was still pounding in my chest. I've dealt with literal monsters, but facing a woman I stole from still hurt worse. When we reached her, Dee was sitting down with a bag of oven-baked chips. She piled a few in, took a drink, then piled in a few more. I didn't want it to, but my stomach growled loudly as I watched her, making the woman look back at me.

"Poor girl, don't worry. We'll get food soon. Let's get this over with first." I nodded, again feeling embarrassed before she called Dee over. "Oh, Miss Dee!" the woman sang excitedly. "Can we have a word?"

"Of course, nice to see you again, Mrs. Lingvil." She put down her chips and practically skipped over to us at the edge of her booth.

"How long have we known each other, Dee? You know better, call me Jill," Jill told her, knocking her cane against the ground.

"Right. Sorry, Jill. What's up?"

"This young lady would like to apologize. Go ahead, sweetheart." Jill patted her hand against my back, and I instantly felt goosebumps rise on my arms as I went to speak up.

"Um... Hi, Dee," I started, picking at the skin on my elbows. "I'm really sorry, but..." I stopped and looked at Jill as my heartbeat went from a drum to a race engine. I was terrified to face her.

"Go ahead, baby. It's okay," she told me, giving my arm a squeeze.

"I stole from your shop," I blurted finally, taking the bag off my shoulder, and holding it out by the straps. At first,

Dee stood straighter and looked between her and me. She looked tongue-tied, as if she didn't know whether to scold me or take the bag back. Then Jill spoke up again.

"Forgive her, Dee. The poor girl is homeless. I'll happily pay you for it, here."

"Oh," Dee responded, taking the bag from my hand. At first, I thought she was going to take it back and tell Jill no, but after a minute, she came back and had one more.

"Wait what?" I asked, completely shocked.

"Your boyfriend came by an hour ago asking about you. He seemed pretty worried. Give the blue one to him, and don't worry about the payment, Jill. I'm happy to help whenever I can." She smiled, and for the first time since this whole mess started, I cried tears of joy.

"Thank you," I said through tears and a sob as I took them from her. "I won't forget this."

"Don't worry about it. Us girls, we gotta look out for each other, right, Jill?" she said, with a wink toward her.

"Oh, definitely. After my husband died, Dee helped me tremendously. I owe her big time."

"No, you don't," Dee responded, closing her eyes with a huge grin. "You're family, Jill. And any friend of yours is a friend of mine. Got that? You're welcome any time." She held out her hand, and after telling her my name and shaking her hand, I left with Jill. I couldn't help but feel nervous when I heard Oliver was out looking for me. I didn't like the idea of him being alone, but Jill took notice.

"Don't worry, we'll find him. Let's get you some supplies first, then I'll help you look." I nodded, and eventually she led me to a food market. It was full of vendors with fresh fish, a butcher with steaks and other fresh meats, and a line of food trucks. All along the middle, I could see people laughing and digging into their food. I wished that I could join them. I wanted to laugh and feel no worries. I wanted to have a bit of normality, but instead I was a scared girl with the Grim Reaper following behind. Shaking my head, I looked around, and eventually after losing her for a minute, found her at the butcher's. She ordered a few different things. Four eight-ounce ribeyes, four baby back rib platters, and a bag of Polish sausage. After the butcher cut them and weighed them all, she told me they were for us and her dinners for the week. I couldn't help but feel thankful that she was doing all of this for us. I was so grateful.

She went to a few different shops, and eventually I had a tote bag full of fresh meats, fresh fish, and fresh produce.

"This'll last us a couple days," she told me. "Now, let's go get you some clothes, those look uncomfortable." I nodded, and after about a half-hour of browsing with her through discount shops, I had enough outfits to last me and Oliver a week or two. Jill wanted to buy us more, but I was so nervous about the meat going bad and having to find him, we left early. She told me about her home and handed me a note with her phone number on it.

"Just in case," she mused, pressing it into my palm. I nodded, and we started to walk back to her place together, until I noticed Oliver stopped in the middle of the causeway, turning his head every which way. I saw him talking to a couple, maybe in their early thirties, with visible signs of distress painted across his face.

"That's him!" I told Jill, pointing him out.

"Go get him. Leave the bags here, I'll wait." I nodded, and instantly started running toward him. I almost reached him when I got distracted by a shop full of TVs. It'd been so long since I was able to watch a regular show that I drifted over that way and clung to the window. The shop was just closing for the day, but the TVs were kept on and tuned to the same channel. At first there was a commercial about car insurance, making me roll my eyes, but then it switched to the news. A younger man came on and started talking about the weekly forecast. It was meant to be a bit warmer in the next few days, but he still recommended wearing a sweater or jacket. When he finished speaking, I almost walked away until I heard, "Breaking news..."

"Good evening, unfortunately I have a startling news story," a woman proclaimed. "The FBI is on the lookout for two dangerous individuals. Police say they are armed and dangerous. Their last known location was Greenburrow, Indiana, before they fled the scene with an AR-15. Luckily no one was hurt, but two bystanders say they saw them walking around with it. Here's Lisa Thomas with the inside scoop." My jaw almost fell open when I saw the story, but it only seemed to get worse from there.

Slowly, I backed away from the shop, until I heard a voice yell out, "Hey!" My whole body froze up the moment I turned and saw a group of officers. Shock didn't even begin to cover it. After everything we went through, I didn't want to face prison time on top of it, so I ran like hell. I couldn't see Jill anymore because a crowd walked in front of where she was, and Oliver walked away in the opposite direction, following the couple.

"Why did I stop?" I said under my breath, staring up at the evening sky.

"You're under arrest, stop now or else!" The last thing I wanted to do was lead the police back to either of them. I didn't have the gun on me, but they knew my face. Our pictures were plastered all over. The moment we found freedom; the chains came right back for us all over again. I knew we were doomed from the moment we left, but I thought we would at least have some time to breathe before it all went bad.

I could only imagine who the two "witnesses" were. In my mind, Simon seemed like the most likely suspect at first, but the more I thought about it, the more I wasn't so sure. He would do anything to take us down after we disobeyed his rules, but would he really risk sending us to jail if he knew we could take him down too? So many thoughts were swarming in my head, but I had to ignore them. I needed to escape.

I ran until the muscles in my legs began to cramp up. They were right on my tail, and I could hear a taser buzzing as they tried and failed to stop me. I must have gone a few miles away from the vendors before my body began to give out on me. My head was pounding, there was sweat pouring down my face and back, and my feet were on fire, as if I was running on a stove top. The shoes I was wearing only made it worse. They were made for work and running around, but after wearing them for the last couple days, they felt unbearable.

I stumbled as I ran down alleyway after alleyway, and eventually, after I turned a corner leading to where we came into the city, I ended up jumping in a trash hopper. All around me, I could hear yelling and stomping footsteps as they tried to find where I had gone, but somehow, I was lucky enough to fool them. The only problem now was how long I would have to stay there, and how I would find Oliver and get us safely back to Jill. *Would this be our downfall?*

Chapter Sixteen: Shipped Away

I don't know how long I was left there, but minutes eventually turned into hours, and they were still swarming around. I was starting to panic. There were flies crawling over my arms and legs, making me squirm, and the smell was rancid. My mind was racing with every imaginable outcome, and all of them were bad.

One, I would come out and they'd immediately cuff me. Two, I'd come out and they'd shoot me. Or three, the worst of them all, I'd come out and Simon would be there. No good options. I felt hopeless, and a moment later, my fears only amplified when I heard a voice I didn't want to hear call out.

"I'm gonna check the dumpster." Immediately I knew it was Simon and cursed silently under my breath. There was nowhere to go, I was trapped, and arming myself would only make it worse, so I held my hands up in pure defeat. A moment later, he peered over the side and shined a flashlight directly into my eyes. I let a whimper escape my lips, causing him to laugh. He knew then that he had won, and worst of all, he had split us up. I didn't want to think about the fear Oliver must have been feeling, so I swallowed that down. I would have to fight this on my own. I thought they'd want me to climb out, so I began to push the trash aside while I stared him down. Right as I was about to put my leg over the side wall, he slammed the lid shut and I heard a lock click on the outside. "I'll take it from here, you've all done well. Give yourselves a pat on the back, the army thanks you personally." I heard the officers cheer, and then little by little the sounds of sirens faded off into the distance.

"No, let me out. Please! He's going to kill me!" I shouted, pounding on the lid and the side of the hopper. I was hoping one of the officers would hear me, but no one responded. I was alone. I stumbled back as I felt the hopper move and heard the sounds of people grunting as it lifted into the air.

"Oliver." I cried, as tears stung my eyes. "Please." Again, no answer. I heard the soft hum of an engine, and immediately felt my heart drop to my stomach. Simon was taking me away, and for all I knew, this was my death sentence. So, I screamed. I screamed as loud as my lungs would let me, and began throwing all my might into the lid, but the car continued down the road. I screamed until my lungs began to burn, but after a while in pure darkness, I gave up trying. The flies still clung to my skin as I was knocked around in the hopper. There wasn't much to hold onto, and they weren't even trying to be gentle with their turns. Simon was an evil person, but I didn't think he'd make me endure this. The bags beneath me had glass bottles in them, and during all the rumbling and sharp turns, one broke and punctured my side.

"Ahhh!" I screamed, and instantly snapped my hand over the wound. It burned, making me think they were alcohol bottles, but worst of all, when I withdrew my fingers, I could see red through the blinding darkness.

"Please, stop the car. I'm bleeding!" I cried out, hoping they would show me mercy. Instead, the driver took another sharp turn I wasn't expecting, causing me to knock my head into the side wall. I felt disoriented as I tried to regain my bearings and failed. My eyes were beginning to blur, and after a couple minutes of lying there, I was out cold.

"Good morning," I heard when my eyes finally opened again. "Looks like you took quite the beating, kid."

"Ugh," I groaned as I tried to form words. My throat stung, and my head was pounding again. Not to mention, the lights above me were making me feel nauseous.

"Don't speak, I have a lot to say, and you're not going to like any of it." I blinked my eyes as Simon and my mom came into focus. They were holding bowls of cold water and rags. I watched as Simon dipped his hand in and grabbed the first one on top before he ran it along the side of my head. I grimaced as the water hit a wound. It felt nice, but it also stung. Then Mom did the same, but this time, along my stomach. "I've had a couple hundred calls about you and that little stunt you pulled in Greenburrow. Telling people about the operation was completely careless!" he yelled, pressing down hard on the wound he was wiping.

"Ow," I whimpered, blinking away spots in my eyes.

"It's time, Mia," Mom said, sitting down next to me. "Oliver is set to die." My whole body froze, and I almost forgot to breathe as the words left her lips. "It's what's best. Clearly that boy has corrupted you, and it's time he faced the consequences of his actions. He had the toxic blood, and instead of living with it, he escaped and turned my own daughter against me. It's time for him to go, effective immediately." She said the last part as if she was telling me to go do chores.

She was condemning the person I loved to die, and he didn't even get a chance to defend himself.

"Y-you can't kill him," I choked out, as bile began to rise in my throat. "I won't let you." I swallowed as I began to taste it in my mouth. A moment later, Simon lifted a glass up to my lips and gently pushed my forehead back to take a sip. "You don't even know where he is." I went to lift my arm to point it at her chest, but it yanked back down. I was chained to the bed.

"You don't have a choice. We're going to find him, and when we do, that's it. No more chances. I've had enough hearing about the atrocities you two have gotten yourselves into. I explained to you in full detail why we couldn't help those people out there, and you and that idiot boy released them? No, never again."

"Once it's done, I'll tell you," Simon said, giving my arm a squeeze as if he actually cared. "Then you're going right back to the army. It's where you belong, and I'm going to drill you until you lose every ounce of fight you have left in you. End of story."

"No, please." I began to sob as I pulled on my arms and legs to try and get out. There was no escaping this, not without help. "Oliver didn't do anything, I did!" I yelled, causing Mom to turn around in the doorway.

"I'm sorry, Mia. But that's just not true." She shook her head, and then left me there crying for someone to help me. After a couple minutes, I managed to regain my composure, and tried to scan my surroundings. I was back in the infirmary wing. Around me, the beds were empty, but then my eyes locked on a bed with a large blood stain and a boy sprawled out across it. It was Indi.

"Indi!" I called out, although my voice came out as a rasp. I tried again, and eventually he began to stir. He groaned and turned on his side before eventually locking eyes with me. A look of shock crossed his face, and he mouthed something at me before he let out a thick cough. I was never very good at reading lips, but it looked like he said, "Hold on." I took a deep breath as I watched him—it was all I could do anyway—and after he turned his head back toward me, he rolled himself onto the floor.

"I'm coming." He coughed, spitting out a mix of blood and phlegm on the ground. I nodded and cheered him on as he pushed himself up off the floor. At first, he seemed stable, but when he went to take a step, he stopped and clutched his head. "Ugh."

"Take it easy, Indi," I told him, although in my head I was screaming, "Go!" He nodded, and after taking a sip of water on the nightstand next to his bed, he mustered up the strength to make it to me.

"You don't look so good," I told him as he fumbled with the straps on my arms.

"I know," he muttered, "they beat me after I blocked one of them from shooting Oliver in Greenburrow. They had a clear shot, but I stepped in the way. I've never seen Simon so...angry."

"When?" I asked, as he managed to undo the first one.

"When you two were in the farmer's market. They found you just as you were leaving, but I couldn't let them do it. I knew what my punishment would be," he told me, giving me a sad smile, "but I never imagined it would be so brutal." Slowly, he lifted his shirt and revealed a large sewn up wound right beneath his ribcage. "They did this to me the moment we got back. I thought for sure I was a goner, but then they brought me back from the brink just so they could torture me all over again by telling me they found you."

"Oh my gosh," I said, covering my mouth. "I'm so sorry you went through that."

"It's okay," he said, letting his smile slip away. "I threatened you both with my gun. I deserved it."

"No, you didn't!" I said, taking his hand to comfort him. "Both of us knew you were forced. You're a good person, Indi. You can't let them take that from you."

"Thanks, Mia. Where's Oliver? Is he okay?"

"I don't know, but...but they want to kill him," I said, hugging my knees into my chest.

"No, they can't do that! He's my friend!" He stumbled back as what I said seemed to hit him. We were both just as shocked. Slowly, he lowered himself down in the bed next to me and ran his fingers through his hair. "What are we going to do?" Hearing "we" made my heart feel warm. He still thought of us as a team, and I was so happy to have that.

"I don't think they're going to let me go so easily," I confessed, "and I'm pretty sure Swinesdale is over state lines."

"We have to think of something, Oliver needs us." I nodded and plopped back on the bed. Next to me, he did the same thing, and we just stared up at the ceiling as I tried to think of ways to save him. Finally, I snapped up, and Indi followed suit with his eyebrows raised.

"Jill! I can call Jill! Do you know if there's a phone?" He looked at me confused before he pointed at a desk by the front doors. It was an old rotary phone. I had only used one once, but I knew I had to try for Oliver's sake. The two of us practically limped up there. We were both in pain, but we supported each other until I got to a seated position in the chair behind the desk.

"Ouch, that thing is a dinosaur. What are you going to do with that?"

"Use it," I said, trying to remember how to. From what I remembered, you had to drag the numbers down, let go, and drag them down again for each one. I did that, and crossed my fingers as the line began to ring.

"Hello?" I nearly jumped for joy when I heard Jill's familiar voice. She sounded distressed, and I instantly knew why.

"Jill, it's me, Mia."

"Oh, Mia, honey," she cried. "Come quick, baby, it's Mia." I wasn't sure who she was talking to at first, but then someone else came on the line.

"Mia?" I knew the moment I heard his voice that it was Oliver. I couldn't help but feel relieved knowing he was safe.

"Indi! It's Oliver!" I yelled, feeling my heart begin to pound in my chest.

"Oh, thank god, my sweet Mia." I could hear him take a shaky breath into the phone, and knew he was crying. "Please tell me you're okay, love. Jill came and found me after she lost you. She was super worried, she said she saw police chasing you."

"They were, I got caught," I told him, pressing the phone against my face to give me comfort. "Simon captured me, and he said he wants to kill you. Whatever you do, don't leave Jill's side, stay put!"

"O-okay," he said, and I began to hear his teeth chatter. I could only imagine how he must have felt. "Are you back at Beacon?"

"Yeah, but don't worry, I'm with Indi. He helped me."

"Good," he said, before the phone crackled with his breath. I knew it was probably right up against his lips. He was scared. "I don't know when I'll see you again, but until that day comes, I love you, okay?"

"I love you too." I began to sob again, prompting Indi to take the phone out of my hand.

"Don't worry, Oliver. I won't let anything happen to her. I've got your backs," he assured him. I don't know what Oliver said after, but they exchanged a few more words, and he eventually handed me the phone to put back on the hook.

"What now?" Indi asked me, as I leaned back in my chair.

"I don't think we have a choice. We'll have to conform. Play our roles until we figure out how to get out for good."

"When that happens, will you take me with you? I don't want to die here with Simon. I had so many plans, and none of them will come to fruition if I let Simon win."

"Of course we will, Indi. You're our friend," I said, taking both his hands in mine over the top of the desk.

"Thanks, Mia. You should know, though, my name is Joque. Joque Adam Indi," he told me with a nervous smile.

"I like that," I said with a chuckle.

"Most people think it sounds goofy." I smiled and assured him that his name was fine. Then we walked toward the door. We were both so nervous, and considering our condition, I wasn't sure if we were making a smart choice or marching to our deaths. Simon told me he'd train me until I gave up fighting, but I was determined to never give in. I never gave in to Polly when she said my name was 851, so I promised I'd never give Simon that satisfaction either. He was a sick, vile human being, and my mom wasn't any better. They both allowed me and Oliver's family to suffer, and I could never forgive them, no matter how much they tried to get me to do so.

Together, we walked across the field toward the barracks. I kept glancing at him as we supported each other, and felt my face grow warm with each grimace. I still blamed myself for the beating they put him through. He was a lot worse off than me. I tried to convince him to go back, but he refused. He said his promise came first. I nodded, but there was a huge part of me that wanted to go back too. If I had the choice, I'd never face Gabby, Polly, my mom, or Simon again, but that didn't seem like a luxury I could have. They were all wicked.

"We're here, Mia," Joque told me as we came to the main doors.

"I know," I responded as I tried to build up the confidence to walk back in. "I don't know if I can do this."

"We have to. It's time to start act I. Just remember, eventually this play will end. Got it?" I nodded with a smile, and after taking a deep breath together, we slid the door open. I wasn't sure how Simon would react when he saw I was up, but I didn't care. He had to know Joque wouldn't leave me there. Slowly, we marched inside with our heads held high. We were both outcasts in the army's eye, maybe even wanted. It scared me half to death to think of it, but I knew it was true. One word from someone higher up could be enough for them to kill us both. I just had to make sure those words would never come.

"Mia?" I heard someone call out as we went back to our beds. It didn't help that mine was right next to Gabby's. I had no choice but to face her.

"Yeah, it's me," I told her, plopping down on my overly familiar rock-hard mattress.

"Wow, I didn't think they'd let rats in here." She snickered, throwing her legs over the side of the bed toward me. "You're lucky you're even alive. If Indi didn't stop me, I would have shot your precious Oliver right between the eyes."

"No way. It was you?" I asked, throwing my legs over the side so we were face to face.

"Yeah. We could have led over a thousand infected back to Beacon and gotten a huge reward from the higher ups, but you," she said, poking me square in the chest, "and that stupid boy ruined it for us."

"Those were innocent people, Gabby. Do you not care?"

"No, I really don't, because I know what I signed up for. This job is thrilling, invigorating, but Simon had to drag you two into it. If you ask me, he made this bed. It'll be sad if he has to lie in it."

"My mom is dating Simon," I told her, although I felt a bit embarrassed to admit that.

"What? Do you think that earns you bragging rights or something? You should have died just like that other soldier when you betrayed our group, but instead you're still alive, and back here as if you did nothing."

"Gabby, you're supposed to be my friend. You helped me, can't we go back to that?" Even saying that felt wrong, but if I had to play an act, I would rather have more allies than enemies.

"You don't have the guts to be my friend," she told me, eyeing me up and down. I felt embarrassed still being in the same dirty outfit, but I just got back. I still had time.

"Yes, I do!" I blurted out, before I saw Joque turn his head in confusion. "What can I do to prove it?"

"OH," she said, loudly standing up to pace. "I have the perfect idea; I'm sure Simon will agree too."

"I won't kill Oliver," I said, crossing my arms.

"I never said that, come with me. Let's see what Simon thinks of my brilliant idea." She looked over her shoulder to make sure I was following as she walked away, and grinned from ear to ear, sending goosebumps up my arms. I had no idea what she had in store for me, but it definitely wasn't good. She walked into the yard where a few soldiers were training, and after a few minutes of following her, she stopped in front of Simon, who was timing them doing exercises.

"What are you doing up?" Simon asked me, though he kept his eyes on the timer.

"I escaped," I lied, staring him straight in the eyes to seal the deal.

"Yeah, right. Private Indi helped you, didn't he?" I went to open my mouth, but he silenced me with a wave of his hand and an eye roll.

"Mia wants to prove herself, Simon. I have the perfect idea how she can do that."

"Oh yeah?" Simon said, finally turning his head toward us. "What's that?"

"Let her clear out her hometown, on her own." I felt my mouth fall open the instant she said it aloud. I couldn't imagine leading an army of infected back that used to be my former friends and neighbors. It was a sickening idea, but Simon's grin only seemed to grow as he considered it.

"I'll have to get more dry-ice bombs from the team, but I'm sure we can do that. And don't worry, Mia. I'll ask your mom for the city name."

"Wait!" I called out as he began to walk away.

"You really don't have the guts," Gabby muttered, crossing her arms.

"I do but let me make a deal first. Oliver's life for my hometown. I'll do it." I swallowed, and saw Simon turn his head with a pensive look.

"On your own? No Indi or Gabby. Just you, and not a single dead infected?"

"Yes," I responded as he held out his hand. Hesitantly I reached my hand out to shake his, but the moment he had it, he grabbed it and pulled me toward him.

"Tell me where the boy is first. I want him under my roof until the job is done." I could smell his rancid breath as he spoke. It smelled as bad as, if not worse than, the trash. His teeth weren't yellow, but they definitely weren't white either.

"How do I know this isn't a trick? I'm not allowing Oliver to come back, just to get him killed. I want a sure thing!" I demanded as I pushed my hands against his chest. Luckily, he released his grip around my wrist and let me put distance between us.

"Fine. I'll have the boy come with you, but he's not helping," he told me. "He'll stay back with us and watch as you kill innocents in his honor."

"He'll understand, he has to." I balled my hand into a fist and turned my face away so neither of them could see me cry again. If he was mad at me for making him a soldier, I could only imagine how he'd respond after the job was done. I just hoped he would still love me. "H-he's in Swinesdale, with a friend of mine," I finally admitted. I was shaking as I spoke; luckily, neither of them took notice.

"Good, so you do know. We'll take you there to find him, but there won't be time for a reunion. We'll load up the helicopter, pick him up, then we're going for... Oh, yes, what city is it, Mia?"

"It's a town, and it's called Juros," I told him, wiping away a large tear that threatened to give me away.

"Indiana?" He asked.

"Yes."

"Wonderful, let's go get your boy." When we were finished, he yelled for the soldiers outside to go back to the barracks. There was a lot of planning ahead of us. For one thing, they had to drop off a shipment of infected in Juros. Then from there, we had to get Oliver, create a police line, wait until the infected did their job, and go in. It wasn't a quick thing, but Simon made it seem like it was. "It'll be over before you know it," he told me as we marched into Beacon. They took a heavy loss thanks to me, but there was definitely enough to go charging back in. I couldn't believe I allowed myself to do this, but as I thought more and more on the subject, I knew I loved him enough to kill if it came down to it. Now was the time.

We marched right to the meeting room, and after Simon came back in and out a few more times, a large group gathered inside. They were all talking, some doctors, some researchers, and some of us from the army. It was weird getting an insider's view from their attacks. It felt wrong on so many levels, but I didn't have a choice. After another hour and a half, Simon and my mom walked down the line straight to the front. Mom's eyes locked on me, as if she was trying to read my emotions. I didn't let her get a good reading, I ducked my head behind another soldier and kept my head down until Simon yelled across the room.

"After yesterday's attacks, we got a lot of infected under our roof and hidden in other facilities. But there's one more town we're going for, and that should give us a huge advantage. Juros, Indiana." The crowd began to murmur. From the chatter, everyone was shocked. Juros was nothing like the other small towns, it was probably the biggest one we faced yet. Close enough to consider it a city, but not that far yet. There were a lot of ins and outs that would need to be covered, not to mention the police force.

"How are we going to do that, sir? Juros is huge!" a doctor yelled as he stood up with his hand raised. He was right, it had a population of 50,000 people. It seemed so overwhelming, and it only made it worse that I was forced to sit next to Gabby as the meeting went on. She kept making excited faces, but Joque was the opposite.

"Hey, Joque," I called out, until his eyes eventually landed on mine. "Breathe." He nodded and took in a deep breath. He was scared, but the one thing he didn't know yet was that I had to face the whole town on my own.

"I'm sure you all have a lot of questions, but I assure you, it can be done. First, we'll start by eliminating their police force, or at least slimming it down. This will be done today." He went on to describe how he planned on sending small amounts of infected into their ranks. A few would die, but they were willing to accept that fact. From there, he explained how they would start blocking off every available exit leading out. There was a total of nine different ways out. Two were bridges that branched into other cities, four were plain roads, and the other three were highways. There were also boat ramps, but he told us that he planned on using military boats to force them back in. He was planning a war, and I would be at the forefront.

Chapter Seventeen: The Battle of Juros, Indiana

We landed in Swinesdale five days later. At that point, the city of Juros was completely blocked off from the outside world. The police force was either slimmed or dead, the electrical towers were cut off, and all planes were instructed not to land there. They were trapped in a giant box. I could only imagine how scared they must be, and I felt even worse knowing what I was going to help put them through. But at that moment, I had to focus on what I'd tell Oliver. He trusted me, and I had to be the one to take him to be locked up. As we approached Jill's house, the tourists made way for us. We were being treated like VIPs, with some people even telling us, "Thank you for your service," as we walked. If I was a real soldier, I would have held my head as high as Gabby was right then, but instead I marched with Joque with my head down.

"Be honest with me, Joque. How do you think Oliver is going to take this?" I asked him, only sharing a quick glance at him.

"Not well," he told me with a sigh. "He's going to feel like he caused you to do this, Mia. I know I would."

"It's not his fault," I told him, stopping just long enough for him to look me in the eyes.

"It's not yours either," he said with a dry chuckle, meeting my gaze before he ushered me forward. "You're trying to keep him alive. Simon is the bad guy here, remember that. We're still playing our roles. Once we get Oliver back, all that's left is the escape. But I have a feeling Juros is going to fall before we get that privilege."

"And I'm going to lead them." I looked down at the overused pavement beneath us and balled my fists again. "I don't want to do this."

"I know, and I don't want to see you do it either, but it's too late. The higher ups are watching you now. This is a war neither you nor Juros can win."

"Can I hug you?" I asked him when the group came to a stop in front of Jill's house.

"Yes, of course you can." He pulled me into him, and I buried my head into his shoulder. I felt so guilty for doing this. I could only imagine what Oliver might say, but if I succeeded, the price on his head would be lifted. This was our only option.

"Go on, go get him," Simon said, practically pulling us apart. "You've got five minutes." I nodded, and after taking a deep, strained breath, I knocked on the door. About twenty seconds later, Jill answered the door. Behind her, I could see him sitting at a table with his head down. He was probably sleeping.

"Mia, sweetheart, you're back."

"Yeah," I said, mustering up a quick smile, "but not for long. I have to take Oliver."

"Oh, where are you taking him to?" she asked, taking a step back as I stepped up to the door.

"Somewhere far," I said, swallowing down the pain in my voice. "Can I come in? He needs to know what's going on."

"Of course. Come on in, sweetheart. Take your shoes off on the carpet, okay?" She gestured to a cute little welcome mat where her shoes and Oliver's army boots were sitting. I nodded and pulled them off before I came over to speak with him.

"Oliver?" I called out as I slowly walked toward him. He didn't wake up at first, so I had no choice but to shake his shoulder. Five minutes wasn't a long time.

"Yeah?" he groaned, wiping his eyes. He finally opened them, and when they landed on me, he tackled me in a huge hug again just like in the basement.

"Mia! My Mia," he cried, kissing me over and over again on my cheeks. I giggled as his lips began to graze my collarbone, but eventually I knew I had no choice but to break it off.

"Oliver, we have to go," I said, holding him out at arm's length.

"Why? It's great here, we really should—" He stopped and glanced out the window. A moment later, his face shifted to pure terror. "Are they here to kill me?" he asked, whipping his head around to face me again.

"No, we're taking you to Juros," I told him, trying to remain as vague as possible. I was too scared to tell him the full thing just yet.

"I don't understand, did you tell them I'm here?" He looked at me with a look of betrayal before his face changed again. "They're forcing you, aren't they?"

"Yes, and I have to do something very bad." Getting it off my chest felt good, but I still didn't get the full thing out yet.

"What are they making you do, Mia? We can fix this, together. We can run!"

"No, we can't. Not anymore." My eyes darkened as I tried to muster up the strength. We were at minute four. To my surprise, Simon was keeping his word. "They want me to lead the infected through my hometown, Juros, in order to keep you alive. They already have it blocked off, but they want you to watch as I do it. Like it's some sick TV show." When I finished, Oliver pushed my arms away out of fear.

"You can't do this, Mia. You have to..." He choked back a sob before he grabbed my arms again and pulled me in close. "Let me die," he finished with a whimper, holding me tight. "I can't let you turn into one of them. It's okay, I can take it. I know you won't be alone. Indi will take care of you, and—"

"No!" I shouted, pounding my fist against his chest. "I need you! Don't you understand? I can't go on without you." Finally, I let the waterworks come, and reached up to hold his face as I finished. He let me. "You are my everything, and without you I'm...a monster. You make me a good person, I'm sure of that now. Juros is going to suffer whether I do this or not, at least this way I'll get you in the end."

"Mia, I—" He went to say something else when the door swung open again. We jumped and separated when the door banged against the wall. He turned his head toward the door only for a moment, then back to me. He wrapped his arms around me again and held me tightly. "I bought you a ring," he whispered in my ear, making my heart leap. He kissed my ear gently as he continued, with quivering lips. "If you must do this, love, then I don't want you to think of anything else. Go dark, cut off your emotions, and when you're done, I'll hold you until you're able to breathe freely again. This is Simon's doing, not yours. Do you understand? Do it." I nodded, and when we walked out together, Simon grabbed him. He bound him and gagged him right in front of me, and there was nothing I could do to help him. Jill came out shocked as she realized what was happening. She held out her kitchen knife and screamed at the men holding him.

"Let my babies go," she yelled, prompting Oliver and I to shake our heads.

"It's okay, Jill." I assured her, but she still looked scared.

"Okay, baby," she said, slowly backing up toward her house. "You're still welcome back any time, okay?" I nodded, and finally we left.

From there, we all made our way back to the helios waiting outside the city. They practically dragged Oliver down the street until eventually we were all ushered inside. They let Oliver sit next to me. He laid his head against my shoulder and closed his eyes. I could only imagine what he was thinking. This was wrong on so many levels.

"I love you," I whispered, kissing the top of his head. "Please don't forget that." I felt him nod against me, and a huge weight lifted off my shoulders. He still loved me. When we got to Juros, it looked like a scene straight out of a horror movie. There were spray-painted signs on all the bridges that said, *go back, dead inside*, and there were walls taller than a small building of barbed wire.

"Come on," Simon said, as they led Oliver forward. "I'll take you to the police line." I nodded and felt all my nerves going nuts at once. There was a blow-up ladder that led to the top of one of the bridges. I was worried Oliver was going to have a tough time, but they cut him loose to climb up there.

"Are the infected already inside?" I asked when I stepped off the final step.

"Yep," Simon responded as he climbed up behind me. Eventually Oliver got to the top, and Simon forced him to his knees to retie him again. The whole time he kept his eyes closed, and I knew that was what was going to happen. He wasn't going to watch what they made me do. I felt slightly better about the whole thing, but not even close to feeling good again. "Gabby, why don't you walk her through this. Tell her what success looks like here."

"Yes, sir," Gabby said, saluting to Simon before she grabbed me by both shoulders. "Here's how this is going to go. Juros is a pretty big town, so we'll wait here until sundown, then we'll send you in with a gun, a radio, a t-shirt cannon, and a box full of dry-ice bombs. There's another police line on the other side of the town where the other half of the army will be waiting to gather up the infected. Don't kill any, and don't hit them directly with dry ice. Shoot the t-shirt cannon in their direction, but don't let it fly at them. Just close enough to push them away. Oh, and there's tons more of those boxes all over the city, make sure you find them." I nodded and risked a look over at Oliver. He looked right back at me and closed his eyes. He was telling me to go dark. I nodded at him and sat down so I didn't have to watch people suffer any longer than I had to. It felt even scarier knowing I was going in at night. If anything went wrong, I would have 50,000 infected gunning for me. Just the thought of that sent shivers up my spine, but it was even worse considering I couldn't kill a single one if something bad happened.

As time went on, I heard the sound of chaos starting. I could hear glass breaking, distant screams, and a lot of loud noises. The only difference was this time, I couldn't hop in to help someone. Instead, I slid on the floor over to Oliver and ungagged him. They looked at me, but to my relief, they let me. We had a lot of time left between then and nighttime, so I felt the need to be with him.

"Hey, love," he said to me as he leaned back against the bridge wall.

"Hey," I responded. He was tied, but he still moved closer to me.

"Hang in there, okay?"

"You're telling me that?" I said with a chuckle.

"I'll be fine," he responded with a shy smile. "It's you I'm worried about."

"Let's not talk about it," I begged. "How about we talk about what you said before we left Jill's." I heard him chuckle and jostle the ropes behind him.

"I wish I could get myself loose, I'd show you." He moved his body a little closer toward me and turned himself to the side. Eventually, I saw a small outline in his pocket and gasped. "Go on," he told me, with an excited yet worried look. I pulled it out and opened a navy-blue ring box to reveal a small amethyst ring. My birthstone, and a piece of paper about the size of a fortune cookie that said, *Be my forever.*

"I know it's not much, but Jill was sure you'd love it. I'll have to work for free for a while, but that's more than fine with me. I'll work forever if it means I get you in the end."

He smiled wide, making my insides feel warm. He had a way of doing that.

"It's amazing, Oliver. Thank you. But I hope you know I don't need a ring to be with you."

"I know," he whispered, pressing his lips into the nape of my neck. He migrated his kisses back up to my ear, making me giggle again. "Wear it for me, please. I want you to feel at peace while you're out there. Look at it anytime you need reassurance."

"I will," I responded, slipping it onto my ring finger. "Oliver? Does this mean we're engaged?" I asked, raising my eyebrows at him.

"Only if you want us to be. I want to ask you more officially, but I can't right now." I nodded, and turned around so that he could hug me with his knees.

"You have me then." I closed my eyes against him and just breathed against his chest as I stared up at the clouds. He made me feel happy, but the noises in the background were starting to get to me. The screams were intensifying, and I could hear distant gunshots. Part of me hoped that the people would win. Maybe then I wouldn't have to go through the city. Simon and the team leaned over the side like they were watching a football game. Instead, they were watching people suffer.

"Oliver, I don't like this," I whispered to him.

"I know, I don't either," he whispered back as he began to kiss my spine. He was trying to distract me, and for the most part it was working. It only seemed to get worse from there, so I tried to fall asleep against him. A few hours passed until the noise died down. I couldn't hear gunshots or screams, just a lot of glass breaking. I could still see thick smoke in the distance, and all over the city, as I peeked my head over the side, I saw abandoned cars. Some crashed into buildings, some just left there. At first, I thought the people would win, but I was very mistaken. I leaned over just a little bit more and saw a whole swarm of *them*, a couple thousand at least, marching through the city. Some were crawling up buildings while others were parading around the ground. The infected won, and I knew that meant I had to be the one to lead them.

"Alright, Mia. It's showtime," Simon told me as he came to stand in front of us.

"Don't make her do this alone, there's too many of them," Oliver pleaded, but Simon immediately shut him down.

"She made the deal, kid. Your life for theirs. Alone. Now it's time for her to keep up her end of it." I watched as Simon grabbed the blow-up ladder and lowered it over the front of the bridge. "Let's hope you make it back. It'd be really sad if this turned into a *Romeo and Juliet* situation."

"Please, we just got engaged. Let me go with her." Again, Simon shook his head as I stood up, and put the gag back in Oliver's mouth.

"No deal," I heard him whisper, sending chills down my spine. Oliver glared at him, but I knew it wouldn't help. The gravity of the situation finally seemed to hit me. This would determine everything. If I died here, they would kill Oliver too. I grabbed a gun out of the crate, although I knew I wasn't allowed to use it, and saw the team lowering the other crate of dry-ice bombs down to the ground.

"I'll make it back," I told Oliver, and a moment later Joque came over to me.

"Keep your eyes and ears open out there, Mia. Don't let them sneak up on you." I nodded and hugged him one last time before I began to climb down the ladder.

"Bye, Mia. Good luck," Gabby said as she hopped up and plopped down on the edge of the bridge.

"If you ever cared about me at all, don't let them break their promise. You may hate me, Gabby, but I don't hate you. Please, can you watch over him for me?" I looked at both her and Joque, and surprisingly they both nodded. Then my feet hit the ground.

"Okay, Mia," I told myself, "you've got this. Oliver needs you." Slowly and cautiously, I loaded the dry-ice bombs into the t-shirt cannon. From the way they were made, only three could fit in at a time. They were small, about the size of a baby bottle, but they packed a huge punch. Just for a test, I shot one off, and gasped as it went up in smoke about forty feet from me. It created a pretty big explosion, so I knew it would definitely work. Before I left the bridge, I loaded another one in, and peered up one last time. When I did, Oliver, Joque, and Gabby were looking back at me. Each with very different expressions painted across their faces. Worried, scared, and unsure. Luckily, they untied Oliver, but I could tell from where I was standing that Simon had a gun to his head. Seeing that made me feel uneasy, but I didn't have a choice but to walk off.

The city was about a mile away. The dry ice would last maybe an hour since the cannon was kept on ice, but once I got into the city more, I knew that time would dwindle. All the crates were filled to the brim with dry-ice bombs, and now that it was nighttime, I had a huge advantage with keeping them cold. I started my walk there with the cannon at the ready. I didn't know how quickly they would find their way here, if at all, but I didn't want to risk being ambushed. There wasn't much action at first, but after walking for about half a mile, I saw a small car flipped on its back. Its alarm was blaring over and over from the accident, and the airbag was blown out. At first, I thought about passing it, but I couldn't let myself pass if someone was hurt.

"H-hello, can anyone hear me?" I put the cannon up on my shoulder and used my other hand to cup my ear. No sound came back. The alarm was starting to annoy me, but I tried again. "Hello?"

"Kid?" I heard a very shaky voice say, followed by a hoarse cough. "It's me. I finally got home to my family, and the infected came here too. Damn monsters. We can never catch a break, can we?" I wasn't sure who was speaking at first until I heard the airbag start hissing. When it finally deflated, I saw Rufus dangling inside. He had blood trickling down his forehead, and I couldn't help but notice he looked sickly pale.

"I could use some help." I saw him yank on his seatbelt, and I immediately nodded and used the knife attached to my A.R. to cut him loose. With a groan, he hit the ground, making me wince. His windshield was completely shattered beneath him, so I was worried he'd cut himself.

"Here, let me help you out." I put the cannon down on the ground and grabbed his arm as gently as I could to guide him out. Once he managed to get past his dented door frame on all fours, I helped him up. He looked shaky, like he might pass out at any moment. He needed help, but that was a problem. Juros was a condemned town, and no one was allowed to make it out alive. *How can I help him escape?*

I can't let him die here; he helped us. He has a family. Wait, where's his family? Oh no.

"Rufus, what happened to your family?" I asked the moment I snapped back to reality.

"Don't worry. They made it out alive. I made them leave the moment they started closing off the city. They were some of the lucky ones. Me, on the other hand..." He stopped and let out a dry chuckle. "Be straight with me, kid. Am I going to die here?"

"Not if I can help it," I told him with a determined look. "I don't care what I have to do, I'm getting you back to your family." He nodded and smiled before he patted me on my back.

"I believe in you. You and that boy. Say, where is he anyway?"

"They took him prisoner, and now I have to guide as many infected to the other side using this," I said, showing him the t-shirt cannon, "or he dies. I don't have much time either, so I need you to follow me."

"You got it." Together, we walked the rest of the mile into Juros. Once we entered the city, we stayed on high alert. He watched my back, while I watched the road ahead. I was scared, but all over the streets, I could see the crates. *Gabby definitely wasn't kidding when she said, "all over."* That put me at ease, at least a little bit, but I was still very scared.

Chapter Eighteen: The Battle of Juros, Indiana II

"Uh, kid, get that cannon ready." I turned to see a huge crowd of them, maybe thirty or forty, huddled by an office building called Gates Plaza. They were wall crawlers, like the ones from the apartment complex, but these had eyes. I began yelling at the top of my lungs, causing the man to look at me like I was crazy. I was drawing them toward us, and luckily it seemed to do the trick. Once they were about fifty feet away, I shot a dry-ice bomb and used the smokescreen to dip behind a crumbled brick wall behind us. All I could hear as I caught my breath was screeches, and when I looked back out, they were all on the run.

"Whew! It worked!" I cheered, pumping my fist into the air.

"Nice work, kid," the man said as he held up his hand for a high-five. I slapped it hard and smiled.

"Two more, and then I'll have to pry open another crate." He nodded, and again we set off down the road. As we continued down the streets, they started to look vaguely familiar. I lived in Juros my whole life but walking through the downtown area felt much different than sitting in the back of Mom or Dad's car. My favorite place downtown was

Fox's Pizza Den. It was a pizza place that had probably the best pizza I'd ever had. Dad used to take me there as a kid, but as we walked past, it looked like a shell of its former self. The glass windows were busted out, the tables and chairs were sprawled around, the walls were covered in black ooze, and there was a body lying on the windowsill right out front. It made me feel sick that someone suffered at a place that used to bring me joy. I was heartbroken.

"Hey, don't look at that, kid. That's not good for you." He put his hand in front of my eyes, and I gently pushed it away.

"It's okay, sir. I'm moving on." I walked away with my head hanging low and heard him sigh behind me. It probably broke him too. We walked on until we came to another small horde. They were huddled around something near the downtown library, but I couldn't see what. Cautiously, I got a little closer, and eventually came to notice a group of survivors huddled on a statue. Somehow the infected didn't think to climb it, but that didn't make them safe. They couldn't move, and I could see the smallest one, a little girl, was bleeding.

"Ahhh!" she screamed. "Someone help! Anyone!" She hugged onto her mom's knee while her brother hit them with a stick.

"We have to do something," the man said, glancing around.

"I-I can't," I told him, feeling like my heart was being torn out. "If I kill even one of the infected, they'll kill Oliver." The man took in my words, but he still glanced around frantically. He wanted to help, but I knew he was just as conflicted as I was. I knew I needed to try something, so I slowly backed up and screamed just like before. Some of them followed the sound of my voice, but some hung around the family. Then I let another bomb rip. When the smoke screen went up, I crossed my fingers that the rest would scurry away too. "Please, please, please," I whispered as it dissipated into the air. When the smoke cleared, my worst fears were answered instead. The infected were sent flying toward the family during the smokescreen, and to my dismay, all three of them were eaten, leaving only the stick behind.

"No!" I cried and fell to my knees on the hard concrete. I thought I helped them, but instead, I made death come quicker. The man looked distraught when he saw what happened. Part of me knew they wouldn't have made it even if I was able to kill the infected, but my heart still shattered knowing I was the reason they died. As I groveled on the ground, the man took the cannon from me and fired off another shot. This time, the entire crowd took off, but it was too late.

"Hey, kid. I-it's okay, come on. We have to...move on." He was careful with his words, and I appreciated that. I didn't want him to say it wasn't my fault, because I would always blame myself for what just happened, but he was right. We had to swallow down the heartbreak and keep going. The man helped me to my feet, and immediately my knees felt like Jell-o. All I could pray for was that their deaths came quick. At least that helped put my mind a bit at ease.

We continued shooting bombs as we pressed on into the city. I opened about ten crates as we pressed farther and farther in, and the darkness crept over us. The streetlights kicked on, but it made me feel uneasy. I didn't see any other survivors as we continued through my hometown, and whether I wanted to admit it or not, I was grateful for that. I couldn't stand to watch someone else suffer. Eventually, we made it to my part of town. I wanted to show it to him. My home. If I could never have that normalcy back again, I wanted to at least show someone what my happy place was. We were about five blocks down when, all of a sudden, I saw a group of infected so big, it made the two groups we saw before look like nothing. They were everywhere. I saw them breaking down doors and windows, busting down fences, and a few were climbing up trees. It was a nightmare, and I knew the dry-ice bombs wouldn't be enough to move them.

"Why are they just huddled here?" the man asked. I wasn't sure, but the air felt unusually cold the closer we got toward the horde. It was strange because they hated the cold, but it felt like walking into the freezer at a restaurant. We had no choice but to sneak through the back alleyways to get to my house. I snuck around my neighbors' yards, dodging the occasional straggler, until we managed to get to my backyard fence. Once we did, I saw exactly why they were gathered. There were holes in my fence where the infected pushed their way in, and I peeked through one of them. I heard all kinds of groaning and moans as I gripped the shattered remnants, but what really struck me was that they were all coming to my house.

"They're in my back yard." I huffed, feeling sad I couldn't show him my house. I thought at first that maybe they were gathered there because they saw survivors, but after I stepped a little farther in, I saw that those things were staring at some sort of dark shape or energy coming out of the ground by my house. It made a whooshing sound, almost like the wind, and they were all transfixed by it. Then I noticed where it was. My sandbox.

Immediately, I knew what was going on. According to Mom, that was where Oliver and his family emerged. This dark energy could be what brought him back. I stepped closer and felt the hairs on my arm stand on end. The infected didn't even look at me, even though I was directly next to one. Despite everything telling me otherwise, I took another step forward. This time, everything felt off. Instead of feeling like I had control, I realized I no longer did. It felt like the infection was pulling me in. *Is this because I was infected before? Maybe being infected again would be nice. This time without immunities. Yeah, there would be no more Simon, or Mom, or Polly. I could be with Dad, and... NO, Mia! Snap out of it!* I was screaming in my head, but my feet kept moving. Behind me, I hoped the man would have stepped in, but I didn't hear a sound. I got within five feet of it before I heard a growl. My head turned, but I kept moving. Finally, my feet stopped about a foot away, and planted in the grass so firmly I swore they were digging into the dirt. My arm began to raise. All I could see was darkness. All I could see was the void. It smelled like death itself. It was worse than the morgue or anything I'd come across so far, and it made every part of my body feel numb just looking at it.

I extended my arm, and right as my index finger stretched out to touch it, I felt something or someone, yank me back. I don't know how, but I went flying across the yard. All the infected parted and forced me to hit part of the fence with so much force, it knocked the wind out of me. When I recovered, I winced and took a couple shaky breaths. The air felt thick, and my head was pounding. I didn't feel any different besides that, but I knew something had happened. Slowly, I arched my head upward again, ignoring a sharp pain that shot up my spine and down my neck, to see the man standing right where I was with his whole hand inside the void. His mouth was open in a horrified fashion and his head was tilted so far back; I was worried he would break his neck. His eyes looked haunted, possessed even. They stared straight up, and he didn't blink once. *Did he do that to me?* I wondered as I used the fence post to pull myself off the ground.

"R-Rufus," I stuttered, as I put my hand against my back to try and soothe the pain. "Please tell me you're okay." As expected, he didn't answer. I was too scared to get any closer, so I went for the dry-ice cannon instead. Luckily it was lying on my back porch when I got to it, and to my relief, there didn't seem to be much damage besides a small crack in the glass.

"Don't worry, I'm gonna get to you. Try and fight it!" I encouraged, although I wasn't sure if he could hear me or not. I shot the first bomb off, and it seemed to do the trick. The infected that were scattered farthest from the mass ran away in fear. I shot off another one to disperse the ones closest to him, and then I aimed one right at the orb. The man was still frozen in it, and I could just start to see his veins turning black on his arm. "No!" I yelled, aimed right at the mass, and shot one straight in. I wasn't sure whether that would help, but it was my last resort. Inside, I heard the bomb go off, but still no change. It didn't seem to do anything. I decided to take matters into my own hands. I closed my eyes and ran forward as fast as I could. When I ran into his body, I reached my hand out and felt for the back of his shirt so that I could use that to pull him back. Instead, I heard a groan.

I opened my eyes, hoping the man was saved and maybe everything would be okay, but instead his head did a full 180 while I wasn't looking, and he was staring back at me with vacant eyes. Again, he groaned and stumbled toward me, making a cracking sound with each step. The only thing I managed to do was melt his arm off. The sweet, kind man I knew was already gone. I didn't have time to grieve his loss, because the infected were starting to come back. So, I let a tear fall into the grass, and smiled at him sadly.

"If I find your family, I'll make sure they know you loved them," I promised, and ran through the last unoccupied hole. I sniffled as I ran to find another crate, but I knew I couldn't focus on him anymore. He was gone. If I didn't survive, no one would be around to stop Simon and possibly even the government too. Just thinking about that made me feel sick to my stomach, but I couldn't dwell on it too long. The infected were coming in droves toward my house. I managed to make it to a crate about a mile back and had to empty the whole crate just to make progress. I got them all running toward the other side, then I heard my radio go off. It made the *bloop* sound, meaning they were calling me.

"Hey, kid, you got five minutes to respond. Do you copy?" I didn't respond at first, because I wasn't close enough to the other side to start making progress.

"She's probably dead, sir," I heard someone snort, followed by the sound of laughter. "Might as well kill that boy now, because—"

"I'm here!" I shouted, cutting the guy off. "I'm still alive." I held the radio up to my lips and breathed as I waited for Simon to respond.

"Nice to hear your voice," Simon said, with a chuckle at my bluntness. "Do you want to speak to the boy? He's really antsy."

"Yes, sir," I responded quickly, before I closed my eyes.

"Mia?" Oliver sounded tired, maybe even weak. "A-are you there?" He huffed into the radio, and then I heard the *beep.*

"Yeah, I'm here. Please tell me you're okay."

"Simon beat me," he responded, letting out another sore breath. "I tried to come down there when I didn't hear from you, but Simon got angry with me and dragged me up the ladder kicking and screaming. He let his soldiers go to town on me. Gabby and—" He stopped and let out another breath, and then a hoarse cough, before he continued. "Gabby and Indi defended me, so he took them away. I don't know what happened to them. I think he—"

"And that's enough of that," Simon finished, cutting off Oliver's final words.

"Please don't hurt them. I swear, I'm doing the best I can." My lips began to quiver as I waited for him. I felt comfort knowing Gabby helped him, despite our argument, and wondered if maybe there was hope for her yet. Simon, on the other hand...

He laughed into the radio, making me feel even more uneasy. "I better start getting reports of the infected going into the containment zone soon, or else I'll hurt them too. I've got them locked up for now, but if you don't make progress soon, Mia, I might just get a little...trigger-happy," he warned before signing off and turning his radio off. I knew that night I wasn't going to get any sleep. All I could do was keep going and hope for the best. Although I was alone, I had to make up for lost time. If I had even a small chance to get my friend back, I would take it. Even after what she did.

I got onto the field at nine and spent all night shooting off dry ice like fireworks. I was fast but careful as I pushed them forward. Around three in the morning, the first few infected ran into the very large cage they had set up on the other side. It looked like a soccer field goal, but there was a large leaf-covered cage door being held above it, waiting to drop. Despite getting a small win, I still had to push on. Eventually, I started sending the infected through the containment zone by the hundreds. No lives were lost, and I even managed to see the man as an infected go through the gate. It broke my heart, but I couldn't save him. There was nothing I could do.

My eyes were starting to crust over, and I yawned every couple minutes as I went on, but I had to keep going until they gave me the green light. Once five in the morning rolled around, I heard my radio go off again.

"Kid, you there?" I heard Simon ask, though I could tell he was mid-yawn.

"Yes, sir," I said, letting my arms fall.

"Good, the soldiers on the other side are going to lower a ladder down for you. I'll count this as a win, but you should know, you, Indi, Gabby, and Oliver are mine now. I expect your full cooperation from now on, and if you fight me again, there won't be a next time. Got it?"

"Yes, sir." Normally, I would have tried to come up with some kind of sarcastic joke to stand up for us, but I was beat. My legs, arms, and back ached and throbbed with each step up the ladder I took. I felt like I just finished working a week's worth of night shifts. I needed sleep and probably therapy.

"Come on," a soldier said as she grabbed my arm when I almost missed the top step. I couldn't see who it was because my eyes were watering, but she supported me all the way back to the helicopter, where I finally let go.

Chapter Nineteen: The Aftermath

I don't know how much time passed, but I woke up in the barracks with drool running down my forearm. Slowly, I sat up, and saw that besides the four of us, everyone else was gone. Gabby was laying on her back in the bed next to me, Oliver was asleep on his side, and Joque was hitting a paddle ball over and over again. I didn't want to disturb either of them, so I slowly peeled myself off my bed and walked over to Joque. At first, he stared absentmindedly into the distance, but then he noticed me approaching and patted the bed next to him.

"Come on. It's support time." I chuckled as he threw the paddle board down and slid over just enough for me to sit next to him. When I did, he pulled my head into his body and hugged me. "How are you?" he asked, taking a deep breath.

"I'm getting there," I answered, trying to ignore the pain I endured in a town I should have felt joy for.

"I can only imagine," he responded, still holding me against him. "We sat there for so long with no answer, I thought... Never mind, I'm just glad you're okay." I nodded against his chest and gave him a forced smile as I sat up. I wasn't ready to muster up a real one again yet, too much went wrong.

"How are they?" I asked him, pointing at the others as I leaned against his shoulder.

"Oliver's pretty beat up. They hurt him badly, Mia. We only got to see the first few minutes of it, but even then, it wasn't pretty. And as for Gabby... She and I got rope burns. We sat in what felt like a cell for hours blindfolded and left in the dark in every way possible. It's nothing compared to what you two went through, but it was still really scary." I nodded and hugged him again.

"I'm sorry, Joque. You shouldn't have had to suffer for us."

"Don't apologize," he responded. "We have to support each other, or we won't make it through this. Now, I know Oliver and Gabby are sleeping over there, but they could probably use a hug too." I nodded and gave his hand a squeeze before I went over to Gabby. I decided to let Oliver sleep a little longer. I could only imagine what shape he was in. He would want me there, I knew that much, but I wanted him to rest, and I knew if I woke him right then, he would have gotten up with me.

Playfully, I went over and pushed Gabby over with my body. I heard her laugh before her eyes came open and she saw me lying next to her.

"Hey," I said, as I crossed my arms over my chest. I wasn't sure how she'd respond at first, but after a second, she pulled me in for a hug too.

"Are you okay?" she asked me, eyeing me up and down.

"Mentally or physically?" I raised my eyebrows, causing her to chuckle.

"Both?"

"Nope, I'm a goner."

"Aw, and here I thought I could fix things between us." She eyed me again, and eventually we both erupted in dry laughter. Maybe it was because of her facial expression or the pain I was suppressing, but it felt good. "Mia, I'm sorry for what I did, really. I just wanted to impress Simon so badly, I became a monster myself. I never should have aimed a gun at Oliver or snapped at you in the helicopter. You and the two idiot boys..." she said, raising her eyebrows, "are all I've got. Please understand what I did back there. It wasn't me, and it'll never happen again. You believe me, don't you?"

"I need to know something first. You don't really think innocent people suffering is okay, right? You stand with us?" I put my hand out, and it brought me great joy when she took it.

"No, it's not okay. I just... I signed up for this place because they said it was a great honor to our country, but what I saw out there was sickening. I don't want to do this anymore, truly, but you know what Simon would do if I tried to check out. Also, I hope you understand that having you go to Juros wasn't my idea. I heard some of the other soldiers talking about it, and...my sick brain thought it was the perfect way to get you on board. I'm so sorry."

"It's okay, I forgive you." She smiled wide and pulled me in for a hug. This time, I felt safe in her arms. She was my friend all over again, and despite what happened, I knew if I could trust her with Oliver, I could trust her as a friend.

"What do we do now?" I asked her when we separated.

"For now, rest. Simon doesn't need us right now anyway, and even if he did, I don't think Oliver could handle very much right now." I nodded and got up to go lay by him. When I got over to his bed, I could hear him snoring again.

I didn't want to disturb him, but I couldn't stand seeing him like that. He was covered in marks. There were some stitches on his arms and a few poking through his shirt on his chest, but his face got the worst of it. I knelt down and ran my fingers across his cheek as I assessed his injuries. His nose was black and blue, and he had a busted lip. It broke my heart.

"Oh, Oliver," I whispered, before I pressed my lips against his forehead. "I'm so sorry." Luckily for me, he was already lying on the edge of the bed, so I laid down beside him and pulled him into me as gently as I could. To my relief, he didn't wake up. His hair fell over his face as he slept, but I left it alone. He looked so peaceful, and for once as I hugged him against me, I was able to fall back to sleep.

When I woke up again, I found myself somewhere completely different. Oliver, Joque, and Gabby were gone, and I was wearing a flower-covered hospital gown. I stood up and glanced around. I was no longer in the barracks; I was in a hospital room. *Am I in Beacon?* I wondered as I got up, and realized there was a feeding tube in my nose. Above the bed I saw a glucose bag and an IV hydration bag hanging on a stand. The water gave me a chill, so I grabbed a thin blue blanket I found draped over the bed's handrail and laid it over my shoulders.

"What's going on?" I mumbled, before my eyes locked on a dry-erase board with my name on it. I grabbed the rolling stand and walked over to it. It said, "Mia Andrews, infection level 1. Doctor: Carmin Junip." My heart leapt when I saw the infection reading, and my eyes immediately jumped to my arms. I saw nothing. Then my legs; again, nothing. I checked my stomach, nothing. Finally, I checked my hands and my eyes widened in fear. The tip of my index finger on my right hand was wrapped in black veins. "No, I didn't touch it. I know I didn't!" Frantically, I ran out into the hall and began to feel dizzy. My legs felt like jelly all of a sudden, and the hallway began to turn in a circle, as if someone put it on wheels.

"Hello?" I called out as I leaned against the doorframe for support. My head felt heavy, and as I tried to pry myself off it, gravity seemed to work against me, causing me to hit the ground. I whimpered as the needle nearly got ripped out of my arm, and slowly managed to look up, only to see a very tall man standing in the doorway. It was the doctor.

"Oh no, I knew I should have put fall risk on your chart." He reached his hand out and, reluctantly, I took it and allowed him to help me up.

"Where am I?" I tried asking him, but my tongue went numb as I spoke, and I slurred my words.

"Don't worry, you're alright. Let's get you back in your bed, and I'll explain what's going on." I nodded, and slowly he helped me walk toward it. I felt dizzy again about halfway there, and he ended up having to carry me. "There you are," he said as he sat me down. I laid my head against my pillows and watched as he connected a machine to make the water and glucose drip faster.

"That's better, huh?" he asked, as he sat down in a rolling chair across from me.

"Yes," I replied, but it seemed to come out as a whisper. *What happened to me?*

"Good," he responded with a toothy grin that seemed to go from ear to ear. "Let's get this started, shall we? First things first, this isn't real. I'm a ghost, and I came into your consciousness," he said, putting his finger against my forehead, "to give you a very important message. The doctors in Beacon finally got the cure together, and if you can get there, you can cure your dad. He's not dead, Mia, but he needs your help to escape that awful hospital." I gasped and put my hand against my mouth. This whole time I thought Dad was beyond saving, but if he was really telling the truth, I knew I needed to try. I wanted to ask him questions, but again my tongue felt numb.

"I know you probably have a million questions, especially about the infection, but we don't have much time. In a strong brain, we have maybe an hour or more, but since you're infected, it cuts our time in half. We only have time for one question. Here, use this." He pulled out another dry-erase board, and the moment he passed the marker to me I started writing as fast as I could. I had so many questions: *Why help me? Who are you? How can I save Dad? Am I still immune? Can I spread the infection?* But I could only ask one, so I had to make it worth my time.

"How did I get infected?" I wrote, and watched as his eyes scanned my board.

"I figured you'd ask that," he told me. "I know this is going to hurt to hear, but you touched the black mass. Only for a moment, but that moment was enough. It will spread slowly for now, since it's only on your finger, but eventually you will be another subject zero again. I'm sorry. Hopefully they can cure you too." He stepped back and did a dramatic bow before I noticed my body had started to evaporate. It looked like TV static was eating away at my feet. It made a buzzing sound as it traveled up to me. I gasped and scrambled to get up, but it stopped me in my tracks. I crawled forward toward the door and screamed out for help, but no one seemed to hear me. The static traveled up my ankles, then my legs, my torso, my hands and arms, then my throat. Somehow, I let out one final scream right in the doorway before it got up to my face and took the rest of me.

I woke up for real in the bed next to Oliver and let out a shriek. I didn't intend to, but I was so startled, I didn't know what to do.

"Mia?" Oliver asked, rubbing his eyes. "Hey, hey, it's okay." He held onto both my shoulders as I started to have a panic attack. I took a deep breath and buried my head in his chest.

"That was so scary," I told him as a shiver traveled up my body.

"It was just a dream, baby. It's okay." I nodded, but I didn't lift my head back up. It felt so real.

"Do you want to tell me about it?" he asked, slowly running his hand down the back of my head. I opened my mouth and then closed it again. I thought it was nothing more than a nightmare, but when I saw my finger through a shaft of light between us, my veins were black.

"No," I cried, and began to sob as I realized that maybe there was some truth to what the doctor was saying. *I have to separate myself from them,* I thought. *I have to do it now.* I sprung up, and without looking back, I ran out the door of the barracks. I knew the infection spread through blood, but I couldn't risk Oliver or any of them catching it from me. Even the hug I gave them made me feel guilty. *Why am I feeling this way? They need you!* I shook my head and ran until I managed to get to a small stream behind Beacon, about a mile and a half back. It was river water, but it was only barely cutting through the ground. I stopped and lowered myself down. I felt so angry with fate. I reached down and swiped the water as hard as I could with a loud scream. No one was around, so I punched a tree until my hand bled. Then I felt someone's arms wrap around me from behind.

"No!" I cried and tried to elbow whoever was holding me, but eventually, she pinned me down. It was Gabby.

"MIA! Look at me, girl, you hurt yourself." I sobbed again and pressed my head against the soft ground beneath me. The leaves crunched against my head, making me flinch until my head finally set down flat.

"I messed up," I cried, as I tried to focus on anything but my guilt. I could see the leaves in the skyscraper-like trees were a beautiful red, brown all around making me feel a bit of comfort. Fall was my favorite season. It was the perfect temperature. Not too hot, not too cold, and the colors were beautiful. I managed to smirk at it before she grabbed my chin and forced me to look at her.

"What happened?" she asked. "It's okay, we can work through this together." I shook my head in response, and tried to fight her again, but she held me in place. "Not letting you go until you tell me. Plain and simple."

"I'm infected again," I admitted, as the numb feeling seemed to travel across my body. It wasn't the same as my dream, but it still felt crippling. "I'm immune, but I can still spread it." She sat up and let out a chuckle.

"That's it? You think I care about that? You're okay, right?" I nodded, and went to open my mouth, but she spoke up first. "Good, then WE have nothing to worry about. No need to panic. We just have to keep your blood away, that's all." She looked at my bloodied hand and widened her eyes. "Yeah, not gonna touch that." I chuckled nervously, and she pulled me off the ground with the opposite hand. "It's okay, got it? You're one of us, who cares if you're infected as long as you're okay." I nodded and felt a relieved tear fall down my cheek.

"Thank you," I said, although I avoided her eyes.

"You're welcome. Now, let's get you back. The boys are probably worried sick." I nodded and followed her back to the barracks. Surprisingly, Simon and the rest of the soldiers were nowhere to be seen. I couldn't help but think he was up to something, but ignored the bad feeling and went back inside, where Oliver and Joque were both looking at us.

"Mia? What happened?" Oliver asked me when I walked back in. He looked me over and eyed me up and down as if he was searching for something.

"It's nothing. She just needed some air, right, Mia?" Gabby raised her eyebrows at me, and even though I didn't want to keep it from them, I nodded.

"Yeah, I'm good." I cradled my hand and heard Oliver gasp before I heard his footsteps. He reached his hand out to grab mine, but I whipped them behind my back before he could connect with them.

"You're bleeding, Mia. Please tell me what's happening." He grabbed my upper arm, so I looked over at Gabby with a startled expression. He definitely took notice, because he followed my gaze. "Did she do this?"

"No, of course not," I replied, lowering my voice little by little.

"Then what happened?" He ran his fingers down my arms until he got to my hands. I instantly widened my eyes and pushed him away just in time, being careful not to get blood on his shirt.

"No! Stop!" I yelled, and watched as he caught his balance again. He looked at me, and I saw his face contort in pain. I hurt him. He was still tired from being beaten, and I was making it worse. I looked at Gabby as if to ask her, *how do I tell him?* and saw her shrug her shoulders.

"Mia, please. Did I do something wrong? If I hurt you—"

"You didn't do anything. I just... I have to get myself patched up, okay? That's all. I'll be right back." I kissed his cheek, and again he eyed me up and down before I jogged away. I thought that would work, but he knew better. He knew something was wrong.

I took the long way to the infirmary wing so I could breathe. Once I got there, I saw Polly at the front desk and stopped in my tracks. I hated her, but what choice did I have? I walked in slow motion, and eventually got to her. She didn't look at me at first, but when she did, her eyes narrowed in anger.

"H-hey," I said to her nervously, "I hurt my hand." I held it up for her to see and gestured to a first-aid kit behind her. "I can patch myself up, I just need some alcohol and some gauze." When I finished speaking, she scoffed and pushed a clipboard toward me.

"That's not how this works, 851," she teased, leaning forward in her chair. "Sign in and I'll examine it." I shook my head and decided to press further. I hated Polly, but I couldn't let her get infected.

"I would much rather—"

"Do you really have to fight me on everything? Do. What. I. Told. YOU." She shoved the clipboard off the desk, and when it hit the floor, I flinched.

"Please understand, I can't. I'm... I'm infected again." I mumbled the last part, but I saw her lips curve up.

"Wow, you really are something special. You get cured and then you mess it up all over again. How pathetic." I felt embarrassed as I picked up the clipboard and put it back on the desk. "Sign in, and then I'll give it to you." I nodded and looked at her briefly, seeing her pick up the first-aid kit and hold it in her lap as I signed my name on the sheet. *Did she think I was going to steal it?* I signed the time too, and then held out my hands. I blew out a breath of air as she rolled her eyes and passed it to me. *Awkward.* I would have rather talked to literally anybody else, but she was the only one on duty.

"Go on." She waved her hand at me, so I picked the first available bed and went to work. After I was done, I balled my hand into a fist and watched the bandage move. It was wrapped tight. Once I felt satisfied, I went back up to her and heard her groan.

"I need to ask you something," I said, looking from her to the desk.

"What now?"

"Is it true Beacon developed another cure?" She looked up at me shocked, and instantly grabbed me by my shirt collar.

"Who told you that? It's supposed to be top secret!"

"A doctor did." I didn't want to tell her it was a dream. Knowing how cruel she was, she would probably use that as an excuse to put me in a mental hospital. I saw her shake her head and gesture to the end of the infirmary wing. I thought she was telling me to leave at first, but then I noticed a large white tarp over the door.

"Down there, they're starting the tests. Not that it's any of your business, but it seems to work so far." I gasped and tried to hide my excitement from her but failed miserably.

"Did they cure my dad?" I locked eyes with her, but she didn't answer me. "Please, Polly. I know you hate me, but—"

"I don't hate you; I loathe you. You escaped your cell where you still should be, aimed a gun at me, stole *my* badge, and now they're telling me you're part of the response team? No, you don't deserve it. You deserve to have that infection take over your body and turn you just like every other sorry sap here. Then have a bullet get shot between your eyes. But since that won't happen, I won't let you get cured. I don't care what happens to me. You're done." I gasped and took a step back as her words seemed to hit me.

"I don't need it." I tried to sound confident as I began to walk away, but she called after me.

"You will, and you know it. You can't keep your distance from Oliver forever, and the day you come asking, I'll make sure it's not there for you. And for your information, no, your father's still rotting away. I guess he won't get cured either, will he?" I balled my hands into fists and glared at her.

"Then I guess I'll have to steal the cure from you, just like your badge." I watched her eyes narrow again and her brows furrowed in anger, but this time I walked out. I walked straight back to the barracks. I intended to tell all of them, but as I got close, I saw a poster outside the barrack's walls.

No Infected was printed in bold, black lettering with a picture of a smeared handprint crossed out beneath it. I swallowed hard and ripped it down from the wall. I knew it probably meant the monsters, but it still made me stop in my tracks. *What would Simon do if he knew the truth?* Part of me wanted to stroll in there and tell both Joque and Oliver, but if it somehow spread, or he overheard me, I was worried he would kill me.

"I really wish I didn't tell Polly," I said to myself as I strolled through the doors. When I walked in, Oliver, Gabby, and Joque were all sitting together in a circle using yard chairs.

"I'm back," I told them, trying to look confident.

"Are you okay?" Oliver asked me. I nodded and stopped a few inches from him. He went to grab my hands but hesitated. "May I?" He looked me in the eyes, and I felt my insides melt. I was a little worried, but there was no blood soaking through. I just had to be careful.

"Yeah." I put my hands in his palms, and watched as he squeezed them gently. Still nothing. I let out a sigh and leaned my head against him. "I'm sorry I pushed you before."

"It's okay." He smiled and ran his thumb across the back of my bandaged hand. It stung a bit, but the butterflies he made me feel overwhelmed the pain. He didn't ask me what happened again, instead he just migrated his hands to my upper arms and pushed my sleeves up with his hands. "God, I love you." He kissed my lips gently and cupped my face in his hands. My heart jumped with guilt, but I kissed him back passionately. After everything I went through in Juros, I needed him. He migrated his lips across my cheek until he reached my ear and began to nibble on it. Then he whispered, "I know why you pushed me, and I don't care.

If you're infected, then so am I." Somehow, I completely missed him moving my bandage aside. He ran his thumb across my open wound and looked from it to my eyes. The moment he grazed it, his finger lit up like a Christmas tree.

"Oliver, no," I gasped, but he cupped my face again.

"We're a team," he told me as he released one of my hands to hold my chin. "We always will be. Even if we have to suffer together." I nodded and kissed him again. I couldn't help but smile in between kisses. For real this time. I glanced over at Joque and Gabby and they were both bright red in the face, causing me to giggle a bit. Oliver noticed too, and chuckled. When I looked back at him, I stood on my tiptoes and whispered three words in his ear.

"I want you." His eyes widened, and after taking a quick glance at Gabby and Joque again with a grin plastered across his face, he immediately grabbed my hand and took off with me. "Where are we going?" I asked with a giggle as he led me toward the far end of the barracks.

"You'll see." He looked at me with a mischievous gleam in his eyes, and instantly made me feel warm. He led me to a side closet room that had nothing but a single twin bed and some supplies. The bed didn't have sheets on it, but neither of us cared. It was clean, that's all that mattered to us. He gently pushed me down on it and took over. I felt him kiss me over and over and he gave me hickeys on my neck as I ran my fingers through his hair. I gasped as his fingers went up my shirt. He moved from the bottom of my stomach to my bra, then stopped and tugged on it gently. "Can I continue?" he asked me, pulling his lips away briefly to get an answer. I nodded and kissed him as if I was desperate for his touch. Almost effortlessly, he unbuckled the clasp and grabbed my breasts. His hands ran over them, and he laughed as my body stiffened a bit.

"Am I making you feel warm?" I nodded, and to distract myself, I moved my hands up his arm. I loved how his hands felt against me, but I was super nervous. I kissed his collar bone, and to tease him, I pulled on his shirt, making him chuckle. A moment later, I pulled his shirt off and stopped for a moment to look at his wounds.

"There's so many," I whimpered, running my hand across his scarred chest.

"I know." He grabbed my hand and pressed it against his lips. "I'll be okay, as long as I have you." I nodded and began fiddling with the button on his pants as I bit my lip. I watched him arch his neck down to look. Then he swallowed and moved his lips back to my ear again. "Are you sure you're ready for this?" he asked, taking a deep breath. "You'd be my first." His lips quivered a bit as he withdrew them from my ear and hovered above me.

"You'd be my first too," I admitted, making him blush. "Do *you* want to do this?" He eyed me up and down again and nodded with a deep exhale.

"More than you know." He slowly unbuttoned the buttons on my shirt, revealing my bare upper body and smiled. Nothing was even happening yet, but we were both breathing deeply. I swallowed as he grasped his hands around my stomach, and then trailed down to my pants, making my skin tingle. He watched me intently the whole time as he undid the button, slowly pushed them down my legs, threw them to the floor and grabbed my bare thighs. "One thing left," he muttered before he wrapped his finger around the side of my underwear.

I blew out a breath and he smiled. Then I unbuttoned his pants. His body drew my breath away. I loved every part of it. Then came the part we were both nervous about. He ran his hands along every inch of my body and took control the moment we both consented. I was sure there wasn't anything he missed. He knew what to do, and honestly did it well. He was slow and methodical with the way he moved, and he made me feel really happy. Our bodies became one, and every step of the way we checked on each other. Fourteen minutes and thirty-five seconds. That's how long we lasted before we collapsed against the bed panting. We were both drenched in sweat. I knew we would probably need a shower, but at that moment, all I cared about was lying there with him. I ran my hand along his stomach and drew circles with my fingers.

"Did you have fun?" he asked me as he put his hand on the square of my back to pull me in close.

"Mhm," I said, trying to catch my breath. "I love you." I laid my head against his sweaty body and listened to his heartbeat.

"I love you too." He held me there and ran his thumb over the engagement ring with a smile. "I couldn't imagine anyone better." I kissed his upper body and heard his head hit the pillows beneath him. We laid there together until I drifted off again. Little did I know that nightmare I had had earlier, was the first of many.

Chapter Twenty: Possessed

Again, I found myself in the hospital, but there wasn't a bed. I was in a plain white room that had padded floors, an outline of a door but no door handle, and a single light that had to be at least ten feet above me. I saw a camera in the corner, so I went to wave to it when I realized I was wearing a straitjacket. It was tight around my body, almost like a corset, and it forced me to hug my arms around myself. I struggled and pulled on my arms, making a grunt escape my lips; it was hopeless.

"Help! Let me out of here!" I screamed, only for the camera to turn toward me.

"Good morning, Mia. Take this as a temporary time out of your life. I gave you an order to save your father, yet you decided to play around with that boy. Now you can sit here. In fact..." He stopped, and a moment later, I felt my legs get dragged out from under me. I screamed as a rope dragged me up to the ceiling and hung me from a dark hole near the light. "Ten minutes, starting now." I saw a timer appear on the wall about a foot from the ceiling and groaned. The blood rushed to my head as I hung there, and I couldn't help but wonder if this was real or not. It felt so real. I was always told as a kid, if you know you're dreaming, it's not usually a good sign. *Is this sleep paralysis?*

"Let me go, you can't do this!" I began to spin a bit as I turned my head toward the camera. Then the door to the room opened, and the light went out. I couldn't hear any footsteps, since the room was padded, but I could hear him take a breath every few seconds and a crunch-like sound, as if he was walking on snow.

"I can do whatever I want. You're supposed to be the hero of this story, yet you're playing games. So let's play." The lights turned back on, so I looked back toward the ground and saw that the doctor from my last nightmare was standing beneath me, holding a carnival mallet. "I can make you feel *real* pain in here, so I suggest you learn to have some manners." With the last line, he pulled the mallet back and swung it as hard as he could at my stomach. I cried out and balled myself up for a second. I couldn't defend myself, so I just cried and hoped he would stop.

"Let's try this again, Mia. What are you going to do the moment I leave your consciousness again?" I drew in a breath and saw a puddle formed beneath me where my tears were falling. I knew I cried a lot, but that was way too much.

"Th-this isn't real!" I huffed as I stared at him and sheltered myself when I saw him drag the mallet back again.

"I don't think you understand, this is real. I possess you, and I'm the worst of them all. Simon, your mother, Polly. They're *nothing* compared to me. I own your thoughts and can make you dance however I please. Just like all my other patients." He waved his arm around dramatically, and the white room disappeared in what looked like a mirage-type fashion. In its place, I saw we were in an O.R. To my shock, I saw the little girl again. I closed my eyes as the same scene repeated itself again, then the little boy came in that we saw being led inside during our escape. He came in coughing and clutching his stomach.

"Come inside, and we'll get started." The boy nodded and tiptoed into the room. He couldn't move too fast from the pain, and every few steps he stopped and let out a cry.

"Don't worry," the doctor told him, "I'm gonna make you all better, okay?" He nodded, then looked up briefly as the doctor patted a operating table surrounded by medicine bottles and one syringe. *The virus.* I gasped and tried to close my eyes, but for some reason I couldn't. He was forcing me to watch. I watched in horror as the man held up the familiar green substance and tapped on it to get the bubbles out. When the boy saw, his eyes widened in fear, and he jumped down only to hunch over on the ground.

"No, I don't want..." He stopped and clutched his stomach again. "I'm scared." The doctor patted the operating table again and smiled reassuringly at him.

"This will make you all better, I promise." His smile was a lot less jarring when he was alive. He was almost convincing me, but I knew better. I watched as the little boy scaled the table again and balled his hands into fists.

"I'm brave," he said as he pinched his eyes shut and lifted his sleeve. Those were his last words. Then, almost as sickeningly quick as he convinced him, he took his life. I watched as the shock from the virus contorted his face just like the man in Juros, and after a few seconds his body began to change. I realized then that, just like the doctors who died due to the little girl, he died due to the little boy. Although it felt wrong, I got some satisfaction in that. Then the image switched again, and again, and again. He made so many people suffer, and each time he lied to them as if their lives meant nothing. The only difference with me was I knew the truth, but I couldn't fight him. He had full control of me and could make me suffer if he chose to. I was his puppet, and I needed to know why.

"Why are you doing this? Why is my father so important to you? And why do you need me?" I looked at him, but my eyes snapped away for a brief moment when the white room reappeared.

"Because the Beacon family is an important asset in destroying this messed-up world, and you've got one wrapped around your little finger. Hell, make that two. You've even got his mom on your side. And as for your father, he can be immune just like you. All he needs is the cure, and *boom*, immunity. Another perfect little soldier. Time to wake him again, and just in time too. Your time's up." I arched my head back up to see the timer hit zero, and then I realized I was falling. I screamed as the ground seemed to get farther away the closer I got to it, then I hit the puddle of tears. It seemed to stick to me just like the infected blood in the morgue. I flailed around and eventually sucked in water as I realized I couldn't surface. I was still wrapped in a strait-jacket. The water seeped into my lungs, and after kicking my feet in a last-ditch effort to get air, I woke up with a loud gasp. Oliver was still lying beneath me, but he didn't hear me. I sobbed and pressed my face into his side. That's when I realized I had to go. Oliver would never understand, but I would have to do this on my own.

Slowly, I peeled myself away from him, gave him one last kiss on the cheek, and threw on my clothes and boots as fast as I could. Once I was dressed, I ran without looking back. I had no idea how much time passed in the real world as I was sleeping, but I could see all the other soldiers were curled up in their beds and Simon was guarding the exit. Luckily, there was a small emergency exit door on my side of the building with no one there. There was no alarm, so I slid it open as quietly as I could, and the moment I was able to squeeze my body through the crack, I ran off into the night. I had to go back around the front, but once Beacon and the infirmary came into view, I began plotting how I was going to do this. Not only did I have to steal the cure, but I also had to get to Dad and inject him without getting myself killed or caught.

"How am I going to do this?" I mumbled to myself, wiping my hand down my face. Eventually, I got the courage to sneak over to the infirmary. The grass made the bottom of my pants wet with dew, and I felt a chill. It was a bit of a colder night, and seeing as it was only a few days before Thanksgiving, I knew winter was getting close. I couldn't help but wonder what they were going to do with the infected for three whole months until spring rolled around. I wasn't sure what to think, but I could only imagine the strings they'd pull to keep infecting people. *I wish I could worry about normal things;* I thought as I hugged my arms around myself.

I almost got there when I saw a group of guards pacing back and forth by the doors. I knew it wasn't going to be easy, but I was hoping I could sneak in unnoticed. I hid behind a riding mower in the field and watched them to try and get their pattern down. Unfortunately for me, the door seemed to be constantly guarded. There were ten guards in total and, like a tag team, they would reach each other and then turn back around. I couldn't help but wonder if Polly made them watch over it. She was a pain, but she definitely wasn't the worst "villain" I'd encountered. If I had to rank them in order, it would probably be the doctor first, Simon second, and Polly and Mom tied for third. I could only imagine them all as a unit. That would be terrifying.

I needed a distraction. I knew I had to get creative to draw them all out, so I decided to try and hot-wire the mower. There were no keys, so I had to use the little bit of knowledge I got from Dad to tear it apart. There was a can of Pepsi laying there, so I crushed it beneath my boot to help me since I didn't have a screwdriver. I ripped the ignition panel off where the key goes in and examined all the wires. There were three. They were wrapped in a thick black tubing almost like a straw, but I was able to tear it off toward the front where it was starting to wear away. Once the wires were exposed, I was able to use two of the wires, a red and a blue one, and the ring of the can to start it. When the engine roared to life, all ten of them stopped in their tracks. There was silence for a brief moment, but then I heard someone say over the radio, "Who started that?" I stayed ducked down behind it, then realized I could use it to my advantage that they didn't see me yet. I'll convince them they saw a ghost. I picked up the closest rock I could find, and after shifting the gear by holding down the brake, I put the rock on the pedal and bolted away. It took off, and they were so busy watching it that they missed me. I ran and hid by the barracks and heard someone in the distance yell, "Ghost!" I couldn't help but burst out laughing as all ten, ran screaming away from the field. I won, and it honestly felt so good.

Finally, I made it to the infirmary and saw a couple beds were occupied. A few soldiers were sleeping there, but they didn't seem injured. Curiosity got the better of me, so I ended up checking their charts.

"No way, they're infecting soldiers now?" I could see by the notes on all their charts that they were testing the cure and the infection, and that Polly had signed off on it. The test was scheduled for the next day, so I knew I had to act. They were all asleep, probably with a sedative, because when I shook them, they didn't wake up. "I'm not letting them get away with this, hear that, Dr. Junip?" I shouted into the air, but no response came. *Don't know why I expected anything different. So far; he's only shown himself in my dreams. Get it together.* I started by picking up the soldier closest to me. There was a doctor lady at the desk, but she had her head down, so I was able to pass by her without much fuss. I wasn't exactly the strongest person, so I had to toss them up every few feet to get a better grip. After a lot of struggling, I walked them over to the closest supply closet and laid them down one by one until all four were inside, then gently closed the door. I knew they would probably be confused when they woke up, but at least I was able to give them a fighting chance. If the cure didn't work, they would all be goners.

Once I finished with them, I tiptoed toward the white tarp at the other end of the building. I wasn't sure what was behind it, but I didn't have to let fear consume me. I pulled it aside and saw rows and rows of locked rolling carts filled with syringes containing a blue liquid. *There's so many of them,* I thought, seeing how full the back of the building was. They all had tape on them with a handwritten note that said, *the cure.* I tried to open one of the drawers, but it didn't budge. Just like the carts inside Beacon, I needed an ID card, and I lost Polly's a long time ago. I groaned and began to pace back and forth until I remembered the lady at the desk. If she had a badge, all I would have to do was swipe it without her looking and I'd be just fine. Cautiously, I went back to the doorway and peered out. No one was there. I let out a sigh of relief and jogged over to her. I looked all over her desk, but I got momentarily distracted when I saw an application for Beacon. There were so many disclaimer messages that I couldn't understand why anyone would want to come here. I flipped through it, and that's when I realized the thing that drew in so many people: it was a non-profit hospital. They were drawing in poor families who couldn't afford to go anywhere else. Absolutely sickening. I folded the application up and snuck another look at the lady. She was still there fast asleep, or so I thought.

I pushed the clipboards with applications on them aside, I peeked behind the computer, I moved the keyboard aside, but it seemed to be nowhere. Then I realized it was probably still pinned to her. With a deep breath, I gently grabbed the lady's shoulder, and turned her over. The moment I saw her face, I screamed. Her eye was dripping down her cheek like it was made of candle wax, and all over her arms, I could see black veins. She got infected, and they shot her. There was no respect for the dead. They didn't care. To them, she was just another casualty, but I started to cry. Somewhere she had a family that was probably waiting for her to come home, but she never would again. *Did they inject her?* I decided to check her over and eventually found the ID card in my search. Her name was Evelyn Drummon. I made a mental note of it, and went back to check her again, but there didn't seem to be any sign of where they stuck her. Then I wondered, *what if the bullet had the infection in it?* I put my hand over my mouth to stop myself from gagging as I moved her head again, and just like I thought, her forehead was extended with what looked like a mushy black mass, and even worse, it was starting to twitch.

"Nope," I said, trying to resist the urge to gag again. I dropped her back down as gently as I could and went to get the cure. I picked one up out of a cart and was about to inject myself with it when I got a massive headache.

No! Don't you dare! I heard a voice mutter in my head. It was the doctor.

"This is really real?" I asked aloud.

He responded with, *yes, now put that away. That's for your dad, not you.* I felt my arm grow weak as if I had just tried lifting a thousand-pound weight, and nearly dropped the syringe. He was pulling the strings again, and I had no choice but to obey. I pulled the needle out and put the vial in my pocket. Now all I had to do was get to the eighth floor and get Dad's cell open. *Beacon...here I come.*

Chapter Twenty-One: Facing Beacon Alone

Usually there would be soldiers waiting at the doors of Beacon, but my distraction earlier seemed to kill two birds with one stone. I was able to sneak inside without anyone seeing me. Since the training field was toward the back door, I had to reorient myself as I walked through. I walked down the halls, and ducked inside a doorway every time I heard the smallest noise. I couldn't risk being caught here, there was too much at stake. Eventually, I reached the elevators again, but when I looked up at the numbered floor lights and saw them going up and down, I realized the stairs would probably be the best bet.

The first few flights felt easy, but then a doctor came out with one of the patients and I was forced to hide on the steps right below them. I could hear her talking about chronic migraines, and how it took away her time with her babies. Two boys, one college age and one in middle school, and one girl. She told the doctor about a ball game she went to about a week back with her youngest son, and how she had to leave right as he hit a home run. It broke her heart. I waited to hear the doctor respond and heard him talk about a treatment plan with a new vaccine. Instantly I knew what he was talking about, and before I could even think of what to do, my legs moved on their own.

I knew it was Junip, and wondered if maybe he was punishing me. *This is too far*, I thought, hoping he could hear my panicked thoughts as both of them turned to look at me.

"Excuse me, who are you? This area is for patients and employees only. Visitors—"

"I'm a patient!" I tried to clamp my hand over my mouth as Junip forced me to speak, but then I realized the doctor saw my veins. His eyes widened, and he turned back to the woman with a face that said, *please go away*. The doctor was trying to make my job harder, and I didn't understand why. He needed me to get Dad back, right?

"I'm sorry, miss, would you mind if I speak with her for a moment. I think she's one of our terminal patients."

"Oh, yes, of course. I'll go back to the waiting room." The woman quickly walked away, making me feel madly uncomfortable. I was hoping she would save me from him.

"You! Come with me, we need to get a wristband on you right away." He reached his hand out to grab my wrist, but I yanked away and stumbled back.

"No way," I snapped, as my eyes darted to the stairs leading up. I had four more floors between me and Dad, and if I got caught before then, I would probably become another subject zero again. I tried to shove my way past him, but he grabbed me and dangled me over the stairway balcony.

"I won't let you ruin our work, you monster. You're going to die soon enough anyway, come with me or I'll drop you." I struggled against his strong grip, and eventually I realized I only had one option. I bit him. The man yelped in pain, and almost made me stumble over the edge. Luckily, the doctor seemed to care enough to keep me alive, because he quickly made me move my feet and regain my footing. I ran as fast as I could, hit with a sudden rush of adrenaline, up the next four flights, and pushed open the door to the hallway. Finally, things started to look familiar again, but some of the cells that were empty before were now filled. It looked like the whole floor was, including my number 851. I sighed with relief when I saw that, and then I went to Dad's cell, 850.

His infected form had gotten a lot bigger since I last saw him, and he took up two rooms now. His body was transformed into a monster like the crawlers, but he had a lot more to him. He had eight arms and legs like a creepy flesh spider, a face full of oval-shaped eyes, a mouth big enough to eat me whole, and a tail so bony I was sure it could cut me. *Is this how that monster in the storage building came to be? The giant fleshy one has to be the latest form,* I thought as I looked him over. At first he didn't seem to notice me, but as I examined him, I saw one of his eyes turn black and the rest follow. He started to growl, so I put my hand out as if to tell him it was me. It seemed to work at first, but then he swiped one of his arms at the glass, making me jump.

"How am I going to cure you, Dad? I'm afraid you'll kill me."

I paced back and forth until I heard a voice yell, "Don't move!" I looked up to see a younger woman doctor, maybe in her late twenties, walking toward me with a tranq gun, until she noticed I was in an army uniform.

"Are you part of the response team?" Slowly, she walked toward me, but my mouth wouldn't open. *Junip, please, not now,* I pleaded in my head, but still my tongue stayed glued to the roof of my mouth as if it was covered in glue. "Answer me! I asked you if you are part of the response team." I tried to nod my head instead this time, but he wouldn't let me. *Why are you doing this?* I said in my head, and this time I got an answer.

"Do as I tell you to from now on or else. No more back-talk."

Okay, please just let me respond before she shoots me.

"Good girl." His words made me cringe, but finally, I was able to speak. I blurted out a yes and saw her stop probably just in time.

"Why didn't you say that before?" she asked, narrowing her eyes at me. "And who are you?"

"My name is Mia, miss. Mia Andrews. If you ask Simon Dreer, I'm sure he'll vouch for me." I wasn't sure what I'd tell Simon when he asked me for an explanation, but since I didn't have an actual ID card on me with my name on it to save me, I had to tell the truth.

"Oh, you know Simon? That guy scares the hell out of me. I'll let you pass for now, but don't do anything stupid. If you see any of those...*things* escape, report it as a containment breach to Polly. She's down the hall in office room 899, got it?"

"Yes, ma'am." I nodded and felt instantly better when she lowered the gun and walked away. It was scary how much power the doctor had. He could make me do whatever he wanted, and knowing how he felt about Oliver, I was worried he would try to use me to lock him back up again. To him, he was nothing more than a vessel for the infection, but to me, he was my future. I had to be very careful with what I did next.

I turned back to Dad again, and I thought of something. Luckily the doctor didn't leave the floor yet. She was watching me from down the hall with her back against the wall. If I could get her gun, I could shoot Dad with it and then inject him with the cure. *Here goes nothing.*

"Um... Miss? I know this is going to sound VERY weird, but I need to use your tranq gun." I held out my hands, but she seemed unsure.

"For what? I can't just give this out, ya know." She lifted it into the air, then looked back at me.

"I have a mission I have to complete with that infected." I pointed at Dad and saw her take a step back. "Please, Dr..." I looked at her badge, and saw her last name was Junip, just like the one possessing me. "Dr. Junip, I know how this sounds, but I'm going to try and cure him."

"Him? I can't let you risk the safety of the staff playing around with the infected. Doesn't matter who you are. I'm telling—" She turned around, but Junip took me over again and made me grab the back of her shirt.

"Let the girl do her job." The man's voice escaped my lips, making me feel shocked. *How much power did he really have?*

"Holy hell, Dad?" She reached forward but hesitated about an inch from me. "How did you do that?"

"I possessed her, now give her the damn tranq." I felt as if I was in the passenger seat of a car as she handed me the gun. Then I got control of my body back. She stared at me in complete shock, and even as I went down the hall, she followed me. She watched as I took a deep breath, swiped the badge, and stepped back as the door opened. Once Dad started to come toward me, I shot him with the tranq, and pulled the cure vial out of my pants pocket.

"Wait, where did you get that? That's top secret!" Ignoring her, I put the needle back in, pushed on the top a bit to get the bubbles out, and stabbed it into one of Dad's arms. At first nothing happened, and I wondered if it was too late, but then, his infected body started to melt away. Me and the doctor jumped as the floor filled with a black goopy liquid much like the morgue, and eventually, as we sheltered our noses, we saw Dad's body starting to emerge again. As if no time had passed at all, he was still wearing the same bowling shirt from when I lost him. It made me feel emotional. "Whoa, who is that man?" the doctor asked, examining him from afar.

"My dad," I replied plainly as I stepped through the goop to check on him. I put my hand on his neck, and nearly jumped for joy when I felt his heartbeat against my finger. *Yes, thank you,* I said in my head, and heard nothing but a dry scoff as I tried to pick him up. *Right, we're just soldiers.* The doctor helped me carry him out and set him down on a dry patch of the floor. Of course, I was happy, but there was so much that Dad missed in the past year or so. So much I would have to fill him in on, and I would have to convince him to be a soldier with us. I knew it would be hard for him. He always was a kind person, but just like me, he would have to give in.

"This is crazy. I didn't even know they approved that cure yet."

"I know. I have to get him down to the barracks outside without anyone here noticing, is there any way to do that?" She took a deep breath and pointed to the window at the end of the hall. "Too high, remember?" I responded instantly, but she chuckled and ran toward it. When we got there, she cranked a lever on the side of the window frame, and revealed a fire escape that went straight down to the ground. "This is perfect, you're amazing." I hugged her, and then I remembered how heavy Dad was.

"Can you get him on your own?"

"Not exactly," I responded nervously. To my relief, she was really kind, and helped me get him all the way down to the first floor. When we got down there, she told me she was too scared to face Simon and that she had to leave me on my own again. I knew it would be hard to get him to the barracks alone, but I nodded anyway and walked on. So far on my journey, I had met so many kind people. Oliver, Joque, Gabby, the man from Greenburrow, her, the little girl, and many others. It felt like I was being guided forward. The only problem now was how I would deal with the four villains. I vowed then that I'd find a way to take them down, and just be plain old Mia again. I'd take my friends and Dad with me when I did...but it wasn't the time to worry about that.

I put my hands under Dad's arms and slowly dragged him toward the barracks. The guards were back in their positions, and despite my want to avoid them, I knew either way I was going to get caught, so I pushed past them. As I pulled Dad along, his shoes made a path behind us, digging themselves into the dirt and making it harder for me to continue. I got pretty close when out of the corner of my eye, I saw Simon come running out with a flashlight in one hand and Oliver's shirt collar in the other.

"Mia, there you are." At first, he noticed me and came running up, dragging Oliver behind him, but then he noticed Dad. "Who the heck is that? What did you do?" he shouted at me in an accusatory tone, making me feel nervous.

"This is my dad. I was able to...save him." Both of them looked at Dad, shocked, and then back at me. They knew I stole the cure, and I had no way to defend myself from that. "I know how this looks, but—" Simon pulled out a pistol and stopped me mid-sentence.

"What. Did. You. do?" he asked, glaring at me. He was always intimidating, even from the start, but right then, as he practically growled his words at me, he made me want to shrink down and hide.

"I didn't have a choice!" I yelled, as my heart began to hammer in my chest. "I was forced to cure him, but look, he's okay now. Isn't that great? The cure works!" I looked from the two of them, and saw Oliver try to force a smile before his eyes locked on Simon. He knew what I did was going to have consequences. I looked back and stared intently at Simon as he pinched the bridge of his nose and balled his hands into fists. He was pissed.

"I'm going to give you five seconds to explain what you mean by 'forced' before I shoot your boy right between his eyes, and it better be good, because I am fed up with you and your crap!" I felt my heart drop to my stomach as he grabbed Oliver and forced him to his knees right in front of me. I didn't know what to say. My mouth froze and I opened and closed it a few times, trying to get the words out. If I told him the truth, I was certain he wouldn't believe me and he'd kill Oliver, but I couldn't think of a lie fast enough. I swallowed hard and tapped on my chest with trembling fingers.

"When I was in Juros," I said slowly, as I inched toward him, "I got infected again, but it wasn't just that. Something...no, someone came along with it." Both looked at me confused, so I continued. "I'm possessed, and the ghost that has me wants me to bring Dad back to join the response team for some reason." When I stopped talking, I saw Oliver glance up at Simon from the ground. I knew he would believe me, but Simon was a wild card. I watched as Simon took a breath and narrowed his eyes, but he didn't speak. Oliver had his hands on the back of his head like he was being arrested, and I could just barely see from where I was standing that he was trembling. I waited an agonizing amount of time before Simon grabbed Oliver's arm and pulled him to his feet, finally ending our standoff.

"Fine, I'll play along for now, Mia, but your mother won't hear a word of this. He is dead in her mind, and if I have anything to say about it, it'll remain that way, got it?"

"Yes, sir," I said, blowing out a breath of air. He pushed Oliver toward me, and I had to let Dad go for a second to stop him from hitting the ground.

"Good, help the girl get him inside, Oliver, and when you're done, both of you are going to come have a word with me. Immediately." I nodded and followed him with my eyes until he was finally out of view.

"Are you okay?" Oliver asked, breaking the silence between us.

"Mostly," I replied, looking back at Dad lying in the grass. "I was so happy when I was able to cure him, but I'm worried this created more trouble for us." Oliver sighed and held out his hand for me to take it. I did, and smiled warmly as he ran his thumb across the back of my hand.

"It probably will, but that's okay. There's so much I want to tell him, like how I'm marrying his daughter for starters." He widened his eyes, causing me to chuckle. "We'll just have to be careful. As for this ghost, is it still there?" I opened my mouth to speak, but before I could, the doctor beat me to it.

"Yes, I'm still here," he replied, making Oliver stumble back. He put his palm on the ground, and sat down with his other hand out as if I was holding a weapon.

"Holy crap," he muttered, before his face turned to a stern expression. "What do you want with her? Leave her alone!"

"Mia is the perfect vessel, for now anyway. I'll be staying right here, but don't worry, boy, as long as she does as I tell her to, I'll let her keep the reins." He laughed wickedly before fading away again and allowing me to regain control.

"I'm back," I said, glancing from him to the ground. I could only imagine what he was thinking. One second we were safe with each other, and the next we were being forced around by two creeps. It was all too overwhelming.

"This is crazy," Oliver said, offering me his hand. I took it, and stood up again. I hadn't even noticed that I fell, but somehow, between the doctor taking control and me coming back, I had hit the ground.

"I know it is, but I can't fight him." I shrugged nervously, and gestured back to Dad. "Can you help me get him inside, please?" He nodded, and together we walked Dad inside to the barracks. I could hear him snoring briefly as we walked and thought back to the times Mom used to make fun of him for talking in his sleep. She always used to say he was a goof, and that she would sometimes listen to him as if he was telling a story. It almost felt nostalgic, but I knew, deep down, I'd never have that back again. It was too late for that.

Mom had a wicked heart, and I could only imagine what Dad would say when he found out what she'd been doing. Then I thought about it some more. *Simon said they were already divorced, is it possible Dad knew this whole time how evil Mom really was?* Part of me wanted to say no. Dad was always the peace keeper of the family, but would he really keep something this big? I shook my head, and eventually we set Dad down on one of the leftover beds.

"Ready to face Simon?" Oliver asked once we backed away from him.

"Not really," I responded, feeling heat rise up in my face, "but I don't think we have a choice." He nodded, and took my hand as we did the walk of shame to Simon at the other end of the barracks. Only a few people were up, but I felt like I could feel their eyes staring into my soul. It felt like being hit with icy daggers from every direction. I loved every second of being with Oliver earlier that night, but I really wished we paid more attention to the time. I walked on with my heart in my throat and eventually sat down in front of Simon waiting for us by the door. He was about to give us the lecture of a lifetime, but the doctor had other plans: Make a fool out of Oliver.

Chapter Twenty-Two: Making a Fool Out of Love

My legs bounced up and down nervously as we sat down in plastic lawn chairs to talk to Simon. He had this annoyed look plastered across his face, like we were the cashiers who got his order wrong at his local coffee shop. It wasn't nearly as intimidating as the look he showed us outside, but it still gave me the creeps. I knew he hated us, and despite him being in a relationship with my mom, he would probably celebrate if we died during a mission. Even if Mom hated him for it, if it happened by his own hands, I was sure he'd laugh. He was that psychotic. He eyed us both, making us shrink down in the chairs. If Oliver hadn't been there with me, I probably would have cried. Instead, I gripped the armrest like it was the only thing keeping me grounded. I hated every second of his little stare down, but none of us wanted to speak up first, so I finally broke the ice.

"I know you're going to lecture us, so can we please get it over with?" He turned his head my way, and leaned back in his chair until he was balancing on the back two legs.

"Alright, let's start with this. Where were you two? And what were you doing?" he asked before he slammed the chair down with a loud *bang.*

"We were—" I went to try and give him an excuse, but then I heard Oliver chuckle next to me. It sounded weirdly deep, as if his voice aged twenty years.

"None of your business," he said, tilting his head to the side. "You may have forced us to be here, but we don't have to answer to you." My eyes widened as Oliver crossed his arms over his chest and shot him an equally uncomfortable glare back. *Please, no.* I tried to squeeze his hand to get him to stop, but he ignored it.

"You listen here, you're only alive because I made a deal with Mia, but if you want to act like a fool, I'll—"

"You'll what? Kill me?" I watched the whole thing through my fingers as they faced off. My whole body felt like jelly, and I almost slid down the chair from pure shock. *Oliver, what are you doing?*

"Oliver, it's okay. We messed up, but we won't do it again. I'm so sorry, Simon." I stepped in between them, hoping to cut the thickening tension, but Oliver used his hands to push me aside. I looked back at him with my mouth open, until I saw his eyes glimmer. This wasn't my Oliver; the doctor possessed him.

"I'm not sorry. You know deep down as a subject zero I held more value than you'll ever amount to. You may be a general or sergeant," he said, using air quotes, "but in the end, you're just grasping at straws that aren't there. I can infect hundreds, you can't infect one without help!" I gasped as Oliver walked over and picked up a vase.

"Doctor Junip, please don't!" I tried to get to him, but before I could, he tilted his arm back like a baseball player and pitched it across the room, causing it to shatter at Simon's feet. I let out a little shriek as glass, some wilted daisies, and water flew my way, but I got pretty lucky. For a moment, he seemed to show concern for me, then the doctor reclaimed him again.

"Is that so? Why don't we take you back there then? You'll be right at home with the other infected." I watched as the soldiers came and formed a circle around us. They were concerned, and they had every right to be. It was starting to get violent.

"No, please, Simon. This isn't him, it's—" I tried to explain, but as I stepped back his way, Simon grabbed a beer bottle and flung it back at Oliver, narrowly missing me.

"He's a useless little brat! I should have known better than to give HIM another chance. It's time he goes back with his family where he belongs." He pulled out his gun, and instantly parted the crowd. The barrel seemed to be pointed directly at Oliver's face, and I knew if he succeeded it would be a killing blow.

"Hold her back," Simon growled. A moment later, two soldiers grabbed me by my arms and made me watch. I made my legs go limp to try and slip out from under them, but they pulled me right back up again. He pulled the trigger, mercilessly, and my fight or flight instantly kicked in. I screamed and covered my face with trembling hands, but when I opened them again, I realized it was a tranq gun. Oliver's body hit the floor, and I stared in pure disbelief as a dark cloud left him and came straight for me. It hit my lower legs and made me feel weightless.

"Simon! That was the doctor, please listen to me!" I pulled on my arms again, but they didn't let me go. The soldiers were talking so loud that he didn't hear me either.

"You'll be better off without him, Mia. He makes you weak." He picked Oliver's limp body up off the floor and carried him away as I screamed. No matter how hard I tried, they didn't listen. Joque and Gabby tried to help me by grabbing my captors, but the two soldiers held onto me like it was their life mission.

"No!" I began to sob, and my knees gave way as they held me. They kept me up and held onto me until Simon came back an hour later with a single sheet of paper in his hands. I looked up at him, but when I didn't see Oliver, I knew what he'd done.

"Let her go," he told them, waving his hands to get them to part. "Back to your beds, all of you!" When they released me, my knees hit the floor with such force, it made me shudder with pain. I sobbed and tried to breathe, but the air felt thick. I could hear the doctor laugh in the back of my head, and had to fight the anger and hatred from making me hurt myself to cause him pain. *Did I really fight all this time just to lose him to the doctor?*

"You won't be seeing him again. Time to let go." Simon cut through my thoughts, and held out the paper. It was Oliver's record, stating that he was reinstated as a patient of Beacon.

"You wanted this," I said with quivering lips, "you hated him, and didn't stop to think for even a second that that wasn't him." I looked up at him and balled my hands against the hardwood floor. "The doctor made him do this!" Finally he heard me, but no matter how much I wanted him to march back there, I knew he wouldn't. This was his opportunity to get rid of Oliver, and I knew, deep down, he wouldn't pass on it.

"Too bad," he responded, "that boy was a ticking time bomb, and you know it. It's time he left so I can shape you into the soldier I need." He grabbed me by my shoulders, so I shoved him back.

"I gave up a whole city for him!" I yelled, before I threw a glass shard at him, hoping it would stick. It didn't.

"Move. On." He narrowed his eyes, and pointed to my empty bed. "Go to bed, Mia, it's over." I shook my head and stared at him as my whole body grew hot with anger and a want for revenge.

"He's my fiancé. My future! I will not 'move on,' I'm going to get him. Now!" I started to walk away when I heard a pop sound and felt a sharp pain in the back of my neck.

"We'll talk again when you wake up. Maybe then you'll have a level head." My legs gave out, and the darkness crept in. It was time to see the doctor again, and I could only imagine what he would have in store for me.

I "woke up" in an empty hospital room this time. There was no bed, no supplies, no window, just a ceiling light that had an abnormal amount of flies swarming around it. I gulped and tiptoed into the hall. I was wearing the flower-covered hospital gown again, but there was a badge pinned to it this time with my name on it. The doctor always seemed to have something up his sleeve, so I knew better than to let my guard down as I walked the barren-looking halls. It was eerily quiet, I was almost certain I could hear my own heartbeat. As I walked on, I started to hear the sound of a ticking clock and felt uneasy. I kept peeking in doors until finally I saw him standing in a room on his own. I peered through the tiny hallway window until his eyes turned and locked on mine. I gasped and tried to hide against the wall, but then I heard his voice.

"There's no use trying to hide, Mia. I know where you are at all times, I'm in your head, remember? Now come in." I felt really uneasy, but I listened, hoping he would show me some mercy. When I walked past the doorway, it slammed shut behind me, making me jump.

"Am I in trouble?" I asked him, as I fiddled with my hair. I tried to peek around him, but he wouldn't let me see what he was standing over. Then he turned back my way, and I saw an empty bed. *What do you have in store for me?*

"No, I'm giving you the luxury of choice."

"Choice? What choice?" I asked him, as I stood on my tiptoes to see the bed. It seemed like an ordinary hospital bed. There were no tools or IV bags, just a bed and one empty rolling cart.

"It's simple really, decide what life you want. I can make it happen, I'll give you three options. All you have to do is choose." I tilted my head, and felt my heartbeat pick up when he gestured to the bed. "Go on." Slowly, I walked toward it, but I kept my eyes on him the whole time. I was already hurting from losing Oliver, I didn't need more heartache. When I sat down, a whole bunch of surgical equipment appeared by me, making me shudder. "Let's get started." He picked up a scalpel, and I watched his every move as he took it and walked toward the wall. He peeked at me over his shoulder, then cut through the wall like it was butter. It looked like the black mass from my back yard, but then he waved his hands in front of it. I saw a picture of Dad, Gabby, and Joque all sitting near each other in the barracks.

"Option one," he said, eyeing me. Then he walked back over to the table and grabbed a blow torch. He lit the edge of the scalpel until it was so hot it turned bright red like an apple, and he used it to cut through the glass window. The sound made me cover my ears as it screeched. It reminded me of those underwater diver videos, where people go into wreckages and have to cut through to get it open. He cut in a round circle, until he got all the way around to where he started and caused the glass to fall. Instead of seeing the clouds, I gasped when I saw Jill sitting at her table crying.

"Is she okay? What did you do?" I stood up, but he gently shoved my shoulders back down into the chair.

"Option two," he said, ignoring me. Then he went over to the wall on my right, and used a hammer this time. He blasted right through the wall, revealing another hospital room, this time with Oliver in it. He was crying too, and I could see he had an IV in his arm and a tube in his nose. He was strapped down to the bed, and there was a group of doctors standing over him.

"Let me go, you monsters!" he yelled, yanking on his straps. They just stared down at him as if they were looking at a zoo animal, and eventually left him there screaming as the blood drained from his arm.

"And option three. Take your pick, but just so you know, once you choose there's no going back. I'll be moving on from you. I don't need you anymore. One of these images is your future. So what'll it be?" I stared at him dumbfounded, and whipped my head around, looking at the three of them.

"How can you make me choose between them? I can't—"

"You can. I saw you crying over Oliver, so why don't you go to him? You'll escape and run far away from this evil place. He's your fiancé, your love, so it should be an easy choice, right? Or you can choose your dad, your friends, and the army. Your father just woke up, don't you want to tell him everything and have him back again? And be with the people who literally risked their safety for you? Or...you can have Jill. She's the mom you need, and a nice safe future. No zombies, no Oliver and his issues, and no doctor. Why not choose her?" I opened and closed my mouth, causing him to laugh. "You and I both know you can't have all three. So, choose."

"Why? Why can't I have all of them? I love them! I choose all of them!"

The doctor shook his head, and gestured again to the three pictures. "The longer you wait, the more likely the others are going to disappear." I gulped and stood up. If I really had to choose, I knew I had to be quick. I glanced at the three choices, and saw a black liquid beginning to pool beneath them. My time was running out.

"Why are you doing this? Are you going to make me forget them?" The doctor's lips curved up, and I felt an icy feeling travel up my spine.

"Why don't you find out?" The liquid began to run into the center of the room, and eventually hit my shoes. It felt goopy, almost like a thick sludge. I did one final double-take of the room. Oliver was suffering again, and my dad had no idea what he was getting himself into. I knew those were my two choices, so I told him that. I loved Jill and her kindness, but I wasn't with her long enough to pick her.

"How am I supposed to choose between Oliver and my dad?" I sighed and paced back and forth. Jill's picture collapsed into the puddle on the floor already, but theirs were getting smaller by the second. He didn't reply, instead he gestured up to a timer on the ceiling that was ticking away. I had sixty seconds to choose my future. *I hate this.* I began to chew on my hair as the seconds ticked away.

Oliver became my everything after I lost Dad. He went through Beacon with me and helped me escape. He infected himself when he saw I got reinfected, he saved me from the water bank and from the park ranger in Hunter's Villa. He even got me a ring, even though he really didn't have to. He was there for me when no one else was, and he made me feel happy.

Dad, on the other hand, raised me to be the woman I am. He raised me to be a hero, to fight until I couldn't fight anymore. He was there for me whenever I needed help as a kid, and he was my protector. He looked after me when Mom couldn't, and he encouraged me to do good things with my life. He didn't shut me down when I wanted to explore Beacon. He made it his mission to make me happy, even if it cost him his life. Not to mention he was the only family I had left. I needed him, but I also needed Oliver.

Finally, with ten seconds left to spare, I made my decision. But I knew it was going to hurt.

Chapter Twenty-Three: Back to Square One

"I choose...my dad. H-he just woke up; I can't leave him." Slowly, I walked over to Dad's picture and saw Oliver's melting away at my feet. *I'll be okay as long as I have you.* His sweet words replayed over and over in my head. I started to cry, but I stepped through the wall and woke up in my bed with Dad shaking my shoulders. It was strange, I could still remember both Oliver and Jill. *I really hope he doesn't do anything bad to them.* I swallowed hard and sat up to rub my eyes.

"Thank goodness you're alright, kid. I was getting worried," Dad said as I came to. When I saw him, I jumped up and gave him a hug. I had missed him so much. He held me tightly and put his hand on the back of my head. "I heard you saved me. You've grown up a lot since I've last seen you, huh?" I nodded and chuckled as tears threatened to fall from my eyes.

"I'm so happy you're back." I smiled up at him, and saw him wipe away a tear.

"Me too, kid," he replied, then he seemed to notice the ring on my finger and I saw his eyes widen. "Whoa, is little Mia engaged?" he asked, causing me to take in a shaky breath.

"Yeah, I'm engaged to Oliver, Dad," I replied, clutching the edge of the bed until my knuckles turned white. "But I think he's in trouble. They trapped him in Beacon again, and I don't know if I'll ever get back to him." I looked down at the hardwood floor beneath my bed, and then I felt two pairs of arms surround me. It was Joque and Gabby.

"Don't worry, Mia, we'll get him back," Joque told me and patted his shoulder. I chuckled and laid my head down on it with a nod.

"Yeah, we'll get your boy back," Gabby said, pulling both of us in for a group hug. I looked up to see Dad smiling warmly when we separated. There was so much he didn't know, but I knew I had to start somewhere.

"I'm guessing you have a lot of questions."

"Oh yeah, I feel like I missed a whole bunch of important details. Mind filling me in?" I nodded and began to tell him everything. I started from the moment me and Oliver ran out of the basement, to me getting infected and finding out I was immune, and meeting Polly, to us going to his truck, and eventually told him the horrifying details of our hometown, Juros. Then everything that led up to this point. The whole time, Gabby and Joque held me while I spoke, and anytime I struggled to speak up, they'd squeeze my hand to reassure me they were there. Never once did he tell me he didn't believe me. He listened and thought about every word.

When I finished and told him about what the doctor did, he shuffled his hand through his thin gray hair and sighed.

"Oh, Mia. I want you to be happy, kid. I'm so happy you chose me, but you didn't have to do that. I would have managed."

"I know, but I couldn't leave you. We're family. My only family now."

He sighed when I said that, and glanced down at the floor. "Your mother disappointed both of us. I can't believe the woman I married did something so...sickening. I'm so sorry, Mia."

"It's not your fault, Dad," I replied. "I've fought so hard just to get to this point, and I won't stop fighting until all of us are happy again. You, Me, Oliver, you two..." I nudged my friends, causing them to laugh. "No matter how long that takes."

"This time, you don't have to fight alone. You've got us now," Joque told me. I smiled, and saw Gabby and Dad nod too. It felt good knowing I wasn't alone anymore, and even better knowing the doctor was gone. Together we all walked outside. I had no idea where Oliver even was, but I was determined to find him and get him back. Right then though, we had Simon to worry about. I was worried how Dad was going to react to him. Especially since Simon seemed to be the exact opposite of him. Cruel, selfish, and sadistic, while Dad actually cared about people. It made me sick that he even had to meet Simon, but I couldn't stop it from happening. We walked out in the yard, and immediately saw him standing out there with a couple other soldiers. He wasn't looking at us at first, but when he did, he shot Dad an icy glare. He didn't move from his post, but he stood there watching Dad like he was going to do something crazy.

"Is that the 'Simon' character you told me about?" Dad asked, using air quotes. I nodded, and chuckled when he rolled his eyes. "What an idiot."

"Please try to be nice, Dad. I know that's going to be pretty hard, but he already hates me. There's no reason for him to hate both of us."

"Oh, he's going to love me," Dad said, before he scrunched up my hair and walked off in his direction. I tried to stop him, but he didn't listen. He marched right up to him and stood beside him like a parent at a school meet.

"So, you're the guy who separated my kids from each other," he said, nonchalantly. "Simon, right? I've heard a LOT about you, and I'm not impressed."

"Is that so?" Simon seethed, squeezing his pen so tight I was sure it was going to break in his hand. "I've heard a LOT about you too, and trust me, if you're going to act like your daughter does, we're going to have a big problem. I'm in charge here. Me. Not you, not her. Me. Get used to it."

I saw Dad nod, and I pulled him away before it got any worse. The last thing I needed was for Simon to hurt him or create an example out of him like that soldier.

"I can't believe we're stuck here. This was supposed to be a one-day trip. Now we're stuck under that idiot as soldiers?" I nodded, causing Dad to groan. "Not if I can help it." He told us he would be back later, and after warning him not to go too far because of Simon, he took off into the woods behind the barracks.

"What do you think he's going to do?" Gabby asked me, as we watched him walk away.

"Not sure, but he'll be back. I know he will." She nodded, and to kill time, we decided to join the soldiers on the training equipment. First I started by racing Gabby up the side of Beacon using the climbing equipment Simon hooked up. After I clipped myself in the harness, Simon pressed play on the timer, and we walked as fast as we could up the wall to the third-floor balcony. At first she was winning, but I was able to push myself to pass her after floor two. I almost got to the top when my right shoe hit a piece of moss and made me slip.

"You know the rules, Mia. Start again." I rolled my eyes and groaned, while Gabby stood on the balcony laughing as she watched me go for round two.

"That was a cute attempt, you know," she said, waving at me with a satisfied smile plastered across her smug face. After eight minutes and twenty-seven seconds, I finally joined her.

"Not good enough, either of you. Go again!" Of course, Simon took everything too seriously. There was no leisure time when it came to him, just work. Apparently, we were supposed to run up the side and get to the third floor in less than three minutes. We tried again, but still we couldn't beat the time he wanted us to. He gave up on us after time four, and moved on to another group of soldiers. After an hour of watching people scale the wall, he blew the whistle he had hanging around his neck and called all the soldiers to the field. Immediately I started to grow nervous. Dad still wasn't back yet, and I knew if I didn't go find him, it might get messy. Which meant I had to face Simon first.

Slowly, I pushed through the crowd, and eventually reached him. He looked like he was about to call attention, but I stopped him in his tracks.

"I need to go find my dad. You'll have to start without us," I told him as bravely as I could. I was scared of him, but it almost felt good being able to face him. Although, what happened next made me regret it.

"Why is he not here?"

"He went into the woods to...to get some air. Yeah, I'll go get him now," I stammered, hoping he would show me mercy. Instead, he yelled in my ear, making my whole body jump.

"Hurry up, soldier!" he yelled, making everyone turn and look at me. I blushed and nodded, with my eyes locked on the grass beneath us. The autumn leaves covered it like a warm, colored blanket and gave me something to keep my mind on: the holidays ahead.

"Yes, sir!" I yelled back. I saw Gabby and Joque look at me when I passed them, so I shrugged, hoping they would know where I was going. My nose began to drip as I ran past the barracks. The frigid wind seemed to swirl around me, and it wasn't any better knowing it was only forty degrees out. It wasn't winter yet, but it was getting closer day by day. The only good thing about the weather was that the infected were probably drawn to shelter by now. That meant no more missions for a while, but that also meant Simon was going to make us run in the snow. I was not excited for that.

I made my way through the woods, stepping over dead branches and leaves until I reached the stream, but there was no sign of him anywhere. I tried to look for footprints, but I couldn't see any. So I called out for him.

"Dad!" I yelled as I stepped up on a fallen tree. I stood on it, and used my hand as binoculars over my eyes. When I didn't see anything, I walked along it like it was a balancing beam and jumped off at the end. "Dad?" I called again, spooking some nearby birds in the area. Still, he didn't answer. I kept on walking until I heard a *bloop* sound, as if something was thrown into water.

"Hello?" I called again.

"Over here, kiddo." I blew out a sigh of relief and trudged through the leaves until I found him sitting on a log, throwing rocks into the stream.

"Hey, Simon is calling for us."

"He can wait. You deserve a minute away." He patted the log next to him, and although I felt worried, I sat down. "I miss being able to take you places like this."

"I know, I miss it too. Maybe...we can convince Simon to let us go fishing or something," I said, nudging his arm.

"You mean ice fishing?" he asked, causing me to laugh.

"Yeah, we can use his stone-cold heart to cut through the ice when it freezes over." I threw a rock into the water, and heard him bust out laughing next to me.

"Very funny, kid." He sighed and threw a thin rock across the water, making it skip three times. "How did we get into this mess?" he asked, wiping his hand down his face.

"I don't know, but some good came from it." I gestured to the ring again, and saw him shake his head.

"I knew I should have kept that boy away when I had the chance."

"Hey!" I yelled, and kicked some leaves at him. He laughed and accidentally leaned back. I tried to catch him, but I couldn't do it in time. He fell onto the ground beneath the log with an *ugh* and laid there staring up at the trees.

"I'm only kidding," he said through laughter. "Oliver seems like a good kid, from what I saw anyway, and if my little girl likes him, then...I guess I'll like him too." I smiled, and plopped down beside him, making the leaves jump up around me.

"Thanks, Dad."

"You're welcome." We sat there for another minute or two in silence before Dad groaned and sat up. "Let's not keep Simon waiting," he said in a mocking tone. I nodded with a smile, and eventually we got back together.

"What took you so damn long?" Simon asked angrily, with his arms crossed over his chest.

"None of your business," Dad snapped back as he came and stood at the front. Both Gabby and Joque jumped forward to distract Simon, but it was too late; he'd already upset him.

"What did you say, Private T. Andrews?" Suddenly he got in Dad's face, and I tried to intervene, but before I could, Dad snapped. I watched in pure terror as he pushed Simon backward and crossed his arms as he looked on in disbelief.

"I used to be a drill sergeant just like you, so I'm not scared of you and your bull. Don't speak to me or my daughter that way." He narrowed his eyes at Simon, and I began to shake when Simon started laughing maniacally. Then, before I could stop him, he punched Dad right in the face. He recoiled in pain, although I knew he wouldn't admit it out loud, then stood back up to face him while we watched on the edge of our seats. At first I thought it would end there. Simon called for attention and moved on, but Dad didn't let it go. He hit him again, ignoring his order, and this time it didn't stop.

"Dad, no!" I screamed when his hand connected with Simon's face. They hit back and forth, each one taking shots at the other until Simon tackled him into the ground. My friends and I tried to stop them, but they wouldn't listen to reason. Then the guards came running. They pulled Dad from him, and the moment they were pulled to their feet, he aimed his pistol at him.

"You stubborn mule," Simon said through deep breaths. They were both red in the face, and bleeding, Dad on his nose, Simon on his cheek and lips. He knelt over and breathed in and out. Finally, he seemed to catch his breath. He lifted the gun again and aimed it at Dad. "I'm going to lock you up. Just like that brat, Oliver."

"No, please." I tried to step in again, but Simon was seething with anger. It was scarier than anything I'd ever seen out of him.

"Don't," he growled through gritted teeth as he wiped blood off his lip.

"There's nothing good about you. You're a wicked man!" Dad yelled as he panted. Simon silenced him by pointing away from the group, making the guards drag him off. Dad was never a violent man, so I knew what happened right then was because of me. Because of the story I told him.

"I just got him back, you can't do this!" I pleaded with Simon, but he was too far gone.

"I'll slaughter you. Don't say another word." He pointed to the group, and although I wanted to say more, Joque pulled me away from him. That was the last time I saw him or Oliver for a few months. Simon took them both from me.

Chapter Twenty-Four: Spring

Winter was long and brutal. I thought the holidays would be nice, but instead it was a brutal reminder of what I couldn't have. For Thanksgiving, we ate the same old dried food, just like normal. A lot of soldiers were upset Simon didn't at least make an effort, but I knew better than to expect him to do something nice. There was no turkey or potatoes or yams, just beef stew or chicken pot pie in a bag. Then Christmas came around. No one was allowed to leave the island to buy gifts, so we all just ate candy canes. At least that was something nostalgic, but it was nothing compared to how it used to be when we could spend Christmas with our families. I was hoping he'd let me see Dad and Oliver, spend the day with them, but he laughed in my face. They were prisoners in his eyes, and he was too stubborn to give them a chance.

I'd spent the last few months staring at the ceiling to plot our escape. Joque would offer up ideas sometimes, but it seemed like no matter what plan we offered up, it was too dangerous. Then spring came along. It was getting closer and closer to mission season, so I knew we couldn't wait any longer. It was time to decide.

"Come on, Mia. You know how Simon is, he'll scream at you if you stay in bed any longer," Gabby told me as she pushed my legs off my bed. I groaned and wiped my eyes. I had been staring for so long, I saw the popcorn ceiling appear in bursts as I blinked.

"Today. We have to decide today." I sat up, and saw her peek around us nervously. There were some others still inside the barracks, but for the most part, most of them had already gone outside. "You know I'm right, Gabby. Dad and Oliver have been locked up long enough. They've suffered long enough. It's time."

"We'll meet later then. But let's not rush this, we need everything to be perfect. We can't leave anything to chance, Mia." I nodded and sighed as I pulled myself out of bed to get dressed. After I grabbed another uniform, I ran to the bathroom with my boots, socks, and undergarments. We didn't have long, so I skipped a shower and just washed myself with a damp cloth. Just like Oliver before he was taken from me, I was covered in scars. One of my shoulders was burnt, I had scars on my arms and legs, and my stomach looked like a war zone. I hated it, but it helped me feel a bit better when I covered it up. At that point, the infection had completely taken over my body. My right eye was black, and there were black veins leading down from it on the side of my cheek. It looked like a lightning strike. Simon tried to hide his distaste whenever he saw it, but it was pretty obvious he was disgusted. I shook my head at myself in the mirror, and pulled my hair into a messy bun. Once I was done, I walked straight outside.

Luckily, the snow was starting to melt away. It was still cooler outside, but it was the warmest day since autumn ended. I could see the mud starting to peek through beneath the snow, and water dripping off the trees. The birds were starting to come back too. A few of us soldiers talked Simon into buying bird feeders, so I watched as a blue jay flew onto a really pretty stained-glass feeder, picked a seed up in its beak, and swallowed it. It was beautiful, but it also reminded me of Dad. It was his favorite type of bird.

Again, I shook my head and walked on. Joque had become a lot more extraverted since the beginning. I was happy that he was out making new friends, but it also hurt more than I cared to admit. That day, he was speaking to a few guys, and he barely seemed to notice we had come outside. He almost seemed like a completely different person, despite his continued effort some days. The two of them were all I had, and I was too scared to trust anyone else, so I just clung to Gabby. Lucky for me, she clung to me too. She became my best friend and protector. Simon picked on me a lot, so whenever he'd give me an unnecessary chore like scrubbing the barracks' walls, she would join me.

When we came outside that day, I decided to pull Joque aside so the three of us could talk before the morning meeting, but Gabby stopped me just before I was about to grab his arm from behind.

"I'm sorry to say this, Mia, but I think we should start plotting without Joque."

"What? Why?" I asked her, as she pulled me away from their group.

"I know this is going to hurt to hear, but... I overheard him telling his friends our plans in the barracks last night," she told me, making my jaw fall open. "I know, I was shocked too. They were gossiping about us, and if he tells any one of them our *final* plan, they could let it slip to Simon." I balled my hands into fists and shot Joque a fiery glare, but he wasn't looking our way. Then I let out a breath, and shook my head.

"No, he's our friend. I'll just have to talk to him. Ask him if he's in or out." She nodded, but I could tell she didn't like what I was saying. I couldn't stand to lose another friend, even if it was turning into a bad situation.

"I'll be here," she said, looking him up and down from a distance. I nodded back to her, and this time I managed to pull him away.

"Hey, Mia," he said, mid-laugh. "What's up?"

"We need to talk, this is important. Okay?"

"Yeah, of course." He crossed his arms over his chest, but he still had this amused look on his face. *Please come back to me, Joque,* I pleaded in my head, then saw Simon emerging from Beacon. I was too late.

"We'll talk later," I told him, before I gestured over to his friends. "Don't want to keep your friends waiting, right?" I didn't mean it to sound spiteful, but I couldn't manage to hide the bitter tone from my voice. His amused look fell instantly, and it was replaced by a heartbroken look like I'd told him I hated him.

"Did I do something wrong?" he asked, running his hands through his hair to hide the fact that they were shaking. I pinched the bridge of my nose as I tried to find the right words, but I knew I wasn't in the right headspace. I wanted to snap at him. "Mia, if I did something—"

Simon's whistle cut through the air like a sharpened blade, and made us both freeze in our tracks.

"Attention!" Side by side, we stood with our backs straight, and while we were supposed to look straight ahead, he didn't look away from me until I reassured him.

"I'm not mad at you, Joque," I whispered, "but we do need to talk whenever we have another moment. Please, come to me. Okay?" He nodded, and turned his head forward.

"Listen up, I've got an assignment for all of you. Normally we'd start with our drills, but this is too important. We have an escapee. Oliver Beacon. He *must* be found and brought back to Beacon Hospital effective immediately. He killed over two hundred infected last night in a fire on the upper levels." He pointed up, and I gasped when I saw a large blackened spot on what looked like the seventh, eighth, and ninth floors. "After he started the fire, he escaped Beacon again and killed three officers along the way. We think he's hiding somewhere on Beacon Island, so we need to stop him before he manages to find a way across the water. Get going!"

"Yes, sir!" everyone yelled in unison, before we grabbed our friends and ran off. Luckily, Joque came with Gabby and I.

"We have to be the ones to find him. This could be our way out," I told them both as we ran along the rocky trail past Beacon.

"Didn't you hear him, Mia? He killed people. What if Oliver isn't...Oliver anymore?" Joque asked me.

"He had to have a reason. He's never killed before." I kicked up mud and snow as I ran. My pant legs were soaked, but I didn't care too much. Oliver was my priority.

"I know you love him, but what if you're wrong. What if he's truly changed? The infection could have done something to him."

"Then why didn't it do anything to me, huh?" I stepped in his path and crossed my arms as he ground to a halt.

"You're different too, do you think we should kick *you* out?" I pointed a finger against his chest and saw him tilt his head with a hurt expression again. "Don't give me puppy-dog eyes, *Private Indi.* Gabby said she heard you telling your friends our plans. Care to explain?"

"Mia, it's not like that." He grabbed my hands, but I shoved his away, making him wince.

"Then what is it like?" I narrowed my eyes, and heard him take in a shaky breath.

"I thought... I thought we gave up, so I was trying to fit in. Yes, I told them a few of our plans. I admit it, okay? But I was only trying to get support. Allies, you know? And if I'm being honest, you haven't been there for me either. I hate being here, but all *you've* been doing," he said, poking me right back, "is staring up at the stupid ceiling. I needed you! Don't you understand?" I stared at him, dumbfounded, and shrunk down under his gaze.

"My family's in trouble, Joque," I said in a very quiet tone, and my eyes fluttered from him to the ground.

"As long as we are here, they will always be in trouble. I get that, but I need you too. I feel scared and alone, and I don't want to feel that way. I want to go home to my family, and watch stupid movies, and eat so many snacks I get a sugar high." He stopped and chuckled before he tucked his hands in his pants pockets and turned his head up to the sky. "But I can't do that. I'm stuck here eating food from a damn bag. We have to train to hurt people, and I've seen so much death since I came here, I feel sick. I will stand by your side, Mia, just as I always have, but I need to know you're going to stand by mine."

"Of course I will... I'm so sorry I ever made you feel otherwise, Joque." I hugged him, and felt him breathe deeply against my neck.

"I'm sorry too," he whispered before we separated.

"I want you to know that I'm glad you have new friends, Joque. That's great, really. But you can't tell them any more of our plans. This is really important."

"Got it. I promise, I won't talk about it anymore." I nodded, and after we contemplated where to go, we continued along the path until we got to apartment 666. It looked like a tornado had blown through it. The windows were broken all around the building, there was black ooze running down the wall almost like moss, and there was a horrible smell lingering in the air, almost like rotten beef.

"Ugh, I really hope he's not in there," Gabby said, waving her hands in front of her nose to dissipate the smell. Some of the other soldiers were already flooding into the other two apartments, so I knew we had no choice but to suck it up and walk in. Unlike the first time I came through, we went through the front door. It was a little disorienting, but I eventually figured out where everything was. "This building looks like it's one kick away from falling to the ground." I watched as she kicked the wall, and widened my eyes when half the wall crumbled to the ground, revealing an apartment.

"Jeez," Joque said, peeking into the gap in the wall.

"Yeah, let's not do that again." I walked on, and heard both of them chuckle behind me. *How did I become the voice of reason?* I thought, rolling my eyes. We opened a few more doors, and eventually were left with only one on the bottom floor. The door where we met. "Okay, this is getting weird."

"Why?" Gabby asked, as I put my hand around the doorknob.

"This is the exact room where we met, room 113. You guys don't think he would hide here again, do you?" I felt an extreme sense of deja vu as I pushed the door open and saw the same scene sprawled out before me. *Oh, how sweet and naive little me was back then.* The only difference I saw in the room was fresh boot marks leading toward the closet.

"Oliver?" I asked, creating my own footprints next to the ones on the floor. "If that's you, answer me, please. It's me—" I got halfway through the room when the closet door burst open. I jumped back, expecting it to be some kind of monster, but to my shock he emerged. He was wearing a pair of jeans and a black button-up t-shirt with the cuffs tucked over. I could tell he got it fresh from the laundromat, because I could smell roses. It hit my nose, almost masking the rot smell from earlier.

"Oliver!" I muttered excitedly, before I ran to meet him. I got within arm's-length of him when he stopped me with his hand.

"Don't touch me," he said, swiping at his shirt as if I smothered dirt on him.

"Oliver? What's the matter? It's me, Mia. Please tell me you remember me." I looked him over, and saw he looked exactly like I did. Black veins all the way up to his eyes, except both of his eyes were black instead of one.

"Of course I remember the pest that infected me," he said, narrowing his eyes. "You know, the one who got me thrown back in Beacon. I'm not dumb." He rolled his eyes, and tucked his hands in his pockets. I could tell they were balled into fists from the outline, and I couldn't help but feel hurt.

"That's not true!" I yelled, as I stepped a little closer to him. "The doctor possessed you, he's the one who got you sent to Beacon."

"Wow, you expect me to believe that? He told me, *YOU* did this. That you chose someone else over me. You could have saved me, Mia, but you choose to let me suffer!" His voice came out hoarse, as if he was crying. I wanted to try to prove myself, but I didn't know how.

"No," I cried, looking to Gabby and Joque for support. They both stepped in, and pulled me behind them. His voice made me shudder. I only got to see his angry side once, and I definitely didn't like it.

"Mia's been fighting for you since the beginning! The doctor is lying to you, Oliver," Joque told him, as he put his hands up to de-escalate the situation. It didn't work.

"No, no, no," he said, wagging his finger back and forth. "He told me that he possessed you to help you get your dad back, and you turned down his help. He's made me more powerful than ever, and I love the new me. I can do things the old Oliver never could. Like this." He put his hand out, and squeezed in the air. At first I thought it wasn't doing anything, until I heard Joque scream. Blood was coming out of his eyes, and he began to gasp for air, but Oliver didn't stop squeezing.

"Oliver! Stop, he's your friend! It's me you want, okay?" I saw Oliver's head tilt to the side, but he didn't stop, so I tackled him. I heard him groan when he hit the ground, but before I could recover, I flew into the wall just like I did in Juros. I couldn't lift myself back up, so I laid there feeling helpless. When I peeked over at Joque, he was gasping for air again, and Oliver was laughing as he skipped over to him.

"You're so right, what was I thinking?" he said sarcastically, before he pulled him to his feet. Joque wobbled as his body fought to stay upright, and I hoped that would have been a wake-up call for Oliver, but the wicked look in his eyes didn't go away. Gabby tried to step in, but when she got within a foot of him, Oliver threw her into the wall next to me. I heard a rumbling sound when her body hit it, then I felt a jolt of pain travel up my legs. Some rubble tumbled on me, making me cry out in pain. "Ooh. That must have hurt," he said in an amused tone, then returned his attention back to Joque, who was stumbling to try and stay upright.

"You can thank Mia for this. Lights out, old friend," Oliver said, before he reached his arm up in the air. I screamed as he used his ability to make the ceiling crumble right on top of Joque, burying him beneath stone and rubble. I heard a groan escape his lips through the smoke, but when it dissipated, he was facing me with blood running down his eyes and forehead. From where I was lying, he didn't move even an inch and I couldn't hear him breathing. *Did Oliver just kill Joque?*

"Joque, no!" I cried, before looking up to see Oliver knelt over me.

"I'm going to destroy you," he whispered, "and as for this...I'll be taking it back." He ripped the ring off my finger and put it in his pocket. The whole time he had this creepy grin plastered on his face like this was all some sort of game to him. He patted the back of my head as I sobbed against the cold hard ground, then he began to walk away until I called after him.

"I loved you..." I said, fighting to breathe. "I didn't have a choice Oliver, I...I had to choose my dad. He made me choose between you two." I felt his lips grow close to my ear, and felt a glimmer of hope that maybe I got through to him, but I was wrong.

"Liar," he whispered, before he pressed my head hard against the ground with the palm of his hand. I whimpered, then he completely shattered me.

"I can't believe I ever loved you," he said as he stared at me in utter disgust. I pinched my eyes closed as his words hit me like a truck. I wanted to give up right there, but I felt Gabby squeeze my hand next to me as tight as she could. She was buried too.

"You've still got me, girl. Don't...don't you dare give up," she told me, as if she was reading my mind. I nodded with tears flowing down my eyes and hugged her as tight as I could.

"Is Joque—" I stopped and let out a sob into her hair.

"I'm sorry, Mia." I nodded and closed my eyes against Gabby's shoulder. I don't know how much time passed after we drifted off together, but Simon and a few other soldiers found us there.

"Oh Jesus." I woke up to see Simon knelt over Joque's body. The stone that was covering him was tossed to the side in a large pile, and my eyes widened when I saw blood covering some of it. Somehow, I slept through all of it. I watched as he put his hand over his neck and gasped, making my heart jump.

"Get help in here, quick!" he yelled to someone outside the door.

"Hang on, kid." He pulled Joque's limp body off the ground and picked him up in his arms. That's when I saw his chest rise and fall very slowly.

"H-he's alive?" I asked, weakly. Only then did I notice a stream of blood coming out of my mouth. I knew the wall crumbled on us, but I didn't expect it to be that bad. As I would come to find out later, all three of us nearly died that day.

"All three of you are here? What the hell happened?" he said in shock. I clawed at the ground trying to get out, but I couldn't move. "We're gonna get you out of there, kid, don't worry." I nodded and laid my head back down facing Gabby. In the background I could hear him yelling to someone, but the sound kept drifting in and out. So did my vision.

"G-Gabby?" I called out through my daze. At first she didn't answer, so I used every ounce of strength I had left to shake her. Luckily, her eyes came open, and she managed to smile weakly at me.

"Hey," she muttered, rolling her eyes into the back of her head. She groaned, and tried to lift herself up, but she failed just like I did. "Ugh." I wanted to comfort her, tell her I was there for her, but my mouth wouldn't open again. I couldn't move anything, and a moment later, I found myself in another soldier's arms.

"Hey...you." He was trying to speak to me, but I couldn't make sense of his words anymore. I laid my head against his chest, and pinched my eyes closed again. This time, I had a normal dream for the first time in a long time.

Chapter Twenty-Five: Recovery

A couple days after Oliver attacked us, I woke up in the infirmary with an IV in my arm and a tube in my nose. I felt like I was trapped in sleep paralysis, and the doctor had captured me again. My body wouldn't move no matter how hard I tried, so I stared up at the ceiling until Polly came and stood over me. She was holding a clipboard in one hand, and a blue pen in the other. I saw her stand up on her tiptoes to look into my eyes, and when our eyes connected, she groaned.

"About time you woke up," she said, rolling her eyes. I tried to snap back at her with one of my signature quips, but my mouth felt so dry, I couldn't say much.

"Mhmm," I responded instead, pressing my head into my pillows. Although it hurt my neck, I managed to turn my head toward the other beds and saw Gabby and Joque lying next to me in a row. We all had IV's and tubes, but Joque was the only one with a heart rate monitor.

"The three of you nearly died four times," Polly said, giving me a look of pure disgust. "Between you and me, I wish you had," she said, not even trying to hide the disappointment in her voice, "Joque got the worst of it, which is why he's still connected to the EKG, but you two dropped twice. No missions for at least a month, and no training. You'll be on bedrest until further notice, got it?" I nodded and felt relieved when she lifted a cup of ice cold water to my lips. It felt like sweet relief as it went down, but my throat still burned from screaming.

We spent the next week and a half in those beds. Gabby woke up after another day passed, but it took Joque two more. With each dip of the line, I felt sick to my stomach. We couldn't help but feel worried for him, but after day four, he got strong enough for Polly to turn the heart monitor off. Polly wouldn't let us get out of our beds until she deemed us "safe," so we had to use bedpans for a few days. Although it felt a bit humiliating to have to use one, the look on her face each time she took the pan away made it all worth it. Pure gold.

After the week and a half period was over, Polly let us walk around on our own, so I went and laid down by Joque. According to Polly, his vision became really cloudy after the attack, and she was sure he would soon go blind. His eyes turned a grayish-white color, almost like ash, and whenever we talked to him, we noticed he would squint a lot. Slowly, I came and stood by his bed and saw him lift his head up to me, but his eyes didn't completely connect with mine.

"Hey, Joque," I said sadly.

"Hey, Mia," he responded, patting the bed beside him. "Sit with me?"

"Of course." I squeezed in next to him and laid my head on his shoulder with a sigh. "How did this happen, Joque?" I asked him, hugging his arm tightly.

"I don't know. Before Oliver did what he did, I would have never even imagined he'd stoop to that level. He is...was my best friend." He shook his head, and lowered his body down so our faces were right next to each other. I swallowed when I noticed how close he was, and felt my cheeks grow warm. "I just wanted to see your face again," he whispered as he slowly brought his hand up to my cheek. He ran the back of his finger hesitantly down the side of my face and let out a pained breath. "Oliver doesn't deserve you."

"I-I love him," I said quietly. "I don't think he did this, I'm sure it was the doctor. It had to be."

"I wanted to believe that too, but then I thought back to his words. He called me 'old friend' before he brought the ceiling down on me. I think the doctor had something to do with it, I'm sure of that, but he didn't attack us back there. Oliver did. The Oliver we knew is gone, and I think it's time we let him go." I sucked in a breath and sat up, feeling frustration building in my chest.

"I can't just 'let him go,' Joque. I gave up everything for him. My hometown, my mom, my dad. I have nothing left but you guys and him. I refuse to believe that he's gone, I—" I tried to say more, but I started to sob and felt Joque pull me in to him.

"Breathe, Mia." I cried into his chest, and felt how shaky his breaths were. I felt safe there with him, but guilty for finding comfort in his embrace. I closed my eyes, and felt him put his hand on the back of my head. "Can you make me a deal?" he asked me as I gathered myself.

I nodded and sat up so I could see his eyes.

"If the Oliver we know really is gone, promise me you'll give me a chance. I may not have known you as long as him, but I've come to know the amazing, beautiful woman you are, and I can't let that go anymore. I think I'm in love with you." A gasp escaped my lips as he confessed his feelings, and I looked over at Gabby, who had her face buried in a book ironically called, *Lovers' Quarrel.* She had no idea what Joque had just said, and I almost wanted to spring up out of his bed and tell her. I was shocked. "Please," he whispered as his eyes jumped back and forth.

"I like you, Joque, but I can't...promise anything. Please understand. I love Oliver," I begged as my lips began to quiver. He took notice, and smiled up at me.

"I understand, but I'm not letting this go. Not yet." I felt my heart hammering in my chest, and stood up. My face felt warm, and my palms were clammy. *What's wrong with you, Mia? You're engaged! Oliver loves you.* I began to pace back and forth until I looked up after the fifth or sixth time and saw him standing there. He chuckled and tucked his hands in his pockets. He knew exactly what he was doing. I shook my head, ignoring the smug look on his face, and fell into a spiral of confusion. *If Oliver really did hurt us on purpose, can I forgive him for that? Can I forgive the awful way he treated me? Can I forgive him for saying he didn't love me? For taking my ring? Would we ever recover from this? Can we—*

"Hey," Joque said finally, snapping me out of the spiral I was drowning in. "It's okay, I'll back off. I know you still have feelings for him, and I don't want to hurt you, but I couldn't go any longer without telling you how I felt. No matter how long I have to wait, I'll do it. You're worth every second of my time, and so much more." He was trying to put my mind at ease, but instead, he made my heart hammer harder. I balled my hands into fists, but I couldn't deny how I was feeling either. My heart was torn in two different directions. I never loved anyone before Oliver, and letting him go felt like a crime, but part of me wanted to give in to Joque right there. Instead, I told him the only thing I could think to say.

"Okay, I promise." I heard him chuckle, and saw him smile wide. His cheeks turned red, and he nodded happily.

"Thank you," he said, and ran his hands through his hair and plopped down on his bed with a groan. I couldn't help but chuckle, despite my chest feeling hollow, and after I calmed down from the shock of what had just happened, I practically tackled Gabby to tell her. Luckily, talking with her stopped my heart from leaping out of my chest. She had a way of keeping me calm.

Despite Joque's confession, our friend group became closer than ever. We started plotting how we were going to escape the island again, and how we planned on taking down the doctor. At first we started thinking about normal ghost-hunting methods, like an exorcism, but then something hit me. If Oliver was more powerful because of the doctor, maybe I could be more powerful, too, if the little girl would help us take him down.

"I love you, Mia, but that sounds crazy," Gabby said. "Besides, how do you even know the little girl ghost you saw has abilities like the doctor?"

"She's right, you know. We have to be strategic about this, and I don't know how I feel about you sneaking back into Beacon to find a ghost," Joque said, crossing his arms over his chest. I looked at the two of them, trying to think of something to say, but deep down, I knew they were right. It was a huge risk. The only problem was that, in my mind, it seemed to me to be the only way. There's no way the doctor would let us get close enough to Oliver to use any ghost equipment. The only problem was how I would convince her to fight her killer, especially since she was only a kid. Then I thought of something even better.

"Okay, what if, hypothetically speaking, I could get two ghosts to fight the doctor?" I heard Joque groan and turned my head toward him.

"Mia, you're my best friend, so I'm going to say this as gently as I can. No." I gasped, and grabbed his shoulders so he knew I was right there.

"We have to try something, Joque. I've recovered as much as I can, so why shouldn't I try? If we can take down the doctor, we can escape Beacon forever and live a happy life. This is a good plan and you know it." I released his shoulders, but he stood up so he could still see me. He wasn't completely blind yet, but his vision was fading more and more by the day. It made me sad.

"It's a crazy plan and YOU know it. Besides, even if we do find Oliver, which is not very likely after his speech, we still don't know whether the doctor has him or not. Oliver could have just picked a side, and that's it." I shook my head and looked to Gabby for support.

"Please back me up here," I pleaded, putting my palms together. I readied myself to hear another lecture, but this time she actually helped me.

"While I think you're crazy, I do think you're right. The Oliver I knew loved all of us. He was a huge sap, sometimes even annoyingly so. I don't see him purposely hurting any of us. And while I'm not completely sure, I know those abilities or powers he got from the doctor don't usually stick around. Unless, of course, Mia is super powerful, and we just don't know about it yet."

"Definitely not," I said with a chuckle.

"So...you think he's still possessed?" Joque asked, raising his eyebrows.

"Yes, I'm almost sure of it," Gabby told him, making him frown. He crossed his arms over his chest again and began pacing back and forth in front of my bed. He seemed lost in thought at first, but after a minute or two of pacing, he stopped and sighed.

"Fine, let's do it, but we need a back-up plan in case this goes south. I care too much about you to lose you to Beacon." I nodded and threw myself down on my bed. I didn't know how to describe it, but it seemed like everything we'd accomplished and endured in the last few months was finally coming to a head. This plan would hopefully be our last one, and maybe, despite Simon helping us in the apartment complex, we could take him down too.

"I think I know what to do," I told them, and sat up again.

"Alright, go on," Joque said, waving his right hand in a circular motion.

"The hospital is still taking in patients for the infection, so what if we send you or Gabby in there undercover to cause a distraction while I find the two kids? That way I wouldn't go in alone." At first, I heard nothing but silence from them. Gabby looked at Joque nervously, and I instantly knew what was going to happen next. Then Joque stood up.

"I'm in," he said, covering his eyes with his hands. "I'll go to them about my vision and use that as my ticket in. While

Mia and I are in there, do you think you can distract Simon for us, Gabby?"

"I can manage that," Gabby said, and she stood up and came to stand by both of us. "Let's get this over with." I nodded, and once again, we got up to sneak out of the infirmary. Slowly we crawled along the floor on our stomachs to keep Polly from seeing us from her desk, and every few feet, I had to help Joque along, so he knew where to go. Everything seemed to be going our way at first as we crawled past the lines of beds, but when we got to the door, I heard what sounded like a tornado alarm go off and saw a flashing red light at the front door. Little did the three of us know at the time that during our extended sleep, Simon ordered Polly to chip us. I froze in the doorway like a deer caught in headlights as an army of guards came running out of the yard straight for us, and heard a clicking sound behind us.

"Freeze," I heard Polly order. "Put your damn hands in the air." I nodded and slowly lifted my hands as high as I could, although I felt pain shoot through my ribs.

"Mia, what's going on?" Joque asked, as he lifted his arms with us. He groaned and cupped his side, making Polly mad.

"We got caught," I replied. "I know it hurts, but lift your hands back up." He nodded, and with a pained expression on his face, he complied.

"I knew you three were going to be nothing but trouble, it seems to follow you like a fungus," she said, shoving her shotgun in my face. "Why should I even be surprised when it comes to you?"

"Leave her alone," Gabby snapped at her, "she just wants to live. She can't help that she's not as wicked as you, Polly."

"Oooh, wicked, huh?" she seethed, making the guards laugh. "I'll show you wicked." Suddenly, as if it was written into a script, the guards grabbed us and began dragging us toward our beds. We fought back, kicking and screaming, but the pain came back for a vengeance. I saw Gabby's face contort in pain as one of the soldiers put his foot against her back to kick her forward. When we made it back to our beds, it didn't end there. The guards pushed us down and tied each one of us to the beds with three thick leather straps. I tried to stop them, but it was like getting a shot at the doctor's office as a kid. They forced us down and began to sedate us. They got Gabby and Joque sedated first, but when they got to me, Polly motioned for the man with the needle hovered directly over my neck to stop. One of the soldiers held my face to the side, and I was sweating as I waited for whatever sick thing would come out of her mouth next.

"I'm going to put you under now, but you should know you're not gonna wake up here, Mia. Simon gave me permission to take you if you dared break his rules again, and I knew the moment I caught you out of bed that I had won. All three of you are going to wake up in Beacon, where you belong. It's game over, and I'm taking control."

"No! Don't, please," I pleaded, but my cries were for nothing. I felt the stinging pain of the needle going in and slipped back into darkness. I wanted to go back to Beacon, but not like this.

Chapter Twenty-Six: Ghostly Encounters

I prepared myself to wake up back in room 851, but instead I woke up in what looked like a mansion. In the distance, I could hear a crackling sound, and I pulled myself out of bed. Besides a small twin bed with a pink blanket, there was nothing else in the room but a nightstand and a photo of the Beacon family hugging each other. There were five of them. I lowered my feet over the side of the bed and picked up the picture frame. I heard an echo bounce off the walls when it left the nightstand, making me feel uneasy. *Why am I in an empty house?* I wondered, as I examined the photo. I saw Oliver's mom and a man with a thick brown mustache that was covered in whipped cream. They were laughing, and I could see a cup of hot chocolate in the man's hand with an indent in the sprinkled whipped cream on top. In front of them were three kids. Two girls and one boy. It was little Oliver at a Christmas family gathering. *Am I in Oliver's head?* I thought, as I peeked around the corner.

In the hall I couldn't see anything but two other doors and a flight of stairs. Slowly, I tiptoed out into the hall and heard the crackling sound get louder. It was coming from downstairs. Before I went down, I decided to try the two doors, but they were locked up tight, making a loud clunking sound as I tried the knobs. After taking a big breath, I descended the stairs, and listened to each sound that came at me. The crackling, my footsteps, the sound of my own heartbeat, and...a muffled cry. Someone was in trouble. I could smell a sweet maple smell as I got to the second landing, but I didn't let that distract me. I grasped the railing going down and peered around the corner, hoping to see someone there. Still I could hear the muffled cries, and I knew I had to toughen up and face it.

I felt like a kid walking into something I knew I shouldn't. I tiptoed down each step and froze when the last one sent a loud exaggerated creak through the house. When no sound came back, I followed the sound of the cries and the crackling and eventually reached the living room. Inside I could see a fire burning away, sending ashes flying around the room like lightning bugs, and a couch with a man in a mask sitting there. I knew I had to be cautious, because he had a knife sitting in front of him. I eyed him as I tiptoed forward and jumped with each sound that transpired. He had his feet kicked up on a coffee table, and his head angled up as if he was looking at something above him. Confused, I followed his gaze and gasped instantly, feeling shock take over. Oliver was hanging above me by his ankles. He was wrapped from head to toe in chains, and I could see blood dripping down his forehead. His nose was bleeding.

"Oliver!" I shouted. He was awake, but I could tell he was going to pass out soon. He made a sound and rolled his eyes back into his skull. I immediately jumped into action. I grabbed the coffee table away from the man, along with the knife, and jumped up. The chains weren't locked around him, so I was able to use the knife to cut him down. When we hit the floor together, the man instantly woke up from the loud boom we made.

"Oh no," I whispered as he stood up and began walking toward us. I ripped the gag off Oliver and tried to carry him away when he spoke up.

"Teleport," he whispered weakly. The next thing I knew, we were at Jill's front door. I couldn't help but smile, but then I looked down at Oliver and saw him crash in my arms. His body went limp against me, and I soon realized that he had fainted.

"No, Oliver," I said, brushing my hand against his cheek. A small trickle of blood came down his lip, so I brushed it away with my index finger. "You're gonna be okay, I've got you." I threw him up in the air to get a better grip and walked up to Jill's door with him. I felt nervous, but after I rang the bell, she came to the door and instantly smiled wide.

"Oh, my sweet babies," she said, rushing forward to get to us. After she saw Oliver, her face turned to a genuine shock, and I saw her eyes dart back to her house. "Let's get him inside, quickly now," she told me, as she held her door open for us. I set him down on her couch and once he was out of my arms, she hugged me tight. "What happened to him?"

"A bad man hurt him," I said, feeling scared. "I don't know if we're safe here, Mrs. Lingvil."

"Oh, of course we are, baby. This is the one place where that mean man can't get us," she said, wagging her finger back and forth. "This is Oliver's happy place. You should see it. There are so many pictures of you, my sweet girl. He really loves you." I couldn't help but smile, and felt my face grow hot as she walked me inside and showed me a whole room full of pictures of me. The first I saw was when we met. I had a grimace on my face as he tried to shove the chair leg toward me. Then I saw a picture of me and him running toward the bridge. All of them were memories of us, and the most recent one was of him kissing me inside the closet in the barracks. Then it hit me. I was starting to lose hope that he still loved me, when this whole time he was trapped in his mind. I felt sick.

"I-I think I messed up." I fell to my knees on her living room floor and felt instantly embarrassed.

"Oh, honey. Don't hurt yourself now, dear, he needs you." I could feel hot tears falling down my cheeks as I realized that he never gave up on me. I was so scared after what he did that I almost gave up on him.

"He'll never forgive me," I cried, burying my head into my hands. Jill put her hand on my shoulder and squeezed to get my attention. She was confused. "I thought he didn't love me anymore," I admitted, putting my hand against my heart. I felt so much pain and anguish, I began to shake.

"That's just not true. I'm an old woman, sweetheart. I've seen love come and go, and what you two have is real. You should go tell him how you feel and make it up to him." She gestured up the stairs, and I felt tingles travel up and down my spine when I saw him awake, leaning against the wall at the top of the steps. I looked at Jill, and she made me chuckle when she gave me two thumbs-up and helped me to my feet. By the time I got to him, we practically met in the middle. I walked up to him, and without a moment's hesitation, I kissed him.

"I missed you," I told him, grabbing his shirt in my hands to stay stable.

"I missed you too." Gently, he ran his finger down my cheek, and when he got down to my chin, he grabbed it and tilted my head his way to kiss him again. Passionately, he kissed me, and when he finished, he pressed his forehead against mine and let out a breath of hot air. "Please tell me I didn't really hurt you and the others, Mia," he pleaded, as he looked into my eyes. I shook my head and cupped his face in my hands.

"Don't you dare blame yourself. The doctor did this, not you." He nodded and sucked in a shaky breath.

"Why were you crying then?" His eyes darted back and forth, as I psyched myself up to admit what happened. It's not like Joque and I did anything, but I still felt sick about it. Oliver deserved better than that.

"After the doctor made you attack us, and you took my ring, and said really heartbreaking things, Joque admitted that he loved me and I... I felt confused. I'm so sorry. You deserve better than me, Oliver." I started to walk down the stairs when I felt him grab me from behind and press me against the wall.

"There is nothing in this world that you could say that would convince me of that. As long as you come back to me in the end, that's all I care about," he said, pressing his forehead against mine again as I began to cry once more. "I love you, and that's not going to change. The fact that you're willing to own up to it tells me everything I need to know. It shows me that I can trust you. Besides, there's no way you could have known, Mia. I was and still am, his puppet on a string, but please understand that no matter what he makes me say or do, I will always be yours. As long as you're still mine. This...is my happy place, and if you weren't in it, none of this would exist. You make me feel hope for the future, our future. I feel like I can take on anything as long as I know I can come home to you, and that's all I've ever wanted."

"You have no idea how much that means to me," I said, pinching my eyes closed like flood gates to hold back the tears. "I will always be yours," I promised, and with a big smile plastered across his face, he dragged me down the hall laughing as he held me by my waist. We laid together for a while on a small bed Jill let us stay on, and just held each other without saying anything. Feeling his hands around me again was enough. He ran them along my thighs, and up and down my back. If we weren't in Jill's place, we might have gone farther.

"I was thinking," he said, bringing his hands up to my arms to hold my mine, "what if we stay here? I know how crazy that sounds, but we have everything we could ever want. A place to stay, a home, no infected, no doctor, no pain. Just you and me...and Jill, of course," he said, causing me to chuckle. "Live with me in my happy place, Mia. Forever." I squeezed his hands and let out a breath. It was definitely tempting, but every part of me knew it was wrong. Slowly I shook my head, making my hair brush against his face.

"We can't, Oliver. Our friends, my dad, all the innocent people affected by this. They need us."

"But what if I hurt you again? I can't control myself anymore, Mia. What if he makes me kill you? I would never forgive myself. Please consider this." He put his hand on my cheek as he waited for me to respond, but again I shook my head and saw a pained expression cross his face.

"I'm sorry. I'm going to fight the doctor, and I'm going to get you back. No matter what, okay?"

"I don't want to fight you, Mia. I'm so scared of what could happen. In here, we're safe, but out there—" He stopped, and sucked in a breath before he rubbed his shaky hands across the back of mine. "What if...what if you kill me fighting him?" he asked, a stream of tears falling down his cheeks.

"I won't kill you, Oliver. I swear."

"I know... it's just...I don't want to die like this. Another casualty of that sick psycho." He sniffled and pressed the back of his hand against his nose. "I want to grow old with you, and—"

Downstairs I heard a cracking sound, and we both sat up. It sounded loud, and as we got up to investigate what was happening, the house began to shake. It felt like an earthquake. We rounded the doorway and raced down the stairs like the house was on fire, but when we got to the bottom, we saw a huge crack straight through the house, splitting the living room in half. It was leaking black ooze, just like the infection, and it reeked like sewer water.

"No, no, no," I heard Oliver say behind me. When I turned around to look at him, he was grasping his hair in his hands like he was going to tear it out. "He's not supposed to come here, this is supposed to be safe. He's breaking in, you have to go, Mia." Suddenly he grabbed me by my shoulders and almost violently shook me back and forth. "Wake up!" he yelled. I was confused at first, but then he yelled it again, and I woke up in the exact place I didn't want to. Room 851.

I looked around again and saw the same layout as before. The speaker, the bed, all of it was the same. I was even wearing the same jumpsuit as before. I didn't know what was worse, being a prisoner or Simon's soldier. Both made me feel miserable.

"Hello?" I called out. I waited a few seconds, but I didn't hear the speaker come alive. "I know you're out there, Polly." Luckily, with my second remark she answered, but she definitely wasn't pleasant.

"What do you want, brat?"

"What have you done with my friends?" I yelled as I balled my hands into fists and stared at the one-way glass.

"You really thought you were gonna be locked up with them? You really are dumber than I thought." I heard her snort and had to stop myself from cringing.

"Oh yeah? Get this in your pea-sized brain. If you hurt them, I'll never stop fighting you. Ever!" I heard her laugh into the speaker, and my face grew hot with anger. I was sure if I could actually see my face, it would be bright red.

"Get this..." I heard the speaker crackle as it turned off, and instantly pressed myself against the wall as she and a guard stepped in my room with the taser. "You're infected, they're not. So why don't you take a guess. What's gonna happen next, sweetheart?" She laced her fingers together mockingly, causing me to widen my eyes. Without a moment's hesitation, I charged at her, but I was met with a prong against my stomach. I yelped in pain and gripped it from the ground.

"Don't do this, please," I pleaded.

"It's okay, 851. I won't, for now, but you're going to listen to my every word from now on. Mess up and they pay the price, got it?" I nodded slowly as I snapped myself out of the pain, and with my eyes locked on her, I stood back up again.

"I'll do everything you tell me to," I promised as I lowered myself down on my bed cautiously.

"About damn time. All it took was me taking your stupid friends." She shook her head and beckoned me to follow her. I didn't want to, but I didn't have a choice. She led me down the hall, passing all kinds of infected who, since I last saw them, grew at least double in size, and made me sit in a large meeting room. At the head of the table I saw a placard with my mom's name on it and grimaced. The guard seemed to notice my uneasiness, so he put his hands on my shoulder to hold me in place. A few minutes passed as I stared up at this very boring-looking clock near the ceiling. Then I heard the door open.

I didn't have to turn around to know who it was. The whole room straightened their backs when she walked in, as if she was a queen. My eyes locked on her as she came around the right side of the table and took her place in front of her placard. She had a cane in her hand, and I could see a wound along her cheek, a long cut. I looked up at her, and somehow, we entered a silent staring match. Neither of us blinked or moved, we just glared at each other. I didn't want to give her the satisfaction of winning, but after about forty seconds of holding her gaze, a guard hit my shoulder and made me lose.

"Ah," I groaned, and looked at the man responsible. He just rolled his eyes and pressed himself against the wall with one knee straight and the other out. If he hadn't hit me, I knew I could have beaten her.

"Congrats," I said through gritted teeth.

"Let's talk, Mia," she responded, ignoring my comment. "I've had enough of the fighting, I've had enough of the threats, and frankly, I've had enough of you. We're launching a grand-scale operation, and now that you're out of the way, there's no one to stop the flood of infected. There's no one to stop Simon and there's no one to stop me."

"Wow, you're a great mom." I rolled my eyes and crossed my arms over my chest. "What do you want to do? Start an apocalypse? There are good people out there. I've seen them myself; they helped save me and Oliver. You have some of them locked up right now. Think about what you're doing. You used to be my hero, now you're nothing more than a villain!" I slammed my hands down on the table and heard it echo through the room. I heard one of them cock their gun and turned to see Polly aiming a shotgun at me. I shook a bit and sat back down.

"Just think about it, what government are you going to have to get orders from if they all turn?" I said, this time in a calmer tone.

"Ours," she said, making me glance around the room in shock.

"What the hell is that supposed to mean?" I asked, feeling scared of her answer.

"It means we're making our own," I heard Simon say as he stepped around the table and kissed my mom on the lips. I hadn't even noticed the door open; I was so distraught; I couldn't concentrate on anything else.

"Who in their right mind would listen to you two? You're sick!" I yelled. It all seemed to hit me at once as Mom slid a clipboard my way with a pile of papers on top. According to the sheet, Simon retired years ago, meaning they were never working for the government. This was all them. I held the papers in my hands and felt a rage so deep building up inside me that I wanted to kill everyone in that room. So many people died as a result of their sick power play.

They hired the doctor, they infected Oliver or worked with the people who did, and they exploited him and his family. I glared at Mom again and imagined every scenario of what I would do next. Part of me wanted to hop over the table and tackle her, but I refused to give her the satisfaction of killing me there.

"I'm going to take all of you down. That's not a threat. That's a promise. You're not my mother anymore, and you... You're nothing to me," I said, gesturing to her and Simon. Again, I heard Polly laugh, but this time I didn't look away. I felt nothing but pure anger.

"Good luck," Simon snickered at me, before gesturing for Polly to remove me from the room. As I was dragged away, I thought of every bad thing that had happened to me. It was all because of her. The sweet man from Juros, the family that died, all the innocents that got bitten, Hunter's Villa. All of it was her fault.

I was being dragged back toward my room by Polly, with a guard accompanying her. Lucky for me, they didn't have their weapons out, so I slammed Polly against the wall and tackled the guard. Once they were down on the ground, I ran as fast as I could past the walls of infected and stopped near the bathrooms when I felt an icy chill cover my whole body. My body froze in place, and I saw my breath in front of my face, as if I had just stepped into a freezer.

Mia, you're okay. I heard the little girl's voice in my head and widened my eyes. All this time I thought I would have to hunt for her, but she found me. I turned my head around through my daze and saw that Polly and the guard were charging at me.

"Please tell me you can take them down; they're going to kill me." I heard her giggle in my head and felt my arm lift on its own. A moment later, they dissolved into the floor, making a fizzle sound like a fresh can of pop, about a foot from me. "Holy crap."

Don't worry, I won't ever let them hurt you, she told me, as she made me ball my hand into a fist in front of me.

"I don't want to ruin the moment, but are they...dead?" I asked, as I got down on my knee and scooped up the sludge. It felt almost like Jell-o, but a little more liquidy. It was gross, and I gagged.

Nope, I just made them melt through the floor like lava, she said as she did jazz hands. ***We gotta move, best friend.*** I chuckled and nodded as I jogged away.

"I know this is going to sound really scary, but how would you feel about helping me take down the doctor? The man who..." I stopped and tried to find a way to say it gently, but I couldn't think of another way.

The man who killed me? she asked in a quiet tone, as if she was reading my mind. ***I wanna be a superhero. I can do it!***

"Thank you, Lilly," I told her.

You're welcome, we should go find my other best friend. He's around here somewhere. I'm sure he'd want to help too! I don't know how she did it, but she helped me slip through doors like they weren't even there, including the keypad doors. We ran straight through the eighth floor to the stairwell and stood at the precipice where the railing was. I expected her to keep running, but instead she used me to call out for the boy.

"Gavin!" I yelled down the steps. I cupped my hands against my ear and waited until I heard a voice yell back.

"Lilly? Is that you?" he yelled back, catching me off guard.

"Yep, I found Mia," she told him, making me lean over the side. I looked down and saw what looked like a small moving shadow near the bottom of the stairwell. It was strange: I was able to see Lilly just fine, but Gavin looked like nothing more than a shape.

"Yes! So, we're going back to the sandbox again?"

"Not this time," she laughed. "It's time for us to be heroes, Gavin. Mia needs our help."

"Got it!" he yelled, and the next thing I knew, I heard a whooshing sound travel up the steps. I peered over again, but I couldn't see him anymore. I scanned each level with my eyes, but I couldn't even catch a glimpse of him. I thought he was gone, until he came flying at me and made me stumble against the railing. Luckily, I managed to catch myself, but the freeze overtook my body as he possessed me too.

I'm here, I heard him say. ***Am I going to be a superhero? Just like my favorite comic book?***

Just like that, Lilly responded. ***We're going to take down the doctor once and for all!***

That sounds scary. His voice became quiet and frail, but Lilly and I reassured him. Somehow all the pieces of the puzzle were falling into place. All we needed to do was rescue Joque and Gabby, and escape Beacon forever. It sounded complicated, but with their help I was sure I could do it.

"Have either of you seen my friends?" I asked them as I chewed on my upper lip in anticipation. "Their names are Joque and Gabby."

Nope, I heard Gavin say.

I'm not sure, I think I did. Were they wearing soldiers' uniforms too? I nodded and heard her gasp. ***Then yep, they're in...dun dun dun, the basement.*** I couldn't help but sigh with her answer. I hoped I'd never have to go down there again, but I knew my luck would eventually run out. I nodded, and slowly made my way down the stairs. Normally I would have rushed to get to them, but I didn't want to face that monster again. If it was still there, there was a huge chance that it was even bigger than before. I got close to the bottom floor when I heard a door creak way above me.

"Check every floor, don't let her get away." I knew it was Polly the moment I heard her voice and felt slightly relieved knowing she was alive. Right then, though, I had to decide which one I'd rather face, the basement monster or the evil witch upstairs. In the end, I chose the basement.

Chapter Twenty-Seven: Hero's Rescue

When we got down to the basement, my heart began to flutter when I opened the door and walked straight into pitch-black darkness. The only light I saw came from the stairway, and it was alarming how little it helped. I swallowed a hard lump in my throat and walked forward, patting the walls beside me. Every single warning bell was going off in my head, but I continued, hoping by some miracle that my eyes would eventually adjust to the darkness. They definitely didn't. A few feet in, I heard a nerve-racking crunch beneath my feet, and felt my whole body tense up. Luckily, I didn't hear any sounds indicating there was anything down there with me, so I pressed on.

After a few minutes of running my hand down the wall, I found the beginning of a doorframe. I decided to try the door, but it didn't do me any good. If Joque and Gabby really were down here, I realized there would be no way I could get to them without turning the power back on. My heart began to pound after I tried a few more doors and still had no luck. After the fourth locked door, I decided to peek inside one, and I couldn't tell if my eyes were playing tricks on me or if I was actually seeing a figure pacing inside. It was so dark, it looked like pixels dancing in front of my eyes. That's when I made a huge mistake.

"Hello?" I called out, as I peered into the tiny window. At first the figure seemed to stop, and I felt a pang of excitement rise in my chest. *Maybe it's Oliver's family.* I squinted my eyes, trying to get a better look. A second later, I saw two bright red eyes peering back at me through the glass, and I screamed. *This is what killed that YouTuber! CRAP, CRAP, CRAP!* Behind the doorway, the infected screeched as loud as it could, and just down the hall I heard glass break.

Oh no, I heard Lilly say in my head, ***something's coming!*** I felt a chill travel down my spine and began walking a bit faster away from the door until my hand dipped down the beginning of another hallway. At the end of it, there was a very dim light revealing the back of someone's head. I inched forward, forgetting the potential horde behind me, and with every single breath that came out of my lungs, my heart skipped a beat as if they would hear that too. I got within fifteen feet when I realized it was Polly and two doctors standing over Joque and Gabby, who were strapped down to medical gurneys. The two of them began to twitch and writhe in their beds, and I heard an inhuman sound come out of Gabby's mouth.

"POLLY, WHAT DID YOU DO?!" I screamed as I ran up to them and felt hot tears begin to fall down my eyes.

"I warned you, didn't I? Maybe you'll learn, now that your friends are dead." I saw them raise guns to their heads and leapt into action.

"No! I won't let you!" I yelled. I grabbed the first thing within my reach and slammed it into one of the doctor's heads. He let out a cry and I froze when his knees buckled.

The kids didn't like what I was doing. They thought I was hurting them, so they took control and made me stop.

You must let me go, they'll kill them, I said to them in my head. *I know this looks bad, but you have to trust me.*

But...you hurt them. That's not what a superhero does, Gavin said with a sad tone. I looked up just in time to see the other doctor click the trigger, and to my relief, it didn't go off. I don't know if she didn't load it, or if she didn't do something right, but I didn't let them figure out their next moves. My friends were infected, but just like Dad, they weren't dead. I could save them, I just had to free them first.

I am a superhero, but I have to get them away from my friends. I have to fight them, or else I'll lose Gabby and Joque forever. They need me, okay?

Okay, we'll trust you, I heard Lilly say before I finally felt my muscles release. I couldn't help but breathe a sigh of relief before I had to jump back into the fray. I kicked the brakes off Joque's bed and managed to take out both Polly and the other doctor. I knew it wouldn't last long, so I scrambled toward the medical table where I saw three cure vials.

"Thank god," I muttered before I plucked them up and stabbed one into each of their arms. I didn't wait even a second for the cure to work. I unbuckled both of them in a blind panic and pulled them from their beds. At first, I heard snarling behind me and pinched my eyes shut. They hadn't turned into crawlers yet, so I had hope they wouldn't hurt me. I dragged them around the dark corner at the end of the hall, then the snarling stopped, and I heard them both groan.

"W-what?" I heard Gabby say as I pulled them away. I couldn't help but smile knowing I had succeeded down there, but I felt uneasy as I remembered the red-eyed infected. I rushed blindly through the hall, and when I heard screeches behind me, I closed my eyes again and decided to see what fate had in store for me. I rushed toward the stairway door, and after an agonizing amount of time I slammed into the doorway. I recoiled from shock as I peeled myself away from it, but when I saw nothing but red eyes behind us, adrenaline kicked in and I rushed with Gabby and Joque up the stairs.

Once we got back to the ground floor, we ran straight outside toward the parking lot where me and Oliver escaped before. I expected it to go the same way: Polly and her guards running around for us for a couple hours, and eventually giving up. But this time it went all kinds of wrong. Together we ran and slid under a rusty red pick-up truck. I covered my mouth as they ran outside, and listened as they ran by. The sound of the rocks tumbling, and their rapid movements were all I heard. As a kid, I was always told to never celebrate too early. I remember seeing a video of a marathon runner who was maybe twenty feet from the finish line, pumping their fist up in the air expecting to cross first, when another runner zoomed past them and crossed just in the nick of time. When Polly and Simon ran past us, I thought we had won too. In my head I was planning our escape. How we would smash the lock again, run along the path, and duck behind trees. We'd stop so Joque could rest, then we'd escape for real. I had it all planned out. We sat there holding our breaths, until I heard the truck's tires scrape the ground beside me. Suddenly, I saw it being lifted in the air, and widened my eyes as all the other cars went up with it, reaching a height of at least thirty feet before they stopped and hovered there. I let out a whimper as I gulped and noticed Simon, Polly, and Mom staring at us, but this time they had help: the soldiers and...Oliver. He had his arm raised in the air, and when he saw us lying there, he tilted his head to the side and flashed an unsettling grin.

"Get up nice and slow and put your hands in the air," he ordered before gesturing to the cars above us. "Or don't and become a pancake. I don't care either way." The three of us shared a glance with each other as we decided what to do next, but after a long pause, we followed his order. I knew I would have to fight Oliver and the doctor eventually, but I never thought it would come this soon.

Mia, what do we do? Lilly asked me as I scanned the crowd Oliver had gathered. They were all armed to the teeth with guns, tasers, and, to my shock, grenades, as if the doctor knew we were preparing to take him down. I could see the soldiers who helped us in the apartments there too, and I couldn't help but feel betrayed, despite their loyalty to Simon.

Don't worry, I'm not going to let them win, I responded after a few moments. *I know you're both scared, but I need you to prepare yourselves. We may have to go to war.*

War? I thought you loved Oliver, Mia. What happened?

I do love him, but the doctor possessed him. That's why he's like this. I heard them both gasp, and I returned my attention just in time to see the soldiers try to grab us. In a panic, I held out my hand and saw them go flying back. On impact, I heard a taser go off, and grimaced as the soldier arched their back in pain. It wasn't much yet, but it was a start.

“Oliver, I know you’re in there," I called out from a distance. "You spoke to me, remember? Don’t let him win! I love you.” A laugh escaped his lips, but it wasn't his voice this time, which helped cement my theory. The doctor still had him.

“Oliver isn't here anymore, sweetheart. And now they won't be either." He took his hand and gestured to Simon, Polly, Mom, and the other soldiers, who seemed completely oblivious to what he just said, making me question if I heard it in my head or out loud.

"Simon?" I said aloud as I saw him begin to pound on his head. I hated him and Polly, but what happened next was a new level of evil. They all began to squirm and cry out as if something was attacking them, so I jumped in. I ran into Oliver’s path as he was expelling some kind of darkness and shoved him backward to the ground. I was hoping to put a damper in the doctor's plans, but it was too late. Right before my eyes, this dark energy formed, looking almost like a fog attached to them, and brutally killed each one. I looked at Simon and saw a large claw mark appear over his ribs. He cried out and clutched it in a panic, hoping to stop the blood, but then it swiped him again and I saw the life leave his eyes as his stomach was torn open.

I tried to stop it, but it didn't falter even a little as I focused my energy on it. All that did was make me feel light-headed. I looked over at Mom next and saw the dark energy attach itself to her face. She screamed so loud I had to plug my ears. She died there too, but I didn't dare watch it happen this time. I pinched my eyes closed as they all erupted in screams of terror, and I tried to imagine something better.

I sank into one of my childhood memories and tried to hide there. I was eight, and we just took a trip to Cedar Point in Ohio. There was this really big ride in the park that was at least three hundred feet in the air, and I knew I had to conquer it. When I saw it for the first time, I felt like I was looking at a mountain. The lift hill went high into the sky, and I was sure that if I reached out at the top, I could touch a cloud. It was called the Millennium Force. There was a huge line that day, since it was the middle of summer, so Dad almost said no. It was hot enough that most people in line bought battery-powered fans, while others were fanning themselves with foldable hand fans. I begged Dad to take me on it so that I could have bragging rights at school. He was fearful, but after giving my best performance, with puppy-dog eyes and all the pleases I could muster, he finally agreed, but Mom stayed behind. I don't know if she was scared or just didn't feel like going on it, but she ended up waiting for us on a bench by the lockers.

After spending an hour using the metal bars as a jungle gym, we finally reached the front of the line and took our places in front of a gate in the middle rows. Although we were brave enough to ride it, neither of us were ready to face the front or back row yet. After a couple minutes, a train rolled in for us, and after the previous riders filed off, we all loaded ourselves inside. Together, me and Dad sat down and locked the lap bar into place. I bounced my knee up and down as the ride operator came around and checked us all. When he got to mine, he gently pulled it up and, to my shock, it lifted. I tried to pull it down again over myself, but even after doing so, it didn't click.

"Sir, it didn't lock!" I yelled as he continued checking the other passengers. He didn't hear me, and when he got to the front, he put his thumb out to a woman at the operating booth. I tried to get his attention again, but the ride took off and rounded the corner to the lift hill.

No, this isn't how it happened at all! I remember that day, this isn't real, I thought, as I tried to remember what really occurred. It felt as if it was being wiped from my memory.

Feeling scared, I grabbed Dad's arm and yanked on it, but he didn't turn toward me. Instead, he just said, "Put your hands up, this is gonna be fun." Panic began to grip me as the ride ascended toward the top. The chain clicked beneath us almost like a clock, and I grimaced as I began to see more and more of the park beneath us. Normally, I would have loved this. I would have pointed out every possible thing to Dad, but my heart was pounding so hard in my chest I couldn't focus. When we reached the top, I gripped the bar in front of me so tight my knuckles screamed out in pain. I pinched my eyes closed, waiting for pain or death or something to claim me, but instead I heard a mechanical sound beneath us, as if a fan cut off, and I opened my eyes to see the whole park went dark. There was no sun, no lights, nothing. I leaned over the front and saw the drop beneath me. It was a lot worse than I thought from the ground. I felt like I was staring down at Earth from a space station, and that I was about to shoot back into it. Cautiously, I stood up with my legs shaking like crazy beneath me and attempted to scooch past Dad to get to the steps right past him. Right as I was about to get there, the lights came back on, and the train car jerked forward. In a panic, I rushed toward the steps and felt two pairs of hands grab my arms and yank me off the car just before it went over the edge.

"Wake up, Mia!" Lilly and Gavin said in unison, as they shook me on the steps. Just like in Oliver's dreamscape, I came to again and saw I was being dragged away by Gabby and Joque.

"Mia! Thank God, he stole their souls! He's going to be more powerful than ever now!" Gabby exclaimed, and as I opened my eyes, I saw the sky darkening overhead and realized we were just barely outside of the darkness. It was changing everything in its path into monsters, including plant life. The trees began to grow sharp vines, the grass turned a gray color and began leaking spores, and the fresh flowers, just blooming from spring, turned into carnivorous plants. It was as if the infection was spreading from Oliver's body. Then it hit me: when me and Oliver got reinfected, we gave the doctor just want he wanted. Unlike Simon and Mom, who wanted to use the infected to start their own government, he wanted to start the end of the world, and we were the only things standing in his way.

Chapter Twenty-Eight: Running from the Grim Reaper

No matter how fast we ran, the doctor seemed faster. His darkness spread over everything, and monsters began to emerge from every corner. When we reached the stone road leading toward the river, the ground became mushy and wet, making it ten times harder to get away. It was like we were on a wet trampoline. Our feet sunk into the ground, and before long we lost our shoes. We managed to make it to the storage building when the crows that were sitting on top of Denny's Diner turned and flew after us. I was almost jealous of the fact that Joque couldn't see them because I wanted to scream each time they came into my view. They looked unsettling, like they were imitating what a crow should look like.

They cawed at us and took turns diving to peck our skin. I yelped as one tore skin away from my forearm, and I had to shelter Joque since he couldn't see what was happening. After swiping at them a few times and realizing it was a useless venture, we ran inside the storage building and locked the door. I felt so tired and disoriented that I let my knees fall and crumbled against the ground. All of us were covered in little wounds, and to make matters worse, the dark cloud coated the storage building and eventually seeped inside. I tried to pull Gabby and Joque away from it, but they were too tired to move, especially since they just got cured. That's when I lost them.

I watched helplessly as the infection claimed them both again, turning them into crawlers. I ran as fast as I could away from them and ducked under one of the shelves. I had to hold my breath as they followed me and tried to sniff me out. I couldn't hurt them, I knew that much, so I had no choice but to find a way to trap them until I could come back and use the cure on them. I looked around through the hazy darkness and felt way overstimulated. My senses were in overdrive. I could smell a rotten stench in every direction, all I could see was pitch-black darkness, I felt like there were pins and needles being shoved into my arms, and there was all kinds of banging and screams outside.

Eventually, I saw a bunch of opened crates on the other side of the warehouse through the haze and realized that I would have to sneak over there and find a way to lock them inside one. Cautiously, I lowered my foot over the side of the metal rack and began walking toward the crates. After I took a couple steps forward, I realized my socks were making a squelching sound from trudging through the mud, so I flicked them off. I cringed when they hit the ground on the other side of me, but they didn't seem to show any sign of hearing it.

Again, I started walking in the darkness. I tiptoed little by little and turned my head in every direction as I went. I had no idea where they were, but so far, they weren't coming for me. I kept walking forward, hoping I would make it, when I bumped into a wheelbarrow and heard it scrape the ground. This time, I heard a screech a short distance away, and felt my whole body tense up. I had no time to waste. The moment I heard their footsteps near me, I took off as fast as I could toward the crates. I bumped into a few things on the way there, but I managed to make it in one piece. When I got close to one, I leaped over it and balled myself up directly behind it. Luckily, my plan worked, and they both hopped in the crate. I knew I didn't have long, so I scrambled to stand back up and slammed a lid over the top. Luckily the nails were still exposed, so I was able to pound it back in with my hands and seal them inside. I felt scared when they didn't move at first, so I peeked inside. *Yeah, I know. That was dumb.* I put my face up against one of the holes, and heard a growl come through the box. With a gasp, I jumped back and fell on my butt. They were both fine, but very agitated. Since the crate already had holes in each side, I wasn't too worried about air, but I was slightly worried they'd hurt each other.

"Don't worry, guys. I'll come back for you," I said sadly as I tapped the crate's lid and left out the back door. I stayed beneath the gutters outside, doing my best to shimmy along the side of the building without being seen. Eventually, I got to the corner of the storage building and peeked out. There were all kinds of monsters and unsettling things around. Then something horrible occurred to me. All the soldiers and guards who avoided the wrath of the doctor were now monsters. I could only imagine how bad the barracks were. The haze didn't seem so bad outside, so I felt a little more determined that I would be safe. I took a deep breath and turned around, only to run face-first into Oliver's chest.

I only managed to scream for a second before he put his fingers to his lips and sealed my mouth.

Mia? What's wrong? Gavin asked me.

"Mmmm." I tried to pull my lips apart and realized I couldn't. *He did something to me,* I told them, and attempted to try and speak again.

"While our little 'escapade' has been going on for far too long, Mia, I don't want you to die just yet. I want to put that brilliant mind of yours to the test," he said, tapping his head with his pointer finger. I watched in horror as the haze seemed to gather around us. It was closing in, and I knew I had to get out fast before I discovered what his plan was. I rushed out of the circle, only to smack into the ground. A chain pulled me right back in, and soon I was trapped inside with him. No matter how hard I tried, I couldn't escape. The darkness became rock hard like a solid brick wall. I pounded my fists on it, but it began to hurt.

As I was distracted trying to get free, he waved his hand in a circular motion, and just like in the nightmares, my feet began to dissolve beneath me. It didn't take me long to realize the seal was gone over my lips. I was pretty sure it happened the moment I hit the ground, as if he was showing me some mercy. I screamed out, but it didn't seem to do me any good. It only hurt me more.

"No! I can't die like this!" I cried out, clawing at the walls. I kept going until one of my nails began to bleed, and I yelped as a searing pain went through my fingertip.

"Calm down, I'm bringing you into his mind again. It's time we play a little game, Mia," he said, and I was able to suck in one final breath before it claimed me. He might have stolen my soul just like the others, but I refused to be his pawn and let him win. I was going to fight him there and put an end to him once and for all.

When I rematerialized, I found myself in pitch-black darkness. I turned in a circle, hoping to see some sort of light or a sign of where to go, but there was nothing. I cupped my hands to my ears, but I didn't hear a single sound. The only thing I could feel was the ground beneath me. Slowly, I walked forward until a light came on overhead, revealing a very familiar rocky road. My heart began to pound as buildings seemed to materialize out of nowhere, and then I was right in front of the apartment buildings again. I took a deep breath in, and heard it echo off the walls and trees around me when I exhaled.

Each step echoed too, and soon it began to rain. The water droplets plopped down, making a calming *splash* sound as they hit the ground. I turned my head up, allowing the water to wash down my face and neck, and put my hands out. It felt peaceful, but I knew it would soon be ruined by whatever the doctor had in store for me, so I took my time. For a brief moment, I was a kid again, hopping in and out of puddles without a care in the world. I always dreamed of dancing in the rain with someone like in the movies Mom and Dad used to watch together. I always thought it was the sweetest gesture. I pretended to bow to someone in front of me, but when I looked back up, Oliver was standing there. I gasped and jumped backward, but to my shock, he repeated my gesture.

"Oliver?" I asked, cautiously. Something didn't seem right. "Is that really you?" I eyed him as he rose back up and saw him nod.

"Of course it is, love. Care for a dance?" he shouted over the rain. He reached his hand out, but I didn't take it. Instead, I stepped back and examined our surroundings. I could hear frogs and toads croaking, the sound of the wind and the rain as it poured, a squirrel scurrying up a tree, then I heard...a stick break. Instinctually, I snapped my head up, and saw the doctor holding his hands in the air about twenty feet away. There was a dark energy surrounding him, and I soon realized it was the same around Oliver's face. I was confused at first until I saw him move one of his hands and Oliver moved with it. He was puppeting him.

"What's the matter? You don't love me anymore?" he asked, making a pouty face at me. "Oh." He lowered his arms and let his face hang there. It felt unnatural, creepy even. I peeked over his shoulder and saw the doctor was making the same face. He had complete control, and I didn't like where this was going.

"I do love you, but—" I tried to step back again, but he seized me before I could and spun me around, so I was facing the doctor.

"Aww, I feel the same way." Before I could even register what he was doing, he wrapped his arms around me so tight it felt like my lungs were restricted.

"Oliver, you're hurting me," I choked out. I tried to wiggle free, but his arms kept getting tighter and tighter, as if he was trying to squeeze me to death. That's when I realized I didn't have a choice. As fast as I could, I kicked his legs out from under him and stumbled away, trying in vain to suck in air. It felt like my lungs were deflated, and I couldn't manage to get any air in. Spots began to pop up in my eyes, and eventually my legs buckled.

"Th-this is h-how you want to k-kill me?"

"On the contrary, I want to see how quickly you can bounce back. If you die here, you weren't the foe I thought you were. Here's a little hint, use your damn head." My arms felt weak, but I tapped my hands against my head to force myself to think. Everything was becoming foggy. My lungs burned, my throat felt tight, my heart was jumping erratically. I needed to think, and luckily the kids helped me do just that.

MIA! I heard Lilly shout in my head, as I began to wobble back and forth. It had been a minute and thirty-seven seconds without air.

HELP ME! I screamed back in my head.

You have to think of something to reflate your lungs. Try, uh...a bike pump! I didn't wait a single second. It may have sounded dumb, but it seemed like my last chance. I laid myself down on the ground and squeezed my eyes shut to focus. The rain was pelting my face so hard, it no longer felt tranquil.

"Come on, Mia. Tick tock," I heard Oliver say as he tapped his wrist. Ignoring him, I thought of the bike pump my dad got me as a kid. It was black with two red stripes on both ends. The tube was lined with red and black-spotted cloth, and there was a black handle on top. I kept imagining it, until finally, out of the darkness, it appeared. Everything burned and I felt too weak to sit up, so I had no choice but to crawl for it. When I reached it, I tipped it over and stuck the nozzle in my mouth. I barely had any strength left, and I soon realized that would be my downfall. I couldn't push the handle down. A minute and fifty-four seconds elapsed.

"Tsk, tsk. You really didn't think, did you?" Oliver mocked. I turned over on my back, ready to accept defeat, but then I heard his footsteps approaching me. I opened my eyes to see him holding the handle of the pump and staring me down with a wide smile across his face. "If you want to live, you're gonna have to beg me for it." He put his hand to his ear and leaned toward me. I was in so much pain, I pounded the ground beneath me, making an indent in the dirt.

"Here, I'll give you a little." He pumped the handle once, and I felt my lungs fill a bit. I managed to get a tiny breath in, but it still wasn't enough. My lungs fell right back down again. "So needy." He rolled his eyes and leaned on the handle, being very gentle not to put his weight on it to give me more. "I'm waiting."

"PLEASE!" I choked out. My face felt like it was on fire, even with the cold water hitting me. I pounded my fist into the ground again, and realized I had to think. He wasn't going to play nice, so I had to play dirty. I thought up a chain wrapped around the closest tree and his ankle. I heard it jangle as I waited in agony and managed to pry my eyes open to see it snatch him.

"Ugh, you brat. Take this off me, now!" he ordered, making me shake my head. "I will let you sit there and die! You're relying on me, remember?" I shook my head again and imagined something much worse. A poisonous snake. When I pried my eyes open again, it was wrapped around both of his ankles, and his face changed from angry to scared. "Are you nuts? It'll kill me, get this thing off!" I managed to smile when I saw the snake open its jaw and hiss at him. In the distance I heard the doctor yell something, and realized what his weakness was. If Oliver died, so would he, because he had attached himself to Oliver's soul.

"P-p-pump the handle, snake goes...*poof*," I stuttered as the pain began to spread to my head. The snake whipped its head back, ready to strike, so he pumped four times. It felt like instant relief. It may not have completely fixed it, but I managed to take in a couple full breaths.

"Now keep your end of the deal!" I nodded, and imagined the chain again. He seemed extremely angry at my little trick, but he still kept his hands on the pump at all times. "If you want to make it through this, you're gonna need ten full pumps, and I'm not giving you crap until you earn it."

"Okay, what do I have to do?" I managed to say. My lungs were beginning to deflate again, so I needed to act fast if I didn't want to lose all my energy.

"Make it to Beacon and I'll fix you right up." My eyes widened as I took in what he said. Beacon was miles away. I could barely breathe, not to mention the fact that my body felt like Jell-o, but I didn't give up. I forced myself to stand, and watched as he lifted the pump to carry with me.

"I suggest you run, sweetheart. Unless you want to give up right here." I shook my head and forced my legs to trudge forward. It only seemed to hit me just then why it was raining. He was trying to make it harder for me to get there. But I had ideas. I pinched my eyes closed and imagined a bridge over the path leading directly to the front door. It worked, and a cherrywood bridge, maybe ten feet up, formed over the pathway. I heard Oliver laugh behind me as he saw what my mind concocted, but he didn't stop me. "I really don't think that's gonna help, but sure."

"I'm guessing you won't let me teleport there," I said quietly, so I didn't waste any energy.

"Nope, but nice try." He winked at me, and I couldn't help but feel disgusted. Normally seeing him do that would make my knees feel weak, but right now, he was making me feel nauseous. Painfully, I walked up the flight of steps to the beginning of the bridge and began to walk toward Beacon. It was so far away, and my eyes were beginning to blur again. Despite that, I forced myself forward until about a half-mile in, when my legs buckled, and I barely managed to catch myself on the railing.

"Awww, poor thing, the pain is starting to set in again, huh?" I pinched my eyes shut again and heard the two kids arguing back and forth in my head. They were trying to come up with a solution, but neither of them could firmly pick one.

What should I do? I asked them as I used the railing to pull myself along.

Ask him for one more pump, then imagine a scooter or something. That's gotta work! Gavin replied confidently. I nodded and turned my head toward him. He was standing there swinging the tube around as if it wasn't my literal lifeline.

"I-I need one more," I said, weakly lifting my hand to get the nozzle. His smile widened, and to my surprise, he actually handed it to me.

"Sure, but it's not gonna save you. You're gonna die here. If I were you, I'd give up and let the doctor take you like he did me." I shook my head and put the nozzle in my mouth again. "Alright then, I suggest you use this wisely. It's the last you're gonna get." While my lungs inflated, I thought up an electric scooter, and the moment I managed to suck in a breath, I hopped on it and zoomed down the path. After a few moments of riding along, he rode alongside me with a tank.

"It's a smart choice, I'll give you that. But that was your last pump. It's simply not meant to go your way." I ignored him and focused all my energy on riding forward. Beneath the bridge, I could see flashes of light, and for a brief moment saw the doctor teleporting along. I wasn't surprised he was following his puppet; he probably had to be close to use him.

That's it! I said in my head, and without a moment's hesitation I shoved Oliver off the bridge and imagined a wormhole beneath us. He screamed as we fell into it, but I didn't stop there. I imagined my home, the only place the doctor didn't know. When we stepped out into my room, I closed the wormhole and pinned him to the ground. For the plan to work, I was relying heavily on the doctor's ability to control Oliver. I sat there and stared at him. He fought me, but unlike me, he couldn't make things appear or disappear for some reason. *Maybe the doctor controlled that too,* I thought. Eventually he stopped struggling, and this blank expression settled on his face. In a panic, I checked his breathing and felt him blow air on my hand.

"Thank god," I said aloud, as I pressed my head into his chest. "Don't worry, I'm going to get you out of this." I grabbed the pump off the ground and did ten full pumps. By the end of it, I was able to fully breathe again, and this time my lungs didn't deflate. I felt instantly relieved, but I wasn't sure how long it would work in our favor. If he found us, he would put me through more of his "tests," and after the first one, I didn't want anymore.

It's time we fought back, I told the kids. *We have to build a completely unstoppable army if we want to take him down and get my friends back. So, I'm going to need all the ideas you got.*

It's time to go to war, Gavin said, and before I knew it my house began to transform in front of my eyes as both of them used my mind. It went from a normal home to a giant castle with tanks, turrets, portals, and a huge moat. That's when I realized the sandbox outside predicted all of it, even the doctor's arrival (a doll), and that I had placed it there.

Chapter Twenty-Nine: Preparing For the End

I thought our final war would start right away, but he didn't move. He stood in front of our base with this menacing look. He could build up just as much as we could, yet he just stood there. My mind instantly imagined cowboy music, as if we were having a showdown. I knew that he was waiting for us to make the first move, but I was too scared to get things started. I paced back and forth up top, seemingly forever, until I heard him shout at me from a distance.

"I could very easily destroy that sad little base of yours, Mia. Make water rain down from the sky like a hurricane and wipe your sad little castle away, boo hoo. But I'll play fair. All I want is the boy." He beckoned with his hand, but I didn't even consider it. I glared at him and saw him shake his head with a sad smirk painted on his face.

"You really don't want to do this. Give me my puppet back, and maybe I'll show you mercy. It'll be us against the three of you, that's fair, isn't it? Oh right, hang on a second." I stared in confusion as he snapped his fingers and made the two kids appear next to me, except this time they weren't apparitions. I couldn't believe it. Lilly stared at herself with wide eyes and spun around, making her dress spin with her like a ballgown. She looked so happy, and so did Gavin. It was like a dream come true, but I realized it came with a cost.

"I can make this a reality for you, Mia. You three against me and Oliver. If you win, all of you live. But if we win, they die again, of course, and you two become my slaves when the world ends." I looked over at Oliver, who was lying in my bed, and felt my heart jump. The two kids looked so happy, but I knew if I gave Oliver up I'd have to fight him. There would be no room for error; even one mistake could mean grave consequences.

"I-I need more time to think," I stammered as I clutched the castle wall for support. My legs felt weak again, but this time for a different reason. *Should I dare sacrifice Oliver's safety again?*

"Sure, take all the time you need, but if you take a shot, even one, the deal's off." In the distance, I could hear building sounds starting up as if construction was going on across the street. In reality, it was the doctor building his base. It looked extremely menacing. It was a dark-colored castle double the size of ours, and it had a giant red flag with Beacon Hospital's emblem on it. When I looked up, I couldn't even see the top of his castle without leaning my whole body out the window. While that may have been impressive, I didn't let it faze me. After all, it wasn't the base that counted, it was our fighting skills and our imagination.

"Mia, I know you won't like this, but you need to say yes," Gavin said as he grabbed my hand, forcing me to look at him.

"I can't. What if we kill him?" I walked over to Oliver and ran my finger down his cheek. Still, he didn't move an inch besides breathing. It seemed to be all he could do.

"Trust us, Mia. We've got this. We'll take down that evil man once and for all," Lilly said, pulling me away from Oliver. "We're going to be an amazing team, all you have to do is say yes." I pinched the bridge of my nose with my fingers and paced back and forth in front of the bed. It sounded absurd to even fathom giving him up, but I found myself wanting to go to the window and give in. The kids deserved a chance to be heroes, and a chance to tell the tale afterward. I couldn't let them die here. I realized I had no choice.

"Okay, Dr. Junip. You win. I'll give you Oliver, but in exchange I want my dad back and for us to play fair. No teleporting or using any abilities! Just what our minds can think up." I leaned out the window and watched as his castle lowered down so his window was across from mine. He had a pensive look on his face, then he leaned out the window to respond.

"If we're doing that, then you'll have to forfeit one kid. Fighting four of you is unfair, so make your pick."

"To join your side?" I asked, as I began to chew on my already short fingernails.

"This is war, Mia. In war you have to make difficult decisions, so what's yours?" I saw the kids look at each other in fear and hug. They both seemed so scared to fight each other, I couldn't imagine splitting them for even a second. Then I thought about Oliver and I. *Could I even bear to split with him? Could I hurt him if it came down to him or us? This isn't fair!* It seemed like an impossible choice, but I knew he wouldn't give me much longer to pick.

"I want you to choose. Help me pick the team you think is strongest to take him down," I told Gavin and Lilly as I pointed at the doctor outside, and watched as they both started pacing like I was. After a second, Lilly's face fell, and she stopped in front of me.

"I'm not very strong, I think you should forfeit me," she said with a sad tone of voice. I wrapped my arms around her, and realized that every part of me hated that idea. I knew Oliver would protect her and that I wouldn't dare hurt her, but it still felt wrong.

"No way, you know Mia better than I do. I think I'm the weaker one here." Gavin began to walk toward the window, but I grabbed his hand and pulled him back.

"I don't want either of you to go," I said, pinching my eyes closed out of frustration. "But if we have to do this, which one of you can hold him off the longest? All we need is to get close enough to defeat him. So, who's got the better imagination?"

"I know something so scary it'll beat him for sure. He'll be so distracted, we'll use that as our cover," Lilly said.

"Then it's settled, I'll go. Hey, creep! Take me before I change my mind." Before I knew what to do, I saw a beam of light encapsulate Gavin. It didn't seem to hurt him, but when I tried to pull him back out of it, it burned my hand. "Do me a favor, Mia," he said. "Don't hold back."

"I won't," I promised, and then he disappeared. The space between our two castles widened too. The ground was torn up as his castle was pushed backward, and eventually it stopped about ten miles away. It felt good having a bit of breathing room, but it also scared me thinking of what he might use it for. Slowly I peeled myself away from the window and saw Dad appear in front of my bed with a disoriented look on his face. I watched as he stumbled for a second before his legs gave out and he plopped down on the floor. As he sat there, he held his hand against his forehead, probably out of confusion, and glanced around before his eyes eventually landed on me.

"Kid!" he yelled and jumped up from the ground to give me a hug.

"Dad!" I yelled back, feeling an overwhelming sense of hope hit me. "I know how this is going to sound, but we need you. Your expertise I mean, ASAP. Long story short, we're in Oliver's head because of a man named Dr. Junip. He possessed Oliver, and in order for us to get him back, we have to fight him...to the death."

"Hey, don't forget about Gavin," Lilly said, crossing her arms.

"Right, Gavin too."

"Whoa, slow down a sec. We have to do what now?" He held me out at arm's-length and raised both his eyebrows. I felt a bit frustrated that we didn't have more time, but I did my best to dumb it down in the fastest way possible.

"I need you to use your army expertise to come up with a strategy to take his team down, and fast! They could strike at any moment."

"This isn't overwhelming at all." He grabbed his chin and paced the floor. "How does this work exactly?"

"Anything you imagine comes to life, sir. It's amazing!" Lilly told him. "Watch this." We both watched as Lilly imagined a basket full of candy. Tootsie Rolls, Skittles, chocolate, and so much more fell on the floor in droves, like it was her Halloween candy haul. I was worried it would give her a toothache, but when I saw her eyes widen in excitement, I knew I couldn't take it from her. "See?"

"That's pretty cool, but where's Oliver then? If we're in his head, shouldn't he be here?" Dad asked, making my face fall. I didn't wish to answer his question, so Lilly spoke up for me.

"Mia had to give him up for our safety, but don't worry; if we take the doctor down, we'll get him back and go back to the real world again!"

"Sounds complicated, but let's do this. The first rule to war is to find a place that's safe that you can hold down. Come on." Cautiously, we followed him out of my bedroom and down the hall. It was a slightly different layout than either of us were used to, thanks to the castle transformation, but we managed to find the stairs to the basement. Surprisingly, a picture of me, Dad, and Lilly appeared on the wall inside golden frames, signifying we owned the place. Although I didn't want to admit it, that was pretty awesome. They even had a plaque with our names on it.

"Keep your eyes peeled," Dad said as we marched down the steps. I nodded and imagined that I could see through walls. Although we agreed not to use any abilities, I knew checking on them wouldn't cause any harm. Eventually I saw all three of them grouped together, probably strategizing, and saw Oliver with his arm around Gavin's shoulder. They seemed to be laughing together, and I felt comforted knowing that Gavin was being treated well. *Hopefully we can get them back and have moments like that more often.*

When we made it to the living room, Dad reimagined the whole area. He transformed the front door into a three-layer reinforced metal door. Then he booby-trapped the whole room. Our couch was converted into a barbed wire barricade that we used to block off the basement steps, the coffee table was turned into a tranq turret, he covered the walls in wooden spikes so crawlers couldn't go around the wires, and he made sprinklers appear on the ceiling that would rain down the cure. It almost seemed like overkill, but if *we* could imagine this stuff, the doctor could be just as sinister.

"I have a bad feeling we're gonna be facing more than just them. I hear all kinds of bad sounds outside. Listen," I told them as I cupped my hands to my ears and leaned against the wall. Outside, I could hear all kinds of shrieks and moaning. I didn't even think about facing more infected. It almost seemed like cheating, but the more I thought about it, the more I realized we could do that too. While I didn't feel like using innocent people for our own game was right, I knew we needed to do something, so I imagined an army of soldiers and expanded the room at least triple the size of what it was before to give them space to defend. I gave them crates filled with more cure vials and tranqs and, in case of emergency, guns.

"My name is Mia Andrews, and we need your help. There's an evil man after us named Dr. Junip, and we need you to help to take him down. Whatever happens, don't let up. I believe in you," I told them as they all gathered around us. "We're gonna need every second you guys can get us."

"Yes, ma'am," they all said in unison, then started gathering supplies.

"Yeah!" Lilly said, pumping one of her fists into the air. It almost felt wrong, like I was a god sending people to die at my expense, but I had to remind myself that they didn't really exist and that they would disappear after the war was over.

"Come on, kid, we've got to prepare the basement," Dad told me, pulling the barricade into place behind us. I nodded, and while we were headed down there, I used my ability again. Not only had they left their castle, but they were headed toward us. Luckily, the space between gave us some time to think, but not much.

"They're coming," I said, feeling my heart begin to pound in my chest.

"Let's not waste any time then," Dad said, and he scooped Lilly up and put her on his shoulders. When we reached the bottom floor, Dad used his imagination to turn the basement into an arena with plenty of hiding spots. It was filled with barriers, thick white columns with spiral stairs leading up a floor, a bright red slide back down to the arena floor, and trap doors. Since they couldn't use abilities, only their minds, we made sure we had every advantage. Dad armed himself with guns and an armored suit, while I held a dagger. We had a plan. Since the doctor wished for me to be his puppet too, that meant he wouldn't kill me. So I decided to risk it all. While Dad distracted Oliver and Gavin, I planned on taking the doctor down. Although the idea of killing someone, even a spirit, would leave a lasting scar, I was prepared to do it for the ones I love.

While we were waiting, I used my vision again, and gasped to see the soldiers upstairs falling like flies. They were being slaughtered like animals. One by one they were killed off, and I felt heartbroken knowing I created them just to get torn apart by monsters. The sprinklers and the spikes seemed to have almost no effect. That's when I realized something. I gave them the freedom to create whatever they wanted. *What if they created something strong enough to shield their monsters?* I grasped my hair in my hands and widened my eyes. I knew then our distraction plan wasn't going to last long at all. I had to do something.

"I have to play bait," I told Dad as I ran to the steps.

"What? Kid, you can't do that. If they get you—"

"Then do whatever you have to do to take him down in my stead. I can't let them die like this, even if they are part of my imagination." I ran up the stairs without looking back and imagined an ear-splitting whistle. It would be so loud, it would disorient anyone or anything in its path, including me. When I reached the top, I pinched my eyes closed and blew the whistle as hard as I could. My ears instantly screamed out in agony, but my plan worked. The creatures and soldiers dropped down. Unfortunately, there was no sign of Oliver, Gavin, or the doctor. I was hoping I could have gotten them in the blast too, but it didn't work out. While we couldn't teleport, he didn't say anything about running away. I wasn't scared of the doctor, but I wanted to hold off fighting Oliver as long as possible. My ears were ringing like crazy, but I managed to create a tunnel through the side of our castle, almost like an underground cavern.

Slowly, I used the wall to pull myself up, and put one foot in front of the other in an attempt to get to our allies. All of them had blood pooling out of their ears, so I checked mine. Sure enough, it felt wet and sticky to the touch. More than likely, I burst my eardrum, but if it helped our cause,

I was willing to deal with it. I pounded the side of my head and forced my feet to move. It felt like my legs had turned to wood. Eventually I reached the first soldier, a young girl who looked a few years younger than me, and gestured to the tunnel that I burrowed through the wall. At first, she looked confused as she rolled over onto her side and eyed the long, narrow corridor, but eventually, after I helped her up, she helped me tell the others about it. Once everyone around us knew, they all took off, but the girl stayed behind.

"Mia?" she said, as I hesitated. Her voice came out as a whisper, probably from our shared ear pain, but I felt extremely relieved that I was able to hear her. Maybe there was a chance I wouldn't go deaf after all.

"I can't run from them forever, can I?" I asked her, as I put my fingertip in my ear. It didn't draw any more blood, but it still felt very sore.

"No, unfortunately not." I nodded and put my palm against my chest.

"Then no one else will die at my expense. I won't allow it. If he wants a fight, so be it. But this is between him and me. Not you guys, not the kids, just us." In an instant, I destroyed the castles and everything we both created, including the soldiers. Then I took out everything around us in my hometown, leaving an empty wasteland filled with nothing but the sand from my childhood sandbox. It felt right, since it was the place where this all started. If we were going to fight, then I intended on doing it my way.

"Dr. Junip!" I yelled, and I saw him rise up in the distance on a dune. "I want to fight you one on one. No monsters, no help, just you and me. The same agreement applies. I'll be your puppet if you win, and you'll cease to exist forever if I win."

"Hmmm," I heard him say, and it echoed over our new surroundings.

"Do we have a deal or not?" I crossed my arms over my chest, and right as Dad was about to speak up, a cage formed over him, Oliver, Lilly, and Gavin. He released Oliver from his binds, and I saw the anger leave his face, only to be replaced by worry.

"Mia!" he shouted, reaching his hand out of the cage. "Don't fight him on your own, please!"

"Let the games begin, Mia Andrews," the doctor announced, ignoring Oliver's pleas. He wiped his hand across the sandy plain and made what looked like a giant Japanese tower that was split in multiple layers, where he stood at the top looking down on me. That's when I noticed that not only was our sandbox still standing, but the tower formed in it too, like it was mimicking real life. *Is it magical?* I wondered, as I squinted at it. Then I was snapped back to reality when a knife narrowly missed my face.

"Come and get me," he sneered from the top. "Don't be a chicken, Mia. Use whatever abilities you have, I'll be waiting. Just make sure you play fair, will you?" I glared fiercely at him and scanned the steps leading up. I could feel Oliver's gaze piercing into me in the final moments as I prepared myself, but I didn't have time to bid him goodbye. It was time for the final battle.

Chapter Thirty: The Sandbox War

"Monsters are real, ghosts are real too. They live inside us, and sometimes they win."
—Stephen King

Clutching my dagger tight in my hand, I ran up the first flight of steps leading to the first of many levels in the tower he created. When I got to the front door, I tried to teleport upstairs to speed up the process, but I felt a blast hit me in the chest. It took my breath away and made my eyes water from the pain.

"Ahh," I groaned as I limped back up to the doorway again.

"I believe I said, 'no cheating,' Mia," I heard his voice echo from a distance. It sounded like he was inside, but I couldn't see him through the windows. Slowly, I sucked in a breath, and pushed the door open. Instead of finding myself in what I thought would be the tower, I was on a street corner. There were four streetlights all around me, a stop sign, and a four-way intersection that was cut off on the ends, but nothing else. He was playing with me again.

"I thought you wanted to fight me? Come on! I'm ready." I stood in the middle of the road and glanced around. At first nothing came; then I saw a strange orb appear, almost like a ghost orb. It flew close to me, making me fall over in shock. It made a buzzing sound like some kind of bug, then it flew away, revealing more of the street. Cautiously, I followed it and watched as a cornfield filled in on either side of me. It stopped in the middle of the road and zipped through the corn. It was my worst nightmare coming to life, being chased in a cornfield. I tried my luck at turning back, but when I turned on my heels, the road behind me vanished and there was nothing left but the corn where the orb went.

"Oh no," I whined, hanging my head low and trudging into the corn. The sky overhead looked ominous and threatening. There were stars lining the night sky, and I could even see a full moon overhead. *Not a good sign, especially in a nightmare,* I thought as I pushed the corn aside. I kept going until my worst fears were realized. The orb disappeared, and soon I was left in pitch-black darkness inside a cornfield. I could hear crickets and an occasional owl hooting, making my hair stand on end. Again, I tried to turn back, but the road had completely disappeared, making me feel like I was trapped in a corn-filled box.

"It's okay, Mia. You've got this. You're a veteran by now. Keep going," I told myself as I continued passing through. My heartbeat picked up as the suspense of what he had planned continued to loom over me. I walked through for maybe a minute or two more until I stepped on a piece of corn and screamed. "You idiot, you're fine." I rolled my eyes and pushed forward again, but this time I noticed it became eerily quiet. There wasn't a single sound around me. "They probably just heard your scream, don't worry."

I swallowed and trudged along until I heard a cornstalk snap behind me. Then another, and another. Something was coming for me, and it was coming fast. I knew if I didn't stand my ground, I would never be able to face the doctor, so I held the dagger out and focused on where the sound was coming from. A few feet from me I saw a stalk move to the right, and charged forward. It was a crawler. I watched as it came straight for me, and felt my body beginning to go weak. Before my legs gave out, I screamed a battle cry and drove my dagger right into the side of its head. It made a kind of choking sound before it writhed and finally stopped moving.

"Whew," I said to myself as I clutched my knees, then heard another twig snap. More were coming. This time I used my abilities to see them through the corn, and saw there were at least twenty of the things blocking a big red door with the number 3 on it at the other end of the cornfield.

"That has to be the exit." I trudged forward and became a real-life warrior. One by one I killed those things as they came at me. After four of them, my dagger broke, so I had no choice but to make something even better. A sword. It was only fitting, considering I was in a war. It had a black-taped handle and a stainless-steel blade with my name carved into the bottom in cursive. It looked badass, and I was thrilled to be able to wield it.

Again I trudged forward, killing any crawler that stood in my way, and eventually came to the door. I had cleared the way to open it, but it was locked up tight. I pushed on it as hard as I could, but it didn't budge.

"I beat your monsters, open up!" I yelled, as I pounded my fist into the wooden door.

"You'll have to find the key first," he responded with a loud cackle.

“Ugh.” I pounded my fist against the door in frustration, then slowly walked back to search the field. Although I didn’t want to, I went through the bodies first. None of them had a key, and I felt disgusted knowing I had to even touch them. My hands were covered in monster blood, and I could smell their stench from across the field. Feeling content in my search, I decided to check around the door. I came up with nothing. It wasn’t under the doorframe or around it. It seemed to be impossible. I knew it would take hours to search the field, but then something hit me, and I looked up. There it was, hanging above me on a rope from a steel hook that extended over the field.

“Are you kidding me?” I said, pressing my head against the door. “I really need to pay more attention.” I used my sword to cut it down, and after putting the key into the door, I opened it and saw steps leading down, not up. With a gulp, I stepped inside and began my descent. I should have known that was going to happen, considering the door said three and not two, but it didn’t occur to me how significant the numbers were. Eventually, after going down three flights of stairs, I came to door number two and pushed it open. Inside I saw another road, but this time there was an old 1989 sports car sitting at the edge of it, and it was running.

“Oh no, you’re gonna make me drive?” I whined, making him laugh.

“Let’s see what you’ve learned, Mia,” he said as I dragged my feet up to the driver's side door and climbed inside. “I’ve learned a lot about you from my time in Oliver’s brain, so I created a...course for you. Hopefully you don’t get yourself killed.”

"How many levels are there to this nightmare?" I yelled out as I examined the controls.

"If you make it through this one, you'll have four more." I nodded and saw the road ahead of me appear out of thin air, leading to a mountain. This wasn't a battle, this was torture. Feeling my heart hammering in my chest, I put the car in drive and gently pressed the accelerator. The car lurched forward, and I grimaced as I tried to remember his tip.

Slowly push down on the gas, don't floor it, I remembered, and I gently pressed down this time and felt the car slowly crawl forward.

"Okay, this is manageable," I said, as it went from feeling like a daunting task to a nice peaceful drive. I was going maybe twenty miles an hour when I heard some kind of rumbling behind me. The road was falling into the void of darkness, and it was catching up to me quickly. I knew he was going to ruin it; nothing was ever easy with him. With my heart in my throat, I pushed down on the accelerator again until I was barely staying ahead of it at fifty miles an hour. I felt like I was going on a trip with my dad, driving down the roads in the country, but this time I couldn't look out the windows to see the sights, just straight ahead. The road began to wind in different directions, and I took a sharp turn, making me squeeze my legs in fear. I felt like I was going to slide off the road. I knew I wasn't, but my driving wasn't stable enough for this yet.

I began to get the hang of it until he threw obstacles at me. As I was driving down what looked like the only way forward, a construction site appeared, blocking the road with orange and white cones.

"How do I get through?" I said, straightening my back to try and see if there was more behind the blockage. It looked like a giant drop-off into nothing.

"Uh oh, looks like you gotta turn around," the doctor mocked as I clutched the wheel in fear. I barely knew how to drive straight, how was I supposed to back up and turn around? Luckily, he seemed to be giving me time; the road wasn't falling away anymore, but I was still scared half to death. I kept my foot on the brake and put the car in reverse. Then came the hard part. I had to use the rearview and side mirrors to back up. I let off the brake very slowly and turned the wheel until the back of the car hit the curb.

"Oooh." I grimaced as I put it back in drive and attempted to fix my mistake. It took me way too long to complete a four-point turn, but eventually I managed and saw a new road had formed leading straight ahead. I felt instantly relieved, and this time as I drove on, he didn't make the road disappear. I went a nice, calm thirty miles an hour down these long winding roads and eventually was shocked to see other people on the road. There were cars on the other side of me, and each one whipped past me like I was going the speed of a turtle. I felt slightly embarrassed, like people could tell I was new, but I kept going strong. Then, out of nowhere, I heard a crashing sound and saw a semi-truck with a plow on the front scraping a car along the road...and it wasn't stopping. That was my next obstacle, avoiding that truck. I picked up speed, this time pressing the gas until I was going eighty to lose it. I zoomed down the country roads, this time being the one to fly by everyone else, and eventually saw a road leading off the path. At the end of it there was a golden door with the number 6 on it, and I knew I had to go for it. If it wasn't another trick door, I could bi-pass all the others and go right into our final fight.

The back end of my car turned in a tailspin as I turned my wheel to the right all too quickly and almost went over the edge into the void. I covered my eyes at first, but when the car came to a stop, I opened them and saw I just barely saved myself. The truck looked like it kept going, so I took a second to catch my breath. Instead of driving down the path, I decided to run for it instead. I scanned my surroundings, looking for a key, but this time there didn't seem to be one. I had about a mile or two to go to get to the door, when I heard an engine roar behind me.

"Uhhh." I froze like a deer in headlights, and slowly, my body shaking like a leaf, turned to see the truck looming over me. It was too late to get back to my car, so I had no choice but to run for it. I ran as if I was a marathon runner on the final lap, but to my shock it didn't follow me. At least not right away. I heard it revving its engine, then...it hit the gas. My muscles burned as I pushed myself to the limit and rushed for the door. I closed my eyes, hoping for the best, and it came down to the wire. The only thing that saved me was that the door wasn't locked. If it had been, I might have lost right then for good. Instead, I rushed into door six and found myself on the roof of the tower, just like I was hoping for. He had moved my friends, Dad, and Oliver up to the roof with him, and he seemed to be examining them like bugs under a lens.

"I'm through playing around," I said through deep, pained breaths. "Let's fight, now!

"Very well. I'm ready for you, pest." I readied my sword, and saw a similar one appear in his hand.

"I'm going to kill you, and I won't feel one ounce of pity!" I screamed, holding my sword out in front of me.

"Are you even trained to use that thing?" he asked, raising his eyebrows as we both circled each other.

"No, but I'm prepared to fight for the people I love. You've done enough!" With that last line, I charged forward and brought the sword up only for him to block it with his own and roll away.

"So easy to manipulate. I mean, really. All I have to do is tire you out and I'll win." I shook my head, and this time took a second to gather myself and look at my friends.

"You've got this, Mia," Joque shouted, rattling his cage with his hands. "I can't see you, but I believe in you. Don't give up." I couldn't help but smirk. Little did he know, all I needed was to hear their voices. They were my motivation, and I refused to give up for their sake.

"He's right. We all love you, Mia. You're our hero, so do us a favor and kick his ass." I chuckled and nodded, steading my legs and allowing myself to breathe.

"Yeah!" the two kids shouted in unison. Gabby and Dad chuckled and joined in, cheering me on. I felt suddenly energized, as if their words were enough to make me stronger. My body still felt sore, but I pushed on. This time I decided to play defense, and when he charged at me, I blocked his blow with my sword and planted my feet firmly on the ground. When he pushed me back with all his might, I nearly went over the roof's edge, but at the last second, I pushed back, making him fall to the ground. For whatever reason, he didn't get back up; he just sat there breathing in and out. I turned my sword back into a dagger and made my way toward him. I saw him look up at me, but something felt off. The look in his eye looked familiar all of a sudden. It didn't look like the evil monster I saw before. Still, I lifted the dagger and pulled it above his head, then I kicked him in the side, forcing him to lay on his back and face me.

"Say goodbye, you monster," I ordered, holding it over him, ready to strike. He didn't respond, so I brought the dagger down like an executioner and stabbed him right in his stomach. When he groaned, I no longer heard the doctor's voice. I heard Oliver's. That's when I knew I was tricked. Mid-fight, I realized then, he had switched with Oliver.

"No!" I screamed. Across from me in the cage, the doctor was bleeding too, but he looked content with it.

"I may die here, Mia," he said with a sinister grin plastered across his face, "but so will he. Congrats on killing your beloved." I watched him spit out blood, and whipped my eyes back to Oliver, who had his eyes pinched shut.

"I'm so sorry." I clutched the blade in my hand until my knuckles turned white and made my mind race trying to think of what to do next. "I can still save you; I know I can. I just have to—"

"No, Mia. I-If you save me, you save him too. Y-y-you have to l-let me go, please." I began to cry as I clutched his hand and felt my whole body cry out.

"I can't," I cried, feeling the weight of what I had done hit me like a brick. "I love you." A stream of tears fell down his face, and I saw his body shake a bit from the pain.

"I love you too, but you knew it had to end this way. I was never meant for this world, my love. I was born a monster, and I'm going to d-die one too." I shook my head and picked him up, determined to do something. I used my abilities to open all their cages and rushed toward my dad, who took him from my arms. The color slowly left his eyes, and I felt my heart shattering with every inch closer he got to death. Dad tried to help him by using one of his shirts, but it bled right through. Then, without warning, we were all sent back to the real world, and I found us all knelt over Oliver's body in the courtyard. I checked his breathing and screamed into the dark around us when I felt nothing.

"No!" I cried out again, as hot tears fell down my cheeks.

"Mia, I know you don't want to hear this, but you...you have to let him go, kid," Dad said, putting his hand on my back.

"I can't! I refuse!" I shook my head and shoved his arm off me. I grabbed him off the ground and, after I reoriented myself, I trudged forward. *The hospital isn't far from us, I can make it,* I told myself, forcing my aching, physically exhausted body forward. My legs gave out, and so did the rest of my body after a few steps, but I forced myself to get back up anyway.

I had to fight off waves of nausea, as the pain hit me in bursts. Dad tried to step in, but I was too stubborn to let him take him from me. I was beyond broken, but he was all that mattered. After what felt like an eternity of suffering, I reached the hospital doors and screamed until I tasted blood in my lungs. To my relief, a doctor came running and found us both at the foot of Beacon.

"Oh my god," the doctor muttered.

"Help him!" I choked out, holding him up to the visibly shocked man. I must have looked awful because his face contorted in horror and concern.

"Okay, I'll, uh...do what I can." He took him from me and ran inside, finally allowing my body to rest. In the end, I won the war, but I gave up everything to get there.

"Kid!" I heard Dad yell as I collapsed and hit my head on the floor. Somehow our story didn't end there, but it definitely should have.

Epilogue

(Oliver's Perspective)

I forced my eyes open and found myself in a hospital bed. Every part of me hurt, but I slowly turned my head until my eyes landed on Mia in a bed next to me with her left foot and right arm elevated in a cast. *That girl doesn't know how to give up, does she?* My face began to heat up.

"Doc. He's awake, come quick," I heard a lady yell from the hall. My neck felt like pure agony, but I turned it toward the door and saw a medical team rush inside.

"Wow, I'm so happy to see you're up. It's been about a week now," a man said as he came up to my bedside.

"W-what about her?" I tried asking, but it came out like muffled garbage. My throat felt drier than Mia's sandbox. I pointed at her and saw the man's confused expression fall away.

"Oh her?" he asked, making me nod. "Don't worry, she's just fine. She's a real trooper. You wouldn't believe what happened to her. We had to put her under anesthesia. She had a broken ankle, multiple fractured ribs, and a broken humerus. It's a miracle she even made it here."

I gasped and tried my best to roll off the bed so I could be with her, but they stopped me. *God, I hate you all right now,*

I thought, rolling my eyes at them. *I need her; why can't you see that?*

"Oh no, friend," the nurse said, catching me before I managed to successfully roll off. "No walking until further notice, got it?" I could feel the frustration building up in my chest, but I took a deep breath and pointed at her bed again. Then I thought of the perfect way to explain the situation. I held up Mia's engagement ring and saw the nurse smile.

"Oh, I see." This time, they all understood.

"Are you her fiancé?" the doctor asked me, forcing me to nod again. "Here, I'll help you. Nurse?" I thought at first, he was going to help me up, but instead they moved my bed right next to Mia's and took the handrails down, allowing me to roll myself into her bed. I'm pretty sure I pissed them off by tangling myself in her tubes, but I felt content just being closer to her, so I didn't care. After they got me settled, they gave me a Styrofoam cup filled with the good kind of ice and water, relieving the Sahara Desert feeling in my mouth. It was so good. I chugged the whole thing down, and after handing the empty cup back to the nurse, I wrapped my arms around Mia and closed my eyes. For a moment, I almost drifted off again, until Mia began to stir.

"Ugh," she groaned, then her eyes locked on mine, and her annoyed expression changed. "Oliver?" she said in a shocked tone, turning her body toward me—as much as she could anyway—to hug me tight in her arms. "My Oliver!"

"Oh, Mia," I said, as I began to sob into her. I kissed her with so much passion, I made her chuckle, and when we stopped, I pressed my forehead against hers and ran my finger down her cheek. "You really did it." She nodded and began to cry right along with me. I looked down at her free hand as I held her and grabbed it to put the ring back on. "I believe this belongs to you," I whispered, fighting back more tears. She nodded again, and gently pressed her quivering lips against mine.

"Thank you," she said, bringing her hand up to my face. "Where's Dad and our friends?"

"Don't worry, they just went to shower and get some food. They'll be back," the doctor said as he stood over us. We both nodded, and I knew right then all I wanted was to be alone with her, so I said it outright.

"Good, because I could use some alone time with my favorite girl," I told them, making the doctor blush.

"Oh, uh...right. Call me if you need anything, alright?" We both nodded again, and when we heard the door shut, we went back to kissing each other.

Two weeks later, we left that hospital for *the last time.* Mia's dad managed to get the crane working again, allowing everyone to escape that horrible island, including my family. It was a whole process getting them released. For a while, the remaining researchers and doctors fought to keep my parents and siblings, but Mia's dad fought tooth and nail for us. It took us about a week, but eventually they all walked free. They were horrified when they learned everything we had gone through, and part of me wondered, even though I had experienced it firsthand, if it was even real.

From there, Mia's dad drove all of us back to Juros in a Beacon medical van, where we helped clean up the abandoned city. There was so much destruction and carnage, it felt sickening, but after a month or so of picking up garbage and rubble, helping reassemble the fallen buildings, and opening the borders again, it started to feel like home.

After a construction crew rebuilt Mia's house, we moved back in and basically became a huge yet very strange family. After four months of normality, the four of us—Me, Mia, Gabby, and Joque—decided to go back to school together. Considering I never got a high school diploma, I had to take GED classes, but they all waited for me like the amazing friends they were. Together, we ended up going to a college in Juros called Skidesdale. It was a small community college, but it seemed perfect for us.

Mia's dad and I had to help Mia around for a long while. After we left the hospital, she was referred to a physical therapist to start walking again. In between classes, either me or her dad would drive her there, and after a few months, she stopped feeling pain when she put pressure on her right leg. Although the doctors said it would never go back to "normal" again, I was proud to see how far she had come.

As for all the poor people that died because of Dr. Junip, the city of Juros banded together with the people from Beacon to host a mass funeral in the town square. A whole bunch of their loved ones showed up, and people came from all around to pay their respects. We only went for the soldiers who defended us, but there were a lot of other people buried that day too. Mia's mom was buried that day, but Mia only stopped to pay her respects to the hero she knew as a kid, not the woman she became in the end. Simon was given a flag ceremony, but we didn't stay for it. He was an evil man, and not many people came to see his final send off.

As for Mia's dad, he became a full-time mechanic to help pay off Mia and I's wedding, although we both got jobs too. Since we didn't have much work experience, we all ended up at an entry-level job at a Save-a-Lot cashiering. While we were there one day, we met up with Rufus again and planned a huge cookout between our families.

In our free time, we'd visit Jill sometimes, and a lot of the time, we'd take Gabby and Joque with us. They basically became our family. After work they'd stop over, and we'd plan out our wedding and study together when we had the chance.

"Mhm, yeah, we'd surely study," Mia mocked, sticking her tongue out at me. I laughed and nudged her gently.

"Okay, okay, we'd goof off. How's that?"

"Better," she replied with a cheeky smile.

We were super happy, just as we deserved after a nightmare like that...until two years later, when things took a turn for the worse again.

It was the ninth of September in what should have been our final year of college. We were taking a test, so the classroom was eerily quiet. I felt a little nervous knowing I finished my test before everyone else, so I began doodling on my textbook. Occasionally I would glance over at Mia, who had her face buried in her paper, or at Gabby, who was tapping her pencil against her temple, or at Joque, who was chewing the eraser off the end of his. Then something weird happened.

The whole class jolted upright when a series of blood-curdling screams came from outside. Confused, we all got up and ran to the windows. At first, we didn't see much besides what we thought was a bunch of stupid college kids causing a ruckus as they ran through campus. Then we saw what was chasing them. Infected. All four of us were in shock.

They chased after the students, and luckily our professor knew something was up and put us on lock down.

Soon, they were everywhere, all over campus. I had no idea how that was even possible, considering we'd killed the doctor, but when I saw the familiar determined glimmer in Mia's eyes, something told me that we were bound to find out.

www.ingramcontent.com/pod-product-compliance
Lightning Source LLC
Chambersburg PA
CBHW020249030826
48979CB00030B/2667/J

* 9 7 9 8 9 9 0 4 7 1 1 1 5 *